ROUGH JUSTICE

ROUGH JUSTICE

Colin Falconer

Hodder & Stoughton

Copyright © 1999 by Colin Falconer

First published in Great Britain in 1999
by Hodder and Stoughton
A division of Hodder Headline PLC

The right of Colin Falconer to be identified as the Author of
the Work has been asserted by him in accordance with the
Copyright, Designs and Patents Act 1988.

10 9 8 7 6 5 4 3 2 1

British Library Cataloguing in Publication Data
A CIP catalogue record for this book
is available from the British Library

ISBN 0 340 75030 8

Typeset by Hewer Text Ltd, Edinburgh
Printed and bound in Great Britain by
Caledonian International Book Manufacturing Ltd

Hodder and Stoughton
A division of Hodder Headline PLC
338 Euston Road
London NW1 3BH

This book is for
Stanley and Barbara Slinger.
With thanks.

ACKNOWLEDGEMENTS

A number of people were kind enough to lend their assistance to this book and I am indebted to them for their help. My thanks to Mark Stobbs and John Lloyd at the Bar Council, and especially Mr Selva Ramasamy who answered many questions about procedures at the Old Bailey. They gave freely of their time and their expertise and I greatly appreciate it.

Thanks also to Alex Bass, at the London Ambulance Service for answering my queries regarding ambulance procedures in north west London.

I am indebted to Martin Fido for his overview of police procedures and culture. A true gentleman. Anyone interested in the Metropolitan Police should look for his Encyclopaedia of Scotland Yard, written in conjunction with Keith Skinner.

My heartfelt thanks goes also to Detective Chief Inspector David Brown for his advice on aspects of police work relating to murder enquiries.

Warm thanks too, to my agent Anthea Morton-Saner, for helping me so greatly with my research. And to Tim Curnow in Sydney for his advice on the manuscript.

To all these people I give my thanks. However any factual errors are mine, and mine alone; and I would like to stress also that no character in this book owes their genesis to any real person, living or dead.

ROUGH JUSTICE

PART ONE

Camden Town.
The early hours of the morning, late summer

Chapter One

The dead man had two small, ovate holes in the side of his polished brown head, and his pleated cotton drill trousers were around his knees. Frank Marenko squatted down beside the driver's window to take a closer look. The tom was still sobbing in the panda car.

'A code 69,' Marenko said.

'What was that, sir?' The uniformed constable looked up. A probationer, barely old enough to shave, Fox thought. Cops get younger every year, as the saying went. As she watched, his expression changed through surprise to bewilderment.

'Code 69,' Marenko repeated. 'I've seen these before. She literally blew his brains out. Sucked so hard his entire skull exploded outwards. Just shows. You've got to be careful. Have you ever gone with a prostitute, son?'

The young man's jaw was slack with confusion. Poor sod. 'No, sir.'

Marenko patted him on his shoulder. 'Good boy.'

For Christ's sake, Madeleine Fox thought. Three in the morning and I'm listening to stand-up comedy in a wet and badly lit street in Camden Town. She felt a drop of rain find its way beneath the collar of her overcoat and trickle between her shoulder blades. She shivered. The tom started dry-retching out of the panda car's door.

I have to be crazy, Fox thought. My father was right. This is no way for a young girl from a respectable family to make a living.

Marenko turned back to the young police constable. 'Have you talked to the tom?' When he didn't answer, Marenko said patiently: 'The prostitute. Have you talked to her?'

The constable shrugged. 'She says she didn't see anything, sir.'

'What?'

'She had her head down.'

Marenko studied the constable's face. 'Sure. But afterwards. She must have heard a bang or something. This guy ejaculated the contents of his head all over her. She must have looked up then.'

The constable shrugged again.

Marenko looked at Fox. 'Do you believe this? She's gobbling his Mars bar, he gets shot in the head and she says she didn't see anything. Christ.'

The Jamaican was slumped in the front seat of the Corvette, a flash American job with left-hand drive. Only it wasn't as flash any more, not with the contents of the deceased's skull sprayed across the dashboard and the passenger side floor well.

Marenko shone the constable's torch into the interior and caught the dull glint of the three heavy gold chains the dead man wore around his neck. 'Got a bit of cargo on board,' Marenko said. 'Enough here to clear Nigeria's national debt.' There was a small packet of white powder on the console, anointed with a glob of congealing blood.

'A prescribed medication, no doubt,' Fox said, her hands deep in her pockets.

'Naturally,' Marenko said. 'What's that he's holding? Looks like a dead cat.' It was known as cadaveric spasm; the muscles of the hands had gone into instant rigor. Whatever he had been holding at the moment of death was still clutched in his fist.

'I think his date lost her wig,' Fox said.

Marenko gave a short, barking laugh. The beam of the torch remained on the dead man's lap. 'What's that on his pork, for Christ's sake?'

'A condom, I think,' the constable said.

Marenko laughed. 'I know what it is, thanks, constable. I *have* seen one before. Hear that, Fox? Safe sex. He uses illegal substances and gets his head blown off in the front of his Yank tank but he practises safe sex. His mum will be pleased.'

There is no dignity in death, Fox thought. At least not violent death, dealt out this way. The dead man was just a piece of meat now. A Home Office photographer had started taking flashlight photographs of the corpse with professional indifference, and two detectives from Hendon Road were standing over him, hands in their pockets, making jokes about his genitals and his sexual practices.

But then, he was very probably a Yardie gangster and a street dealer. He would get no respect here.

A Scenes of Crime officer wearing overalls and latex gloves was carefully checking the corpse's pockets. He passed the contents to a colleague, who stood beside him with plastic evidence bags; there was a roll of fifty-pound notes as thick as a hamburger and a crocodile-skin wallet.

The SOCO flipped open the wallet and examined the driving licence. Fox scribbled down the details in her notebook. Crawford, Elmore Joshua, born 15 July 1975. An address in Islington.

'Someone called Gravedigger?' Marenko asked.

Gravedigger: Professor Aloysius Graveney, the Home Office pathologist. Death had already been certified by the divisional surgeon. 'He's on his way,' the constable said.

The cul-de-sac led off Kentish Town Road and faced a block of council estate flats. Some of the residents were standing on their balconies watching the early-morning entertainment, jeering or shouting suggestions. There was a carnival atmosphere.

Fox's arrival had created an extra buzz. CID in a skirt. This had to be good.

Fox looked around. Scenes of Crime had set up arc lights, and the immediate area was illuminated like a film set. Four Borough of Camden dump bins had been lined up beside two vandalised telephone boxes. There was an ancient chestnut tree and beyond it, stranded by the developers, a single, narrow two-storey house with iron railings. It appeared to be derelict.

On the opposite corner was a public house, the Green Man. Its wall appeared to be the local lavatory, and the smell of urine mingled with the stench of ripe shit from the car. Elmore Crawford had voided himself in death.

'Anyone see anything?' Fox asked. She spoke the words without expression, like a mantra. No one ever saw anything at three o'clock in the morning.

'There was a woman standing at those railings when we got here,' the constable said, gesturing across the way towards the house that Fox had thought was derelict. 'She went back inside before I had a chance to talk to her.'

Marenko made a face. Nah. Life isn't like that.

'I'll check it out,' Fox said.

Even at that hour a crowd had gathered on the other side of the police tape. They were kept back by uniformed police who had been dispatched from Kentish Town police station. They parted only grudgingly for the mortuary van when it arrived. There were a few Rastas, one of them in a rainbow-coloured woollen hat, an elderly man in a dressing gown, an umbrella shielding him from the rain, another man with a plastic mac over his pyjamas. Fox noticed a teenage punk in jeans and Doc Martens, his head shaved, the two strips of hair on either side teased into horns. He had a ring in his ear and another in his lip. His face was ghostly in the blue strobe of the emergency lights as he strained for a look at the corpse.

'Oh, look. Satan,' Marenko said. 'How appropriate.'

The Rastas were shouting jokes to each other and catcalling to the tom. Now they turned their attention to Fox. One of them whistled as she pushed her way through the crowd. Fox ignored them.

The tom stared up at Fox from the front seat of the panda car, all cleavage and belligerence. She had the body of a super-model and the face of a slaughterman. The WPC who had been assigned to watch her caught Fox's glance and her eyes glittered with amusement. The tom had her legs crossed, her blood-stained body sock riding high around her waist. Fox didn't think she was wearing underwear.

She had evidently recovered from the shock of having one of her johns executed right next to her and her attitude was back in place. She popped a wad of pink chewing gum. 'Can I go home now?' she said.

'I'm afraid not. We'll need to talk to you about this.'

'Look, I been sitting on me business 'ere for the last hour. This is costing me, know what I mean?'

'We won't keep you any longer than necessary.'

'You don't understand. I can't sit here on my arse all fuckin' night, you bitch.'

Fox proffered a pack of Wrigley's. 'Would you like some more gum? It's good for the jaw muscles.' The girl knocked it out of her hand on to the ground. Fox shrugged and walked away.

She stood on the front stoop of the house. Her nose wrinkled at the smell of rubbish and dog shit from the dark corners of the tiny front garden. She looked up at the windows. The house was in darkness. The occupants had gone back to bed. Squatters, perhaps.

She pressed the doorbell but it appeared to be broken, so she hammered with her fist three times on the door. She waited almost a minute and was about to knock again when a light went on inside and the door inched open. A black woman, a dressing gown clutched at her throat, peered out. Her eyes glittered with fear.

Fox held up her ID. 'Detective Inspector Madeleine Fox,' she said.

'I didn't see sod all,' the woman said.

'One of the police constables said you were standing out here by the railings when he arrived,' Fox said, her voice betraying her weariness.

'It's the middle of the night,' the woman said. Her voice was soft, frightened rather than aggressive. Fox felt sorry for her.

The woman tried to shut the door, but Fox held it open with her foot. 'Can I talk to you for a moment?'

The woman looked past her at the crowd of faces turned in their direction from the street and the shadowed brick balconies of the council flats across the way. 'About what?'

'A man's just been shot in that car over there.'

'I didn't do it.'

'Did you see anything?'

A child started crying inside the house. 'I told you. I didn't see sod all. You woke my baby up!'

'For God's sake. A man's just been murdered. Do you understand?'

Inexplicably, the woman started to cry. 'Can't you see I got enough troubles?' she whispered.

And the door slammed shut.

Chapter Two

The team was assembled in the Incident Room at Hendon Road by eight the next morning. As soon as everyone was there, Marenko made his entrance. He was a big, lumbering mess of a man, with the body of a wrestler gone to seed, his suit hanging on him like it had been thrown carelessly over a chair. His shock of grey hair trailed over his collar and his moustache needed a trim. He was six feet and three inches of bad attitude and irritable behaviour, and when he was tired and pissed off, as he was now, he entered rooms like a stormfront, banging open doors and scattering papers off desks.

'How did you go with the tom?' Fox asked him.

Mistake.

'That lying little tart!' The door slammed behind him. He threw a cassette tape on Fox's desk. It slid off on to the floor. He crumpled a polystyrene cup in his fist and threw it across the room.

'That slag's as hard as a frozen chicken.'

'What did she say?'

'She really expects us to believe she didn't see anything? What is this? Dumb and dumber? Do I look that stupid?'

'Not in profile, guv.'

Marenko studied the younger detective. 'Don't be a smart arse, Fox.'

He sat on the edge of the desk and briefed the team on the events of the previous night. He showed them the videotape from SO3, the stark image of a red Corvette, Crawford's body slumped across the passenger seat, the dark puddles of blood in the passenger side floor well; then he talked them through the facts of the case, the anonymous telephone call to Kentish Town police station at around 2 a.m. the panda car dispatched to the scene to investigate, finding Elmore Crawford dead and the tom throwing up on the pavement a few yards away. The possible eyewitness in the nearby house. The fruitless interview with the prostitute at Holmes Road a few hours later.

'So,' DC Honeywell said when he had finished. 'This slag who was with him. She does oral, but she doesn't do verbals. Is that right?'

'Maybe she was thinking of something else,' DS James said from the other side of the room. 'The toms do that, you know.'

'Do what?' Marenko said, joining in the game.

'I hear they sort of turn off when they're doing it. I suppose they get bored. Maybe that's why she never noticed her john was shot. When it happened she thought she was Celine Dion and she was going down on the *Titanic*.' He mimicked a girl performing fellatio and started to sing the theme tune from the movie.

Marenko grinned. 'You're diseased.' The tension broken, Marenko slumped into a chair and threw his head back. 'We've got to nail this one. There is no way this is going to get away from us. We have an eyewitness, for Christ's sake.'

'Yeah, but she was looking down the wrong eye,' James said.

Everyone in the room liked that one. But Marenko was right to feel frustrated, Fox thought. All right, Elmore Crawford was no loss to society. No taxpayer, as James would say. They now had his previous off the computer; the print-out was ten pages long and included drugs possession, dealing in narcotic substances and grievous bodily harm. But the case should have been a lay-down; as Marenko had pointed out, there was an eye-witness.

Why then did Fox get a bad feeling about this one?

Perhaps because the girl who had had her head buried in Elmore Crawford's lap when his head was blown off didn't give a shit about him either way, and they would have to get some other drug-world identity in an arm lock to come down to the Junkyard and ID the body. The murder weapon would even now be sinking into the silt somewhere in Camden Lock or the Regent's Canal.

Elmore Crawford would be page-three news tomorrow in the tabloids, but his associates in Islington would already be going about their daily business, which no doubt consisted of dealing in cocaine and amphetamines, without giving his passing another thought. It seemed to Fox that the only person in the whole of London who really cared about Elmore Crawford was DCI Frank Marenko.

And professional interest aside, he didn't care a whole lot either.

'What about the woman the uniform saw standing at the railings?' someone asked.

'Her name's Flora Ellis,' Fox answered. 'She said she was woken by the police siren, that she didn't see anything before the panda arrived.'

'This whole city should be walking around with white fucken' sticks,' Marenko hissed. 'Pardon my French, Fox.' She smiled. It was almost quaint the way he kept apologising for his language in front of her. And he had a point about the white sticks. Once, when she was a DC at Vauxhall, she had attended a murder scene at a rave party where five hundred of the two thousand patrons had claimed to have been in the lavatory at the time of the incident.

'We start off with the door-to-door enquiries. Someone on the estate must have seen something. We still don't know how the shooter got away from the scene. Did he drive, did he walk —

what? I also want to know everything there is to know about this Elmore Crawford. Obviously he's upset someone very badly. James has pinned the duty roster to the board. Meanwhile me and Fox are going to pay another visit to this Mrs Ellis.'

Chapter Three

'I told you already. I didn't see sod all.'

Flora Ellis was prettier than Fox had imagined in the darkness the night before, a delicate woman with nervous, bird-like movements. Her dress was Marks & Spencer, but it was clean and had been freshly ironed. A toddler, no more than twelve months old, was playing on the floor. His hair was brushed and his face had the scrubbed, pink glow that suggested regular baths.

The house was narrow and dark. It had been built in the days of Queen Victoria; in its time it had been perhaps even somewhat grand. Sometime in the 1950s the council had built an estate on the allotment across the street, and then in the 1960s developers had bulldozed its neighbours to build more flats. It appeared that someone had bought it with a view to renovating it, for the floorboards had been pulled up in the parlour and had been left in a pile beside the stoop, reinforcing the impression of decay and abandonment.

The kitchen contained a bath concealed behind a plastic curtain decorated with bright yellow flowers. The only other downstairs room was a tiny living room that looked over a cluttered and overgrown yard. There was rising damp on one of the walls, and in places the wallpaper was peeling away. The floor was covered with ancient linoleum, and children's toys were scattered on a thin rug. There was little furniture; a two-seater sofa of faded floral chintz with wooden armrests, a battered armchair of red imitation leather, a veneer sideboard. Handmade cushions prettied the sofa. There was a souvenir plate of Charles and Di gathering dust on the wall beside a framed needlepoint:

> Bless this house, O Lord we pray.
> Keep it safe by night and day.

Fox noted a photograph on the mantel, in a plastic Woolworth's frame. A smiling, handsome man had his arm around Flora. She was holding a small baby. It must have been taken less than a year ago, Fox decided.

'Is that your husband, Mrs Ellis?'

Flora nodded, her face sullen.

'Could we speak to him?' Marenko asked her.

'Long as you don't want him to answer you back.' She turned back to Fox. 'He's dead.'

'I'm sorry.'

'You don't have to be sorry. You didn't do it. Happened just before Christmas. He had a job at this paint factory in Clapham. Pallet came loose off a fork-lift and he was standin' under it, weren't he? Miles here was three months old.' There was a difficult silence. 'He was goin' to do this place up. He was good wiv his hands. No point now, is there?'

Marenko leaned forward. 'Mrs Ellis, last night at around 2 a.m. a man was shot dead just twenty yards from your front door. We need to know if you saw or heard anything around that time.'

'You already asked me that. I told you . . .'

'I know, you saw sod all.'

'I was asleep, weren't I?'

'A policeman said he saw you standing on the porch out the front when he first arrived on the scene.' Another long silence. 'We need you to help us, Mrs Ellis.'

'Why should I?'

I suppose there really is no good reason, Fox thought. Elmore 'Eli Dread' Crawford was a Yardie and a drug dealer whom no one was going to miss.

'We've checked our records, Mrs Ellis. Your husband, Michael, was arrested in Dover in 1996 trying to smuggle a large quantity of cannabis resin into this country. He was sentenced to two years in prison.'

'He did his time! Anyway, what's that got to do with it?'

Marenko's face gave nothing away.

Somehow, in a way still not clear to Fox, Marenko had struck a nerve. Flora Ellis's defences started to come down. 'If I say anything, someone'll do me. Not that I care about that, but what about Miles?'

Miles, her little boy. Yes, Fox thought, you've got a point there. Her heart really wasn't in this.

'How do you know what happened to your husband the day he died, Mrs Ellis?' Marenko said softly.

Flora Ellis gave him a puzzled look. 'Because everyone in the factory saw it happen, that's why.'

'That's right. But what if they all said they didn't see anything? Perhaps because they were frightened of getting into trouble, losing their jobs. How would you have ever known that what happened to him was just an accident?'

'What happened to him in that car was no accident!'

'So you *did* see what happened?'

Flora Ellis seemed to deflate. Marenko had trapped her into admitting she had seen the murder. Still, there was nothing they could do to force her to give a statement. Yet it seemed to Fox that it had taken all of Flora's resolve just to remain silent to that point.

'If I tell you,' she whispered, her voice very small, 'they're gonna do me.'

'No one's going to hurt you, Mrs Ellis,' Marenko said. 'I guarantee it.'

'I don't know.'

Flora Ellis hesitated. To her surprise Fox realised that she just wanted to grab her and shake her: Don't do it. You know he can't guarantee anything! Think about the kid and shut up!

Flora put her face in her hands. 'Oh, Jesus.'

Marenko knew he had won. 'If people turn their heads away when someone gets murdered,' he said, 'what kind of world is that going to be? You want Miles to grow up in that kind of place? Somebody has to start to change things, Mrs Ellis.'

His voice was hypnotic. Even Fox was seduced by it, and she'd heard this speech countless times before. She bit her lip and willed Flora Ellis to keep silent.

Instead Flora took her face from her hands and nodded towards Fox. 'Last night when she knocked on the door, I thought: I'll be a bit clever for once and mind me own business. Mick always used to say to me, you're didgy, Flora, you got to learn to keep your nose out of things. Never did learn, did I?'

She took a deep breath.

'That bastard.'

'What bastard, Mrs Ellis?'

'It was 'is fault my Mick got banged up. I know it. It was easy money at first, and Mick thought he was a really big man, being part of Pat's firm.'

'Who are we talking about, Mrs Ellis?'

'Capper. You know who I mean.'

Marenko looked at Fox. She held her breath. They both knew where this was leading.

'Tell us what you saw last night.'

'All right. This is it, OK? I was awake. I was feeding Miles his bottle. I heard these two bangs, like a car backfiring in the street. I went to the window. I saw this geezer running past the window. Right past the house. I saw his face, clear as day, the streetlight was still on. He jumped in a car, up by the estate there. Then I looked where he was running from, and there was this flash car parked under the old tree out the front and I heard some girl screaming. I didn't see anyone shoot nobody. I just saw him running. That's it.'

'Would you know this man if you saw him again?' Marenko prompted gently.

'I didn't see him shoot nobody, I just saw him running. OK?' She lowered her head and started to cry softly. 'OK?' Flora Ellis put her face in her hands.

'Was it Capper you saw? Patrick Capper? You're sure?'

'I'd know that bastard anywhere. He was him that got my Mick banged up.'

Marenko put a hand on her shoulder. 'Thank you, Mrs Ellis. Perhaps we can get a statement.'

She nodded, still sobbing into her hands.

'You did the right thing to tell us.'

Fox looked out of the window, at the council flats, the satellite dishes, the bicycles parked on third floor balconies, a window box of petunias the only wink of colour on this grey morning.

The right thing. I hope it was the right thing, Fox thought. But she could see the future rushing towards them all.

Chapter Four

The mortuary, aka the Junkyard, aka Gravedigger's Slice and Dice.

The pathologist was a tall, bespectacled and rather fussy-looking man who looked more like a literature professor or a pharmacist than someone who spent the greater part of his working life dissecting corpses and examining the detritus of human misery. His name was Aloysius Graveney, but he was known more affectionately and very obviously to the local divisional CID and the 2 Area AMIT as Gravedigger.

Fox waited with Marenko in the anteroom of the main laboratory knowing the mortuary stench was going to be on her clothes and in her nostrils for the rest of the day. She wished now that she had not chosen her best Jaeger raincoat that morning.

'You're not looking too clever, Fox.'

'I'm fine.'

He silently dabbed a little Vick's Vaporub under his nose and passed her the jar. She did the same. A few minutes later Gravedigger's assistant emerged from the doors to fetch them.

Marenko thrust his hands into his pockets and looked around. The detritus of a Wednesday night in the city of London. 'Stiffs on parade,' he said. 'I wonder which ones went to heaven?'

Fox said nothing. She wasn't shocked by what he said, she never was. This was just another murder scene; you made jokes, you separated yourself from it, you stayed sane. But she wasn't of a mind to join in. The cold, sweetish smell made her nauseous.

Another of Graveney's assistants passed them pushing a stainless-steel trolley, the body covered with a green sheet.

'He'd like a table near the window,' Marenko said.

The attendant shot Fox a wearied look. He had heard all the jokes before. 'Lung cancer,' he said to her, nodding to the corpse.

'Better make it in the non-smoking section then,' Marenko shot back and gave a short, barking laugh. Diseased, Fox thought as she followed him down the corridor towards the sluice room.

Graveney emerged from his office with a clipboard under his arm, dressed in regulation green gown and white wellington boots. He looked at them over the top of his half-moon glasses. 'DCI Marenko. One of yours here?'

'Crawford. Last night's shooting in Camden Town.'

'Right. The PM's finished. Come and have a look.' He led them down the white-tiled corridor. There was a wall of drawers set into the wall. One of the drawers had E. CRAWFORD chalked on the tray. He pulled on a lever, released a hinge and slid it out.

He drew the sheet back. The body had been cleaned, but from what Fox could see not a great deal of Elmore Crawford's skull remained after the two bullets had done their job.

'Many are drilled, a few are frozen,' Marenko said.

Graveney ignored him, consulting his clipboard. 'Death was instantaneous, occurred around 2 a.m. as you know from the . . . witness. Two gunshot wounds to the head. One bullet entered the left temple at a trajectory of around forty-five degrees. It was fired from behind the victim and exited through the orbit of the right eye. Powder marks around the entry wound indicate that the shot was fired from very close range. The window was halfway down. The assailant would have simply leaned in and fired.

'There is a second gunshot wound just above the left ear, also fired at an angle of approximately forty-five degrees, but from the side and with an upward trajectory, indicating that the victim was already lying on his side across the passenger seat, probably already dead, in the position that he was found.'

Marenko nodded. 'Thanks. When the report's ready, send it over.'

Graveney nodded. 'No more Elmore,' he said as he slid the drawer back into the bank.

Fox stood at the washbasins staring at her reflection in the cold light of the fluorescent tubing. What a way to earn a living. Why did she love this job so much? Not for the money, that was for sure.

What was it she was trying to prove? Thirty-two years old. This morning you could pass for ten years older than that, she thought. Your make-up's disappeared already. And look at that, around your eyes, the start of crow's feet. Jesus Christ. There are bruises under your eyes; you look like you've been in a fight.

She studied herself critically, as if her reflection was a stranger she was meeting for the first time. She knew men found her attractive, but men being what they were she was not always as flattered by their attentions as she might have been. Most of the men she knew would buy drinks for a duck if it had a skirt, lipstick and showed willing. Some of her colleagues found her height intimidating; at five feet and nine inches she was taller than Honeywell. Other women resented her figure – no exercise to speak of and doughnuts every day for morning tea and she never put on a pound. It wasn't her shoulder-length ash-blonde hair that was her favourite feature; it was the slate-grey eyes. She knew the effect they had. She had heard Marenko say she had a stare that could melt plastic, and she took it as a compliment.

The door opened and Fox stood back from the mirror as WPC Stacey walked in. Fox pretended to wash her hands. Stacey didn't go straight to one of the cubicles but joined Fox at the washbasins and started re-applying her mascara.

'Still here, ma'am?'

'I like working sixteen-hour days, constable. Good for the skin.'

'Do my eight hours chained to the wheel, then I'm out of here.' She watched Fox in the mirror. 'You OK, ma'am?'

'Just tired. I don't know if I'm cut out for this job any more.'

Stacey looked embarrassed by this admission. Rank, I suppose, Fox thought. I'm not one of the girls because I'm a DI; I'm not one of the boys because I'm a girl. I don't fit in in this place. I must like being a loner.

Stacey crossed to the cubicles. As the door closed, Fox heard her sit down and rip off two sheets of paper. 'You should go home and get a good night's sleep, ma'am,' Stacey said from the other side of the cubicle door.

'A solid eight hours would be nice. I didn't get home last night till eleven and I was called out again at two-thirty.'

'Jesus. What do you do for blokes?' There was a pause as WPC Stacey realised what she had said. 'If you don't mind me asking, ma'am.'

Fox grinned. 'The closest I get to real men are TJ and Honeywell.'

The lavatory flushed and the cubicle door swung open again.

'What do they say about me, Angela?' She dropped the 'constable', hoping to make Stacey feel more comfortable with her.

But Stacey was still wary. 'Ma'am?'

'I know the men have a nickname for me behind my back. Would you mind telling me what it is? Please,' she added.

Stacey looked at her, unsure.

'Between ourselves,' Fox said.

'Foxy,' Stacey said. 'As in foxy lady. Or just The Fox.'

'Not that one, Angela. I know about that one. What do they call me that they don't want me to know?'

Stacey took a deep breath. 'Sometimes it's Corporal Plonk. Or the Bod Squad. The ones that don't like you call you Elliot Ness. As in *The Untouchables*.'

Fox took a deep breath. Well, she had asked the question. 'It's all right, Angela, I'm not going to ask for names.'

'I wouldn't tell you, ma'am.' Stacey stopped with her hand on the door. 'By the way, ma'am, is that right what I hear about DCI Marenko?'

'That he's human? No, just an ugly rumour.'

'I heard his daughter's getting married on Saturday. Didn't know he had a daughter.'

'He keeps it quiet. She's a PLO terrorist.'

'That's what I thought,' Stacey said and went out.

Chapter Five

Marenko burst into the Incident Room.

'TJ, Honeywell, meet here tomorrow morning, 5 a.m. We're going to make an early-morning call. I've got an armed assault squad from SO19 lined up.'

James turned to Fox. 'Christ, he's really pissed off with his ex-wife this time.'

The house-to-house enquiries had yielded no more witnesses. Two people admitted being woken by the sound of the gunshots and seeing a man running from the scene and getting into a car. No, they wouldn't recognise him if they saw him again. Too far away. Too dark. No, they didn't get the registration number of the vehicle. One thought it was a black BMW, the other a red Toyota.

The news from ballistics was no more promising. Elmore Crawford had been shot with .38 hollowpoints, probably from a Smith & Wesson revolver. But both bullets were too badly mutilated to match to any particular weapon.

Enquiries among Elmore Crawford's family and associates had not progressed the investigation. He was a good boy. Had a thirteen-month-old daughter by his girlfriend. He would maybe smoke a little ganga to relax, but he would never touch drugs. Why are you here asking us all these questions? Why aren't you out there catching the bad men who did this to him?

It's because we're black, isn't it?

At this stage everything depended on Flora Ellis.

'I'll come with you,' Fox said.

Marenko hesitated. 'These are dangerous people.'

Fox just stared at him. For Christ's sake.

'OK. But stay out of trouble.'

Patrick James Capper was better known on the street as 'Knee Capper'. In his youth he'd had a string of convictions for assault and grievous bodily harm, but these days he passed himself off as a legitimate businessman. He ran his own security company, hiring doormen to various North London pubs and nightclubs; some of the clubs he owned himself. When Fox had been with the Drug Squad they had raided one of Capper's premises after a tip-off and netted a cache of cocaine and amphetamines, as well as several automatic weapons. Charges against Capper himself had been dropped for lack of evidence. An employee had taken the fall.

For a boy born and raised in a thirteenth-floor council flat in Stepney, Capper had done well for himself. His main residence was down a quiet lane near Waltham Abbey, in The Grange, a six-bedroom mock-Tudor house with blackened oak beams and trailing ivy, the latticed windows looking out over a private golf course. His neighbours were a corporate lawyer and an arms dealer. There was a sign at the entrance to the lane: PRIVATE ROAD. RESIDENTS ONLY.

But that morning Capper and his wealthy neighbours had their jealously guarded privacy temporarily disturbed as a police van and two police cars skidded to a halt on the raked gravel driveway of The Grange. James deliberately drove his Granada into the flower beds, and he and Marenko and Honeywell charged out, leaving the doors swinging open behind them.

Fox took her time following them. This was definitely not her territory. Three armed police in dark-blue body armour were attacking the front door with a sledgehammer, better known as a universal key. The heavy oak splintered and gave way and the team sergeant led his men inside. Jesus, she thought, you could probably smell the testosterone in Colchester.

'Nice place,' Fox murmured. Stone eagles and heavy urns of flowers flanked the doorway. There was a three-car garage, its doors open; in the grey dawn light she counted off a silver XJS, a sky-blue Rolls-Royce Corniche and a black left-hand-drive Mercedes 190E. No, crime doesn't pay. Sure.

The assault team's sergeant gave them the all clear and Marenko led the way inside.

Fox stepped over the door, employing a more leisurely pace. She looked around, as if she was thinking of buying the place. The cavernous hall had been redecorated in the gaudy and eclectic style favoured by East End gangsters in their country retreats. Fox was dimly aware of lurid marble statues of naked black women under nineteenth-century oils, a marble fountain bubbling below the staircase, a gilt Renaissance chair upholstered in rose silk positioned on a leopardskin rug. Even a crystal chandelier.

One of the SO19 had a tall man with bleached hair and a black leather bomber jacket pressed against the wall, while his partner searched him for weapons. He straightened, triumphantly holding up a Glock automatic pistol he had found in a shoulder holster.

Fox made her way up the stairs, following the stamps and yells of Marenko's vanguard.

Most of the noise was coming from the bedroom. Capper had been dragged from an imitation four-poster bed. He was stark naked, but he still had on enough gold chain to bankroll Ghana. An armed constable was holding his face into the Chinese carpet, his knee pressed into his spine. His wrists were cuffed behind his back. A blonde girl was shrieking hysterically in the bed and trying to cover herself with the black silk sheets while Honeywell formally read Capper his rights.

Capper screwed his head around and saw Marenko standing at the door. 'Bastards! I'll fuckin' do you for this, you bastards!'

James grinned. 'Is that a gun you got there, Pat, or are you just pleased to see us?'

As they hauled him to his feet, James was still slouching in the doorway. 'And cover that thing up with a blanket in case it goes off.'

'Filth! Fuckin' arseholes!'

'Mind your language,' Marenko said. 'There's ladies present.'

Capper's girlfriend was trying to struggle into her underwear on the bed. The sheets fell away.

'Nice tits,' James said.

There was a dressing gown on the back of a chair. Fox threw it to the girl. 'Show's over,' she said to James.

'Who's side are you on?' James snapped at her, disappointed, and walked out.

Marenko was at his desk, reading through the case file. Elmore Crawford had a file at Islington CID, where criminal intelligence placed him as a low-level drug dealer. Capper, on the other hand, had attracted the attention of the Drug Squad and had a file at the Organised Crime Task Force at New Scotland Yard. One of James's informants had told him that Crawford and some of his friends had been involved in an altercation with Capper in a public house in Kentish Town the night before Crawford was murdered, and that Crawford had 'dissed' him, called him a pussy.

It seemed pretty clear to Marenko what had happened from there.

Fox came in, carrying two coffees and two sausage rolls. She sometimes brought him these peace offerings, if she was in the mood. But sausage rolls! He was trying to lose weight, for Christ's sake.

'You seem well chuffed,' she said.

'Long way to go,' Marenko said prophetically.

That was her feeling also. The search of Capper's home in Waltham Abbey had been fruitless. Both of his minders had been armed but neither of their weapons were .38s; both had flash nine-millimetre pistols with lightweight plastic moulded handles. They had taken away a number of items of clothing for forensic testing, but Fox considered it was harassment, pure and simple. There were no bloodstains.

She sat down, pushed a polystyrene cup across the desk, and tore open the bag with the sausage rolls. 'Doesn't make sense.'

'What doesn't, Fox?'

'Why didn't he get someone else to top Crawford? Some hard man from out of town?'

'Reputation. Some of Capper's competition reckon he's going soft. They've been saying it for years. So along comes this smart mouth Yardie with big ideas, reckons he can take on his firm. Maybe he was dealing on Capper's patch, or maybe he was one of his distributors and he was creaming off the top. You know what Capper's like. Once he gets charlied up, he's a total nutter. He wants certain people to know he did this, show everyone he's still hard.'

'We don't have much. One witness twenty yards away at night. A good defence counsel will have a field day.'

Marenko looked at her, his face sour. 'This is different. He's known to her, and we have a statement. It will stick.'

The door opened and WPC Stacey leaned in. 'There's a Susan Delahunty to see you, sir.'

'Fuck it,' he muttered and then looked back at Fox. 'Pardon my French.'

'She's down at reception,' Stacey said. 'Shall I bring her up?'

'No, I'll come down.'

Stacey closed the door and Marenko looked at Fox. 'Christ Almighty.'

'Good news, guv?'

'Capper's brief,' Marenko said and walked out.

*   *   *

She was late forties, early fifties. If pressed he would have described her as tidy rather than handsome. There was something well scrubbed about her, belonging to another world, a world long gone, where she would have been the wife of a wealthy man instead of wealthy in her own right, as she now was. He found her intimidating; he always had. But he never let it show.

Today she wore a dark blue suit with a white blouse, a gold Piaget on her wrist. There was a burnished leather briefcase on her lap. When he walked into the foyer she was sitting on one of the bench seats flicking through a Filofax and talking into a burgundy mobile telephone the size of a pocket calculator. He was met by an assault wave of expensive French perfume.

When she saw him she cut short the telephone call and got to her feet. 'What the hell do you think you're doing?'

'Hello, Susan,' he said.

'I have advised my client to lodge a complaint against you and this department.'

Marenko glanced at the desk sergeant, who looked quickly away. 'Let's discuss this upstairs.'

'You break down the door, terrorise his fiancée—'

'—slut.'

'—put guns in his face, and drag him down here naked. Where do you think you are? Russia? Iran?'

'If it was Russia I'd have electrodes attached to his private parts by now. And yours as well. Would you like a coffee instead?'

He led her back upstairs to his office. Fox had taken her cue and removed to the Incident Room. He ushered Susan Delahunty inside. As he closed the door behind them he was uncomfortably aware of the litter of polystyrene cups and pastries and the smell of his own sweat on his clothes.

'Now. What's your problem, Susan?'

'I intend to lodge a formal complaint with the Metropolitan Commissioner of Police about your reckless disregard for my client's civil liberties.'

He settled himself behind his desk. A barrier, of sorts. 'We had reason to believe he was armed and dangerous.'

'He was in bed asleep.'

'Not exactly asleep, Susan. And he was armed. In fact, he was brandishing a large weapon at a naked woman.'

'Spare me the smut, Frank. What evidence do you have against my client?'

'We have an eyewitness placing him at the scene of a fatal shooting in the early hours of Thursday morning.'

'At what time exactly?'

'Around 2 a.m.'

'My client has instructed me to inform you that he was playing cards at a friend's house in Highbury until 3.30 that morning, and he has three independent witnesses who can corroborate this.'

'Three other well-known drug dealers.'

'Business identities.' She opened her briefcase and threw copies of the depositions on his desk. 'You have no cause to hold my client.'

Marenko tapped on the desk with a biro, a fast tattoo beating to a quicker time as his patience evaporated. This was what was wrong with the criminal justice system; there was no justice. There were just solicitors and barristers fucking with everyone. What did she care? She lived in Hampstead.

'For Christ's sake, this bloke makes his living from dealing in cocaine.'

'If that's true, why isn't he in jail?'

Marenko got to his feet and leaned across his desk. A small vein had popped at his temple and was outlined against his skin in an angry purple knot. 'Because of people like you! Is that why you wanted to do law, *Ms* Delahunty? To keep these scrotes on the street?'

Susan was not intimidated by his size or his anger. God knows, she had witnessed this performance enough times during their married life. She crossed her legs. 'If we don't uphold the law, we might as well go back to the jungle.'

'Go *back* to the jungle? What do you think Brixton is? What do you call Clapham? *Civilisation?*'

'All you had to do was make one phone call and my client would have accompanied me to the nearest police station voluntarily. Instead you deliberately dragged him out of his home in this humiliating manner. You haven't heard the last of this.' Susan Delahunty got to her feet, snapped the locks on her briefcase and walked out.

Marenko shouted after her, 'Have a nice day!' but she had already slammed the door behind her.

Patrick Capper was sitting on the bunk in his cell in Tottenham police station, his arms folded across his chest, thin-lipped with rage. One of his minders had delivered his clothes to the reception; pinstriped trousers, Italian leather shoes, a black silk shirt and a waistcoat, which was also silk and had a paisley pattern in violet and black. Another of his many street names was Dapper Capper.

Crims, Marenko thought sourly. They always mistook being obvious for being clever.

When a uniformed constable opened the door and asked Capper to follow him to the interview room, he rose without a word, his eyes brimming with sullen malevolence.

Capper leaned forward and directed his answers to the built-in microphone, displaying his contempt for the two detectives. 'When this Elmore Crawford geezer was shot, I was at a friend's place playing cards.'

'At 2 o'clock in the morning?'

Capper spared a glance of contempt for Marenko. 'Just because you're tucked up in bed with a cup of cocoa after the 9 o'clock news doesn't mean other people don't have a life.'

Fox broke in, her voice soothing, her smile forced. 'We're trying to help you with this, Mr Capper. If you cooperate with us, I'm sure we'll soon have this sorted out. Now, these friends of yours. They would be willing to testify in court that you were with them at that time?'

Capper returned his attention to the microphone. 'Yes.'

'Can we have their names, please?'

They already knew the names from Delahunty's depositions. She wanted to know if Capper remembered them. He reeled them off. James Strong. Charles Whitten. Vernon Taylor. Fox recognised two of them as Capper's minders. The other was his accountant.

'You sure the Three Stooges have got their stories straight?' Marenko said. 'Charlie Whitten needs three goes to spell his name right.'

Delahunty, Capper's brief, raised an eyebrow in warning. Marenko did his best to ignore her. He leaned across the table. 'We have an eyewitness who saw you shoot Elmore Crawford in the head.' he said, elaborating the truth a little.

'They must have mistaken me for someone else,' Capper recited into the microphone.

'Come on,' Marenko went on, probing for a reaction. 'What was it? Was he trying to deal on your turf?'

'I have never met this geezer. OK?'

'We have other witnesses who say that you and Crawford were involved in an argument in a public house called the Crooked Billet on Tuesday evening.'

'Yeah? Why aren't they here, then?'

'What was it, Pat? You were supplying and he was holding out on you? Was that it?'

'I believe my client has answered your question, Chief Inspector,' Delahunty said.

Marenko kept his eyes fixed on Capper. 'You really made your point, didn't you, Patrick? Showed everyone you were still hard.'

'This is harassment! My client has answered your question!'

But Marenko went on, ignoring her. 'This wasn't just business, was it? This was personal. He'd been putting it around that you'd gone soft so you—'

'Chief Inspector Marenko! If you are going to browbeat my client I am going to end this interview right now! My client has made it quite clear to you that he did not know the deceased, and there are three independent witnesses who can corroborate that he was elsewhere at the time of the murder. You clearly have a case of mistaken identity.'

Marenko sat back in his seat. There was sweat on his upper lip.

We're in trouble, Fox thought, unless we can put him at the crime scene some other way; another witness, a murder weapon with his prints on it.

He might still slip out from under this.

Marenko forced himself to smile. Christ, that was an effort, Fox thought. It's like he's holding a two-hundred-pound bench press. 'I don't think so, Ms Delahunty,' he said. 'We have a statement from an eyewitness to the shooting. I would caution Mr Capper's associates about perjuring themselves.' He turned back to Capper. 'I hope you've packed your jammies.'

'This is preposterous,' Delahunty said. 'This won't even get to court.'

Marenko rose to his feet. There was an air of menace about him when he was quiet like this. Fox felt safer when he was raging and throwing things. 'Interview terminated 3.15 p.m.' He snapped off the tape and turned back to Delahunty. 'Why don't you get yourself a short leather skirt and stand out on the street and earn a decent living?' He stamped out of the room.

Delahunty stared at Fox, her face pink with shock and rage. Even Fox was appalled. 'That was uncalled for,' Fox said. 'I apologise.' She stood up and nodded to the police constable who was standing at the door. 'Take Mr Capper back to the cells, please,' she said.

'Don't apologise for him,' Delahunty said to her as she left. 'Once you start, you find you never stop.'

Chapter Six

Fox led Flora Ellis to the observation room. She moved stiffly, almost rigid with fear, a shoulder bag clutched white-knuckled at her side. She's not going to go through with this, Fox thought. She's going to change her mind and run right out of here. And there's a part of me that doesn't want to stop her.

'Where's Miles, Mrs Ellis?' she asked.

'Neighbour's looking after him for an hour. But I have to get home soon. She goes to work at seven.'

'We'll be through well before then,' Fox said, trying to make the whole process sound no more threatening than a routine trip to the dentist. If she's going to point her finger at Patrick Capper, Fox thought, the guv'nor had better get her some protection.

They went into the observation room. Susan Delahunty was in there with a DC from another squad, Jennings. Flora stood stiffly to attention, staring in horror at the glass.

'It's all right,' Fox reassured her. 'You can see them, but they can't see you. It's one-way glass.'

'Why didn't I just stay away from that sodding window?' Flora Ellis muttered.

Fox gave her a reassuring smile and tested the microphone that linked them to the identification room.

There were twelve men standing in a row facing the

observation window. Each held a number in front of him. Capper was number seven; he was staring at the glass with a crooked smile and a look of seasoned contempt on his face. The other men all had reddish hair like Capper and were more or less the same height.

Fox put a hand lightly on Flora's arm. 'If you see the man you saw that night you just have to tell the detective constable here and he'll do the rest. If you want the men to do something to help you make an identification, he'll give the instructions over the address system.'

'Won't you be here with me?' Flora Ellis asked her.

'I'm too heavily involved with this case, Mrs Ellis. I have to wait outside to remove any question of bias. But I'll be right outside that door. Now, just take your time. Do you have any questions?'

Flora Ellis shook her head. There was a sheen of sweat on her upper lip.

Fox went out and closed the door behind her. Marenko was leaning against the wall, chewing on a hangnail. 'Is she going to be all right?'

Fox shrugged her shoulders and crossed her arms. They would have to wait and see.

Three minutes later the door opened. Delahunty walked out, her face an inscrutable mask. Jennings guided Flora Ellis out, a hand gently on her elbow. He shook his head. Flora Ellis had been unable to make the identification. Marenko walked away without saying a word to her, his face pale with anger.

It was 6 o'clock at night and the reception area was chaos. A woman was in tears because her Volvo estate had been stolen from a local car park. She slammed her hand on the counter, both angry and terrified at once. 'What's my husband going to say?' A young woman was being released after being arrested and charged with shoplifting. Her father led her through the crowd, white-lipped with fury.

The men from the identity parade were leaving, a few pounds richer. And a story for the pub tonight. Not every day you get to stand in an identity parade next to Pat Capper.

It was raining when they got outside. Still only the middle of September. So that was summer for another year.

'Thank you for your help, Mrs Ellis,' Fox said.

Flora could not meet her eyes. 'I'm sorry. I couldn't do it. It was him all right, but I couldn't do it.'

'I'll get a patrol car to take you home.'

'I don't want the neighbours to see me with the Old Bill,' Flora said. 'I'll take the bus.'

'We can't let you do that,' Fox told her. 'I'll call you a cab. I can give you a voucher to give to the driver. It won't cost you anything.'

She called a cab from the front desk. When she got back to the foyer, Flora was staring vacantly at a missing persons poster. They went out through the doors and stood in the shelter of the forecourt. Flora Ellis said nothing, staring at the rain splashing from the eaves, her face as grey as the evening sky. The streets were slick like the belly of a snake.

Friday. Poets Day: Piss Off Early, Tomorrow's Saturday. Not now. With an unsolved murder in their lap they'd all be working overtime for the next couple of weeks.

'I hope I done the right thing,' Flora said.

'I'm sure you did,' Fox forced herself to say.

'Only I worry about my Miles.'

What could she say to her? If she had been in her position, would she have had the guts to have gone through with it?

They waited in silence, listening to the rain.

A few minutes later a black taxicab pulled up, its diesel motor ticking over. She handed her the docket for the taxi, helped her into the back seat and closed the door.

As the taxicab pulled away Fox looked across the street and saw a black Mercedes 190E pull away from the kerb. There were two men in the front of the car. She recognised the man behind the wheel. He had bleached hair and a leather bomber jacket, the man she had seen that morning with his face pressed against the wall of Capper's mansion.

The man in the passenger seat was Patrick Capper. He smiled and flashed a wave.

Chapter Seven

'Maddy?'

Fox felt her knuckles tighten around the phone. 'Ginny.' Her big sister. Christ, what had she forgotten now? Ma's birthday? No, she was pretty sure that was some time in November. Perhaps one of Ginny's kids? She fumbled on the desk for her Filofax, thumbing quickly to the Year Planner, where all the birthdays and anniversaries were noted, keeping her guard up, trying to sound relaxed.

'You still OK for tonight?'

'Tonight.'

'You haven't forgotten?'

Here it was. September. Fifteenth. Ian's birthday. Hard enough to remember when her own family had birthdays, never mind in-laws. It wasn't that she was selfish; one year she had forgotten her own birthday and Ginny had even reminded her about that. The job did that to you.

'No, I haven't forgotten.' *Forgotten what?*

'Seven-thirty.'

'Uh-huh.'

'You *have* forgotten.'

'No. You're having a party.'

'Dinner.'

'At Ravanelli's.'

'Here. Just bring a bottle of wine.'

'Yeah. Right. Here it is in my diary.' *Christ.* She checked her watch. Better get into town and buy him something.

'I've invited George and Siobhan. You remember them? George was Ian's best man at the wedding.' Oh, vaguely. The wedding was a blur. She'd drunk too much champagne on an empty stomach and had been poured into a taxi just after they cut the cake. 'And one of Ian's old friends from school. He's just moved back to London. You'll like him.'

Oh, shit. She was being set up with a blind date. Ginny, you *cow.* 'Uh-huh.'

'Don't be late.'

'Me? Never.'

'See you then.'

Fox hung up the receiver. Family. Impossible to forget you had one; it was like having chewing gum on the bottom of your shoe. And she had distanced herself. Families held you back, told you what you couldn't, or shouldn't, do. Families were the keeper of secrets long outgrown.

Her eyes wandered to the family photographs on Marenko's desk. Lighten up, Madeleine. Perhaps you should arm yourself with a few personal touches. After all, if Marenko had them . . . Hard to think of the Big Man with a family. She wandered through to his office to take a closer look.

Two young girls grinned from an ancient Kodachrome. They were both grown women now, by all accounts, just a little younger than herself. But there they were enshrined on Marenko's desk, permanently frozen in braces and school uniforms, icons from a time when Marenko was still married and ate his dinners at tables instead of takeaway boxes at his desk. If there ever was such a time; if legend could be believed.

She looked at her watch. One o'clock on a Saturday afternoon, and here she was pushing paper around her desk. Only contract killers and drug dealers valued their leisure time, apparently. She picked up her leather shoulder bag, found her keys and tucked the chair into the desk well with a gesture of finality.

She walked out of her office and down the corridor, through the swing doors to the lifts. She found her Vauxhall Cavalier in its space. What a mess. There were dents in the rear wing and in the passenger door. That was Marenko's handiwork: he had parked too close to her one day and thrown open his door, in a hurry as usual. She thought she might try to take it to the carwash this afternoon. Get the bird mess off the back window. Perhaps get some of the takeaway chicken boxes out of the back seat too.

She slumped behind the wheel. She put the keys in the ignition but did not switch on the engine straight away. There has to be a time, she thought, when you ask yourself what you're doing with your life. And this is as good a time as any.

She stared at the windscreen, a mist of grime on the glass. She turned on the windscreen washers. It just made it worse, smearing the mud and dirt in an opaque arc across the glass.

Like my life, she thought. I try to get things clearer for myself and all I succeed in doing is making everything worse. Is it because I'm a woman that being a cop is so hard, or is it just hard being a cop anyway? Most of the guys she knew in the department had been through a number of marriages. She had never married, but like them she really had no private life of her own. Police work was like a drug. She couldn't get off it and couldn't imagine living without it. It was the root of all her problems and the source of all her highs, the occasional adrenalin rush of a murder scene, an arrest, a conviction; and there was something else, this need to prove something to someone, God knows what or why.

She supposed the fact of it was that she was a true believer. She always had been, from her time as a WPC at Shepherd's Bush and Leyton, the three years as a DC at Southwark, another two years at Vauxhall, then as a DS with the Robbery Squad in Finchley. She had earned her reputation as a high-flier with the

Flying Squad, an elite unit based at Scotland Yard that handled organised crime.

She had been attached to the Area Major Incident Team at Hendon Road for just six months. Still cutting her teeth in the job. She loved the force, and she loved being a detective. She didn't care about money, and despite the constant proposals apparently she didn't care about sex either. She cared about justice and doing something that really mattered.

Justice.

Absently she turned on the radio. The Radio 1 news led with the story of the Macclesfield Monsters, as the press had dubbed them, a husband and wife who had been arrested that morning for the rape, torture and murder of four teenagers who had gone missing in Lancashire over the last twelve months. The report said that the police believed the couple were involved in the disappearance of at least three other young girls.

They won't see light of day again, Fox thought with grim satisfaction. At least there are some crimes still too heinous for even the best defence barrister to bargain down.

She asked herself once more about the system of justice that she sought to serve. Too many times she had seen cases where justice had been ill-served by clever barristers, and in the end the victims went forgotten and unavenged. There was the nineteen-year-old she had arrested following the fatal bashing of a taxi driver only to see his brief argue the charge down to GBH. He was somehow back on the street within nine months. She had had murderers make full confessions without duress only to have a court-appointed solicitor persuade them to retract their confessions and in one instance had the case dismissed on a chain of evidence irregularity. She knew the man was guilty, and his brief knew it, and the judge knew it. But the man was put back on the streets, and fifteen months later he shot a petrol station attendant during an armed robbery and left the man in a wheelchair for life.

She was sick to death of lawyers educated beyond their

conscience or their ethics, of a critical press, of crushing hours with little value or reward from society beyond her own brotherhood of police, and even there she was isolated because she was a woman.

But as her father had said, on the day she announced she was giving up her nursing training to be a policewoman: 'Maddy, I hope you never regret your choice. This is not going to be easy.'

Her old man. If he was alive today it would kill him.

Chapter Eight

Marenko examined his reflection in the mirror on top of the dressing-table. Jesus, the monkey suit had shrunk since the last time he had worn it. He fiddled with the carnation in his buttonhole. I look like a complete prat in this. Like a stand-up comic in a Bradford working-man's club.

His eyes flicked to the photograph on the dressing-table, a man and a woman and two small girls, on a seafront somewhere, standing against the sea wall, the wind blowing a gale. Must have been taken in the summer. The girls were still small, Jules no older than ten — that would make Donna maybe seven. Donna was giggling, Jules was standing self-consciously and ramrod straight. Her blonde curls were in her face. The man was shirtless, beefy; he had a flat stomach and his hair wasn't around his collar and turning to grey.

Just look at me now, Marenko thought. Suck your guts in, son, you're not Mr Universe any more. They were better days. Just not enough of them, that was the trouble. Can't relax, never could. I bet I was standing there, looking at Susan behind the camera and mentally ticking off items in the evidence folder back at the office.

He traced the outlines of the two small girls lovingly, with a fingertip. Too late now, you stupid bastard.

✲   ✲   ✲

Marenko walked into the Incident Room, acutely aware that the office had fallen silent and that everyone was staring at him. He kept his head down and tried not to catch anyone's eye.

A wolf whistle from somewhere. James and Honeywell were both at their desks, DS Terry James – TJ, as he was known – in his usual sartorial elegance, a charcoal double-breasted suit and burgundy silk tie, black Oxfords polished to a mirror under the desk. Across from him, Honeywell, looking like a bag of shit, bastard hadn't even combed his hair. Probably been up all night walking the baby.

James was the first to speak. 'Are we doing cases in Belgravia now, guv?'

'There's a penguin gone missing at the zoo,' Honeywell said, 'and he's going undercover.'

Marenko looked around, his stare hard, preparing to deck the next man who spoke. WPC Stacey was fighting to keep her face straight. Two other DCs found things of incredible interest on their computer screens.

He heard James say to Honeywell: 'What's he doing here? I thought his kid was getting married this afternoon.'

'He'll probably take his mobile with him and chase leads at the reception.'

'What are you two muttering about?' Marenko said.

'Nothing, guv'nor. Just comparing notes.'

'Well, as soon as you've finished doing that I want you to write up search and seizure warrants for every pub and every nightclub that Capper owns. When you've done that I'm going to try to find a magistrate to sign them.'

'But haven't you got a wedding to go to this afternoon, guv?'

'I've got time.'

James and Honeywell looked at each other. Jesus Christ.

Chapter Nine

Donna and Martin had decided against a formal church wedding; trying their luck on an English summer they had settled on a garden ceremony. Marenko drove down North End Way towards The Hill and parked his brown Sierra between a BMW convertible and a black Saab turbo.

A young couple got out of the Saab. The man was dressed casually in a shirt with grandfather collar and jeans. Marenko felt suddenly shabby in the monkey suit. He worked the collar of his shirt. Overdressed and underpaid again, he thought grimly. The story of my life.

The weather had been kind. It was a warm Indian summer, the water in the pond like liquid mercury in the late-afternoon sun. He broke into a trot across the grass. He was late. The ceremony was already under way.

'. . . and I'd like to welcome you all here today to the wedding of Martin and Donna. It's a joyous occasion, a day in which we all can celebrate the very nature of love.'

Christ Almighty. It was going to be one of those weddings. Susan had organised most of it, he should have suspected. That was the trouble with the legal fraternity. Six days a week they twisted your balls by the roots, toiling away to put drug dealers and rapists and murderers back on the streets, and on Sundays they went to church and it was all things bright and beautiful.

It was why he never trusted religion. He didn't like the sort of people it attracted.

The marriage celebrant was a woman with dark hair, long strands of grey through it. She wore it like a teenager, wild and falling around her stooped shoulders. She had been mugged by a long and shapeless frock, there was a shawl around her shoulders and what looked like a daisy chain on her head. She was standing under an arch of flowers reading from a bound red leather book. A superannuated hippie, Marenko thought sourly. If I strip-searched this old bird right now I guarantee I'd find a couple of ounces of cannabis cached up her arse.

'Before we start,' the celebrant was saying, 'I think it might be a good idea if we all really tune in to the nature all around us in this beautiful setting. There is love energy in even the flowers and the trees, so let's all close our eyes and really feel ourselves at one with nature and the love principle.'

Marenko felt himself starting to sweat.

'Now I'd like you to turn to the person next to you and give them a really big hug.'

Marenko looked to his right. One of Donna's friends. An overdressed young man reeking of aftershave. There was a diamond stud in his left ear.

'You as much as fucken touch me,' Marenko whispered, 'and you'll be eating your piece of the wedding cake through a tube.'

'Perhaps at this stage everyone might like to come forward and congratulate the bride and groom.'

Marenko hung back as the guests milled around his daughter and her new husband. Most of the faces were strangers, though he recognised some of Susan's family here and there. It seemed he was the sole representative of the Marenko clan, or what was left of it, his parents gone now, his brother dead of a stroke at forty-seven.

'Hello, Frank.' He looked up. Susan.

'Hello, Susan.' Well, make an effort, he told himself. 'I guess I owe you an apology.'

'Oh?' When she wanted to, she could cut through ice with her voice.

'The crack about the leather skirt and that. Said in the heat of the moment.'

'That's all right, Frank, I forgive you.'

A lie, he thought. Women are genetically incapable of forgiveness. They store up hurts like a squirrel caching nuts, saving them all up until the day they have your balls in a wringer, then they smile and run them through. She came forward and kissed him lightly on the cheek. That perfume again.

'Well. That's both our daughters married off. We'll be grandparents next.'

'Give me a break.'

'What did you think of the ceremony?'

'It was different. I suppose you organised everything.'

Her face was deadpan. 'I'm just here to read through the contract.'

'Feeling the energy of the flowers and the trees. For Christ's sake.'

'They're young, and they're in love. They'll learn.'

'Yeah, we did.' Stop, Marenko thought. Stop now. This is not the time or the place. You're spoiling for a fight. Give it a rest for once. Make an effort, be nice. But instead he heard himself say: 'I see you got Capper back on the street. Does he commune with nature too?'

'Not today, Frank. It's a wedding.'

A young man in a grey suit walked towards them, smiling. Young men get younger every year, Marenko thought. On his arm was a girl with red hair and a face at once pretty and challenging, her mother's Irish colouring, her father's cheekbones and swagger. Jules. My Jules.

'Hello, Tom. Jules. How's it going?'

Tom shook his hand. 'Hello, sir.' Sir. Sir, as in sir, my wife's father. Also sir, as in Detective Chief Inspector, sir. Tom was at police training school. Still proud of it.

Julia leaned forward and gave him a rather cool peck on the cheek. 'Daddy.'

'Hi, Jules. Haven't seen you for a while.'

Julia ignored him, turned to her mother and hugged her, close in. The two women moved away.

Marenko turned to Tom. 'She still mad at me?'

'At both of us, sir. She still isn't used to the idea of having another cop in the family.'

Marenko turned back to the thinning crowd around Donna, watched them a little resentfully. I'm her father, he thought. But I just don't figure with this lot any more. I have to wait for a son-in-law before I get any respect.

'What did you think of the wedding, sir?'

I should really stop him calling me sir. No, bollocks, I like the sound of it. 'Fucken brilliant. Especially the bit about being one with the trees. I really got it together with that horse chestnut over there. We're going to dance later.'

'That's just Donna, sir. She collects crystals too. Takes all sorts.'

'My day we got married in a church. You got a sermon about not taking the pill and then all the blokes got paralytic at the church hall. Whatever happened to religion?'

'God knows.'

'Right.'

'Martin seems a decent bloke.'

'He's a barrister. A cop's kid and she marries one of the enemy. Might as well have hitched up with a Triad or one of the Krays.'

Marenko saw his chance. The crowd around the newlyweds had finally started to drift away. 'Excuse me a minute,' he said to Tom and walked over. Donna saw him, took a step towards him and threw her arms around his neck.

'You look beautiful, Dons.'

'Thanks, Dad.'

As Marenko pulled away Martin grabbed him and started to pump his hand. 'This is the best day of my life, Frank.' *Frank.* Marenko felt his face freeze into a grimace.

Then the photographer moved in, hurrying them away. Marenko turned around. Tom was standing there, watching.

'Let's go and get a drink,' Marenko said.

Chapter Ten

It seemed to Marenko that Hampstead was aloof from the rest of London, perched awkwardly there on its hilltop, prime real estate, its nose stuck in the air. A Georgian village in its own time loop. The reception was held at Susan's place, a Victorian villa with a narrow garden and a view over the heath. When daddy died, Susan, as the only daughter, got the lot.

Marenko had a flat in Swiss Cottage.

The lawn in the back garden had been freshly mowed; it looked like a bit of Wembley on Cup Final day. A small marquee had been erected at the end of the lawn, open at one end, with tables and chairs set out in a U-shape. The caterers were busy setting the final touches, while the guests stood around the tent and on the lawn sipping champagne. Not cheap stuff either, Marenko thought. French, Veuve Clicquot.

He was standing on his own, watching Susan work the room — or, in this case, work the lawn; room, lawn, she was always good at it — saw the couple approach him from the corner of his eye. Grey hair, tinted bifocals, a good suit. All those things that made him uncomfortable and angry.

'Lovely wedding,' the man said.

'Yes, it is.'

'I don't believe we've met.' He held out his hand. 'My name's Michael, Michael Williams. This is my wife Sarah.'

Sarah held out a soft, white hand. Immaculately groomed, a grey silk dress, an emerald brooch, a soft face, eyes ceaselessly searching for imperfection. They were sizing him up; these people, he thought, are accustomed to making quick judgements on the social scale.

'Frank Marenko.'

Williams's embarrassment was immediately obvious. 'Ah. So you're Susan's—'

'I'm her ex, right. I think I remember your name too. Barrister at Stawell Pateman, right?'

The man looked wary.

'One of my guys told me about you.'

'Oh?'

'Rape case he had. You gave the victim such a hard time on the stand she threw in the towel.'

Michael Williams licked his lips. 'I don't think this is the time or the place.'

'Neither did she.'

'Well, if I'd been the victim I don't think I would have dropped the charges — if they were true.'

'You're not sixteen and you've never been raped.'

'Perhaps another time. We're here to enjoy ourselves.'

'You're right. Yeah, let's enjoy ourselves. Hey, I've got a joke for you. What's the difference between a lawyer and a catfish?'

Williams took his wife by the arm and started to lead her away, but Marenko grabbed his arm.

'One's a bottom-dwelling, scum-sucking, ugly little shark . . . and a catfish is just a catfish. Sorry. Got to go now. Think I've been called to the bar.'

Marenko let them go then. At the top of some steps, on the stone-flagged patio, was a trestle table covered with a cloth of Irish linen. It was attended by a young, dark-haired man in a white shirt and a bow tie. Oh, look at that. Someone else with one of these damned things on.

'Having a good time, sir?' the man asked him.

'Sure. This is right up there with my brother's funeral.' He handed him the empty champagne flute. 'Look, I'm pretty sick of drinking lolly water. Got any Scotch?'

Fox stood in the off-licence staring at the racks of wines, her hand hovering over the bottles without a clue. The French stuff was too expensive and the Frogs didn't need the jobs. The labels on the Australian wines were nice, but she kept thinking about Les Patterson and it put her off. Besides, their economy was healthy enough. That left Bulgaria or Chile. They were both in a bit of a mess, and she was sure some grape picker in the Maipo valley or Plovdiv would appreciate her custom. A vigneron might be appalled at her methods of judging a suitable wine, she thought, but as a determined gin and tonic drinker she had to form her own methodology somehow.

The Indian proprietor was sitting behind the counter in what appeared to be a comatose state, staring at the television set mounted on the wall above his head. It was a news bulletin, coverage of the arrest of the Macclesfield Monsters. There was the usual footage of enraged men and women shouting from behind a police cordon, then shots of a man and woman, handcuffed and with jackets thrown over their faces, being hurried out of a police van.

'What do they hope to achieve?' she heard someone say. She looked up. A tall, fair-haired man was standing at the counter watching the news pictures. There was a bottle of wine on the counter and he was reaching inside his jacket for his wallet.

The proprietor offered no comment but took the wine and slipped it inside a brown paper bag. Fox brought her own selection – a Chilean Cabernet Sauvignon – over to the cash register.

'They're just giving vent to their anger,' she found herself saying.

'No better than a lynch mob.'

'Those people tortured four young girls to death. What do you expect?'

'And that makes us a civilised society, does it?'

I don't believe this, Fox thought. I am not getting into this argument in public. She shrugged her shoulders and was going to leave it at that, but the proprietor wanted his say now. 'I think castration would be better. Cut his bloody nuts off.'

'And what about the woman? Ritual rape followed by a disembowelling?'

The proprietor looked up at the fair-haired man, his spectacles catching the reflection of the TV screen. 'Well, why bloody not?'

'I don't believe this. This is the twentieth century. Or did you miss it?'

'You don't have daughters.'

'I do, actually,' the fair-haired man said. 'I just don't think that killing people is any solution. They murder someone so we murder them?'

'Cut his bloody todger off and he won't go raping anyone again, will he? If it was my daughter, that's what I'd do.' He held tight to the bottle of wine, almost daring the fair-haired man to go and take his custom somewhere else.

'Well, why don't we all go back to the Middle Ages?'

These two are going to start hitting each other in a minute, Fox thought. Nothing like the high moral ground to make the testosterone start to flow. She decided to try the role of peacemaker. 'I think what he's trying to say,' she said to the fair-haired man, 'is that it's easy to distance yourself from a problem when you're not directly involved.'

The man gave a deep sigh of forbearance. 'Well, I think I shall go and enjoy my dinner before the rule of the mob becomes law and I have to dodge lynching parties on the way home.' He slammed a five-pound note on the counter. 'Four pounds ninety-nine, I believe. Keep the change.' He took the wine and stormed out, the glass door slamming behind him.

The proprietor glared after him. 'At least in India we know how to deal with criminals,' he said to Fox. 'We leave them to rot in prison or we make them Prime Minister. But either way we get them off the damned streets!'   •

Chapter Eleven

Ian and Ginny lived in a semidetached house in Worcester Park, mock Tudor with gabled loft and carriage lamps in the porch. Ian was an accountant in the city, Ginny had been a nurse until the twins arrived. They had a new Ford in the garage, took holidays in France every year, had a dishwasher in the kitchen and a dustbuster in the utility room. They lived a decent, normal life. Unlike Ginny's little sister, Fox thought, who drove a filthy, dented Cavalier, never took holidays, had dirty dishes piling up in the sink and washed her clothes at the launderette.

Fox loved Ginny and she liked Ian, but she always felt uncomfortable around them. They were nice people, members of a public she had pledged to serve and protect, but she knew she made them nervous. They didn't understand her, and she didn't understand them. For a start Fox did not know how to make small talk. The last time she had seen them, at Easter, she had spent the afternoon helping to retrieve a three-day-old suicide from Camden Lock. Hauling the body on to the bank, the victim's arm had come away from the torso, leaving her holding a disembodied limb.

How did you respond when a member of your family asked you how your day had been. *It was a bitch. I unintentionally dismembered a corpse. How about you?*

In fact, that was precisely how they looked at her, as if she might indeed absent-mindedly pull some decaying body part from her jacket pocket at any moment. *Oh, damn, I meant to leave this at the office.* There had never been a cop in the family before, and Ginny treated her with the gentle but patronising deference she might afford a member of another race, a Jamaican, perhaps, or, God forbid, a Scot.

She parked her car a little down the road – there was, incredibly, a space right in front of the house but she ignored it. Ginny wouldn't have said anything, but she would have noticed the dirt and the dents and a week later, when she next saw her mother, it would be: 'Ginny says you can't afford a new car.'

It was a warm September evening. In the distance she heard the rattle of a train pulling into the station; a 747 flying overhead left a white plume of vapour in the sky. Clutching her bottle of wine and the gift-wrapped CD she had bought for Ian – Chris Rea never offended anyone – she took a deep breath and marched resolutely down the road.

The garden was neat, a rectangle of lawn, a few rosebushes, a paved driveway. There was the homely glow of table lamps through the lattice windows. Ian threw open the door with a cry of 'Maddy!' and encircled her in his arms as if she had just returned from a special airborne mission over Iraq. His good humour was infectious and also irritating, depending on your mood. He almost carried her inside. She heard the toddlers fighting upstairs, drowning out the old Dire Straits CD on the stereo. The warm smell of cooking drifted through the house.

'Happy birthday,' Fox said and handed Ian the gift and the wine.

He shouted his thanks as if a present was absolutely the last thing he had ever expected to receive from her – possibly not an unjustifiable reaction if form was anything to go by – and then Ginny came forward and wrapped her arms around her. Beautiful Ginny, dark hair in a ponytail, elfin face, a figure to die for –

though perhaps a little more cuddly since the twins, she thought with sibling spite, and immediately hated herself for it.

'Maddy,' she gushed. 'How are you? It's ages since we've seen you.'

'Fine,' Fox said. 'Just fine.'

'We thought you might forget.' Then she added in a stage whisper, 'Ian was *sure* you'd forget.'

Ian grinned and shook his head in that charming way of his that let her know he was absolutely stunned she had even remembered where they lived.

'How could I forget my favourite brother-in-law's birthday?' she said, going along with the charade.

A long, oak table was set for six, heavy, solid-silver cutlery, willow-pattern place settings, candles. There was a bottle of French champagne on the table, and Ian poured some into a flute and handed it to her. George and Siobhan were already there, and she prayed that Ian was not going to leave them in the room alone. Siobhan was a teacher, George a sales rep for a chemicals company. She had absolutely nothing in common with them, and she was useless at small talk. In fact, she sometimes wondered if police work hadn't eroded all her social skills. She could keep up an interrogation for hours but a few minutes' talk around a dinner table and she was exhausted.

She sipped her champagne and looked around. It was all so different from her own flat off the Bayswater Road; there were no knickers on the floor, no piles of old newspapers waiting to be thrown out, no car keys or bank statements strewn around the hall table. The lamps lent a muted glow to the living room, there were bookshelves full of paperback novels and hardbound books, collectors' plates on the walls. So this is how normal people live.

'Dinner's nearly ready,' Ginny announced and disappeared back into the kitchen.

'Anyone else coming?' George asked.

'Simon. Old mate of mine from school days. He's just moved back down to London. In fact, there he is now.'

Ian went to the door. As it opened, the final guest stood framed in the doorway. He wore a black rollneck jumper under a tan leather jacket, and charcoal slacks. His eyes were a startling china blue. He was tall and fair-haired, and, as Fox had already ascertained, was keenly interested in the question of civil liberties.

Ian embraced him with the enthusiasm he reserved exclusively, it appeared, for about a quarter of the world's population and almost dropped the proferred bottle of wine.

'Sorry I'm late,' Simon said. 'I had trouble finding the street.'

'No problem. Come on in, I'll introduce everyone. This is Simon. Simon, this is—' He stopped.

Fox's eyes locked with Simon's. Ian caught the stare. 'Met, have you?'

'In the off-licence.'

'What a coincidence,' George said.

Fox nodded. 'Yeah. Life's crazy, isn't it?'

Ginny served a chilled gazpacho and then a home-made pasta dish with shrimp and fresh mushrooms; there were medallions of veal with baby potatoes for the main course. Ginny had always been a fantastic cook; Fox was the one who always broke the eggs and overcooked the roast. But then we all have our talents, she thought. Ginny can baste a chicken to perfection. I can turn over a three-day-old corpse without it bursting.

'So what do you do?' George was asking Simon.

'I'm a doctor.'

'GP?' Siobhan asked.

'No, I work in the accident and emergency department at the Royal Free at Hampstead.'

'You must see some terrible things,' Siobhan said. 'I don't think I could do anything like that.'

Fox smiled sympathetically across the table. She had had people say the same things to her. Simon did not smile back.

He turned back to Siobhan. 'You get used to it,' he said. What else could you say?

'Where's Sandy?' Ian asked.

'Is that your wife?' Siobhan wanted to know, taking a little more interest in their dinner companion than her husband would probably have liked.

'She's my daughter,' he answered and turned back to Ian. 'She's staying over at a friend's place.'

'How old is she?'

'Thirteen?'

There was a long silence. Oh, come on, Fox thought, who's going to say it? But no one did. Looks like it's going to have to be me. 'Where is your wife?'

'She's dead,' he said, and everyone immediately found it necessary to concentrate very hard on slicing small pieces off their medallions of veal.

'I'm sorry,' Fox said, and had to stop herself adding, 'for your loss.' It became a habit after a while. *I'm sorry for your loss. You can be assured we will do everything possible to find the person responsible for this.* This is ridiculous, she thought. People die all the time. Even in the borough of Kingston. If he's not going to tell us, I'm going to ask. 'How did she die?'

For some reason Ian felt the need to apologise for her. 'Maddy's with the Met. CID. She always asks those sort of questions.'

She glared at Ian, but he ignored her. Simon looked up. She knew the look. It said: *That explains everything.*

'You're a detective!' Siobhan almost shouted.

For smiled. She hated this, hated explaining what she did for a living. It sounded either glamorous or grubby, depending on how she did it, and the truth was it was neither. It was what she did and she enjoyed it. End of story.

She still wanted to know what happened to Simon's wife.

But George was already saying: 'That can't be easy. I mean, are there many female detectives in the Met?'

'There's a few.'

'Do you specialise? I mean, like a doctor. You know. Rape? Burglary?'

'I'm based at Hendon Road. Area Major Incident Team. At the moment we're working on a murder investigation.'

'Anyone like more veal?' Ginny said, too quickly.

Oh, she hates me talking work as much as I do. She's afraid I'm going to ruin her dinner party for her. No one's going to want the veal if I start discussing corpses.

Ian took his wife's cue and dutifully asked for more. Meanwhile George and Siobhan contemplated their fellow guests, whether in disgust or admiration she couldn't be sure. The trauma surgeon and the murder detective. Fascinating. Two freaks who spent their working days up to their elbows in gore.

'Funny you haven't run into each other before,' Siobhan said.

Fox was beginning to warm to her. It was apparent she had an unfettered curiosity and a wonderful imagination. It seemed she had already visualised Fox running in beside a blood-stained trolley shouting to Simon: *I found this one in an alley, but don't touch that artery — there are fingerprints all over it.*

'Yes,' Simon said, and for the first time she saw him smile, 'it is a wonder our paths haven't crossed before.' His smile gave her a warm and unsettling sensation in the pit of her stomach. 'The ones I mess up on she gets to keep.'

They all laughed, but she wasn't entirely sure if he was joking.

Chapter Twelve

'I was going to be a police officer once,' George said.

Fox nodded and said nothing.

'How do you go about becoming a detective?' Siobhan said. This one's like a dog: she gets hold of something, she won't let it go, Fox thought. 'Do you have to pass a test. Like Cluedo or something?'

'I'm not very good at Cluedo,' Fox said.

Siobhan looked disappointed.

'I started on the beat. I took examinations to become a detective. I like to think I worked my way up through merit, though some would allege it's pure tokenism. I've been an inspector at Hendon Road for only a few months.'

'I don't think I could stand it. Looking at dead bodies.'

She felt Ginny give her another warning look. This is not my fault, she thought. I didn't start this. 'You get used to it pretty quickly. For me, a dead body is just a piece of evidence.'

'What made you become a detective?' George asked her. There was a patronising smile on his face.

'I like slapping cuffs on a man and telling him to spread 'em,' Fox said.

She saw Ginny flush, her cheeks filling from the bottom like a thermometer. Siobhan bit her lip. Then Simon threw down his napkin, threw back his head and laughed. Guffawed, really. So, he did have a sense of humour.

'Well, you can arrest me any time,' he said.

'I need a reason,' Fox said.

'Non-payment of parking fines?'

'You'll have to do better than that.'

'What about exhibitionism?' Ian said.

She raised an eyebrow.

'When we were at school—'

'For Christ's sake,' Simon said.

'—When we were at school he ran across the girls' play-ground wearing nothing but a pair of football boots.'

'It was a dare,' Simon said. 'Anyway, there was nothing to see. I was only eleven years old and it was freezing cold. It was shrivelled up like an acorn.'

'From little acorns mighty oaks do grow,' Fox quoted and then she looked away, realising what she had said.

Ian grinned. 'And a few lovehearts were carved on the bark in his day.'

Fox was relieved to see that Simon had the decency to appear embarrassed by this remark. 'That was all a long time ago,' he said dismissively.

She looked up. He was watching her, speculatively, for the first time. Well, about time. Most men gave her the look as soon as they met. He was a good-looking man, no doubt about it, not that she put great store in looks on a man. The long fair hair and the ruddy glow to his cheeks made him seem younger than he must surely be if he had a thirteen-year-old daughter. In fact, he was a little too good-looking in some ways, like a male model. In other circumstances she might have considered him soft, but there was a hard edge to his voice when he spoke and an aggression about his movements that belied this.

'Is anyone doing any carving these days?' Siobhan asked him, with a transparency that even shocked Fox. George studied something of interest on the ceiling. Ginny gave Ian a hard stare.

But what was he supposed to do about one mate's wife flirting with his other mate? Hardly his fault.

'These days I'm too busy raising a teenager to raise hell.'

'It must be hard juggling a job like yours with a daughter,' Fox said, wresting control of Simon's attention from the shameless Siobhan. Now why did I do that, she asked herself. Was it for Ginny, or am I, you know, a little bit jealous?

'Sandy's grown up to be very independent. I don't know whether that's a good or a bad thing. Having a kid with a free spirit is just as emotionally and physically wearing as being sole guardian of a couch potato.'

'How long have you been a single parent?'

'You mean when did my wife die?' he said, deliberately rephrasing the question. It was apparent that, like her, he did not like to tiptoe around a subject. 'Three years ago. Car crash.' He fell silent and no one spoke for a while. Somewhere behind the china-blue eyes Simon was busy cutting and editing the memories, perhaps searching for suitable phrases. Finally he discarded them all and fast-forwarded his account to more recent and less painful history. 'I was working in a Leicester hospital when it happened. But a few months ago I got the opportunity to move back down to London. I wanted to be closer to Sandy's grandparents.'

'That's sad,' Siobhan said.

'It's life. People die tragically all the time. You just have to be in the wrong place at the wrong time. Don't you, Madeleine?'

Their eyes locked. 'That's right,' she said. She felt another warm gelatin buzz in the pit of her stomach. What was happening here? she thought. Didn't I start off this evening hating your guts?

The bride and groom had left an hour ago. Just the drunks and the desperate and the newly divorced still hanging around, Marenko noted. Which I suppose explains why I'm still here;

why I'm still here and dancing under the stars with my former wife, who, incidentally, I loathe.

How romantic.

The DJ Susan had hired was playing an old Smokey Robinson and the Miracles song: 'The Tracks of my Tears'. 'Listen,' Marenko whispered in Susan's ear, 'they're playing our song.'

'Frank. I have to ask you. Are you drunk?'

'A bit.'

'I hope you behaved yourself tonight.'

'I was the perfect gentleman. It wasn't easy.'

'What's that supposed to mean?'

'I noticed you stacked the meeting. Couldn't move this afternoon without tripping over a brief. If I was the caterers I'd be shitting myself. One stomach ache and they'd be sued out of business.'

'Please, Frank.'

'Right, change the subject. You seeing anyone?'

'No. How about you?'

'And cheat on my job?'

'Silly of me. Forget I asked.'

'Look at all these people. I hardly know anyone. I'm a stranger in my own family.'

'You can't blame us for that.'

'No,' Marenko said. 'I don't.' The music stopped. They stepped away, staring at each other, awkward. 'Remember when we last did this?'

'Danced, you mean? Probably our wedding. That horrible little hall in Hornchurch.'

He nodded. 'You think Donna and Martin will be doing this in twenty-five years?'

'What? Dancing? Or asking each other who they're going out with these days?'

'Well, what's your money on?'

'I shall say a prayer for them.'

'All these solicitors in the family. They'll be right for the divorce, anyway.' He looked at his watch. 'I'd better go.'

'I'll get you a cab.'

'I'm right to drive.'

'Cops. You're the worst offenders I know when it comes to drinking and driving. I'm calling you a cab. I'll pay for it if you like.'

'Shit. You still know where to put a knife, don't you, Susan?'

She looked abashed. She hadn't meant to hurt him, which made it worse. 'I'm sorry.'

He took the car keys out of his pocket.

'What if you get arrested?'

'They'll pension me off and I'll have more time to spend with my family. That's what you always wanted. Wasn't it?'

She watched him go. Holy hell. It was always worse when they tried not to stagger. Whisky robbed a man of his dignity. If he crashed his car, killed himself, God forbid killed someone else, would she ever forgive herself? But then, she was no longer in any position to stop him doing these stupid things. God damn him. God damn him for always. He had broken her heart.

'Did you see they caught the couple that murdered those four girls?' Ian said. He had waited until Ginny was in the kitchen fetching the dessert to bring it up.

The ball was rolling and George caught it. 'We should bring back the death penalty.'

Fox looked at Simon. Here we go. 'Do you think so?' he said, his voice deceptively mild.

'Hanging's too good for them,' Ian said.

'What do you suggest, Ian? Have them drawn and quartered first? Or perhaps a crucifixion outside St Paul's?'

'I think they should pay for what they've done.'

'You think we have the right to take another human life?'

'What gave them the right?' Ian countered.

'There is no doubt they are both deranged and we, the public, should be protected from people like that. But do we kill them? That makes us no better than they are.'

'Yes, it does,' George said, looking sombre. 'We'd be doing it for a reason.'

Ian turned to Fox. 'What do you think, Maddy?'

What do I think? I think I should keep my opinions to myself. But she couldn't help herself. 'Wrong person to ask. What would I know? I only lock murderers away just to have some senile judge give them five years or watch a parole board release child rapists back into the community after two. I agree with bleeding-heart liberals like Simon here. Let's take it easy on criminals and keep our hands clean.' Bleeding-heart liberals? Whoops, that last bit just slipped out.

He glared at her across the table. 'I don't think appealing to basic humanity is the same as being a bleeding-heart liberal.'

'It's probably because you don't have a bloody clue what you're talking about.'

An icy silence in the room. Ian and George sat back; having tossed their two bob in the ring, they suddenly found the stakes too rich for their blood. Siobhan leaned forward, critically interested. Obviously one of those girls who was right up the front at school when the boys started fighting.

'Because you're a member of the police force does not make you the arbiter of public morals,' Simon told her. 'It doesn't give you the right to sit in judgement. Far from it. You could justifiably be accused of bias.'

'Hmm. Interesting. So even though I sit in an interview room with a murderer for six hours and hear him pour out every detail of his poor twisted mind so that I know him better than his mother, I should still keep my mouth shut. Is that what you're saying?'

He leaned across the table, his fair cheeks turning beet red.

'It's not at all what I'm saying. I don't think any of us have the right to play God.'

'Depends whether you believe in God, I suppose. Others might just say that if you have a mad dog, you shoot it. Or perhaps you'd just like to put rabid dogs into behavioural therapy?'

'There is a difference between dogs and humans.'

'Not in my parish, there isn't. I see people do things to other people that even animals wouldn't do.'

'Don't preach to me! I don't exactly live a sheltered life working for the NHS!'

'Typical doctor! You treat a couple of assaults and suddenly you're an expert on the London underworld. Dickhead!'

There was a sudden long silence. Fox turned around. Ginny was standing in the doorway with the birthday cake. The candles were fluttering in the draught. She had a look of utter horror on her face.

'Are we all ready to sing happy birthday?' she said.

PART TWO

Islington.
A winter morning, just before dawn

Chapter Thirteen

The dead are not supposed to be beautiful, Fox thought.

The brown eyes were wide, the face creased into a frown of surprise and confusion. A mop of long, fair hair, streaked with grime, lay across her face and was splayed around her shoulders, partly concealing the livid purple bruising on her neck. The blue eyes were half-lidded and unblinking. Small droplets of rain played on her face, giving the illusion of tears.

Like a rag doll, left out in the rain by a careless child.

The petechiae around the eyes and the trauma to the tongue confirmed the manner of death: strangulation. Lividity along her right cheek and temple told Fox something else. The little girl had not died here. Someone had dumped her.

Her hips were twisted, her right knee angled into the left. Her fingers were cupped, but stiff with rigor this wet December morning. She lay on her back, her arms outstretched, as if inviting one of the assembled watchers to reach out and comfort her. Instead they stood in shuffling silence, with their hands in their pockets, alone with grim and private thoughts.

'Jesus wept,' Marenko said.

And He undoubtedly would, Fox thought, if He could see us all here now, our breath freezing on the air, rain dripping off our coats, trace evidence disappearing in the rain. So much for the season of goodwill. And on the tenth day before Christmas my chief inspector gave to me.

She heard scrabbling in the darkness, a rat perhaps. The alleyway stank of urine and dog shit and garbage. The headlights of a panda car cast long shadows, the body of the dead girl centre stage, against a backdrop of chimneypots and tumbledown wooden palings. Like a scene from Dickens.

The deceased was wearing a green raincoat over a claret school blazer. Underneath she had on a white blouse and a uniform tie, the child's crooked knot skewed across the collar. She wore white socks over sturdy brown leather shoes. Her grey skirt was hooked up around her waist, and her underwear was missing. Fox fought down the impulse to cover her up.

She heard Marenko's voice from when she first joined the department. *A dead body is not a person. A dead body is your best, and sometimes your only, piece of evidence. That's all.*

Ten years old, Fox decided. Eleven, tops. How can an eleven-year-old girl be just a piece of evidence?

There were no jokes this cold, wet morning. The voices of the other detectives were hushed; there were no routines as with Elmore Crawford. They were in the presence of a true victim. Even James struggled to keep the emotion from his face. In the background a PC stood ashen-faced, rain dripping from the peak of his cap.

'Jesus Christ,' Marenko repeated.

The forensic team was putting up plastic sheeting to keep out the rain. Graveney, wearing waterproofs and green wellington boots, bent down beside the little girl, his face impassive as he tied paper bags over her outstretched hands. If she had tried to fight off her killer, scrapings from under her fingernails might reveal blood or human tissue that could be cross-matched for blood type and DNA.

Fox turned away a moment, a small respect for the dead. Graveney was using an internal thermometer to calibrate body temperature, so that he could calculate time of death on an arcane degrees lost per hour formula. He would also be looking for first stage rigor.

Her schoolbag had been dumped next to the body. Library books spilled out on to the pavement, along with a cheap compact case. He flipped open the satchel and read out the name. 'Kate Mercer. 17B, Tolway Court, Islington. Jesus, she's only eleven years old,' he added.

Fox swallowed down a burning in her throat. She copied down the address in her notebook, the rain smudging the ink, and tried to stay detached.

Graveney closed the satchel and left it where it was. A flashbulb popped as the Home Office photographer started taking photographs of the scene.

'Was she raped?' Marenko said to Graveney.

'You know I can't tell you anything just yet,' Graveney said, his voice soft.

'She *was* raped,' Marenko said, certain in his own mind what Graveney would find.

The pathologist shook his head. 'Poor little mite.'

'We've got to catch this bastard,' Marenko said.

Kate Mercer reached out, her arms wide, looking for comfort.

Two attendants in green overalls lifted the little girl on to a stretcher. She was covered with a green sheet and wheeled towards the waiting mortuary van.

A uniformed sergeant walked over from one of the panda cars and stood beside Marenko. He spoke in a flat monotone, reading from his notebook, reciting the dispatch he had taken down from the control room at Tolpuddle Street.

' "Katherine Rachel Mercer, reported missing yesterday evening, report received 7.38 p.m. Her mother made the report in person." Christ, sir, we get dozens of these. Half the time the kid's stayed over at a friend's house and forgot to tell Mum.'

Fox shivered inside her rain-streaked coat. There was silence, except for the gentle rhythm of rain.

'It's like a scene from hell,' she murmured.

'You haven't seen anything yet,' Marenko said.

Fox felt suddenly nauseous. She knew immediately what he wanted her to do.

Chapter Fourteen

Dawn announced itself with the leeching of shadows from a monochrome world of grease-grey, London now in the chill grip of a Northern winter. Tolway Court was a cluster of trim, khaki-brown council flats half a mile from the Angel. Already the noise of traffic on Upper Street was starting to build. In the forecourt a skeletal tree was illuminated under the sick yellow light from a sodium lamp, like the hand of a half-buried corpse stretched towards the sky.

The icy wind was funnelled up the concrete stairs. Honeywell and Fox stopped outside a green-painted door on the third floor and Fox took a deep breath, her hand hovering a few inches from the door. She took out her badge and held it in her other hand.

Honeywell shuffled his feet, hands deep in the pockets of his trenchcoat. Marenko had chosen him as the family liaison officer. A naturally hangdog expression, a good listener, a hide like a rhino. It seemed to work well most of the time.

Fox rapped with her knuckles. The door was flung open just a few moments later. They've been waiting, Fox realised; they've been sitting up all night waiting for this knock on the door. What did you expect? Fox asked herself. Their daughter has been missing all night. Why would they go to bed?

A big man, balding, with the body of a docker, stared out at them, his face etched with strain and grief. He was dressed in dark jeans and a thick woollen jumper.

Fox held out her ID and saw a look of utter despair cross his face. He had been hoping to see his daughter. Now he knew. 'Brian Mercer?'

The man put his hands together in an attitude of prayer. 'Please,' he said to Fox, as if she possessed the power of life and death, as if she could reverse what had been done.

She felt her throat tighten. You just have to do this, she reminded herself. You've done it before, you know there is nothing that will make it easier. 'I'm Detective Inspector Madeleine Fox. This is Detective Constable William Honeywell.'

A woman appeared behind Mercer in the hallway, small and dark-haired, her face chalk-white with dread. Fox realised with shock that she recognised Kate Mercer in her. Other faces appeared in the hallway, Kate's sisters and brothers.

'She's gone, isn't she?' the woman said.

Fox looked up at Honeywell. He wasn't going to help her with any of this.

'She's gone?' the woman repeated.

Suddenly Fox didn't trust her voice. She nodded.

The man slumped against the wall and gasped, open-mouthed, as if he had been punched in the stomach. He was talking, but none of the words made sense, because he was crying and praying all at once, his hands still clasped in front of him.

His wife came forward and held him, the tiny bird-like creature enfolding this giant in her arms. She led him back inside the flat, leaving the door open. They followed them inside, Honeywell shutting the door gently behind him.

The flat was cramped, messy with the detritus of a large family, homework spread on a kitchen table, kids' toys on the floor, clothes scattered over a sofa, cups littering the coffee table. But it was clean. No empty beer bottles on the tables, no overflowing ashtrays, no takeaway boxes piled on the floor. Somehow it made it worse.

Fox heard Kate's father screaming from the bedroom. He was beating his fists against the walls.

Please God, let this be over soon, she thought. Give me a nice drug murder, one of Capper's runners sprayed over the wall of a pub, a derelict clubbed to death with a beer bottle at King's Cross Station. But not this. Not this raw pain. I don't mind the blood, the eviscerations. But spare me this.

A child's paintings were fixed to the refrigerator with magnets; a picture of a block of flats, Mum, Dad, brothers and sisters leaning out and waving. Even a garden, for Christ's sake. A leap of childhood imagination from the single stunted plane tree in the concrete forecourt. There were framed photographs on the bookshelf. Fox stared at them, absently picked one up and looked at it, her eyes unseeing, her mind focused on Kate's father, the sounds of him choking on his pain in the next room. It sounded like he was bringing his heart up in there.

'She's a beautiful little girl, isn't she?'

Fox turned around. Kate's mother was standing in the doorway.

It occurred to her that Mrs Mercer was waiting for her to answer. She returned her attention to the photograph in her hand. She realised with shock that it was Kate. It was a confirmation photograph. She was dressed in white and was grinning self-consciously at the camera.

'Yes, she was . . . she is very beautiful,' Fox said.

'You must excuse my husband,' Mrs Mercer said, as if he had committed some unpardonable breach of etiquette.

Honeywell and Fox waited, staring at the floor.

'How . . . what did she . . . ?'

'We think she was abducted, Mrs Mercer. We found her about two hours ago, in an alley behind MacNaghten Row.' She cleared her throat, struggling with this. 'She had been strangled.'

Mrs Mercer nodded, her Adam's apple bobbing in her throat as she fought back emotion. 'Did she . . . suffer . . . ?'

Honeywell rescued her. 'No, I don't think so,' he said. It was a lie, for they could not possibly know that yet. There was a long silence. 'I am sorry for your loss. I want you to know we will do everything possible to apprehend the person responsible for this.' He paused. Having finished the familiar speech, he was floundering. 'Look, Mrs Mercer, I know this is a bad time for you, but we need to talk to you, find out exactly what happened to your daughter. Also you or your husband needs to come with us . . . for identification. I hate to ask you right now, but—'

'Of course.' Mrs Mercer went back into the bedroom. From another room the faces of Kate's brothers and sisters appeared, staring. To Fox their expressions seemed almost accusing, as if she was responsible for what had happened to Kate. The eldest was about seven or eight, the youngest still in nappies.

Mrs Mercer reappeared with her coat. 'I've rung my brother. He only lives in the next street. He'll look after the children and . . .' She looked towards the closed door, where it seemed that big Brian Mercer was destroying the bedroom brick by brick.

They waited there in silence for what seemed like a hundred years. Finally, a knock at the door. Mrs Mercer hurried to answer it. But it wasn't her brother. It was one of the neighbours complaining about the noise.

Finally her brother arrived. He and Kate's mother held a whispered conference by the door. He looked around once, staring white-faced at the two detectives. Then Mrs Mercer nodded, indicating that she was ready to leave. Fox hurried out of the door. She could think of no words of comfort for anyone, wanted only to get out of there. As they shut the door she heard Kate's father wailing again, and she felt like the shadow of death itself.

They already had a suspect. His name was Henry Lincoln Wexxler and he owned the sweet shop on the corner of MacNaghten Row. It was Wexxler who had found the body, and his telephone call to Islington police station had been logged at 5.06 a.m.

Marenko had already interviewed him. Wexxler said he woke early and went downstairs to take out some rubbish and had seen what he had at first thought to be a dead animal lying near his back fence. He had gone over to investigate, taking a torch. That, he said, was when he made his grim discovery.

Marenko could find no obvious discrepancies in his story and the facts thus far established, but it was his private opinion that Henry Wexxler could not lie straight in bed.

Scenes of Crime officers in white overalls were still at work in the lane behind MacNaghten Row, searching for discarded clothes, tyre marks, blood trails, any piece of physical evidence that might be related to the dead girl. Marenko watched them, his grey hair matted across his skull by the rain. Fox knew what he was thinking. The worst possible crime scene. If you found someone murdered in a house, you could establish certain facts because the killer has to get inside, either by force or by invitation. Straight away, you learned something; your murderer's blood was left on a smashed window, there might be fingerprints on a windowframe, cloth fibres in the carpet. If there was no forced entry, you thought, right, these people knew each other.

Inside a building, a bullet might lodge in a wall, you could find a bloody handprint smeared on a tabletop. You could vacuum a three-bedroom home and the pointyheads in Lambeth could practically describe the wardrobe of anyone who had ever stepped foot inside the house. You learned something else.

But life wasn't as straightforward when your crime scene was in an alleyway that was already littered with used syringes and old beds and black bags of decaying rubbish. The bullet you were looking for could be in a factory wall two hundred yards away, footprints and tyre tracks can get washed away in the rain, curious onlookers tramp all over your crime scene. And there was no relationship established between the victim and the murderer. You learned a whole lot less.

Marenko reached in the pocket for his mobile. He punched

in a number and waited. 'Fox? Where are you? All right, stay there. I'll see you in about a quarter of an hour. I need to talk to you.' He folded the telephone away in his pocket with a grim smile. The PM would be under way in about an hour, but sod it, he'd let the bitch have breakfast first.

Chapter Fifteen

Fox fought back the taste of bile in her throat. The whiff of corpse-gas combined with disinfectant immediately made her regret the fried bacon sandwich she had wolfed down at the sandwich bar across the road from the station. Of course, that was before Marenko had told her that she was to accompany him to the morgue for the postmortem.

There were two open bodies in the dissection room. Fox looked at the case sheets on the ends of the trolleys. A derelict and a futures broker, side by side in death, the divide that separated them in life insignificant now. The derelict was found outside King's Cross Station with his skull caved in; the broker had stumbled into the path of a taxi on Euston Road. Both now lay naked on the silver-tray tables, cracked and spread. You could tell which one was the meths drinker by the stubble on the chin and the different shading of their livers, but otherwise there did not seem much to choose between them.

Blood dripped into buckets set at each end of the trolley. An assistant was busy closing up the broker's chest. On any other day, Fox thought, Marenko would have made a joke. *He went short on his own futures.* Not this morning.

Graveney silently nodded a greeting. His half-moon glasses caught the fluorescent lights. He could have been a bank teller.

He was standing at the metal sink with an organ tree that he had removed from one of the cadavers on the trolleys. His green gown and elbow-length gloves were stained a dark red.

'You see this, Frank? This is what a lifetime of smoking does for you.' He sliced through one of the rich-red blood vessels and squeezed.

'What is that?'

'Fats that have built up in the walls of the aorta.'

'I gave up a couple of months ago.'

'Good for you,' Graveney said cheerfully and carried the organ tree back to the gaping chest cavity on the table.

Marenko stood there with his hands in the pockets of his overcoat, a green plastic disposable apron over the top. Fox stared at the faces of the two corpses. No matter what condition they found their victims in the street, they were mostly still recognisable as people, she thought. But this place had the humanity of the abattoir. In here the dead were as near to being human as hamburger was to a cow. But the postmortem was as necessary to the process of homicide investigation as the scanning for fingerprints.

'Let's get started,' Graveney said, and he took off the stained gown and put on a fresh one.

An attendant pushed a stainless-steel trolley into the room. The child's shoes protruded from beneath the green sheet. The sheet was removed and the body transferred to the sluice table.

Graveney studied the dead girl over his half-moon glasses. A camera was mounted on a tripod at the foot of the steel table, and the photographer went about his work, for a time the whirring of the electric drive motor the only sound in the room. The pathologist's forehead creased into a frown. 'This is a tragedy,' he said to Marenko, as if he were lecturing one of his students.

He took a folder from a steel counter in the corner of the room and scanned the typewritten sheets. 'On examination this morning at 6.15 a.m. she had a rectal temperature of 93.5 degrees and rigor had commenced in the small muscles. If the body cooled at approximately one to two degrees per hour, that means she could have been dead two to three hours. I would put time of death between 3 and 4 a.m. However, it was a cold night. That could postpone rigor. It could feasibly have been as early as two.'

Marenko nodded.

Fox took one last look at the killer's small, pale victim. Kate Mercer looked so tiny in this world of steel and tile, her skin so pale, the ugly purple bruises around her neck livid against the marble flesh. But from this moment she became just another piece of evidence. This was what it meant to be a professional, Fox thought. Easy to turn off your humanity to the derelicts and the drug users and the dealers shot to shit in their red Corvettes. If you had the stomach for it, that bizarre other world could appear just that way — another world. Harder to be quite as coldly professional now.

'Shall we begin?' Graveney said, laying aside his notes.

There was an overhead microphone in which Graveney addressed himself, giving the date and the time and Kate Mercer's full name, and then he began to speak in a low monotone. All his findings were spoken aloud for later transcription, a copy of which would find its way into the case file on Marenko's desk and one day, Fox hoped, into a courtroom with the man who did this.

Graveney began with an external examination of the body. He moved slowly around the corpse, noting bruises and contusions, all visible signs of injury. Kate Mercer was still dressed in her school uniform, as she had been when she was found. Her hands were encased in paper bags, and Graveney examined these first, clipping her fingernails and placing the clippings into sealed plastic bags for later examination in the forensics laboratory in Lambeth. If Kate had fought her attacker, trace evidence such as hairs, blood or skin might give them a match to their killer.

'The fingernail of the third finger on the left hand is broken around the quick, and there is a dark substance driven up underneath the nail. It may just be dirt from the alley.'

Fox could also see there were fingernail marks in her palms.

Marenko caught her eye and said nothing. They both knew what that meant.

Fox heard Mrs Mercer's voice. 'Did she suffer?'

Fox took a deep breath. She had witnessed a number of postmortems; none of them promised to be quite as rough as this. I hope I'm up to it, she thought.

Graveney examined Kate's clothes for blood or fibres. They were caked in dirt from the alley. But Graveney was meticulous and picked off several tiny particles and placed them in clear plastic evidence bags and labelled them. He took his time. This would be done just once, and it had to be done correctly. Marenko shuffled his feet impatiently. Fox realised he wanted to get this over as much as she did.

When Graveney had finished he started to remove the dead girl's clothes. Cold in here, Fox thought, as unloving a place as you could find. There was an age-old impulse to throw a blanket over the naked child, as if she could still feel the chill in here. As if anyone could mother and protect her now.

When he had finished, an assistant tied a label to the big toe of her left foot with her name and a number.

Graveney examined her entire body looking for lesions, bruises, unexplained marks. He noted the ligature marks around the wrists, the bruising around the throat and the genital area, the lividity on the right side.

He straightened, stretching his back muscles for a moment. 'Death caused by asphyxia. Strangulation effected by a fibrous material such as rope or plastic cord. Bruising to the limbs and the genital areas effected ante-mortem.'

He made oral and vaginal swabs for semen.

'Small vaginal tear just here,' Graveney said. 'No seminal fluid apparent.'

'He didn't rape her, then?' Fox said to Marenko.

Marenko shook his head. 'Doesn't mean anything either way. Sometimes these people can't ejaculate. They can kill, but they can't come.'

Fox looked up sharply, but she saw from his expression that it wasn't a joke.

Graveney was about to take an anal swab. He paused. 'She's been split,' he said, reverting for a moment from the detached monotone required for the autopsy notes.

At first Fox did not understand what he was referring to. Then, as he lifted the legs, she stifled a gasp. There was a two-inch tear in the child's anus.

The external examination over, Graveney took a scalpel and made a Y-shaped incision on the chest, then used an electric saw to cut through the ribs and remove the sternum. The organ tree, heart, lungs and liver, were lifted out together and carried to the steel sink at the rear of the room, where Graveney studied them for haematomas or abnormalities. Fox looked away, concentrating her gaze on the white polystyrene tiles on the ceiling.

A loud buzzing made her look back. Fox knew what was coming, hated this part, but was drawn to it by a terrible fascination. Graveney was using the electric saw to cut around the skull, prising back the crown with a steel lever. It came free with a loud pop. The skin was then folded across her face; de-gloving, they called it. As the face disappeared beneath its own scalp, Fox thought of one of her nephew's rubber monster masks, all folded up on itself in its toy box.

Fox blinked. Screw the job, she thought. There goes another little part of me. She had wondered if she was up to this; the answer was yes. But it had cost her, as every day of the job cost her another part of herself, the last vestiges of innocence she had retained after years of investigating rapes and assaults and murders. There was something about the death of the very young that even now struck her as obscene. An image came back to her, unbidden, from her own childhood. It was a wall-painting in her Sunday school in Repulse Bay, Jesus surrounded by all the little children of the world. Hard to believe in a beneficent God after you had spent an hour in the autopsy room with Professor Aloysius Graveney and all that remained of Kate Mercer.

The brain was removed, weighed and examined separately. Graveney routinely drew phials of blood from the heart, bile from the gut and urine from the bladder. The contents of the stomach and intestine were removed for laboratory examination. The presence of food in the gut could establish not only what the little girl last ate, but its stage of digestion might help confirm the time of death.

At last he had finished. He peeled off his gloves and gown and walked away. The assistant cutter returned the organ tree to the chest and replaced the brain inside the skull. He pulled the scalp back into position and began to suture the incisions.

Graveney finished labelling the blood samples, swabs and nail clippings and handed them to Marenko to ensure chain of custody. 'Good luck,' he said and walked away back to his office.

Fox got outside and leaned back against the wall. She craved fresh air, a coffee, people, light, traffic. Marenko looked resentfully at the NO SMOKING sign above the doors. She knew what he was thinking. What a time to try to quit.

'I don't know how he does that job,' Fox said.

'Somebody has to,' was all she got from Marenko. They drove the samples to Lambeth and then headed back to brief the AMIT at Hendon Road. They didn't talk much. Neither of them felt like it.

Chapter Sixteen

There is a science to murder investigation, Marenko had told her; but there is art as well as organisation, and a detective requires talent to be good at it, in the same way that it is talent that makes a good doctor or physicist or astronomer. Talent is something that is merely added to a sound technical knowledge and a thorough grounding in procedure.

First, he said, you learn the science behind your craft and learn it well, if you expect to be paid at the end of the week. Sure, there is a place for intuition, but only as an adjunct to all the other skills. It can never take the place of thorough, solid, often tedious police work.

You learn the basics, he said to her. Then we'll see if you have what it takes to lead a murder squad. Everything else is cream.

So here it is. The Gospel according to Frank.

In a murder investigation, he had said, you always start off, by definition, with one less witness than you usually have. The victim, in such circumstances, cannot plead their case, cannot give you a description of the man who held up their off-licence and took all the money from the till; they cannot go to an identity parade and pick out the fellow Rasta who beat them senseless with a cricket bat in an argument over a woman; they cannot refute the suspect's alibi that he was playing cards with Mickey when Sean had his face remodelled with a broken bottle;

they are not able to give you a description of the young man who took them out for a drink and then brutally bashed and raped them in the back of their car. In a murder investigation the victim is not lying in a hospital bed or on a trolley in a casualty ward. What they are doing is lying in a soggy mess of blood on their bedroom carpet, or in an alley like Kate Mercer, or in a shallow grave in a public park, mute testimony to the most terrible of human sins.

And what do you do when you arrive at the scene of this terrible crime? Marenko had asked her.

What you do is stand there.

You stand there and you stare. You stare at the scene like it is one of those 3-D puzzles; you ignore the obvious picture and look for the other one, the one that will come into focus if you look and stare hard enough and long enough. You ask yourself questions.

Why is the body in this particular place?

Did the murder take place here or somewhere else?

Is there a blood trail, or blood spatter, and if there is what does it tell you about how the victim died?

When you've seen all that there is to see, you look for the one piece of evidence that the Home Office photographer and the pathologist and the SOCOs cannot, by definition, find – *what isn't here that should be here?*

And also, because the first few hours after a murder are critical, you don't wait for Graveney to tell you that there are defence wounds on the left hand or that there is lividity on the right side when the body is actually lying on its back. You look for yourself. You find out if the victim's wallet and jewellery are still there. You look around for a knife, or shell casings from a gun.

After you've done all that, you take out your little notebook and you make a sketch of everything you see, with a little stick figure of the victim as the centrepiece of this scene. And then, when you've done that, pinpointing the location of furniture or dustbins or trees and every piece of critical evidence recovered, and even after it's been photographed and videotaped from every possible angle by the Home Office photographer, you still stare at that scene some more until it's imprinted on your memory.

While you do that, the SOCOs will be combing the room or the street or the park for evidence of the exchange that the textbooks say is left behind at any crime – the hairs, the blood, the semen, the loose fibres from clothes – and putting them in plastic bags to send down to the forensic laboratory in Lambeth. They are taking prints from doors and door handles, from the furniture and the eating utensils, digging bullets out of walls and picking shell casings and bloodied knives from the floor. They are measuring off key distances and angles of trajectory.

While they work you look for anything that appears out of place – a beer can, a loose pillowslip, a pair of scissors – and you send that down to the lab as well. And only when you are sure you have every piece of physical evidence that is to be gleaned from the scene, that the SOCOs have missed nothing you may need later, then and only then do you turn your back on the body and go in search of the second elusive spirit in Frank Marenko's Holy Trinity: witnesses.

You talk to the crowd of spectators first, because blue cordon tape attracts gawkers like sticky paper attracts flies, and sometimes your killer will be right there too, watching, enjoying himself. If you are lucky, the uniforms who were first on the scene have grabbed someone who saw the whole thing and they are now sitting inside a panda car waiting to give you an identikit picture or even, God help us, a name. If not, someone who looks very much like a detective constable will have to trudge from door to door looking for witnesses while not allowing himself to be wearied by a succession of blank faces peering out at him from darkened doorways professing disinterest and total lack of knowledge.

And then you drag in your suspects. You talk hardest to whoever found the body, for often they are your first and most promising suspect. Then you interview everyone who knew your victim: the family, the flatmates, the workmates, the boyfriends and girlfriends and wives and husbands and lovers. You get to know your victim and the way they lived their foreshortened life as well as someone from your own family. Better. While you talk to them you look for little lies and half-truths and pick at them like loose threads on a jumper. Sometimes people unravel and sometimes they don't. And when you have done all that you go back to Lambeth and put modern forensic science to the test.

Repeated month after month, he told her, it is tedious and frustrating work. Like investigating a burglary or a car theft when you were with the CID. Only with a murder at least you have a better chance of finding the culprit, because people still care more about people getting trashed than they do about videos and cars getting fenced, and because the Met will allow you far more time and resources to do the job. Also, because, at least at this moment in time, there are fewer murders than there are stolen televisions.

So far. But watch this space.

As you have already discovered from your years in the CID, there are no car pursuits or fistfights as there are on the television. Sorting out the Saturday night pub brawls and chasing joyriders or fighting squatters is the preserve of the uniforms on the beat. As a detective you must learn to use your brain, not your brawn, Marenko had told her, looking disparagingly at Fox's seven and a half stone. You get a six-foot-three uniformed sergeant to haul in your suspect, if you have one. Your weapon is not a baton or, God forbid, a revolver; you arm yourself with the two Ss, science and psychology.

That was how she learned to play to type when she was running an interrogation with Marenko or James; she sweet-talked, understood, tried to help, while they asked their questions cold-eyed, oozing menace. It isn't confessions we're looking for, Marenko said – that happens sometimes but not as often as the cop shows will have everyone believe and certainly less often now that the PACE laws have restricted the more imaginative approaches I learned in my day — it is witnesses.

It's not the *OK-I-did-it*s you're hoping for, Marenko said. What all this posturing may get you is the *OK-he-did-it*s. Because at the end of the day, when your case goes to court it's living, breathing, credible witnesses that impress juries, not fibres and blood types and cross-matching DNA on a strand of hair.

If science cannot always pinpoint a suspect, Marenko said, it should at least be able to help you identify your victim. You can't move on to whodunnit until you figure out whowasit. The pointyheads can also make the call on time of death, which you absolutely have to know. A nice girl like you doesn't want to know how they do it, but as you asked I'll tell you. Rigor mortis sets in two to four hours after death. It starts to disappear after twelve, and the muscles become flaccid again. The rest of the calculation is done with a thermometer. In the deceased's rectum.

If the body has been there a while, then there are other ways of calculating time of death. For example, maggots take twenty-four hours to hatch. Decomposition sets in after forty. Depending on the weather.

If the place where you find the body is not the scene of the crime, the guys in the lab coats may help you identify where your victim met his or her grisly end, and that may lead you to your suspect, although it may not help you convict him.

Remember that forensics is never on your side when the scene is hot. You may have to wait days or weeks for results. For the most part, forensics is bluff. *We know that this is the deceased's blood on your shoe.* Well, we will when we get the report back next Christmas. In the meantime you say what you think is the truth to your suspect, and sometimes they break. Or they call for their brief and start bargaining their position right away, and you flick the file the way of the CPS and clear the Incident Room for the next case and go down the King's Head and celebrate.

Murders will get sorted, Marenko told her, because of, and sometimes despite, your best efforts. Most murders happen in the heat of the moment, and most murderers are mostly stupid. They leave witnesses or they brag to their friends or they unburden themselves to their family and they leave behind incontrovertible evidence to boot. Most people, most of the time, don't mean to kill their victim. It's when they do mean it that you've got a problem.

It's the professionals and the enthusiasts who are hardest to catch. The work of true professionals often goes unsolved because they have no relationship with the victim and because they have time to plan the murder, usually in some detail, so it is rare for them to leave behind witnesses or even trace evidence. And besides, no chief super is going to write a blank cheque for unlimited overtime on some shot to shit drug dealer or underworld figure. The victims of professional executions are usually 'known to police', as they say at press briefings, and the only one crying at their funeral is the victim's mother and some slut with peroxide hair and a black dress with cleavage.

It is the enthusiasts who try a detective's mettle, Marenko said. Monsters like the Yorkshire Ripper or Frederick West. They are cold and they are cunning and they choose their victims with care. Like the professionals, their crimes are premeditated, so there is often little in the way of physical evidence. But unlike the professionals, their victims are innocent of any crime other than being in the wrong place at the wrong time. A lot of people die and a lot of careers fall over before those case files are closed.

There are no Agatha Christie denouements. Only go looking for a motive, Marenko warned her, as far as it might lead you to a suspect and because it will keep the CPS and the trial jury happy. In his experience people did cruel and senseless things all the time and you never found out why. But juries, before they convict on a charge like murder, like to have the whole thing tied up with a bow, they want to understand the reason behind the crime. They look for rational behaviour from men whose brains are fried with amphetamines and even in more lucid moments regard the laws of the country in which they live as no more than an inconvenience to their daily lives.

Generally people do not break down and confess when confronted with their manipulations, as they do in the final five minutes of a one-hour cop show. What they do when they are cornered is scream for their brief.

And what you need at that moment is physical evidence or a witness, preferably both, or you'll have the civil liberties crowd crawling all over you.

And that's the job, Marenko had told her, that first day she arrived at Hendon Road. And it is my personal and professional opinion that you do not have what it takes to perform it satisfactorily.

I guess it is up to you to prove me wrong.

There were nearly three dozen people crammed into the Incident Room. To Marenko's disgust there was a fug of tobacco smoke hanging in the air. Perhaps it was a conspiracy. They all knew he was trying to quit.

There was a large bulletin board at the end of the room. On it were photographs of Kate Mercer; at the centre a colour print taken recently by a school photographer, in her school uniform, captured halfway between childhood and a woman-hood she would not attain. The other photographs were the shadowy three-by-fives from the SOC unit, Kate lying twisted on her back in the alleyway, her tongue swollen and her skirt around her waist. The ligature marks at her wrists and the bruising on her throat were highlighted with red and green arrows.

There was a danger, Fox thought, that staring at these photographs every day you could become too familiar with them. Desensitised, they called it, another word for losing your basic humanity. Or there was Marenko's point of view, as he had stated it to her so many times. *No matter what you see, it's all just evidence.* She heard James and Rankin laughing at the back of the room. She turned around and gave them a hard stare.

You can't help your victim if you cry, Marenko had also taught her. The most you can do for them now is do your job.

But she did want to cry for Kate Mercer. Perhaps it was because she was a woman. It was also the reason she tried hardest to hide her remorse. Any show of emotion in this job and you were weak. If the men did it, it was a sign almost of pride. *Even hardened detectives shed a tear*, the newspapers would sometimes report.

But if a hardened woman detective shed a tear, it was not despite the fact that she was hardened; it was because she was a woman.

The rest of the noticeboard was cluttered with the other detritus thrown up by the investigation: diagrams of the crime scene, maps of the area.

As Marenko had predicted, the shit had hit the fan. Within three hours of Frank Marenko and Madeleine Fox having been summoned from their beds in the early hours of that December morning to the freezing alleyway in Islington, the Commissioner of Police was on the phone to Marenko demanding to know if they had a suspect. Merenko was to attend a press conference later that afternoon at Scotland Yard to field questions from the city's major newspapers, radio and television stations. Kate Mercer was news.

The room had fallen quiet when Marenko walked in. He sat down on his desk, his big hands wrapped around the edges, knuckles white.

'What we have is this,' he said. 'Kate Mercer left school at 3.40 yesterday afternoon. The victim was reported missing by her parents at Tolpuddle Street yesterday evening when she failed to return home. She normally walks home from school and gets home around 4.15. Sometimes she stops over at a friend's house and on this occasion this is what the parents assumed – hoped – had happened. However, at about six o'clock, after ringing around all her friends, they became anxious. They drove around the streets themselves for over an hour before making a Missing Persons report. Police officers were sent to interview the family, but a full-scale search was not scheduled to begin until this morning.'

Marenko paused, tapped his jacket pocket, looking for the cigarettes he no longer carried, before he remembered himself.

'Recently she had begun walking home from school with a friend, Sarah Eastham. This particular day Sarah was kept behind at school for detention, so Kate went home alone. We believe she always took the same route and we have now established that she was last seen alive on Caledonian Road at around 3.50. Her body was found in the alley behind MacNaghten Row at five minutes past five the next morning by the man who owns the sweet shop on the corner of the street. Death was by strangulation, effected by a piece of rope or cord. The pathologist's report states that there were also ligature marks on her wrists, indicating that she had been tied up. There was extensive bruising and lacerations to the vagina and anus, indicating that she had been sexually molested, but tests were negative for semen on the oral, vaginal and anal swabs.'

Fox was disgusted at herself for being disappointed. But it was one critical DNA clue they would have to fly without.

Marenko had stopped. Someone coughed at the back of the room and there was a lot of shuffling of feet.

James looked up from his desk. 'Did Graveney find anything from the oral swab?'

Marenko nodded. 'Negative for semen also. A couple of fibres for analysis. Looks like he used a gag.'

Fox tried to dissociate herself from her logical mind, choke off her imagination from the gut-wrenching facts of the case.

'What's the time of death?' Rankin asked.

'The report puts time of death at around 3 a.m., but it could have been an hour earlier. It means her assailant kept her somewhere for around ten hours before murdering her. The question is, where?'

'Could have been anywhere,' James said. 'Ten hours. That puts it anywhere in . . . what? A five-hour radius of London.'

Marenko shook his head. 'If he drove her away from where he picked her up, he's not going to drive all the way back again just to dump her.'

'You don't think there was a car involved?' Fox asked him.

'SOC are checking the alley for tyre prints. But the rain has made the chances of a result unlikely.'

'He must have known her,' Honeywell said.

'That's what I think too,' Marenko said.

'Why?' Fox asked him.

'No one snatches a girl off a busy street without someone seeing him. She must have gone with him willingly. If there had been a struggle, it would have attracted attention. Once she was off the street he did his thing.'

'It was raining that afternoon,' James said. 'Perhaps he offered her a lift.'

'Her parents said they'd warned her about strangers time and time again,' Marenko said. 'No way they see her getting in a car with someone she doesn't know.'

Fox shrugged. What parents told their kids to do and what their kids actually did were always two different things, in her experience.

'Whether he knew her or not,' Fox said, 'to keep her invisible for nearly twelve hours he must have some sort of hidy-hole somewhere.'

'That's what I think too.'

But James was still not sold on Marenko's theory. 'Perhaps he picked her up in a car, took her somewhere, some woodland outside the city.'

'If he did this somewhere else, he wouldn't bring her back to dump her. No, he did this right here, some place between school and home. No one drives all night with a dead kid in their car, even in this fucken' city. Pardon my French, Foxy. I'm telling you, our boy lives within two hundred yards of where we found her.'

No one spoke, some of the detectives making notes, others sitting with their arms crossed, just listening. Fox thought it was too soon to be making these assumptions but said nothing.

'The body was reported at five o'clock this morning by a Mr Henry Wexxler,' Marenko went on, 'who owns a sweet shop that backs directly on to the alleyway where the girl's body was found. I've checked his previous.'

There was a sheaf of print-out lying on his desk. He read: 'Deprivation of liberty and carnal knowledge, 1973. Sentenced to seven years at Colchester Assizes, paroled after three. Child molestation, 1982. Three-year suspended sentence. Also acquitted of a rape charge in 1980. Alleged victim was sixteen years old.'

'What do we know about him?' James asked.

'Lives alone in a one-bedroom flat above the sweet shop. Honeywell has talked to the family. Kate went in there a few times for chocolate bars on the way home from school. He could have snatched her in the shop. Dumped her in the early hours of the next morning, then called in to try to deflect attention from himself. Happens often enough. He has to be favourite.'

'Do we bring him in?' James asked.

Marenko shook his head. 'I've already interviewed him, this morning, in his flat. This man is seriously weird. I had a quick look around when I was there, but I want to get a search and seizure warrant as soon as I can. Meanwhile, next time I speak to him, I want to be prepared. Fox has drawn up a duty roster for today. A number of you will be on door-to-door enquiries. I want you to speak to everyone whose houses back on to that alleyway, and the estate across the road. Someone must have seen or heard something last night. If they've got kids, ask them if they've had any problems lately. I want to know if Mr Wexxler's name comes up in any conversations. Fox, I want you and WPC Stacey to go to the school, talk to her friends, her teachers. I want to know if she mentioned being bothered by anything or anyone lately.'

Marenko grimaced, as if he had stomach acid.

'What we have here is a little girl who's been strangled and sexually assaulted, probably sodomised. We have to get a result on this one. We will be assisted on it by uniforms from Islington who are going to make enquiries along the route between her school and MacNaghten Row and find out if anyone saw her yesterday afternoon. We have to establish where she was last seen and when.'

He looked around the room.

'I don't need to tell you, ladies and gentlemen, that you can forget about weekends, you can even forget about sleeping. This one has to get sorted. All right?'

Chapter Seventeen

The first twelve hours following a murder were critical to the success of an investigation. In that time blood-stained clothes were dumped in a skip or thrown in an incinerator, guns and knives dropped into rivers or sewers, stolen cars torched. It was when alibis were honed and lies perfected. Twelve hours to haul in your prime suspect, three days to put the case to bed. That was the accepted wisdom around the old hands. If you didn't have someone banged up after three days, you were in for the long haul.

Kate Mercer's mother had been interviewed at length by Honeywell, though Brian Mercer was under sedation and was still unable to talk to them. It was unlikely he could tell them anything they had not already learned from his wife. Fox spent most of the day at the little girl's school, talking to her schoolteachers and schoolfriends and her schoolfriends' parents, taking statements. Most of Kate's schoolfriends were too shocked to be coherent, and a team of counsellors had been called in to talk to each of the children in her class.

When Fox went back to the alleyway early that afternoon, the blue police tape was still up, a television camera crew were shooting footage, a knot of locals still stood vigil at the end of the street. Fox showed her ID to the uniform on duty and ducked under the tape. A sniffer dog was being used to search the alley and the adjoining back yards, nosing among the accumulated plastic and paper rubbish and the discarded bottles and cans. The handler's voice was hyptnotic. 'Look–look . . . look–look . . .'

Fox looked around; a crisp bag trapped against a wire mesh fence, coils of dog excrement, a rusted Coke can, a scrap of newspaper. Her gaze travelled along the row of terraced houses that backed on to the alley. Someone had drawn a snowman on their loft window with spray-on snow. Almost Christmas.

She saw James walking towards her and nodded. 'Anything?'

He shook his head. 'Nothing, ma'am. Seven syringes, a Reebok, size eleven, eleven beer cans of various age, and eighteen condoms. Used. Must be the local lovers' lane.'

'I'm going to look around.'

He nodded. 'Good luck.' No innuendo, no baiting, not today. Kate Mercer's murder had infected them all.

Fox came out of the alley and stood on the corner of MacNaghten Row, her collar turned up against the bitter wind. An eddy of leaves and swirling rubbish engulfed the onlookers at the end of the alleyway and moved on like a wraith towards the distant bedlam of Upper Street. The rain had cleared, but the sky was uniform grey.

She was assailed by the smell of garlic and fat from a Turkish takeaway. All this and doner kebabs too.

She peered through the windows of the sweet shop. They were almost opaque with grime. There were a few ancient posters in the windows advertising Mars bars and Golden Wonder crisps.

There was a newsagent's on the other side of the road. She saw an *Evening Standard* placard outside: SCHOOLGIRL SLAIN IN ISLINGTON. Better see what the papers are saying. She hurried across the intersection. A bell rang as she pushed open the door. A clutter of cheap greetings cards and paperbacks, a rack of comics and football magazines, some girlie mags hidden away in a corner.

She picked up a copy of the *Evening Standard*, held out her coins. The woman behind the counter was mid-fifties, West

Indian perhaps. She had permed hair going to grey, and a pair of thick-rimmed black spectacles that flashed in the light.

'You be a policewoman,' she said, with a clipped West Country accent.

'That's right.'

'It's about that little girl. My husband said you lot been in. Asking questions.'

Fox nodded. Instinctively, she asked: 'Did you know her?'

The woman nodded. 'Poor little mite. She came in here sometimes to buy magazines. *Dolly*. That sort of thing.' She made a clucking noise with her tongue. 'In the paper there, they do say she was raped.'

'Yes.'

'What sort of man does that to a little girl?'

'That's what we want to find out.'

'I know what I'd do to him if I found him.'

'Did the police interview you this morning, ma'am?'

'Not yet. I had to visit my sister in hospital. I'm sure my husband would have told you lot everything you want to know.'

'Did you hear or see anything unusual last night?'

'No, luv. Sleep like a log, I do. Can't help you, I'm afraid.'

'You said you knew Katherine Mercer?'

'Well, she came in the shop sometimes, like I said. Didn't really know her. Just her face, if you know what I mean.'

'She used to come in on the way home from school?'

'Sometimes. But always in the afternoon. Never the morning.'

'Did you ever see her with anyone else?'

'Now and then she was with some other kiddie from the school. I never took much notice.'

Fox continued, following her instincts. There was something about the woman, something in her manner, that made her suspect she had something on her mind. 'Do you have any children?' Fox asked her.

The woman shook her head. 'Mine is all growed up. Just me and my husband live here now.'

'Do you have any problems with anyone in the neighbour-hood? Anyone who makes you nervous?'

The woman hesitated. Fox waited. So, she was right.

'It's just that . . . I shouldn't be saying this, it be just gossip.'

'It could be important.'

The woman nodded through the window towards the shop on the other side of the street. 'The man who owns the sweet shop over there. He comes in here sometimes.' She lowered her voice. 'He was in here this mornin'.'

'And?'

'He just acts funny. I don't know.'

'This morning. Did he seem nervous?'

'He'd been drinking. I could smell it on his breath. Eight o'clock in the mornin'!'

Fox pondered. He had just discovered the body of a school-girl in the alley behind his shop. Perhaps he had needed a drink to steady his nerves.

'He comes in here sometimes, looking at them magazines. You know the ones.' She nodded her head towards the *Hustler*s and *Penthouse*s at the end of the rack, next to the biker and trucker magazines. 'Never buys them, mind. Just looks. Gives me the creeps.'

Fox waited. Sometimes silence was the best question.

'Look, I don't want to get him in no trouble. But I don't know. There's something funny about him. Well, you asked me what I thought.'

'Did you ever see Kate Mercer go into his shop?'

'All the time.'

'Did she go in yesterday afternoon?'

'I didn't see her. But we was busy yesterday.'

'All right. Thanks. You've been very helpful.'

'I hope you catch who it was did it. They should bring back hanging, you ask me.'

Fox went outside and looked across the intersection to the sweet shop. Perhaps Marenko was right. But rumour and innuendo alone did not make a man a monster. What they needed was evidence.

Chapter Eighteen

Marenko stared moodily at the muddy remains of his coffee in the bottom of the polystyrene cup. 'I need a cigarette.'

'Lung cancer. Heart attack. Emphysema.'

'Yeah, OK, OK.' He rubbed his forehead with his hand.

Marenko had interview statements and SOC photographs piled on his desk and was painstakingly going through each one. The rest of the available space was taken up with sealed evidence bags; Kate's torn and muddied clothes, her shoes, all that remained of a little girl's life. They were still waiting for the results from forensics on the scrapings Graveney had taken from under the dead girl's fingernails that might yet yield blood and tissue for DNA checking, the latent print analysis on her satchel and books. Graveney had also found fibres on her clothes which might be relevant or might reveal nothing. The two hairs Graveney found on her school uniform, for example, might have come from the SOC unit, from one of the cutters at the mortuary or from Marenko himself. If they did find a hair from the perpetrator, Lambeth needed the root intact to match the DNA code. In any case it was all irrelevant unless they had a prime suspect to match it to.

It was past eight o'clock but detectives were still hunched around computer terminals, punching information into one of the four HOLMES – Home Office Large/Major Enquiry System –

terminals, or calling up the criminal records on every man, woman and juvenile in the two-hundred-yard zone that Marenko had declared around the crime scene. The result was a stark reminder of the realities of modern urban life; of the seven hundred and eighty-three people on their target list they had so far discovered a hundred and forty-three with prior criminal convictions, ranging from disorderly conduct to assault occasioning grievous bodily harm.

Already the team had interviewed over eight hundred and fifty people, and WPC Stacey and four typists were working twelve-hour days to keep up with the paperwork.

The newsagent had not been the first to point a finger in the direction of Henry Wexxler. Two other families in the street had specifically told their children not to go into the shop because they thought the owner was 'iffy' — the word one mother had used — and 'a sleaze', as another woman had said.

He had been the one to find the body and alert the police; not the first time a murderer had done that to cover his tracks. It looked as if Marenko was right. The man they were looking for was right under their noses.

Fox pinned a list of the detectives assigned to the case to the noticeboard and beside their names the duties that had been allotted to them the next day.

James looked up from his desk. 'This is some evil prick we've got here,' he said.

'Has to be Wexxler,' Honeywell said.

Fox shook her head, still not convinced. 'I've just been checking the statements. Number twenty-four thought he saw a black saloon driving out of the alley in the early hours of the morning.'

'He'd just got home from a nightclub. He was paralytic,' James said.

'You think he imagined it?'

He shrugged. 'Like the guv'nor says, it doesn't make sense. So he carries the body from wherever to the boot of his car, drives around London and then thinks, right, I'll dump her in this alley over there? You can't see it from the road.'

At that moment Marenko came out of his office, shrugging on his jacket. 'OK, let's go,' he said.

'Where to?' Fox asked him.

'I reckon we've got enough. Let's go talk to him.'

'Who?' James asked.

'Who do you think?' Marenko said, and then spoke the two words that were to become a litany and a curse over the next fifteen months. 'The Candy Man.'

Chapter Nineteen

Marenko nodded to Fox. Fox hammered on the door with her fist. Nothing.

Twice more.

'Mr Wexxler,' Marenko shouted. 'This is the police. Open the door.'

Marenko looked at Fox. He wanted to go in the hard way, but as yet they did not have a warrant. But then the door opened and the Monster of MacNaghten Row peered out.

Wexxler wore a threadbare dressing gown, loosely tied, revealing a pair of grey-white underpants with an off-yellow stain at the crotch. His sparse grey hair was woolly from sleep, his eyes pink and drooping like an old dog. He reeked of sweat and booze.

Fox held out her ID. 'Henry Wexxler? My name is Detective Inspector Madeleine Fox and this is Detective Chief Inspector Frank Marenko, Detective Sergeant Terry James and Detective Constable William Honeywell. Could you get dressed and come with us please sir? We would like you to come to Islington police station and help us with our enquiries into the murder of Katherine Mercer.'

As Fox was talking, Marenko, Honeywell and James pushed past him into the shop. They had no search warrant, but they could state truthfully that Wexxler had allowed them plain view entry.

He blinked in surprise. 'What time is it?'

'Can you get dressed please sir?' They took a quick look around – dingy shelves with haphazard piles of sweets and crisps, a tiny cubby-hole office at the rear – and then went upstairs, Wexxler shuffling after them.

He passed a hand over his face and stared at the detectives who were already walking right through his one-bedroom flat, switching on all the lights.

'What time is it?' he repeated.

'It's ten o'clock. Can you get dressed, please?'

This is wrong, Fox thought. This guy doesn't look like a child killer to me. But what do I know? What does a child killer look like?

'I go to bed at half-past nine,' he mumbled.

'Will you get dressed, please?' Fox persisted.

'Do you have a search warrant?'

'We don't need a warrant, sir. You allowed us free entry and the detectives are merely waiting for you to get dressed. We would like you to accompany us to the station and answer a few questions. It won't take long.'

'What time is it?' Henry Wexxler said.

'It's ten o'clock,' Fox repeated. 'Can you get dressed please?' What am I, the talking clock? How many more times do we have to go through this?

'I told you everything I know,' Henry Wexxler mumbled. 'I told everything I know to him.' He pointed to Marenko.

'We need to clarify some things.'

Wexxler finally turned around and went back into the flat, to the bedroom. Fox followed him inside. It stank.

'What the Christ is that smell?' James said to Honeywell.

'Cats, skipper.'

He was right. There were cats everywhere, as well as evidence of cats. The carpet in the corner of the room was sodden with urine, and the tray of litter behind the armchair looked as if it had been there for years. Fox followed James and

Marenko into the kitchen. There were empty catfood tins on the draining board next to a stack of dirty dishes and a mewing gaggle of cats fighting over the scraps that had been left in the sink. Fox put a hand to her mouth and nose and went back to the living room.

Honeywell came out of the bedroom. His face was pale. 'What a dump.'

Marenko gave him a questioning glance but he shook his head. 'Nothing in the bedroom, sir.' He saw James kneeling on the floor. 'Jesus, TJ, get up off the floor. You'll catch a disease.'

'Last time I do a plain view search with you, guv,' James said.

'What's the matter? Never had pets in your family?'

Henry Wexxler came out of the bedroom. He was wearing brown trousers, the fly buttons undone and gaping open, a shirt with a dark rim around the collar and a red woollen cardigan fraying at the sleeves and elbows.

'Christ, look at him,' Fox whispered. 'He's unravelling as he walks. There won't be any of him left by the time we get to the station.'

'What time is it?' Henry Wexxler said.

A miasma of stench surrounded Henry Wexxler in the interview room. Marenko had left him sitting alone in Room 4B for almost two hours and now he stared blank-eyed at the two detectives, his jaw loose, scratching a pit as he tried to comprehend their unsmiling, unfriendly faces.

Fox pulled up one of the hard wooden chairs and sat down. 'Henry, I'm Detective Inspector Madeleine Fox and this is Detective Chief Inspector Frank Marenko and that's Police Constable Wells by the door. We just want to ask you a few questions, Henry, so you probably won't need a solicitor or anything. It's just routine.'

Henry Wexxler blinked like an owl caught in the beam of a car's headlights.

'Where were you between 3.30 p.m. of the fourteenth and 5 a.m. of the fifteenth?'

'What time is it?' Henry Wexxler said.

'What is it with you and the time?' Marenko asked him. 'Have you got an appointment some place? Am I interfering with your busy schedule?'

'Why are you shouting?' Henry Wexxler said.

'Where were you between 3.30 p.m. of the fourteenth and 5 a.m. of the fifteenth,' Marenko repeated slowly.

'When was that?'

'That was the day before last, Henry,' Fox said gently.

'I don't know.'

'You don't know?' Marenko said. 'That was the day you found the body of a little girl in the alleyway behind your shop. You don't remember that? You were the one who called us, remember?'

'I told you everything I know about that.'

'Well, tell us again. What were you doing the afternoon before you found the little girl?'

'I was in the shop. I'm always in the shop in the afternoons.'

'Did Katherine Mercer ever come into your shop?'

A slight nod of the head. 'Sometimes.'

'Did she go into the shop that Tuesday afternoon?'

He shook his head.

'Are you sure?'

'I didn't see her that day.'

'What time do you shut the shop?'

'Half-past five. I always shut the shop at half-past five. Exactly.'

'And then what do you do?'

'Then I watch the television. I have dinner at half-past seven.'

'Exactly?' Marenko sneered.

Henry Wexxler nodded, oblivious to the irony.

'And then what?'

'And then I watch the television again. Until nine-thirty. Then I go to bed.'

'So what did you do between 3.30 p.m. of the fourteenth and 5 a.m. of the fifteenth?'

'I don't remember.'

'Jesus.'

'Can I go home now?'

Fox leaned forward, her voice gentle. 'Mr Wexxler, you do remember finding the little girl?'

Henry Wexxler nodded.

'What had you been doing that night?'

'I was watching television, I suppose. Until nine-thirty—'

'Then you went to bed,' Marenko finished for him.

'So you are telling us that you had been watching television all evening?'

'I don't remember.'

Marenko's hands were gripped around a plastic Bic, the knuckles white. A muscle rippled in his jaw. He took a deep breath. 'OK, Mr Wexxler. Let's talk about something else. In 1973 you were charged with depriving the liberty of a fourteen-year-old girl and carnal knowledge. Would you like to tell us about that?'

It seemed Henry Wexxler remembered this well enough. 'She seduced me,' he said, reaching through the gaping fly of his brown corduroys and scratching himself. 'I was innocent.'

'She seduced you?' Marenko said, making no attempt to keep the incredulity from his voice.

Henry Wexxler sniffed his fingers before replacing them in the pockets of his trousers. 'Yeah.'

'Nineteen eighty. You were charged with rape.'

'What time is it?'

The Biro Marenko was holding between his fingers snapped, but his voice remained even. 'Tell me about the rape charge, Mr Wexxler.'

'I don't remember.'

'The girl was sixteen years old. This was when you were living in Colchester. Her name was Sandra Jane Morrison. You remember now?'

'I was innocent,' Henry Wexxler said.

Marenko looked at Fox. Fox shrugged. That was what the jury had said too.

'Nineteen eighty-two. Child molesting. You're one bad boy, Mr Wexxler.'

Henry Wexxler wiped his mouth with his sleeve. 'Can I go home now?'

'Do you like little children, Mr Wexxler?'

'I didn't molest her. That was a lie. A dirty lie!' For the first time Henry Wexxler became animated. His fist banged on the tabletop.

'Did that little girl accusing you make you angry, Henry?'

'Yeah, it did.'

'Why did it make you angry?'

'I didn't do it!'

'According to our records, the victim was just eleven years old. What happened, Henry? Did she seduce you?'

Henry Wexxler stared back at Marenko, eyes dull and uncomprehending. 'What time is it?' he said.

Marenko and Fox stood in the basement corridor and stared at their chief suspect through the glass panel. He was examining the contents of his nose with a thumbnail. 'I seen some scrotes in my time,' Marenko growled, 'but this bloke is something else.'

'That is the sorriest excuse for a human being I ever saw,' Fox said, 'but I don't think he's our boy.'

Marenko shook his head and gave Fox a look of seasoned contempt. 'What do you know, Fox? What were you doing before you came here?'

'I was with the Flying Squad . . .'

'The Flying Squad,' Marenko said, with a sneer that let her know that in his opinion the Flying Squad were all Masons and queers. 'Suddenly you know everything about child killers. That right?'

Fox was not prepared for this sudden venom from her superior. Marenko was as volatile and unpredictable as sweating gelignite. 'Just my gut instinct,' she said, backing down.

'Women don't have a gut, they got e-motions.' He pronounced the word deprecatingly, like it was a lyric from a Motown song. Marenko stepped closer, so Fox could smell the vinegar on his breath from the fish and chip supper he had eaten at his desk earlier that evening. 'You've got a lot to learn, Fox.'

'Well, I'm trying to do it your way,' she said, meeting his stare. 'You told me there are only two things that matter: witnesses and physical evidence. And we don't have either. So why is Henry Wexxler in here?' When Marenko didn't answer her, she said: 'Could it be I'm not the only one around here who likes to follow their instinct. Or is that e-motion?'

Marenko stared at her. 'I hope my instinct's wrong about you,' he said and shambled away.

Chapter Twenty

Fox sat at her desk and drained the contents of a polystyrene cup. The coffee left a bitter aftertaste in her mouth. Caffeine was a drug like any other; you didn't like what it did to your body but you needed what it gave you. In this instance, kept you awake and alert another few hours.

In the four days since Kate Mercer had died Fox had slept a total of maybe fifteen hours, tops. The investigation had now found a focus. Marenko had his suspect and a *casus belli*. Its name was Henry Wexxler.

They had retraced the girl's route from school to home, and the team had now checked every house, every flat and every shop along the way, showing copies of the same photograph that now smiled so poignantly from the pinboard in the Incident Room, asking the same question over and over again. *Did you see this girl on Tuesday afternoon?*

They had found four people who thought they had seen a young girl in a school uniform answering Katie's description that day. But all of the sightings were vague, and none of them could fix her at any place on her route at a given time with any certainty.

And no one had seen her enter the sweet shop.

They had found five schoolchildren and three adults who had all been in the sweet shop after four o'clock that afternoon.

None of them reported seeing anything unusual. As far as they could ascertain Henry Wexxler had not closed the shop early, had not interrupted his usual business hours in any way.

Not a single witness.

The paperwork on Marenko's desk was still growing, witness statements piling up beside the print-outs on the criminal records of every living soul within a two-hundred-yard radius of MacNaghten Row, correlated in street and number order: those with sex offences had been circled in red. There were just two others apart from Henry Wexxler, one a thirty-three-year-old father of four with a previous for rape in 1983, the other a forty-seven-year-old unemployed factory worker with three indecent assault charges dating from 1976. But all these cases had involved women and not minors, and Marenko had discounted them as genuine suspects.

'Rape is something that can happen to any bloke if he drinks too much,' Marenko had said. 'Rock spiders are different.'

Fox had looked up hard when he said that, but he just smiled at her and shrugged his shoulders.

'Sorry if that's not politically correct, Foxy,' he said. 'But it's true.'

They still had no crime scene; the forensic lab had found flakes of brick on her blazer and some sort of mould. From this it was concluded that she had been held for a time in an unsealed room, probably under ground. A basement, Marenko had hissed.

Forensics had given the murder priority, after a phone call from the Commissioner. But they had nothing: there were no latents on any of her belongings, there was no blood or hair or tissue that might have excluded Wexxler as a suspect or confirmed him as their prime suspect.

If they lacked hard evidence they were overwhelmed with suspicions and innuendo. It seemed that people in MacNaghten Row had been talking since the murder, and they must have reached a consensus among themselves. The telephone in the Incident Room started to ring as neighbours decided to share their suspicions with the police; Wexxler was a loner; certain kids were frightened of him; some kids said he'd tried to persuade them to go into his back room to watch videos. No one had made any official complaint to the police at the time, but now, with the murder of Kate Mercer, tales of his misdemeanours became legion.

Fox and Honeywell had been back to Kate's parents, had gone into the little girl's room, read through her diary. It was a profoundly depressing experience, and in the end they had found nothing.

'So how did he do it, guv?'

Marenko tapped a Biro on the edge of a desk and chewed on his lip. He shrugged his shoulders and said nothing.

'She goes into the sweet shop,' Fox went on. 'He grabs her somehow. This had to be around a quarter to, ten to four. He doesn't shut the shop until the usual time. As far as we know the last customer came out of there at around twenty-past five. By this time he's had the little girl nearly an hour and a half. It doesn't make sense.'

'The way I see it is this, Fox. She comes in the shop, alone. He grabs her. Puts a hand over her mouth, ties her up, dumps her somewhere in the back of the shop. Takes how long? Couple of minutes. It's a risk, if someone came in the shop right then, they would have seen him. But he gets away with it. He knows if he closes up the shop he's as good as putting a sign in the window: "I just did something really bad." So he stays cool, shuts up at the normal time. And he's got the next eleven hours to play.'

'But how did he dispose of the body? He must have carried her down the path at the back of the shop and scrambled over the fence, dragging the body or holding her in his arms. Surely he would have left footprints something. The SOCOs found nothing.'

The telephone rang on her desk. Fox withdrew reluctantly from this debate and snatched up the receiver. 'Fox.'

'Madeleine?'

'Who is this?' she snapped.

'It's Simon. Simon Andrews. We met a couple of months ago at your sister's house.'

Her mind a complete blank. Her sister's house. Like waking from a dream, unable to differentiate between vivid night and grey morning, between a nightmare world of dead children and rain-soaked alleyways and a vague and distant world of suburban houses and dinner parties and conversations that did not have at their centre a matter of violent death.

She blinked, trying to refocus on this other life. Her bewilderment and confusion were mistaken for some other emotion, more malevolent. 'I suppose you have a right to be mad at me,' the voice on the other end of the line told her. 'I don't blame you.'

'Sorry, who is this again?'

A long silence. Oh, *that* Simon, she thought. Her mind finally responded, dragging the image of a handsome, fair-haired man from the misty archives of a long-ago weekend. A lifetime past. Kate Mercer's lifetime.

'I've rung a few times. Left messages.'

'It's been pretty busy in here.'

'Of course. Look, I've thought a lot about that night. I behaved badly, I admit it. I'm not condoning what you said, but . . . what I did wasn't right either. I wanted to say I'm sorry.'

'Oh. Right. Apology accepted.'

What had he done? What had *she* done? Was it as bad as raping and murdering an eleven-year-old girl? And if it wasn't — why were they even discussing it?

There was another long silence. 'Well. Perhaps I'll see you around.'

'OK.'

'Goodbye. And once again, I'm sorry.'

He hung up. Marenko looked over. 'Well, either your chief witness just emigrated or you just got dumped by your boyfriend.'

Fox ignored him. She stood up and walked down the corridor to the women's locker room, thinking she might be about to cry for Kate Mercer. But she didn't. She just stood looking in the mirror, her face set like stone, and when she walked back into the Incident Room the only thing she felt was fatigue, down to the marrow of her bones.

The church was built of chocolate-brown brick. There were a few ancient graves overgrown with weeds, and an ornamental pond with water the colour of sump oil and a Sainsbury's shopping trolley upended in it. It was just four hundred yards from where they found the body of Kate Mercer, in the shadow of a hundred-year-old biscuit factory.

It was bitterly cold inside. Men fidgeted in sombre black suits, the women giving themselves openly to weeping. Fox followed Marenko through the porch and took a seat near the back. Fox closed her eyes and said a small prayer to a God she did not believe in.

She caught a glimpse of a woman in a shapeless black dress slumped against a huge, balding man in an ill-fitting dark suit. The man's face was set like stone, his eyes glassy and unfocused. Today it seemed the roles had reversed. Brian Mercer was back in control.

Fox could not concentrate on the service, her mind wandering to the details of the investigation. It was two weeks now since they had found her body. That morning's *Daily Mirror* had featured a photograph of little Kate smiling out from page five. The headline said:

LEADS ELUSIVE IN KATE MERCER MURDER:
POLICE APPEAL FOR WITNESSES.

Marenko had thrown the net again, sending members of the team over an ever-widening area armed only with desperation and a photograph of Katherine Mercer. So far this week Fox had devoted over a hundred hours to the case, as had most of the detectives on the squad. A television re-enactment, using a child actor with a resemblance to the dead schoolgirl, had been shown twice that week on prime-time television asking for anyone who recalled having seen a girl answering Kate's description on the afternoon she went missing to contact the Incident Room. For a few days the telephones had run hot. But at the end of two weeks Marenko was still no closer to issuing an arrest warrant for the Candy Man.

The forensic report on the stomach contents had set the needle flickering again, and like a compass it always pointed in the same direction. Kate Mercer's intestinal tract contained a fully digested meal of bread, peanuts, flour and sultanas. Her mother confirmed that in her lunchbox the day she was murdered Kate had peanut butter sandwiches and fruit cake.

But her last meal, the report stated, consisted of chocolate and caramel. The last thing she had eaten had been some sort of chocolate bar. No, Kate's mother told Fox on the telephone, I never gave her sweets for her school lunch. I told her it was bad for her teeth. Perhaps she bought some with her pocket money on the way home from school.

But on its own it proved nothing.

In the last couple of days the members of the AMIT team had started snapping at each other, exhausted and scared to admit, even to each other, that a sense of desperation had overtaken the case. Henry Lincoln Wexxler, the owner of the sweet shop that bordered the alley not twenty yards from where Kate was found, was still their prime suspect.

But there was no clear evidence against him. Except DCI Marenko said he was the killer. And as any of the veterans in the department would tell you, Frank Marenko was never wrong.

The memorial service for Kate Mercer was almost over. The mayor followed the parish priest to the pulpit to express the council's outrage over the murder of an eleven-year-old girl within their boundaries. Then Brian Mercer got up to speak.

He leaned on the lectern, staring out over the heads of his family, his friends and neighbours, as well as a dozen ranking officers of the Metropolitan Police Force, strangers from newspapers and radio and television stations, men and women he had never seen before, whom he would never see again. His hands trembled as he began to speak.

'My Kate,' he said into the microphone. For a moment Fox thought he was going to break, but then he composed himself. 'She was just a kid. What can I say? She was doing well at school. She was bright, and most of the time she was pretty happy. Like every other kid. She was good at drawing, and we figured one day she might go to a college and make something of herself. She was going to be a very pretty girl someday. She was going to have a good job, boyfriends, all the rest of it. I prayed for her, like every father. I wanted her to have a good life. But that's it, she's gone . . . what am I going to say?

'Maybe all I can say is there's something wrong with living in a place where we can't look after our kids no more.' He paused. The only sound in the church was the muffled sobbing from Mrs Mercer in the front pew. Jesus looked down from His own agonised situation on a Cross. Pity me, pity her. 'I remember she stood right there when she took her communion . . .'

The memory overtook him, and his voice broke and he was unable to go on. Two of Brian's brothers helped him from the pulpit. The priest led the congregation in a hymn. And that was it.

And we still have no murder scene, Fox thought. And no one who can definitely say they saw her after she left the school gates at three-thirty that afternoon. It was as if she had vanished off the earth, sucked into the devil's torture chamber to die a horrible death and then be spewed back from the ether into a North London alleyway.

As they left the church Fox spotted the surveillance van

parked on the other side of the street. Inside it, one of the technicians would be photographing the crowd, hoping the killer might make an appearance out of remorse or out of some twisted sense of triumph. They would examine the video later, hoping for the lucky break they were all praying for.

Fox and Marenko walked in silence back to their car. Marenko got behind the wheel, and they drove back to Hendon Road.

'You know who we work for?' Marenko said, breaking a long silence.

'What is this, guv, *Mastermind*?'

'Hey, Fox, your superior officer asked you a question. Who do we work for?'

'We work for the Metropolitan Police.'

'No, wrong, Fox. That's why you're still in nappies. You do not work for the Metropolitan Police. You work for God.'

'Run that by me again, guv?'

'Who's going to avenge that little girl, Fox? Us. We talk for the dead. This is not a job, it's a vocation, a sacred mission. We are all that stands between the public and the devil. Us.'

'Yes, guv.'

'You'll see, Fox. You'll see the light or you'll be back investigating hold-ups inside the year.' He drummed his fingers on the wheel. 'Christ, I need a cigarette.'

Chapter Twenty-one

It had been a day very much like today. It was her first day at the new school, and after Hong Kong the grey English skies and damp chill had made her feel lonelier than she had ever felt in her whole life. A skinny, mousy-haired girl sat down next to her in the school yard and offered her a peanut butter sandwich. What she remembered most about her was not her face but the hand that held out the sandwich: the nails were bitten down to the quick and the fingers were covered with ink.

They had been friends ever since.

Her mother was a Hollies fan, and she had been named after a Hollies tune that had been popular when she was born: Carrie Anne. Carrie Anne Kennedy. It was a long-standing joke between them; what if she had been born a few months earlier or later? 'Bus Stop Kennedy,' Fox had suggested.

'Jennifer Eccles,' she had countered, and they had laughed themselves sick in Carrie's bedroom. They were thirteen.

Almost twenty years had passed since then, not all of them good ones.

Carrie was thirty-two now but she could have passed for ten years older. She had always been angular, all collarbones and knees, with bony wrists at the end of arms that seemed too long for her. Her Oxfam discards and the dark rings under her eyes only accentuated the effect. There were curd stains on her shoulder, the baby clinging to her like some parasite that had locked on, sucking her dry. She looked more like a refugee staring out from the cover of *Time* magazine than her oldest and best friend, a single mother in an anonymous Chingford flat.

The morning was chill as death, and a fine drizzle had settled over London like a malevolent gas. The little flat was cold, the only warmth coming from a single-bar electric fire in the tiny living room. There were baby toys scattered on a rug on the floor, washing-up piled in the sink, a discarded nappy on the floor. All the clutter of single motherhood.

Carrie Anne had recently broken up with the child's father, Sean. A charming and erudite man when he was sober, when he was drunk he screamed abuse and slapped her around the face. Fox had told her time and again to throw him out. The last straw came when Carrie found a bruise on the infant's arm after Sean had been left looking after the child for an hour. She didn't mind the slaps herself, but she wouldn't accept them on her baby.

Carrie was in the kitchen, pouring hot water on two PG Tips teabags. 'He keeps coming round. Sometimes he just sits in his car watching the flat. It gives me the creeps.'

'We can talk to him for you,' Fox said.

'We? You mean the police?'

'I can show him my badge and be a cop for a few minutes. If that's what you want.'

Carrie shook her head.

'Has he hurt you?'

'No. I told him. Like you said. I told him I'm not taking that from him any more.'

Carrie had had a string of go-nowhere relationships with men who abused her, hit her, cheated on her, drank too much. Was it possible to be that unlucky, Fox wondered, or was there something else, some masochistic streak in her that loved what hurt her most? Not that she could lecture anyone about men and relationships.

'Funny,' Carrie said. 'I still miss him.'

'After what he did to you?'

'It wasn't all bad.' She poured milk in the teas and handed one to Fox. 'He was great, you know, when he wasn't drinking. He kept promising to give up. I knew he couldn't.'

Fox said nothing. She knows what I think about Sean.

'It's just waking up in the morning with no one in the bed. God knows I don't miss the sex. But I hate rolling over and there's no one to cuddle up to. Starting the day on your own, it guts me. Don't you ever feel like that?'

Fox shrugged her shoulders. But the answer was, Oh, yes.

'I don't get you, Maddy.'

'What?'

'Look at you. You could have been a model. You should have blokes hanging off you. I mean me, I get everybody else's leftovers.'

'A bloke would be lucky to have someone like you, Carrie.'

'Yeah. Right.' She got up to find some biscuits. 'Did you see that bit on the news about the little kid that got murdered?' She put her head around the door. 'One of yours?'

Fox nodded her head.

'I don't know how you do it. Hope you get the bastard.'

She sorted through the cupboard and found a half-eaten packet of digestives. When she came back into the living room Fox was staring vacantly out of the window.

'Maddy?' Carrie said. 'Are you all right?'

Not really, she wanted to say. My private life is a mess. Professionally, I think I'm a stress case. I work too hard, I don't play enough, I'm coming apart out of loneliness and I don't think I can cope with the demands of my job. No, I'm not all right.

'Yes,' she said, smiling. 'I'm fine.'

The King's Head on Station Road had been a decent pub once. There was a solid oak bar running the length of the room, old highback chairs, dark panelling on the walls, ever beer barrels in the centre of the room where you could rest your pint of Carling or London Pride or Caffrey's Irish Ale.

But sometime in the 1980s a new publican had had a CD player mounted on the wall and now Tina Turner's 'Simply the Best' competed with the jangle of a Baywatch pinball machine and a garishly lit Monopoly one-armed bandit and the television mounted on a bracket above the bar.

But it was still considered the local among the uniformed officers and CID at Hendon Road and, despite some misgivings, they had remained loyal.

Marenko had taken his post in the corner, a Guinness in his left fist, the nicotine-stained fingers of his right hand tapping an impatient tattoo on the polished oak bar. Beside him, holding a pint of Young's, was a young man in a black leather jacket, open-necked shirt and jeans. He was good-looking, with short black hair and a powder-white smile. Fox found herself involuntarily smoothing back her hair and looking for somewhere to check her reflection.

'Hey, Fox,' Marenko said. 'I want you to meet Tom. Tom, this is my DI, Madeleine Fox. Known to the troops as Foxy, as you can see for yourself. This is Tom, latest addition to the Metropolitan's finest.' He put an arm around the young man. There was a stain on Marenko's shirt. Not drunk, but on the right road to it and speeding. 'Tom has just joined the ranks of the uniformed constabulary at Kentish Town. We are celebrating his elevation from civilian to the exalted ranks of this city's police force. Passed first in his class. Also happens to be my son-in-law. Not only a future police commander in the making but he had the good sense to marry a Marenko girl.'

Tom held out his hand and she took it. Marenko's son-in-law, she thought, smiling in the young man's direction. Well. He returned her smile, slightly diffident for all his good looks. Twenty-three, twenty-four tops, she thought. Well, a little too young for me anyway. 'Welcome to the Good Guys,' she said.

'What are you drinking, Fox?' Marenko asked her.

'I'll have the usual,' she said. The usual, she thought; a microwave dinner and a bed for one.

'Frank's talked about you a lot,' Tom said.

Fox glanced sideways at Marenko, surprised. 'He has?'

Marenko had a ten-pound note in his fist and had attracted the barman's interest. 'I said you were the best woman DI I'd ever worked with.'

'I'm the *only* woman DI you've ever worked with.'

'Still works,' Marenko said.

'I guess there aren't many women that high up in the CID.'

'Let's put it this way, if I run out of tampons there's no one to borrow from at Hendon Road. And I don't get many takers to my Tupperware parties either.'

Marenko handed her a gin and tonic, slopping a third of it on to the carpeted floor. 'Excuse me, got to see a man about a dog,' he said, and staggered towards the Gents.

Tom smiled, embarrassed.

There was an uneasy silence. 'So you work with Frank,' Tom said finally. 'I don't envy you.'

'You're related to him. I don't envy *you*.'

'At least I had a choice.'

Nice guy, Fox thought, warming to him. Charming, good-looking, a shy smile. And married. She remembered that old saying about policemen and decided it applied equally well to married men. They were getting younger all the time as well.

'How long have you been a cop?' she asked him.

'Three months. Still haven't got used to talking to my left shoulder yet.' Constables on the beat had radios attached to the lapels of their jackets for easier communications. 'I do it at home, for practice, and my wife thinks I've gone crazy.'

'It doesn't get any easier. I start off every conversation with "You have the right to remain silent".'

He laughed, which was nice of him, Fox thought.

'So, what made you join the force?'

'I was a rep with a pharmaceuticals company. I guess I was looking for something with more of a challenge.'

'Did Frank talk you into it?'

'He was an influence, sure.' He looked at her over the rim of his glass. Nice eyes. A long time since she had looked deep into a man's eyes that weren't fixed and dilated and non-reactive to light.

'How do you get along with Frank?' he asked her.

'Fine,' she said, and he nodded and seemed to understand the subtext of her smile. 'He's a legend around the department. But he's probably already told you that himself.'

'I'm always up for another story.'

Stories about Frank Marenko were legion. Despite his relentless litany of orthodox police theory – witnesses, physical evidence – Fox had heard countless anecdotes from other members of the AMIT about his unorthodox methods, his blind hunches and his stubborn refusal to admit he was wrong after he had established a particular theory about a case. 'One of the detective sergeants remembers working under Frank on the shooting murder of a drug dealer when they were both stationed at Rotherhithe. The man's partner had gone missing and Frank was sure he was the shooter, that he had killed him in an argument about money and then skipped the country on a fake passport. But as it happened, their Super had been given high-level intelligence that in fact both men had been murdered by a rival dealer and that the bodies had been dumped in the Thames near Southwark. Police divers searched the river, and after an hour they found the body and it was winched to the surface in a net. As it came on board there were four mud crabs still hanging on to the corpse. The Super turned to Frank and said: "Well, Inspector, what do you have to say now?" Frank just shrugged and said: "You have two. I'll have two and we'll set him again." '

Tom liked that one. 'It's a joke, though, right?'

'I bent the truth a little.'

'I'll tell you my first experience of Frank,' Tom said, 'and this is true, swear to God. I'd been going out with Jules for about three months when she took me over to his place to meet him. He looked me in the eye, shook my hand, a grip like iron, and he said: "If you're studying law I'm going to have to kill you right now." '

Fox laughed and thought: three months for him to meet Frank. Interesting. She knew her boss was divorced, of course, but she didn't realise he was practically estranged from his family. Frank didn't talk about his private life. She would have liked to have pumped Tom for more, but by then Marenko had returned. He threw an arm around Tom's shoulder and said, 'He's like a son to me, this boy.' He said to Fox, 'Did I tell you he graduated top of his class?'

'Yes, you did,' Tom said, clearly embarrassed, disentangling himself from the big man.

For the next half an hour Marenko held court, regaling them with his own experiences as a beat policeman in the 1970s. He told his favourite story, how he had once arrested John Lennon for speeding. Fox finished her G&T and looked at her watch. She felt like she was standing on a slope, the combined effects of fatigue and alcohol. When was the last time she had caught eight hours' sleep?

'I have to go home,' she said. 'It was nice meeting you, Tom. See you in the morning, guv.'

As she was leaving, Marenko said: 'We're going to get him, Fox.'

She nodded, knowing who he was referring to. 'You bet we are,' she said, but she no longer felt quite so certain.

James took the call. A delivery driver for a soft drinks company had seen the re-enactment on the news and now thought he had seen a schoolgirl like the one on the television going into a sweet shop on the corner of MacNaghten Row. He guessed it was sometime between quarter to four and four o' clock in the afternoon.

An hour later he came into the station and gave a written statement. He remembered her clearly, he said, because she looked so much like his own daughter and he had done a double take.

'That's all we need,' Marenko said to Fox. 'I'm going to get a search warrant.'

Chapter Twenty-two

Fox was cold, cold to her bones. The damp chill seemed to emanate in waves from the dark brick walls as they climbed the back stairs of the Candy Man's flat above the sweet shop. She slapped the glass door with the flat of her hand. When Henry Wexxler opened the door, Marenko thrust a copy of the search warrant in his face. 'Get out of the way.'

Henry Lincoln Wexxler wore a stained T-shirt and under-pants – the same ones he had worn for the interrogation two weeks before, by the look of them. But he was not so drowsy this time, Fox thought, and not so drunk.

'You can't come in here,' he said, his tone belligerent.

Marenko took the target copy of the search and seizure warrant out of his jacket pocket and thrust it into his hands. 'Yes, I can. Read this.'

Fox, Marenko and James pushed past him into the shop.

During the next half an hour the flat yielded many gruesome finds, none of them related to the case: an ancient tin of catfood, empty but not clean, which had somehow rolled under the bed; dark and turgid lumps that had dried to the linoleum, and which Marenko guessed to be faecal material, hopefully animal in origin. A sheet with a large crimson stain was found in one corner of the bedroom and caused some excitement until one of the SOCOS sniffed at it and pronounced that the stain was almost certainly cheap sherry. They took a sample anyway.

While they worked, the Candy Man returned his attention to the television, slumped in an armchair with an ashtray balanced on the armrest beside him, the target copy of the search warrant unread on his lap. He was watching a rerun of *The Bill*.

'Nothing here,' Marenko finally announced. 'Why don't we take another look at the shop?'

Fox nodded. 'I'll tell him to get the keys.'

'And Fox . . .'

'Guv?'

'If he asks what the time is, I swear to Christ I'm going to kick the shit out of him.'

The sweet shop. The last place Kate Mercer was seen alive.

Fox stood inside, transfixed, as if in some arcane and holy shrine. The racks of boiled sweets and chocolate looked both sad and sinister in the flickering, dusty strip light. She remembered from her childhood the tales of the witch in the gingerbread cottage. She conjured up the image of the little girl being drawn into the back room with the promise of some treat, then battered unconscious, hog-tied and smuggled out. But the mechanics of the abduction still gnawed at her. *How* had Henry Wexxler smuggled her out? And where had he taken her? He did not own a car.

So how was it done?

The Candy Man stood by the door, in his dressing gown, muttering unintelligible protests as the search continued.

'What the fuck's this?' Marenko put his head around the curtain that divided the small office at the back from the shop.

'Have you done?' Henry Wexxler said.

'No, I'm not done. I'm not done with you at all. I want to know what the fuck this is.'

Fox grabbed the Candy Man's arm and dragged him into the

strip-lit office. There was a trap door in the floor, with a ladder leading down to dark and fetid depths. The other detectives crowded around. Marenko had pushed aside an ancient wooden desk to reveal it. That was why they had not seen it on their first visit.

Marenko leaned closer to the Candy Man so that his face filled his vision. Sweat glistened on his upper lip like dew. 'Well?'

'It's the cellar.'

'What do you need with a cellar, Mr Wexxler?' Fox asked him.

'The cellar's always been here.'

'You never go down there?'

The Candy Man looked scared. Fox felt a thrill in her stomach and saw Marenko grin wolfishly.

We've got you now.

James handed Marenko a torch. He eased his bulk through the trap door and went down the ladder into the pitch black. The beam of the torch caught a cord hanging from the ceiling. Marenko tugged on it, and the cellar was illuminated in the dirty yellow glow of a forty-watt bulb.

'Why didn't you tell us there was a light, Mr Wexxler?' Fox said.

'You never asked me.'

She heard Marenko swear. 'You find something?'

'I don't know.'

She pushed the Candy Man down the ladder in front of her. The cellar was as cold as a tomb and stacked ceiling high with cardboard boxes. Marenko tore one of the boxes open: baked beans. He tore open another one: toilet rolls.

'What the hell is this?' Marenko said.

Henry Wexxler looked embarrassed. 'It's my fallout shelter.'

'Your what?'

'I started storing gear down here a few years back, when the Gulf War started. I thought there was gonna be a nuclear war.'

Marenko shook his head in wonder. 'This is the future of mankind,' he said to Fox. 'A pre-nuclear mutation.' He straightened and looked around the room. 'This is pretty much soundproof, I imagine,' he said to no one in particular.

'I suppose so,' Henry Wexxler agreed.

Marenko turned back to Fox. 'Get the SOCOS down here now. I want this place dusted for lifts, every atom sucked off the floor for blood and hair. Mr Wexxler, why don't we go back to the station and have a cup of tea and talk about this?'

Chapter Twenty-three

'Listen to me,' Marenko said, leaning forward.

The Candy Man looked up.

'You did it, didn't you, Henry?'

The Candy Man was silent.

Marenko leaned across the desk. 'You killed her, Henry. Say it. It will make you feel better.'

'What time is it?'

Fox thought Marenko was going to explode. The colour had left his face. He took out a packet of Benson and Hedges and laid them on the table between them. He casually stripped off the cellophane and put a cigarette in his mouth. He lit it, deeply inhaling the smoke. The Candy Man looked hungrily at the box. Marenko left it there, on the table between them, a symbol of his control. He casually flicked a piece of ash into the ashtray.

'The last time we interviewed you, you said Katherine Mercer did not come into your shop the afternoon she disappeared.'

Henry Wexxler stared. The Adam's apple bobbed in his throat, a cork on a stormy sea.

'We now have a witness who is willing to testify he saw her enter your shop between quarter to four and four o'clock.'

'I don't remember.'

'You knew her quite well, didn't you, Henry? She used to go

in your shop a lot. Young Kate. Can you say her name for me? For the tape.'

'K-Kate.'

'Hard to say her name, wasn't it, Henry? You stumbled over it just then. Painful memory, was it? Say it again.'

'Kate.'

'Kate. What did you do to little Kate?'

'I didn't do anything.'

Marenko blew out a long stream of smoke. 'I know you, Henry,' he said. 'I know how you think. I know what you do when you're alone. I've had lots of blokes like you through here. Rock spiders.'

Fox watched the Candy Man's face, waiting for him to betray himself. But there was no expression.

'No one lies to me, Henry. They try. They start off with half-truths and deceptions, but in the end they tell me everything. You know why, Henry? Because you can't hide anything from me. I don't need a lie detector, I can smell it. I've been doing this job a long time. I never miss, Henry. I know it was you who killed her.'

'I want a solicitor,' the Candy Man said

Fox shrugged. She was about to get up, but Marenko put a hand on her arm. He opened the file in front of him and slid out a picture of Kate Mercer, a glossy colour ten by seven, taken the year before by a portrait photographer in the High Street. For her Communion.

'Look at her, Henry. Look at what you did.'

The rock had shifted. Peering beneath, Fox was afforded another view. For a moment the Candy Man shuffled aside and she caught a glimpse of the orange eyes of a predator. 'I want a solicitor,' he repeated.

Marenko opened the file again, and like a poker-player sliding a card from the deck he slid the glossy colour crime-scene photographs across the table and flipped them over. He spread them out in front of Henry Wexxler, never taking his eyes from the other man's face. Then he took out the photographs from the autopsy.

'Guv,' Fox said.

A hard look. Shut up. He turned back to the Candy Man. 'Look at her, Henry. Look at what you did.'

The Candy Man looked. He shook his head.

'What is it, Henry? You want to tell me something?'

'He's asked for a solicitor, guv.'

'Shut up, Fox.' He leaned further across the table. 'What is it you want to tell me, Henry?'

For a moment Fox thought she saw a muscle twitch in the other man's cheek, waited for some deep-seated emotion to bubble up to the surface, for the dam to break. But then it was gone and Henry Wexxler was back in control. 'Can I go home now?' he said to Fox.

Marenko told the custody sergeant to send for a solicitor, then told Honeywell that when he arrived he was to stall him downstairs in the foyer. And so it went on.

Marenko asked the same questions again and again. He left the room, came back, left again, working in tandem with Fox, then sent James in, trying different tactics all the time. It was the way he approached any investigation. Once he decided on a suspect he was relentless, worrying the target like a dog with a bone. And sometimes it worked, sometimes he went at it in that same monotone, over and over, working at tiny flaws and inconsistencies, and ended up hours later with a signed confession.

But this was not to be one of those times. Henry Wexxler kept insisting on his right to legal representation, showing not a trace of fear or distress. He sat there like a stone. He offered no alibi, would admit nothing.

When the custody sergeant called Marenko out and said there was a court-appointed solicitor raising hell downstairs,

Marenko told him to send him home again, that the interview was already over. They had fired their best shots, and the Candy Man had taken them all. They had no leverage, not one solid piece of evidence linking him to Kate Mercer.

Everything now was down to forensics. There had to be something in that cellar. There had to be.

PART THREE

North London.
A late afternoon in the middle of winter

Chapter Twenty-four

Frank Marenko walked into the King's Head, hoping to find James or Honeywell or one of his fellow DCIs but there was only a couple of uniformed sergeants in civvies, leather jackets and jeans. One of them leaned on the pinball machine, his beer glass resting on the surface, desultorily jerking the flippers. Marenko scowled. It had been a black day when they allowed pinball machines and video games and, worst of all, karaoke machines into British pubs.

A grey-haired woman in the uniform of the Salvation Army moved around the room rattling her collection tin.

Marenko hoisted himself on a stool. Henry, behind the bar, picked up a pint glass and started to draw off a Guinness.

'How was your day, Frank?' he said, setting it on the bar in front of him.

'Don't ask.'

He nodded, sensing that the big man was in no mood even to sound off. He moved away. Marenko put the glass to his lips and drained half of it with one pull.

Marenko knew that by now he should be eating a TV dinner with his feet on a stool. But these days his home away from home was here, sharing the familiar shop-talk of the other detectives from Hendon Road over the jangle of the poppers on the pinball machine. Here, at least, he was never lonely, here with the other members of the Metropolitan Police Force he had a place to belong. He could brood about Kate Mercer and was guaranteed a sympathetic ear, and the ache in his gut would submit for a while to the anaesthetic of beer and brotherhood.

He finished his Guinness. Henry set another on the counter in front of him and moved away again without a word.

Kate Mercer had now been dead for over two months and the case was still open. The cellar below the Candy Man's shop had revealed nothing. Forensics had identified not one drop of blood, not one human hair or fibre that could be linked to the little girl. Moreover, the flakes of brick forensic had found on her blazer did not match samples taken from Wexxler's cellar. So where had they come from?

The case was stalled, and his failure nagged at him constantly. The enquiry had been wound down, although the case remained open. But most days it seemed to him that only Frank Marenko kept the torch burning for the little girl who had died horribly, and alone, in that Islington alleyway.

Kate Mercer stood as a black mark against him, against the Metropolitan Police, against all natural law.

His desk at Hendon Road was surrounded by three large cardboard boxes, and some days he felt as if he was carrying each one of them on his shoulders; two boxes were devoted to the witness statements from the hundreds of people who had been interviewed in the week after the little girl's body was found; the other box was filled with five-by-three photographs of the crime scene, lab reports, the transcript of Graveney's postmortem examination.

And one thick manila folder, the weight of a housebrick, was devoted to the Candy Man

Behind Marenko's desk was a bulletin board, and on it were diagrams of the crime scene and maps of the MacNaghten Row area, which he had taken from the Incident Room to remind him of those heady days when the case was still viable, and everyone on it was convinced it would close. Pinned in the middle of the board was the photograph Marenko remembered from the morning they had gone to Kate's home to break the news to her family; a little girl he had never known in life, dressed in her school uniform, grinning shyly and without guile at the camera.

It was not grief that bothered him, for he had never known Katherine Mercer. There had been no pain as he stared at her wounds that early morning in the alleyway; they were merely points of evidence, footprints on the trail he thought would lead him to her killer. He was shocked at the brutality of her death, certainly, but it was the same detached horror he had experienced countless times before. He was no stranger to unnatural death.

Yet her case had become a personal obsession. For the last two months he had worked sixteen-hour days, seven days a week. He had developed a cough, and the coughing fits sometimes went on for several minutes, while his cheeks turned purple and Honeywell slapped him on his back and told him he should have given up cigarettes years ago. James had laughed and told him that if he felt something round and furry at the back of his throat he should swallow hard because he was about to splutter up his arse.

He had quit smoking twice more in that two months. He was now on his third attempt.

He was constantly tired. He went to his doctor thinking he finally had the big C. And the doctor did every kind of test he could think of, and a few days later when Marenko went back to see him, braced for bad news, he told him he could find nothing physically wrong, but was he under any kind of stress at the moment?

No more than usual, Marenko had answered.

Frank Marenko knew what was wrong. It did not have to do with his lungs; it had to do with justice. If some groid got charlied up and chopped up his old lady, or some junkie overdosed behind King's Cross station, well, he couldn't care less. If some pub doorman ended up in a pool of blood and vomit on the pavement on a Saturday night, well, too bad. Shit happens.

But when the tortured children and the raped and murdered women went unavenged, then the angels wept, and Frank Marenko wept with them. The devil had won. More than that, it made him a failure, no longer of use to the gods that were watching this shitty little morality play in which he had cast himself as star turn.

He had felt this way before, but the black dog had not had its claws in his back for so long. It had started with the Capper case. Not that he gave a damn about the life of Elmore Crawford – he was hardly a taxpayer – but Capper had walked because his witness had feared his system of justice more than she had feared Marenko's.

Now he recognised the Capper case for what it was; the one case that might take him over the hump from fatigue to burnout.

It was why he had sent James and Rankin back down Kentish Town Road to talk to Flora Ellis again. He still hoped she might change her mind. While the file on Elmore Crawford stayed open, she was still their best shot to finally get Pat Capper banged up.

Someone sat down on the stool on his left. He looked up hopefully, then saw that it was Fox. He ignored her and kept on drinking.

'Still on that double murder, guv?'

'What double murder, Fox?'

'Kate Mercer.'

'That was one murder.'

'Looks to me like it's killing you too.'

'You talk a load of shite.'

'Want another Guinness?'

'Women don't buy me drinks.'

Fox stared at him, her face a study in frustration. 'What is it you have against me, guv?'

'Apart from you being a woman, you mean?'

'Apart from that?'

Henry drew off another Guinness and put it on the polished

bar in front of Marenko. Fox pushed her money across the bar, a five-pound note. Marenko tore it in half and handed it back to her.

'I suppose you don't think women should have the vote either.'

'I know, I'm a dinosaur. And it'll be a sorry day when I go.'

Fox drained her glass and put it back on the bar. She nodded to Henry for another.

'Oh, please,' Marenko said. 'Is this another part of the performance?'

'What performance?'

'When I first saw you, I knew you were a show pony. It's not just because you're a woman, although that's a part of it. You're here for the glory, Fox; you're trying to prove something. That isn't what all this is about.'

'What is it about?'

'If you don't know, I can't tell you.'

'You won't push me out, guv.'

'We'll see.'

She took the torn halves of the five-pound note and shoved them in his Guinness. 'You'll drink my money whether you want to or not,' she said.

She walked out. The off-duty constable at the pinball machine was grinning at him. Marenko scowled and looked away.

Chapter Twenty-five

Two ambulances were pulled up at the emergency entrance to the Royal Free, unloading victims from a head-on collision on West Heath Road. Two green-uniformed crew went past her, wheeling their bloodied patient on a stretcher, an oxygen mask clamped across his face. He was transferred to a stretcher in Casualty, and the doctors and nurses moved in, going to work with intravenous lines and cardiac monitors and blood-pressure cuffs.

Fox stood in the middle of it, forgotten in the wash of the emergency, lost. She stood in the overheated corridor, assailed by the hospital smells, disinfectant and the faint metallic smell of blood from the other side of the Casualty doors.

Two men had been stabbed in a fight in Gospel Oak. One of them was already dead when the paramedics had arrived. The other man had been brought here in an ambulance, and Fox hoped to talk to him.

She saw a familiar figure moving towards her. He was tall, with tousled fair hair and a distinctive combative stride. He was in shirtsleeves, a stethoscope draped around his neck, and was unhitching a disposable plastic apron.

He looked up and their eyes met. His expression changed from astonishment to pleasure. 'Madeleine,' he said. 'What are you doing here?'

'Ambulance-chasing, I'm afraid. I was looking for a Muhammad Obasanjo. Brought in here about half an hour ago.'

'He's still in X-ray. But he's stable. No damage to vital organs or blood vessels. He's lucky.'

'So he's going to be all right?'

'If you mean by that, can he give you a statement, I'm not sure. We've pumped him full of morphine, so he may not make much sense for a while.' The corners of his mouth creased into a crooked grin. 'What happened to him? Wouldn't he pay his parking fine?'

'You know how it is,' she answered, deadpan. 'Once one person does it everyone thinks they can get away with it. You have to set an example.'

He took off the latex gloves and tossed them in a bin, serious again. 'You meet some nice people in your line of work, don't you?'

'His mate's dead. So we really want to catch the nutters who did this.' She stared at the apparently organised chaos around her. 'Am I keeping you from something?'

'I'm up for the next ambulance through the doors. They've called in a spinal with a suspected pneumothorax. Be here in three minutes.' She followed him through the emergency ward. He changed into a new apron and put on another pair of latex gloves.

On a nearby table the doctors had intubated their head-on victim but he had arrested. One of the nurses had commenced heart massage while the doctor held the defibrillator paddles, staring at the green and black screen, waiting for it to charge. 'Two hundred joules. Everyone clear.'

Another one for Gravedigger, Fox thought.

'How have you been?' Simon asked her.

She forced herself to look away from the drama unfolding a few feet away. 'Well, I've had a bit of a head cold all week, but this doesn't seem the right place to look for sympathy.'

'You look great.'

'Thanks.'

'I'm really sorry we had that argument. At Ian's.'

'You've already apologised for that. It was months ago and, anyway, it was as much my fault as yours.'

'Well, it was *all* your fault, really. I was just being gracious.' He grinned again.

She smiled back. He did have a sort of charm, she supposed. Was this going somewhere?

'I know this isn't the time or the place. Would you like to go to dinner with me on Friday night?'

'Charging three-sixty,' the doctor shouted before replacing the defibrillator paddles. The body on the table jerked. The doctor looked hopefully at the green ECG screen.

'This is so romantic,' Fox said.

'Isn't it?'

'Why now? Why haven't you rung me and asked me before?'

'Well, the last time we spoke on the phone you sounded as if you barely remembered my name. And you have to admit, we didn't get off to a flying start.' Again the boyish grin. 'But here we are, now, and I look so . . . hot . . . with this stethoscope around my neck and exuding charm and confidence, I didn't think you'd be able to resist.'

Fox grinned. 'You're absolutely right. Why not?'

He grabbed a pen from the nurse's station and scribbled his address on the back of an admission form. He handed it to her. 'Seven-thirty?'

'OK.'

They heard the sound of a siren, another ambulance pulling in to the hospital forecourt.

'Better not keep you from your bleeding chest,' she said.

'Your man should be coming out of X-ray right now. Go down that corridor there, first room on the right, ask for Max. He's the radiologist. He'll tell you where they're taking him.'

'Thanks.'

'See you Friday.'

'Right.'

'You don't mind if I bring my daughter?' he said and moved away.

It was a security apartment in Wimbledon. She buzzed up and took the lift to the second floor. It was open plan, there were cedar blinds instead of curtains, the furniture chrome and leather. A black Swedish sound system in a smoked glass cabinet.

Perhaps he saw the look on her face. 'It's only heart surgeons who have the Hockney prints and views over the Thames,' he said, almost apologetically. He was wearing a navy-blue dressing gown and his hair was wet. He looked at his watch. 'You're early.'

'I thought you said seven.'

'I thought I said half-past.'

'Darling. Our first fight.'

His face creased into a familiar grin. 'Sorry. You're right. That was rude.'

'Yes,' Fox said. 'But I'm getting used to it.'

A girl appeared on the stairs. She was thirteen or fourteen years old, Fox guessed, with short, sandy-brown hair and a look of exquisite curiosity on her face. She wore a long shapeless jumper and torn blue jeans. All her fingernails had been carefully varnished in different colours, and there were silver rings on every finger of both hands, including her thumbs. 'You don't look like a cop,' she said.

Simon appeared embarrassed. 'Madeleine, this is my daughter, Sandra.'

'Sandy,' the girl corrected him.

'This is—' He seemed unsure how to introduce her. 'This is Madeleine.'

Sandy held out a hand. 'Hey.'

'Hey yourself,' Fox said.

There was a dramatic silence. 'Like a drink?' Simon asked her. 'White wine? Vodka? Gin?'

'Just a beer.'

They went through to the kitchen and Sandy watched, fascinated, as Madeleine took the can of French lager from her father, set the glass aside, and swallowed straight from the can.

'I'd better finish getting dressed,' Simon said. She heard him hiss, 'Be nice!' to his daughter before he went to change.

'So. You're the detective,' Sandy said.

'So,' Fox said. 'You're the daughter.'

'Do you have a gun?'

Madeleine shook her head, and Sandy looked disappointed.

'So what happens if you're at dinner tonight and you see someone you recognise from a Wanted poster?'

'I'd have to hide under the table with everyone else.'

Sandy considered this answer carefully. She cocked her head to one side like an inquisitive spaniel and went in for the kill. 'Why aren't you married?'

Madeleine took another pull at the beer and considered best how to answer this.

'I mean, you must be old enough,' Sandy persisted.

'Your dad's not married.'

'My mum died. Did your husband die?'

'I've never had a husband.'

'Why?'

'This sounds like a formal interrogation. Should I call my solicitor?'

Fox glanced upstairs. The flat had raked ceilings and a mezzanine floor. She saw Simon emerge from the upstairs bathroom and walk into the bedroom, naked except for a towel. Sandy caught the direction of her stare and their eyes met.

'Nice bod, hey?' Sandy said.

Fox caught the play of a smile about the young girl's lips. I've been set up, she thought. This is some kind of a test. Young daughter meets father's new girlfriend and takes her for a spin around the block, see if she's suitable.

'What case are you working on right now?'

'Little girl. Murdered by her father's new girlfriend for asking too many personal questions. Tragic. No one found her for weeks.'

If Sandy understood the joke, she didn't show it. Fox glanced nervously upstairs, hoping Simon would come down soon.

Sandy folded her arms, and Fox felt herself being carefully assessed. 'Dad said you do murders.'

'I don't *do* them,' Fox said, correcting her gently, 'that's illegal. I have investigated several, as part of something called an Area Major Incident Team.'

'Must be great.'

'No, it's not great. People getting killed is not great. And the work is mostly very tedious. You spend a lot of time just asking people questions.' Fox took another sip of beer.

'Do you think I'd be good at it?'

'Definitely. Very, very good.'

'How many GCSEs do you need to be a murder detective?'

'Can you write your name and chew gum at the same time?'

Sandy knew she was being had on. 'Yeah.'

'You're in.'

'OK. Because Simon wants me to do chemistry and physics and I told him it's all a waste of time.' At that moment the father in question came down the stairs, dressed casually in jeans and a cable-stitched black jumper. Fox felt a curious, oily sensation in the pit of her belly. Not bad.

'Madeleine and I have been discussing my career prospects,' Sandy said when he came back into the kitchen. 'She doesn't think I should do chemistry or physics either.'

'Really?' he said and raised an eyebrow and looked at her hard.

Oh my, Fox thought. This young girl is going to get me into a lot of trouble.

But she didn't know right then just how much trouble a lot of trouble could be. Which was possibly just as well.

Chapter Twenty-six

There was an Italian restaurant called the Café Dorigo on the corner of the High Street. It was what Fox categorised as authentic fake Italian, black and white marble tiles, small wooden tables, dark panelled walls, the menu scribbled on a blackboard. They squeezed into a corner table by the window. It was hot inside after the bitter cold of the February night, and the windows were steamed over.

The place was crowded. A harried-looking young man in a white apron hurried over and garbled the evening's specials, his rehearsed speech so rapid they caught hardly any of it. After he had gone, Sandy looked at her father. 'What did he say?'

'He said the specials are off, just read the menu.'

'He did not. He said something about ravioli alla pesto. I *love* ravioli alla pesto.'

'Well, that makes it simple, then. What do you want to drink?'

'Frascati.'

'You're thirteen years old.'

'Next year I'll be fifteen.'

'In twenty-one months you'll be fifteen. That still makes you just thirteen any way you look at it. Ravioli alla pesto and coke. Perfect combination of Italian and American cuisines. OK?'

Sandy crossed her arms, pouting. Simon stared at the menu, embarrassed.

'Sara rang earlier,' Sandy said. 'She's having a party tomorrow night. I'm invited.'

'Are her parents going to be there?'

Sandy's silence seemed to affirm his suspicions.

'*Everybody's* going.'

'Salman Rushdie? Benjamin Netanyahu? The Prime Minister of Norway?'

'Sara doesn't know the Prime Minister of Norway.'

'Then not *everybody* is going.'

'I can't miss this party, Dad.'

Fox bit her lip. She recognised the tactical switch from bullying to wheedling, Simon to Dad. The next move would be tears and 'Daddy'. Then threats and a tantrum. She knew, because she had done the same thing to her own father.

'You're thirteen years old. You are not going to a party in Fulham without parental supervision.'

'You make Fulham sound like . . . Bosnia.'

'For an unsupervised thirteen-year-old, it might as well be Bosnia.'

Sandy looked at Fox, imploring her to come to her aid. Fox suddenly found herself fascinated by the range of antipasti offered on the menu board.

'I bet you went to parties when you were thirteen,' Sandy said to her.

Fox shook her head. 'I went to my first one last year.'

Sandy was not deterred by this response. She shrugged her shoulders dismissively. 'Things were different in the 1980s. What Simon fails to realise is that young girls today grow up faster. If you were my mother and I promised to be home by midnight at the latest and I offered to pay for the taxi home, wouldn't you let me go?'

Fox thought: the irony. A young girl barely older than Kate Mercer asking me if she thinks it's OK to take risks. Before she could reply, Simon broke in: 'Madeleine is not your mother and it is not fair to put her on the spot like that.'

'You never let me do anything.'

'I let you breathe. I let you eat anything that's in the fridge. I let you live in my flat.'

Sandy banged her fist on the table, making the cutlery rattle. Several heads turned in their direction. She was close to tears. 'When I leave school I'm going to be a prostitute!' Sandy hissed and she got up and stormed out, past a sign that said TOILETS. Heads turned in their direction. Simon took a deep breath and concentrated on the wine list. His hands were shaking.

'This is the last time I take her out with me. She uses every available opportunity to embarrass me. She wouldn't dare behave like that at home.'

Fox was relieved Sandy had left the table. She felt her jaw muscles relax and her face creased into a smile.

'It's not amusing,' Simon said. 'She's grounded for a month when I get her home.'

'She has you over a barrel.'

He raised an eyebrow. 'How so?'

'You're a single father. If you say no to her, there's an unspoken understanding that if she had a mother she'd be able to work it out with her. That was why she was asking me my opinion. Just another version of the same tactic. And if you do give in to the pressure, against your better judgement, you end up feeling shitty anyway. It's a lose-lose situation. Right?'

He nodded. 'I spend my entire life feeling frightened or guilty. She doesn't have a mother and her father works ridiculously long hours. I feel bad enough about that. Which makes me vulnerable to juvenile blackmail, I realise. But if I give her more freedom I'm scared she's going to get into trouble. I just want someone to take her off my hands and give her back to me, safe and sound, when she's twenty years old.'

'And then?'

'And then I want her to get engaged immediately to a six-foot-six karate instructor who goes with her absolutely everywhere and maintains a current first-aid certificate.' He let out a long breath, leaned back in his chair and grinned at her. 'Now do you see why I'm prone to getting into stupid arguments at dinner parties? Between fatherhood and the emergency department there isn't a moment in my day when I can relax.'

Sandy came back from the ladies. She slumped into her chair and sat there sulking, arms crossed. Simon looked at Fox, who shrugged her shoulders and smiled encouragement. It was a ploy children learned from the aisles of the supermarket when they were barely able to walk.

They daren't touch me in public.

Fox finished her penne alla arabiata and pushed the plate away, replete. She took a sip of the Bortioli and smiled at Simon. A long time since she'd been wined and dined. She'd forgotten what it was like to be with a man. A proper man, anyway. Drinking coffee in the Incident Room with Marenko, Honeywell and TJ didn't really count.

Fox thought about what WPC Stacey had said to her: *Elliot Ness. As in* The Untouchables.

Tonight perhaps she would make herself a little more touchable. She would wait and see how things panned out. For the moment she was enjoying the evening, despite the scowling thirteen-year-old in the corner and the obnoxious young man at the next table who was drinking too much and talking too loud.

He was power-dressed in a dark blue woollen suit and spent a lot of time shouting into a mobile phone. He had loosened his burgundy tie, almost as if to advertise: hey, look at me, I'm drunk. A commodities trader, Fox thought, categorising him. Too rich, too much. He was spoiling to impress his girlfriend, a blonde girl with a ring through her eyebrow and showing too much cleavage even for a peepshow doorway in Wardour Street, never mind a high-street restaurant in Wimbledon.

The couple had started on their third bottle of wine. The

man reached into his pocket, produced a packet of Marlboro and lit up.

'I thought this was the non-smoking section,' Simon said.

Fox shrugged. Just let it be.

But Simon was coiled tight as a spring. Probably because of the fight with his daughter, or because of the avulsed aorta that had arrested on him that afternoon in emergency, or because his first date in months was not going as he had planned. He leaned across to the man and said: 'Excuse me. I think this part of the restaurant is non-smoking.'

'I don't really give a fuck what you think,' the man said and turned away.

Simon persevered. 'Would you mind putting your cigarette out?'

'Yeah, I would mind,' He grinned at his girlfriend, who screeched with laughter.

Simon looked at Fox, frowned and shook his head. The diversion at least brought Sandy back from her gloomy intro-spection. She nudged Fox's arm. 'Arrest him,' she whispered.

Fox ignored her.

'He's smoking in a designated non-smoking area,' Sandy persisted. 'We could all get lung cancer here.'

'I'm off duty.'

Sandy glared at the man, her eyes emitting death rays.

The waiters and other diners were throwing worried glances in the direction of the Marlboro Man, but he was determined to prove himself the dominant male in Wimbledon. God help us if Vinnie Jones walks in, Fox thought. The garlic will be drowned out with the smell of testosterone.

Fooling around now, the man took a drag on his cigarette, turned his head at an angle, and, still with his eyes on the Pamela Anderson lookalike across the table, blew the smoke in Simon's direction.

This is going to go too far, Fox thought. I have to stop this right now. 'I think you've had too much to drink, sir,' she said.

Simon shook his head. Having started something he could not finish, he wanted to let it go. Too late for that. The man twisted around in his seat.

'What did you say to me?' he asked, seizing on it like an angler with his first bite of the day.

'You are drunk and you are making a fool of yourself. Why don't you pick up your bottle of wine, call a taxi and go home before someone gets hurt?'

He swivelled right around in his chair. His eyes were unfocused and his lips were wet. 'And why don't you go and fuck yourself, blondie.'

The tables around them fell silent. One of the waiters hurried off to find the proprietor; another hesitated with his hand on the telephone, about to call the police.

'Arrest him,' Sandy urged her.

Oh shit, Fox thought. Me and my big mouth. 'How about you leave quietly? You're causing a disturbance.'

'I've got a better idea,' Simon said. 'Why don't *we* go?'

But the Marlboro Man had lurched to his feet and now stood between them and the door. He leaned forward and put both hands on their table. His breath reeked of garlic and alcohol and tobacco. 'Yeah. Why don't you and your nancy boy fuck off.'

'Let's go,' Simon said, and he took Sandy by the hand and pulled her to her feet. Fox fought back her anger. She heard her father's voice: *Madeleine, one day that temper of yours is going to get you into a lot of trouble.* She finished her red wine and got slowly to her feet. She took her handbag off the back of her seat and followed Simon towards the cash register by the door.

And there, against her baser instincts, she was willing to leave it, if only Marlboro Man hadn't put his hand up her dress as she went past. Almost without thinking, she whirled around, her right foot angling into his groin. He doubled over, gasping, and she hit him, her hand shooting out bent-knuckled from her hip in one blurred movement.

There was a gasp around the restaurant followed by a deadly

silence. As he crumpled to the floor she stepped back, a little astonished at her own violence. The man was thrashing among the chairs, clutching at his testicles and his face. His girlfriend started to scream.

Simon pushed her aside. 'For God's sake!' he shouted. He knelt down beside the injured man. Marlboro Man had drawn his knees up to his chest, keeping one of his hands clutched between his legs. He was fighting for breath and there was blood frothing from his nose and mouth.

Simon rolled him on to his side. He looked up at Fox and threw her his keys. 'Take Sandy home. Now.'

Fox was furious, with the man in the blue suit, with Simon, with herself. I could have killed him, she thought. Insane. She grabbed Sandy by the hand and hurried out of the restaurant.

This is not going to look good on my record.

Chapter Twenty-seven

'That was just awesome,' Sandy said as they hurried across the street, still struggling into their coats.

'It was stupid. Violence isn't the answer.'

'Depends on the question,' Sandy said. 'If the question is: what do you do with a drunk who wants to fight you in a restaurant, I'd give you an A-minus.'

'I could have killed him.'

'That would have been a loss to the future of mankind,' Sandy said, hurrying to keep up with her. She was buzzing. 'Where did you learn to do that? I didn't even see you hit him.'

'I've been training in martial arts since I was a kid. I grew up in Hong Kong. It's nothing to be proud of. It's smarter not to fight. I don't like to use force unless I can't possibly avoid it.'

'If I could do that, I'd use force every chance I could. I'd never have any spare time. I can think of hundreds of people I'd like to beat up.'

'That's my point,' Fox said.

She made herself a cup of coffee in the kitchen. Sandy watched her, sipping on a coke from the fridge. Simon buzzed up and Sandy let him into the apartment. His face was set like stone.

He stood in the middle of the kitchen, his hands in the

pockets of his jeans. 'You'll be pleased to know he's not going to press charges.'

'I don't give a damn what he does,' Fox said, though she could have almost shouted with relief.

'I think he felt humiliated enough. I suppose you can hardly go to the police and say that a woman beat you up.'

'That's sexist,' Sandy said, but Simon ignored her.

'There was no damage to the restaurant so Marco was happy to let the whole matter drop,' he said.

'Marco?'

'The proprietor. He's a friend of mine. Well, he was. I don't think he's in any hurry for me to go back to his place again.'

'Well, there's a McDonald's on the corner.' Fox picked up her leather shoulder bag. 'I'd better get going. Perhaps we can do it again sometime.'

'What? Beat up complete strangers?'

'I will not be humiliated by drunks, OK? I will give them a certain amount of latitude, but when they physically assault me I draw the line.'

'How did he assault you? Did he hit you, did he try to strangle you?'

'He put his hand up my dress.'

'And that would have killed you?'

'So it's OK, is it? Because he's drunk? Hey, OK, grab a quick feel, humiliate me in front of everyone in the whole place. What am I supposed to do? Shout, "Here big boy, grab my tits too, if you like." '

Simon flushed and threw a glance at his daughter, who was grinning enthusiastically, hugely enjoying herself.

'Violence never solved anything,' Simon said.

'Sandy and I were just discussing that same point. It's my view also, funnily enough. But I'm afraid I lost my temper just then.'

'You'll be pleased to know you broke his nose.'

'I'm neither pleased nor displeased, thank you very much.'

'God knows what damage you did . . . elsewhere. That sort

of blow can cause a serious haemorrhage. Is that how you question your suspects?'

Fox flushed. 'Talking of hitting below the belt.' She pushed past him. 'But with any luck I interrupted the flow of testosterone for a while.' She looked at Sandy. 'Good night.'

'Way to go, Madeleine.'

'Your father's right. What I did was inexcusable.'

'As inexcusable goes, it was brilliant.'

'Go to bed, Sandy,' Simon said.

He turned away and she made a face behind his back.

'I'll see myself out, shall I?' Fox said. She went to leave but then came back into the kitchen. 'By the way, just for the record, I wasn't the one who started it, OK. I would have put up with the smoke for the sake of the peace.'

'I intended to reason with him. But I don't believe in caveman tactics. That's your department, apparently.'

'Cave*person*. I'll thank you to be politically correct.' Jesus, Fox thought. No date for months and the one night I go out to enjoy myself I get into a fight. Dad was right about me. I should have been a boy. Fox drew back her shoulders. 'You have a lovely daughter. I still like to think if it was her bottom he grabbed you would have broken his nose instead of me. Goodnight, Simon.'

And she went out.

Black plastic binbags had been piled outside the entrance to the flats, a rat scuttled away into the shadows as she approached. She opened the glass door with her key and nodded to the Chinese porter as she made her way to the tiny lift. Everyone called him Charlie. No one knew his real name.

He was a Hong Kong Chinese and every time she saw him, twice a day, coming in and going out, it reminded her. It had been the happiest time of her life, she decided. She could still smell the frangipani in the garden, the exotic aromas of garlic and star anise drifting from the kitchen, the magical perfumes of the incense coils in the Tin Hau temple where the great tigerskin still hung on the wall.

Like many of the other *gwailos*, they had lived in Stanley village, a privileged world of *amahs* and private schools and views of the bay through the gardens.

Her father had his yacht moored in Causeway Bay, and he would take them out to Tung Lung Chau or around Lamma Island. Her mother and Ginny both got seasick, so she was the only female in the Fox family allowed on board. She still remembered the crisp blue waters and the deep greens of the islands, the great ocean freighters cutting past them in the deep-sea channels.

It was a magical time, before the realisation came to her that her father did not love her in the same way that he loved his boys. If she had been more like Ginny it would not have mattered, for her sister never tried to compete with her brothers, as she did. But Fox had been good at maths and at sports, and it wounded her bitterly that her father never took the same delight in her achievements as he did in those of her brothers.

But that was another world, far removed from the rain-dark streets off the Bayswater Road. The toms had been kept inside by the weather tonight, and the doorway of Boots the Chemist was occupied by a solitary bag lady, curled asleep under a few pieces of cardboard. A miracle if she didn't freeze to death. But who would care?

Fox shivered, waiting for the gas fire to take the chill from the room, her forehead pressed against the glass. So Simon was not the one. Hardly a surprise. But what was it she did want? She told herself she wanted a man who could combine intelligence with sensitivity, but when she did find such rare souls they were always a disappointment to her. What you want, she murmured, almost embarrassed by the admission, is a bit of rough.

A bit of rough. A black prince. Someone with a soft smile and hard eyes, a pianist's fingers with calloused palms. Perhaps it was the real reason she had never married David. Perhaps it was the reason she was still alone.

Chapter Twenty-eight

Satan was back, in his brown boots and rainjacket. She spotted him in the crowd; this time he had his girlfriend with him, a stout girl with spiked hair, her ears bristling with rings. Uniformed officers were keeping Satan and his fellow spectators at a respectable distance.

There were lights on all over the estate. Nothing better than a murder to keep people from their beds. The residents were getting used to this; it was becoming a regular early-morning event. No doubt they would miss it when the bodies stopped dropping. The Rastas were back too, laughing and rapping to each other across the cordon. The same carnival atmosphere as last time. The Camden Town Homicide Festival.

Marenko's Ford Sierra was parked in the street between two patrol cars. An ambulance stood at the kerb, beacons flashing, its rear doors open. The mortuary van had not yet arrived.

Fox held up her ID as she stepped through the cordon. A young PC led the way into the house. She remembered her previous visit.

If I say anything, someone'll do me. Not that I care about that, but what about Miles?

Marenko was standing on the pavement smoking a cigarette. The third time he'd cracked in as many months. Their eyes locked, but neither of them spoke. They didn't have to. He knew what she was thinking. He brushed past her, flicked the still-glowing cigarette into the darkness.

'Ready, Fox?'

She nodded.

They went inside, struggled into white overalls and white overshoes and went up the stairs to the bedrooms. Fox hesitated, steeling herself, knowing what they would find when they entered the bedroom. Marenko stared at her, impatiently. She followed him in.

Graveney was speaking into a tape recorder. 'She is lying next to the double bed, next to the window, away from the door. She's half covered by a cotton duvet. The window is closed. There is a sheet covering half her face. She is lying face down, one arm twisted beneath her. She is wearing a nightgown, polyester.'

They entered, careful where they put their feet. Fox saw that the sheets and duvet had been dragged over the side of the bed. There were dark stains on the mattress.

A flashbulb popped. A white-overcalled SOCO was on his hands and knees beside the bed, carefully placing hairs from the sheets into evidence bags.

The ancient wardrobe had a cracked mirror. Fox saw the stippled reflection of Flora Ellis in the glass, a mass of blood-caked hair, her face grey-blue in death, jaw extended at an unnatural angle. A pool of red-purple blood had coagulated around her head.

Graveney was still talking into the tape recorder. 'There are two gunshot wounds to her head, two more to her back. There is a lot of blood matted into her hair. The room temperature is cool, around ten degrees. The curtains are drawn, the windows are locked from the inside, there is no sign of forced entry to the bedroom.'

He crouched down beside the body and felt the arms and legs. 'Body exhibits absence of rigor.' Fox saw him lift Flora Ellis's nightgown and stare at something out of her view. 'Deep rectal temperature is thirty-five point eight degrees. Time is now 3.35 a.m.'

As he rolled the body, two white-clad men moved in to examine the carpet where Flora Ellis had been lying.

Fox stepped closer. The entry wounds on her back were small, neat and with little blood. There was soot around the entrance holes, indicating the gun had been fired very close. The back of her skull had disintegrated. Probably hollowpoints, Fox decided.

There was blood and brain matter everywhere. What a mess.

'Was the light on or off when she was found?' Marenko asked.

'On.'

Fox imagined the scene: the killer entered the room, turned on the light. Flora Ellis sat upright, experienced a moment's terror as she stared at her killer in the sudden light. Perhaps she had time to scream, started to rise. The first gunshot wound most likely to her head. She would have crumpled sideways off the bed, already dead. But the killer got in close, fired three more rounds, one to the head, two into the torso. A professional hit.

Her duty done, Fox looked for a last time at Flora Ellis the woman, not Flora Ellis the cadaver. The dilated black pupils were hidden beneath half-lidded eyes, but the look on her face could not be denied. *You did this to me,* Flora whispered. *I told you I didn't see sod all, but you kept on at me, you made me tell you what I knew. I put my life on the line for some Yardie gangster who didn't matter anyway, and look what happened to me.*

Fox stood up.

If I tell you anything, they gonna kill me. I don't give a shit about that any more, but what about Miles?

'Time of death?' Marenko said to Graveney.

'Between midnight and 1 a.m., at this stage. I'll know more after the PM. As far as I can ascertain there's no indication that she was sexually molested ante-mortem.'

Marenko shook his head. 'I know why she was murdered,' he grunted.

'Body bag,' Graveney said to one of the attendants, who was

hovering by the door. 'Let's get her out of here and down the mortuary. Quicker I get to her, the faster you get results.'

Marenko and Fox peeled off their overalls and went back downstairs.

The living room had been ransacked. All the drawers had been pulled out of the dresser and now lay upside down on the carpet to make it appear that the intruder had been searching for valuables. As if. They went through to the kitchen. Flora's handbag had been thrown on the linoleum, and her purse lay open on the kitchen table, empty.

'Looks like a robbery,' a uniformed sergeant said.

Marenko looked at him in disgust but said nothing.

Their man had come in through the kitchen. The wooden frame around the window was splintered. He had used a crowbar to prise it open. Fox watched the SOC boys at work, dusting for prints around the windowsill and all the flat surfaces so that everything was covered in a film of grey, shining dust. They won't find a thing, Fox thought. The man responsible for this was wearing gloves. This was not an amateur; this was a professional trying to look like an amateur, a contracted murder made to look like a robbery.

She looked up at the wall.

> Bless this house, O Lord we pray.
> Keep it safe by night and day.

'Who found her?' Fox said.

'She has a young child,' the sergeant said. 'Someone heard him screaming. It went on for a couple of hours before anyone thought of calling us. Said they thought she was murdering him.'

'How long do they think it takes to murder a kid?' Marenko muttered.

'Patrol car got here about two-thirty,' the sergeant went on.

'They found the open window at the back here and effected entry. They found the small child sitting in the bedroom.'

'He saw his mother like that?'

'That's why he was screaming. Must have got out of his cot.'

'Oh, for God's sake. Where is he?'

'There's a woman up the street, she's sitting with him in the panda outside. Only one who can do anything with him. Babysits him from time to time, she reckons. We've called Welfare. They've got someone on the way.'

Fox looked around the drab little kitchen. She felt suddenly depressed. 'Has anyone talked to the neighbours, guv?'

He shrugged. 'They thought they heard a scream about midnight, but then they didn't hear anything else so they went back to sleep. Didn't hear any gunshots. Our man was using a silencer.'

'A burglar who breaks into the house, steals a few pounds from an unemployed single mother's purse, then shoots her four times with a silenced pistol. Does that make sense to you?'

'If you're Patrick Capper, it does.'

'He didn't do this.'

'No, not this time. London to a brick when this happened he was in the middle of Wembley Stadium playing "Chopsticks" on a white grand piano to a sell-out all-ticket crowd.'

The SOC unit had set up arc lights in the garden, concentrating on the path around the back of the house, and three men in white police overalls were crouched over searching for footprints.

Marenko went back to his car. There was nothing more he could do here. 'We'll get the team together in the morning.'

Two SOCOs were carrying some evidence bags out of the house. Behind them two of Graveney's men pushed a stretcher with all that remained of Flora Ellis to the waiting mortuary van.

The blue strobe of a patrol car flickered on Marenko's face. 'This is my fault,' he said.

'Your fault, guv? How is it your fault?'

'It was a week ago today I sent TJ and Rankin back here to talk to her.'

Fox stared at him. 'Why?'

'I thought I could make her change her mind. About Capper. Perhaps someone saw them, got nervous.'

She closed her eyes. 'Couldn't you have got her some protection?'

'Not unless she made herself a witness.'

'Christ Almighty!'

One of the constables at the cordon was watching this exchange with great interest. Marenko gave her a warning glance.

Fox lowered her voice. 'This was a contract. Capper's off the hook. And we've just created an orphan.'

As if on cue they heard a baby crying in one of the panda cars. A woman in a dressing gown was sitting in the front seat with a child on her knee. Miles was squirming and crying. There was a dummy tied with a safety pin to his blue jumpsuit.

Marenko would not meet her eyes. 'I know what we've done, Fox. You don't have to tell me. You just get on with your job, I'll get on with mine.' He got in his car and drove slowly through the cordon, brake lights glowing as he stopped at Kentish Town Road. Fox heard the squeal of tyres as he accelerated too fast around the corner. The Rastas gave an ironic cheer.

Fox leaned against the patrol car. Show me some justice, she murmured to no one in particular. Show me the daylight and the way to put this right.

A light rain started to fall. It was spring, but clear skies and a warm sun were a long way off.

Chapter Twenty-nine

They found Patrick Capper drinking in the saloon bar of The Pieman, a theme pub he owned on Upper Street in Islington. He was dressed well for a Sunday morning: a waistcoat of violet silk with a gold fob, a hand-tailored suit. His long ginger hair was combed back in a ponytail. There were several chunky gold rings on his fingers and a gold chain nestled among the hairs on his chest. He was reading the *News of the World*.

Jesus, Fox thought. Some of these characters are a parody of themselves. He's auditioning for his own part.

If the pub had a theme, she didn't get it. There were leaded windows on to the street, blue stars on a burned-orange ceiling, wooden bench seats, floorboards in Baltic pine. Cocktail prices were chalked on a blackboard, the barman's own invention by the looks of it: Seven Inches of Heaven, Virgin's Arse. The television was on but was drowned out by the music system.

Capper was holding court in a corner. The light was better for reading by the door, but when you were Patrick Capper you never sat too close to a window, and you always had your back against a wall.

She recognised one of the minders. The tall one with the bleached hair had been out at the house in Waltham Abbey the morning they had picked up Capper for the Crawford shooting. Today he was wearing a black zippered leather jacket and a white cotton shirt with a grandfather collar. He had positioned himself between Capper and the bar. On the other side of the table another man, older and less sartorial than his counterpart, his balding head shaved to the skull, was toying with the ashtray. If the Cro-Magnon forehead is any indication, Fox thought, he's trying to figure out how it works.

A black girl in a leather dress, her hair bleached with peroxide, was sitting on Capper's knee, playing with the hairs that sprouted from his open collar. He was ignoring her. Another girl, a redhead, was chewing gum and swirling the ice around her glass.

Capper looked up as they came through the door. He smiled and lit a cigarette. Then his eyes shifted to Fox. The lips split back from the teeth into a leer. 'Brought a bird with ya, Frank?'

'This is Detective Inspector Fox.'

'Nice tits.'

Marenko's hand moved quickly to his jacket, which produced a predictably twitchy reaction from the minders. Marenko brought out a packet of Benson and Hedges and took his time lighting one. He dropped the discarded match on the floor. Capper watched him grind out the match on the polished boards with his heel, but he said nothing. 'Wish I could say the same about your girlfriend, Patrick. Like flat-chested women, do you?'

The girl gave Marenko a look that could have buckled steel. There was a deathly silence. Fox hoped Marenko knew what he was doing. Someone had just turned up the central heating in here.

Capper leaned back in his seat and grinned. The minders took their cue and seemed to relax. 'You're right, Frank. I'm forgetting me manners.' He looked at Fox. 'That was out of order. Here, let me buy you a drink.' He stood up and guided her towards the bar, a hand lightly on her elbow. Very smooth, she thought.

'What will you have, darlin'? You look like a vodka sort of girl to me.'

'I don't drink when I'm on duty.'

'Oh, this is official, is it? I thought it might be a social call. What about you, Frank? Guinness with a couple of whisky chasers, if I remember right?'

That struck a nerve. 'Can you tell me where you were last night between 11 p.m. and 1 a.m.?' Marenko asked him.

He looked at the two girls in the corner. 'Just so happens I do know where I was, and I have two witnesses who can vouch for it. They can tell you *exactly* where, though I don't think they'd be willing to show ya.' He leaned forward and added in a stage whisper, 'Unless you got a torch.'

Oh, a class act. No doubt about it.

'These two slags be willing to tesify in court, would they?' Marenko asked.

Capper's smile fell away. 'Watch your mouth, Frank. This is my turf.'

'What are you going to do, Pat? Going to set your dogs on me?' Then he added, his voice low, 'What happened to Flora Ellis? Did you send one of your bumboys over to do the dirty work for you?'

'Who?'

'As God is my witness I am going to lay this one right on your doorstep. You are not going to walk away from this.'

'I don't know what you're talking about, Frank.'

Marenko still had his hands in his pockets. The minders were standing behind Capper, arms crossed, looking hard. Marenko looked as if he couldn't care less, but Fox felt her own heart bouncing against her ribs. OK, so she doubted they would go for a cop in Capper's own pub. But still. They were dealing with prime nutters here.

Marenko leaned on the bar, one foot on the brass footrail. 'That's funny, Pat. Must be the light. I hadn't noticed.'

'Noticed what?'

'You've gone prematurely orange.'

He had him. His weak point, his vanity. Capper put a hand

self-consciously to the designer ponytail. Marenko was right, Fox noticed. Capper got his hair colour out of a bottle.

'Dye your pubes as well?'

Oh, *shite*. Might as well poke a bear with a stick. Because Marenko had shown no emotion in Flora Ellis's bedroom, she had made the mistake of thinking he didn't care. But here he was, baiting one of London's foremost headcases on his home ground. Her DCI must be mightily pissed off.

'You'd better fuck off out of here while you can still walk,' Capper said.

'You did Flora Ellis and I'm going to get you for it.'

'You've got shit, copper. You want to charge me with anything, you let me know and I'll come down with my brief any time you like. Otherwise this is police harassment, and I'll have you on a charge before you know what's hit ya. Don't want to lose your pension, Frank.'

Marenko pushed away from the bar. He nodded to Fox. 'We're out of here.'

Thank God.

'We'll be back, Pat,' Marenko said.

'Hey,' Capper said.

Marenko turned at the door.

'My brief. Used to be your missus. That right?'

Marenko stared.

'Still got you by the nuts, hasn't she?'

They drove back to Hendon Road. He didn't say another word.

Chapter Thirty

Fox walked over the road to the King's Head and there was Marenko propped on his favourite stool at the end of the oak bar, a Guinness in his fist. He sat there brooding, froth on his grey moustache and a don't-fuck-with-me look in his eye. He wanted a fight, he wanted some punks in leather jackets and torn jeans to walk through the door and aggravate him. He wanted somewhere to relieve his frustrations. And the reason for his black mood was Patrick Capper, and the Case of the Ultimate Head Job, as James had called the Elmore Crawford murder, and its corollary, the Ultimate Cockup, the Case Where the DCI Blames Himself for the Murder of a Witness.

There were only about a dozen customers at that time of the day, most of them staring slack-jawed at the three o'clock from Cheltenham on the wall-mounted television. No doubt Marenko had logged this in: *met informant in King's Head and bought him liquid refreshment.* Fox slapped her money on the bar and nodded to the young barman in the crisp white shirt. It was Henry's day off.

'Two pints of Guinness,' she said.

'Guinness is a man's drink,' Marenko said.

'Well, let's pretend,' Fox told him.

'Pretend what?'

'Pretend I've got one of those ugly, droopy things down there that you blokes are so proud of. Let's pretend that me having better skin and a cuter arse doesn't put a barrier between us.'

Marenko downed his Guinness and reached for the drink she had just bought him. 'I didn't say you had a cuter arse.'

Fox stared at him hard. 'You still think I can't do this job?'

'Jury's still out. I don't know. It's not a woman's work, my opinion. But you do show some aptitude.' He said the last word slowly, having some difficulty with it.

'Aptitude.'

'I don't know if it's going to be enough, Fox. This is a men's club. It's like the priesthood. It seems funny when a woman does it.'

'They said that about women doctors. I know I can make a good detective.'

'Sure you can. Do it better than any man, right?'

Marenko swallowed the rest of the Guinness. Christ, she thought, where does he put it all? He must have a bladder like a barrage balloon. She forced down the rest of the Guinness and ordered two more.

'I'll get them,' Fox said.

'Why?'

'Because you've had a bad day.'

'We're pretending, right, Foxy? We're pretending you and me are men. That means it's my round. So put your money away.' He pushed it back across the counter.

The young barman poured two more Guinness and placed them on beer mats.

'Here's to justice,' Marenko said. He downed half a pint in one swallow, the froth glistening on his moustache. He sucked at it with his bottom lip, savouring it. 'The sweet taste of defeat,' Marenko said. 'Nothing like it. Is there, Fox?'

Fox checked her look in the mirror. A black silver-studded biker's jacket, dirty blue Levi's – she had never washed them –

high-heeled cowboy boots. There was a special drawer in her vanity and she opened it and took out the cosmetics case she kept for her creation, whom she had christened Janie. Cherry lipstick, purple eyeshadow. As she applied the heavy make-up Janie emerged from the mirror. A catharsis of sorts, perhaps, for the Madeleine Fox who rarely wore cosmetics, preferred pink to any other colour and would never be seen dead in black. A private pleasure masquerading as the necessities of work. The slut, the biker chick, the fantasy.

She was wired, as was required procedure. The leather jacket hid the recorder, which was fitted to her broad black leather belt at the back.

When she had finished she looked in the mirror, satisfied. She had not washed her hair for two days, and it hung straight and lank around her shoulders. She popped a slice of Wrigley's in her mouth and shrugged on the attitude as easily as the leather jacket. Overplaying the part, no doubt.

But what the hell. People overplayed their parts in life all the time. Look at Patrick Capper. And *his* friends took him seriously.

She walked out of the flat in the direction of Lancaster Gate tube station. She was aware of Charlie leering at her through the cubbyhole window of his tiny office. She knew what he was thinking, that she was a tart, ten quid for a relief massage in some spit-dirty upstairs room on the Bayswater Road. *As long as she doesn't bring her johns back here*, she could hear him wheedling to the librarian on the second floor, *as long as she pays her rent*, to the retired insurance assessor in flat 1A. *Don't care what she does.*

In a way she enjoyed her notoriety. Being regarded as some sort of deviant living on the fringes of the sexual underworld was a lot more interesting than being a female detective, though perhaps not a lot different.

It was not yet midday and there was just a handful of early customers in the café, a muddle of chrome and Formica tables and chairs where customers could sit and stare at the traffic on King's Cross Road. Piles of snow, blackened with grit and filth, were piled against the kerb.

A balding man with a Mediterranean complexion sweated over the fryers behind the counter, under a blackboard menu advertising spring rolls and samosas and crab sticks. Fox could still remember when a fish and chip shop meant cod and haddock and skate. How quickly the world turns. There was the over-whelming smell of grease, and when the number 24 to Hampstead rumbled to a stop outside it drowned out all conversation.

Not that the customers in the fish and chip bar were all debating Proust and international monetary theory. An old man with greying whiskers was slurping noisily at a cup of tea out of a china mug while two black kids in the inevitable joggers and hooded track jackets were sitting in the corner and arguing in broad cockney accents about Arsenal's recent loss of form.

A passing taxpayer may have glanced briefly at the skinny giant in a dirty denim jacket huddled at a corner table beside a sluttish young woman in her early thirties, wearing a black leather biker's jacket. Drug addicts, this same taxpayer may have thought, before passing on.

Fox watched her guest devour the cod roe and chips. Her best-kept secret, her snout, her budgie; he went by the improbable name of Michael Joseph Angel, better known on the street as Ferret. A beanpole of a human being, six foot four inches of him and rail-thin, with huge bony wrists and an Adam's apple that bobbed in his throat like some small animal knotted in a bag. His teeth were cracked and brown in a mouth full of receding gums. They looked like tombstones.

'Looking good, Michael,' she said.

'You reckon?' he said, and looked pleased. A fine spray of half chewed cod roe landed on the table. Michael was sur-rounded by a miasma of secretions and bodily fluids wherever he went. On slow days she tried to calculate her chances of contracting a hepatitis strain just from talking with him.

'Back on the programme,' he said, as if this alone was an achievement on a par with selection for the Olympic track team, and shovelled more chips into his mouth. Fox had lost count of the number of times that Michael had checked himself on to the methadone programme. He would kick the habit for three months, sometimes six. Then one day something would snap and he would go back out on the street and score some more heroin. But he never let his addiction take him to the point where he lost control of his extraordinary life. It was a game of brinkmanship he had perfected − so far.

'Looking real good for it.'

'Goin' to keep with it this time. I mean it.'

He devoured the last of the chips, then sat back and lit a cigarette. The tremor in his fingers was not as pronounced as the last time they had met. Some days he couldn't even hold a coffee cup. 'My old lady's back in hospital.'

'Overdose?'

'She got an infection. You know, women's shit.'

'Right.'

'She reckons she got it from me, but she didn't.'

Behind the counter the proprietor was arguing with a small dark-haired woman the size of a refrigerator. She said she gave him a ten-pound note; he said it was a fiver.

'Gonna make a break soon,' Michael said. 'Get away from all this shit in the city. It's dragging me down. Know what I mean?'

'Yes, I know what you mean,' she said. It was an endless refrain. One day he was going to get his life together. One day. Early on in their relationship she had even tried to help him do just that. Some men tried to reform whores, some cops got emotionally involved with their grasses. Fox had learned soon enough that Michael was past helping and now he was just too valuable to reform, even if it were possible. How he had made the long journey from Guildford to the North London underworld she did not know. His father was a computer consultant, his older brother a sales rep for a publishing company. Michael had made a rapid descent from a comfortable middle class into hell in just a few short years from getting A-levels in mathematics and applied science.

Now he lived on the edges of the criminal fraternity, prostituting his genius with computers to the highest bidder. Fox had never learned if it was his addictions that led him to this life, or his life that required and supported his addictions, which were mainly heroin and alcohol. But it was the grassing that paid the regular money, and it was money that kept the Ferret dancing on the end of her string.

What he knew he told her, and what he did not know he could find out, and what he could not find out he fabricated, which made dealing with the Ferret such a pleasure and such a perilous journey. Fox's job was to sort the rubies from the rocks.

She stirred sugar into a tepid cup of coffee she had no intention of drinking. 'A woman was murdered in Camden Town a couple of nights ago, Michael.'

'I heard,' he said. Nicotine-stained fingers tapped an in-determinate tattoo on the table.

'She was a witness to a murder a few months ago. A Yardie by the name of Elmore Crawford was shot in the front of his car right outside her house. She at first identified the assailant as Pat Capper and then withdrew her statement a few hours later.'

His eyes went to a corner of the room. 'Is that right?'

Fox leaned across the table. There was a plain brown envelope in her right hand, his reward claim from a successful conviction of two men who had tried to hold up a Securicor van in Holborn six months before. 'Who did it?'

The envelope was smoothly transferred to Michael's denim jacket. 'I heard Mac was in town.'

'When?'

'The night she got done. There was talk Capper had him brought down for a job.'

Mac. Fox had heard his name mentioned once before. A professional. Marenko would know his real name. She could check his records on the computer.

'Is that all?' Fox said.

Ferret shrugged. What did she want? 'I don't know if you'll see me again,' he said. 'I'm thinking of going up north. This is the last time.'

Michael said this every time. Like all snouts, he lived in constant fear of being grassed up himself. But Fox knew he wasn't going to get out of London, and if he didn't leave she knew he'd be back for the money. 'OK,' she said to him. 'You take it easy. If you need anything, you know my number.'

She went outside. A BMW went past, Middle Eastern music thrumming through the windows. The sky was grey, the air bitterly cold. The sun was trying to break through but it wasn't trying too hard, and she couldn't really say she was very surprised.

Chapter Thirty-one

The mirror reassured her that the transformation was complete. She searched for vestiges of her alter ego in the fearful manner of a Jekyll looking for evidence of Mr. Hyde. But she was satisfied. Return of the Ice Maiden, she murmured.

She had changed into a high-necked Victorian blouse in pink silk and a black skirt with a hem below the knee. Her hair was perfect. She put a touch of pale pink gloss to her lips and then, on an impulse, smeared it off. She took out a grey blazer and put it on. There. She was ready for the enemy.

Marenko was in the canteen eating lunch: sausages, bacon, baked beans, chips and two fried eggs.

'Back on that health food diet, guv?' she said as she sat down.

Marenko wiped his mouth with a paper napkin.

He ignored the jibe. 'Just had a phone call from forensics. The bullets were nine-millimetre hollowpoints, probably fired from a Glock model 19. The one they got from the skirting board isn't too bad. They think they can get a match if we can find the weapon.'

Fine, but they all knew that wasn't going to happen. Marenko pulled a plate of spotted dick and custard towards him.

'Anything else?'

'They got a footprint from the side of the house. He wears size ten and a half.'

'That narrows it down a bit. We could go around London with a size ten and a half shoe; the first match we get, that's our man. Like Cinderella.'

Marenko gave her a sour look. 'Thanks for that.'

'I've had my ear to the ground,' Fox said.

'Your supergrass,' he said, intrigued. He knew Fox had a squeal, but the Chief Superintendent was the only other CID who knew his identity.

'And?' Marenko said.

'Evidently Mac was in town the night it happened.'

Marenko ran a hand across his face. It was as it had looked to them all from the beginning. A premeditated and professionally undertaken murder, the hardest to close.

Mac: real name Stuart Anthony Grayden, 39, an SAS veteran who had been decorated in the Gulf War, and who now ran a small building company in Leeds. A high-class body. New Scotland Yard's organised crime task force had a file on him. Before he joined the army he had two previous for GBH. Since his discharge, and the lethal and expert training the army had given him, he was believed to be responsible for four murders in London and the Midlands in the last two years as well as numerous assaults. He was still yet to be formally charged in any of those cases.

He wasn't a professional in the strictest sense, for there were no full-time assassins in Britain. The going rate for a murder was ten thousand pounds, though occasionally a well-protected target might attract as much as double that sum. For a fee they would also put the 'frighteners' on a victim, break an arm or a kneecap to persuade the target to repay some outstanding debt. It was a nice sideline, but most of the hard men had other businesses that supported them. By all accounts Mac kept himself busy, what with building houses and killing people, both good businesses in the new Britain.

Men like Mac were careful, experienced and sometimes even well trained – Mac's SAS training being a case in point – which made it very hard to put together enough evidence to take into court.

'I did a routine check with the Gestapo,' Fox said, using in-house slang for the traffic police. 'He was booked for speeding on the M25 near Waltham Abbey the afternoon the murder took place.'

'Waltham Abbey,' Marenko said, like he had indigestion. 'This isn't going anywhere, is it?'

'Not unless forensics come up with some DNA evidence that puts him right there.' Fox stared into her mug of tea.

Marenko massaged his temples with his knuckles. Finally he sighed and sat back in the plastic chair. 'Go and talk to him, Fox,' he said. 'Take TJ with you.'

Chapter Thirty-two

Stuart Grayden lived in a detached house in a comfortable neighbourhood five miles from the centre of Leeds. There was nothing about his home that suggested the gaudy or the sinister: a well-kept garden, a blue-grey Ford in the driveway, an executive model, not flash like Elmore Crawford's red Corvette or Capper's sky-blue Roller.

The living room where Fox and James now sat was similarly innocuous; there was a pastel-blue sofa, three china ducks in flight on Laura Ashley wallpaper, and a few cheap souvenirs from Spain, a bullfight poster and an empty sangria bottle. Through the net curtain Fox saw the distant moors merge with a sky of uniform grey.

They had driven up the M1 early that morning, before dawn. Stuart Grayden had opened the door wearing a silk dressing gown, salt and pepper stubble on his chin. He had of course shown no particular pleasure at finding police on his doorstep before he had even eaten breakfast, but neither had he been hostile. With gruff civility he had led them inside and his wife had made a pot of tea.

He was a big man, almost six foot three, and now he sat with his bare shins against the coffee table, a mug of lukewarm coffee on his lap, and waited patiently for them to begin. He knew the form. He had sparred with the Old Bill plenty of times before.

Fox's eyes went to the suitcases in the hall. 'Going on holiday, Mr Grayden?'

'Aye. Off t' Spain this afternoon. Takin' a few weeks off. I hope this isn't going to take long.'

'Let me guess. Marbella.'

'Ibiza.'

'Work on your tan.'

Grayden smiled with his mouth but his eyes were hard. 'Aye. That's right. Work on me tan.'

'I need to know where you were on the morning of the twenty-seventh,' Fox asked him.

'Which month?'

'Two days ago,' Fox said, not rising to the bait.

'Why? Am I bein' charged with summat?'

'No, Mr Grayden, we are just conducting a preliminary interview.'

'Only maybe I should call my brief.'

'You may certainly call your brief, and we can continue the interview at the local police station, if you feel it's necessary. But that may well be wasting everyone's time.'

Grayden's wife returned from the kitchen. She wore a gaudy housecoat and her hair and face were perfectly made up. Fox sniffed expensive perfume, but too much of it. At this time of the morning, Fox thought, feeling somehow shabby in her plain grey suit with the motorway coffee stain on the skirt from when she had swerved through a traffic lane.

'Did you hear that, love?' Grayden was saying to his wife. 'Came all t' way from London for a routine interview. But I still don't need my brief, they reckon.'

'Mr Grayden, where were you on the morning of the twenty-seventh of March?'

'I were in bed. I had flu.'

'You were not in London?'

'I told you. I were in bed.'

'Can anyone vouch for that?'

Grayden patted his wife's bottom as she left another coffee on the arm of the sofa. 'Tell this nice lady where I was, love.'

'He were in bed. With the flu.'

Fox consulted her notebook. 'Did anyone drive your car that day?'

The hard grey eyes flickered. He knew where this was going. 'Maybe.'

Fox raised an eyebrow.'

'I lent it to a mate.'

'Can I have his name?'

Grayden grinned and leaned forward. 'I think,' he said, 'that I ought to call my brief.'

'If that is what you'd prefer.'

'Oh, aye,' Grayden said. 'That is what I'd prefer.'

As Fox had anticipated, it had been a complete waste of time. Grayden had called his brief and they adjourned the interview to the local police station, where they met the solicitor, an impeccably dressed man in his late forties with spectacles that flashed disconcertingly in the strip lights of the interview room.

Once again Fox had asked Grayden where he spent the night of the twenty-seventh. This time, however, Grayden said he was in London, on business. Yes, he had the name of an associate who could corroborate their meeting and would say that at midnight on the twenty-seventh of March they were in a nightclub near Piccadilly.

'Earlier today you told me you were in bed with the flu,' Fox reminded him.

'He was confused as to the dates,' Grayden's brief told her.

It had not been the answer she wanted. On the afternoon of the twenty-seventh a patrol car on the M25 had stopped Grayden for a speeding violation. It proved Grayden was in London a few hours before Flora Ellis was murdered, but that was all. Now he was no longer even attempting to deny it, and there were no more bullets left in her gun.

She heard Marenko's voice. *Physical evidence. Witnesses.*

The interview ended abruptly after ten minutes. They had no probable cause to detain Stuart Grayden, and the solicitor reminded them of this fact. His client was a law-abiding citizen, he said, without even a trace of irony. He had never met anyone called Flora Ellis and could help no further. Mr Grayden had a plane to catch.

Fox had to let him go.

On the way back to London their day stayed in character when they were caught in a traffic jam. Accident perhaps, or road-works. They crawled along in second gear while James toyed with the radio.

'I can't believe Jimmy Young's still alive,' Fox said.

'He's not.'

He found Billy Ray Cyrus. 'Christ,' she said and switched it off. James leaned back in his seat, put his hands in his pockets and stared at the English countryside; pylons marching relent-lessly across snow-patched fields, the brick and tile of suburbia encroaching along the valleys.

'They reckon there is nowhere in England now where you can stand on a hill and not see either a motorway or a nuclear power plant,' James said.

'You're cheerful.'

'What do you want to talk about, ma'am? How well things went with Stuart Grayden back there?'

'Don't call me ma'am. It makes me feel about a hundred years old.' She tapped a nail on the steering wheel. 'What do you think about him?'

'We're firing blanks.'

She nodded. They needed something to place him at the

scene. What were they going to do? Ask him his shoe size? The clothes he wore that night would have been in an incinerator within hours of the murder, the gun he had used dumped in a canal or a sewer.

'We don't have due cause for a search and seizure warrant, and if we did we wouldn't find anything,' James said, echoing her thoughts.

'But Michael was right,' she said. 'He *was* in London.'

'So were a few million other people.' James sucked on his teeth, restless. They were down to first gear. The traffic had slowed to a crawl, snaking over the hill ahead of them, no sign of a break.

He whistled tunelessly, drumming on his thighs with his hands. 'How's things,' he asked her after a while.

'With what?'

'Generally.'

She gave him a glance and shrugged her shoulders.

'You know what? You and I should get it together.'

She gave a short, barking laugh. She hadn't meant to.

But James did not seem offended. 'Beneath this crusty exterior there's a marshmallow,' he said.

'If you're talking about your head I'd have to agree with you.'

'When's the last time you went out and had a good time?' James went on.

'That night we arrested those Yardies at the crack house in Ashfield Street and one of them turned round and kicked you in the groin. I enjoyed that.'

'I mean, really.'

'Why is it you think I'm joking?'

'You're a hell of a woman.'

'So are you, TJ. And you know what? I've changed my mind. I think I'd prefer it if you called me ma'am from now on.'

He shrugged. 'Yes, ma'am,' he said. Then he reached forward and turned on the radio. Kylie Minogue. She shot him a glance. He grinned and started to tap his feet in time.

Chapter Thirty-three

A sparkling, ice-cold day in Holland Park, the daffodils out in a riot of yellow but the trees bare, not a bud or leaf showing. Squirrels scampered and darted across the grass, taking refuge in the oaks and horse chestnuts when someone came by.

Fox sat on a park bench, watching a man kicking a football to a small boy. A woman sat nearby, rocking a smaller child in its stroller. Fox was suddenly stricken with an assault wave of loss and of longing.

Thirty-two years old, it was time to make up her mind about certain things. The biological clock she had heard her sister talk of had become a time bomb ticking in her head. Soon she would have to choose between a life she loved and a life she needed. But she could not have both.

How had it rolled on her so fast? When she was twenty-three, there had been plenty of time; twenty-four she met David and they started living together. It had still been too soon, for both of them. He did not want kids, and that had suited her perfectly because she was still chasing a career. As the years went by, the decision was deferred because the choices never became any easier for either of them. And then one day she was thirty and all the rules changed. She realised that she was mortal. Until then she thought she had all the time in the world.

Three weeks after her thirtieth birthday David left her for a younger woman, or so some people said, but that was wrong for she was only a girl. She was just nineteen, a sometime receptionist and underwear model. And Madeleine, faced with the shock of the betrayal, looked at her own life and realised that suddenly there were too many miles on the speedo.

When he left he tried to imply that it was her fault. You're married to your work, he shouted at her; I never see you any more. That could have been part of the truth, but what he did not say was that he was thirty years old too and the Peter Pan in him did not want to leave his youth behind. He clung on, fingers clawing for a handhold in the wash of the tide, and the rock around which his fingers closed was nineteen years old. After all, he worked in advertising, an industry that had youth and beauty as a god, right up there with money. What had she expected?

Well, for one thing, when she had been a little girl she had not expected to spend her life in the kitchen like her own mother. But in her grandiose dreams neither had she expected to reach the age of thirty-two and be sitting here on a cold afternoon in Holland Park watching other women with husbands and young children and feeling this rage and sense of grief. She had not expected to come this far and still feel that somehow, for all her success in her chosen career, life had passed her by.

And what was her life? A one-bedroom flat in Bayswater with a collection of Mahler and John Lee Hooker CDs. How had it happened? She had elbowed her way through the crowd into this man's world and had proved herself just as smart and tough and intelligent. What had been her reward?

She was alone. She was alone because she had hair on her chest, as her elder brother had once said. She faced down drunks in restaurants, she spent her life in mortuaries and alleyways staring at corpses and blood spatter patterns. What was it David had said to her once? You're growing balls in that job, Maddy.

One of these days you're going to open the door for me and it'll be over.

And just a year later it was.

There were only a few Chinese among the tourists and pre-theatre crowds roaming through Chinatown, the Cantonese and Szechuan restaurants side by side with herbal chemists and basement peepshows. It was Sunday evening and the Gerrard Street restaurant was packed. White-jacketed waiters burst in and out of the kitchen like tag wrestlers, shouting warnings and instructions, the huge room rich with the pungent aromas of ginger and garlic and roast duck.

Marenko stared at the banquet laid out on the round table, the crisp grilled pork, the flower rolls, the steamed dumplings and chilli chicken, and thought it best not to mention that he did not like Chinese food. After all, they were there to celebrate his elder daughter's birthday.

He looked at the faces around the table; Susan, matriarch and ruler of the clan now that the patriarch had lost his approval rating and his credibility; Susan's latest, an antiques dealer from Richmond; Donna and her new husband Martin; Tom and Jules.

He had arrived late and Susan had made a weak joke about putting the enemy on one side – she meant him and Tom – and the good guys on the other. Everyone had dutifully laughed, although Marenko didn't think it was particularly funny.

Tom was finally allocated his place between Jules and Donna, and he was left to swing between Martin and the antiques dealer. The dealer, whose name was Graham, attempted desultory conversation.

'Do you collect antiques?' he asked.

'I married one,' Marenko said, looking at Susan.

Graham then tried talking rugby, but Marenko had even less interest in sport than he did in antiques. Graham mentioned the latest production at the Globe. The last dramatic production

Marenko had seen was *Lethal Weapon II* on the Movie Channel. Finally the two men gave up and concentrated on their food.

Marenko bit down hard on a chilli and through watering eyes he stared across the table at Susan and wondered what they had ever seen in each other. It had been a Beauty and the Beast match back then. She had been a legal clerk with the CPS and on his side of the wire. When he set out to court her, his friends thought he didn't have a chance. He was clumsy, unsophisticated and no oil-painting. She looked like Audrey Hepburn.

But he had won her over with persistence and what she later referred to disparagingly and in retrospect as a sort of brutish charm. The marriage had worked well for a while, until Donna and Jules started school and Susan decided to go back to university and do law. Marenko was a traditionalist, and the move took him off balance. At heart Susan was liberal and took her life philosophy from Gloria Steinem and Germaine Greer.

When they finally split up, ten rancorous years later, it was blamed on the long hours Marenko put in at work, but it went much deeper than that. In Marenko's world policemen came home late to a burned dinner and their wives understood that was part of the job. Marenko came home to no dinner at all and a wife still poring over law books.

'How's things, Frank?'

He shook himself from the uncomfortable memories and turned to his left. Not enough that he had to make small talk with Graham; now it was Martin starting in on him. Donna's new husband would not have been his choice. Everything about him galled him; the designer spectacles, the Christian Dior suits, the expensive aftershave, the soft leather boots. He had a supercilious air that made Marenko's teeth ache, something both sharp and soft all in this same package that he was now pleased to call part of his family.

'Things? Things are fine, Martin.'

'Keeping you busy?'

'Well, we're not going to be made redundant, that's for sure.'

'I'm going to be part of the defence team on one of your cases soon. My first time in the Old Bailey.'

Marenko smiled and bit his lip. Christ.

'Michael Charlton.'

'Turbo,' Marenko said.

'Excuse me?'

'Turbo. It's his street name. Because he's always charged up on coke and speed. He put one of his dealers in the morgue when he ripped him off in a crack deal.'

'We intend to plead that it was self-defence.'

'Is that how you're playing it?'

'You have no proof of premeditation.'

'His life wasn't exactly threatened. Two of his minders held the guy down while he beat him. His jaw was broken in five different places.'

'There is no evidence that he was being held during the fight.'

I can't believe this is happening, Marenko thought. Bad enough that Susan turned on me. Now I have a son-in-law in the profession. But he guessed that was his ex's fault too. Martin had met Donna through her. Susan put quite a bit of work through his chambers in Lincoln's Inn.

'There was a witness,' Marenko said.

'She's retracted her statement.'

'I thought she might.'

'She will testify that it was obtained under duress.'

'Yeah, I thought that thumbscrew was a bad idea. I warned my DS at the time, but he wouldn't listen.'

Martin didn't smile. That was Martin's main problem. No sense of humour.

'So there's two in the family now,' Marenko said.

'Two what?'

Arseholes, he was about to say, but it was Jules's birthday. 'Briefs.'

'It must be difficult, I suppose. Having your wife and your son-in-law on the other side of the fence, so to speak.'

'No. I cope. You enjoy the work, do you, Martin?'

'It's worth my time,' he pronounced, as if he was billing about as much per hour as God. 'I find it fulfilling. I have to draw on every ounce of talent that I have. Every day I see the ignorant and the uneducated and I realise that the people who appear in our courtrooms, year in, year out, are simply a product of their environments. They need, no, they deserve, our help and under-standing.'

Oh my, Marenko thought. I think the chilli chicken's about to make a reappearance.

'I mean, you rap—'

'Rap?' Marenko said.

Martin ignored him. '—with some of these so-called har-dened criminals for a while, you discover they're victims too, as much a casualty as the victim of the crime they've committed. The state is supposed to be the plaintiff, but our society is very often the defendant, and those charged with the crimes are the victims.'

Marenko turned away. He was too stunned to speak.

Just then the waiters brought out the cake that Susan had delivered the previous day to the kitchens, and they all sang 'For she's a jolly good fellow' which surprised Marenko, because it sounded politically incorrect. And then they all talked some more, and Susan announced Martin's promotion at work, though Marenko noticed Tom's career change didn't rate a mention. And then Jules announced she was pregnant and there was bedlam, everyone getting up and hugging everyone else. Marenko took the opportunity to congratulate Tom on his impending fatherhood and managed in the fuss to switch seats with the antiques dealer.

He ordered two more beers and hoped this would all be over soon. 'How long's she been seeing that bloke Graham?' he asked Tom.

Tom shrugged. 'I don't know. Maybe a couple of months.'

'Jesus.'

Tom looked embarrassed. 'This must be hard for you.'

'Funny, that's what Martin reckons.' Their beers arrived and Marenko raised his glass in toast. 'When's the baby due?'

'September.'

'Here's to life.'

'Yes,' Tom said. 'Life.'

Chapter Thirty-four

Half-past three in the morning and Fox was in a black and bottomless sleep. The shrill alarm of the phone beside the bed jerked her awake. She fumbled for the light, knocking the receiver off its cradle on to the floor. She groped for it on the carpet.

'Fox.'

'It's TJ, ma'am. Sorry to wake you. There's a break-in on Kentish Town Road. There's a constable down. I'm heading out there now.'

'How are we involved in this?'

'They don't think the uniform's going to make it.'

'All right,' Fox said. 'I'm on my way.'

She stumbled out of bed and into her clothes. She was still half asleep when she fumbled the key into the ignition of her Cavalier and accelerated through the gears along the Bayswater Road.

She heard the sirens wailing across the city when she was still in Camden High Street. There seemed to be flashing blue beacons all along Kentish Town Road. When she got there she leaned out of her car to show her ID, and a constable waved her through the cordon.

The glass shopfront of a large electrical store lay in shards across the footpath. The alarm was still wailing, and no one had yet managed to shut it off. There were rubber tyre marks on the pavement. A ram raid, Fox thought.

There was not much traffic at this time of the morning, a taxi, and a red Royal Mail van slowing down to take a look. A fat robber's moon hung over King's Cross.

On the other side of the road she saw a PC sitting in the passenger seat of his patrol car, his right arm in a sling. Another uniform was squatting down talking to him, but he hardly seemed to be listening.

There were two senior CID from Holmes Road, but neither of them had seen James. They pointed down the road towards one of the side streets.

She heard the crackle of a police radio. The second crime scene had been marked out with police tape, a lane at the junction of Crossland Walk and Anderson Way. There was the usual crowd of spectators.

She saw the red and blue stripes of a panda, James leaning against the doors, his head resting on the roof.

'TJ?'

He raised his head, but he did not look at her. He ran a hand through his hair. His face was caught in the ghostly strobe of the ambulance beacons. He looked like hell. 'This is a mess.'

'What's happened?'

'They've taken him to the Whittington,' he said.

Fox stood there and experienced the first thrill of alarm. What was wrong with him? OK, a cop's got himself badly hurt. Let's get down to business and get it sorted. 'What the hell is it?'

He shook his head. 'Christ Almighty,' he said. 'What are we going to tell Frank?'

Chapter Thirty-five

There was a cold silence in the Incident Room when Fox walked in.

The detectives sat in groups, drinking coffee, waiting. There were no jokes. Marenko was still at the hospital. Fox had been given provisional responsibility for the investigation until a new DCI could be brought in to head the team.

The Chief Superintendent, Radford, didn't like it, would have preferred to have given the case to one of the other squads. James had originally been notified about the incident by an old friend of his who was night duty officer at Kentish Town. Now their AMIT was involved, and none of the other three squads were exactly sitting on their hands, so the Chief was going to let it play.

She looked around the room at the grim, angry faces. 'You've all heard what happened last night,' she said.

She briefed them on the facts of the case.

'The initial incident took place at Brightwell's store on Kentish Town Road. The premises have an alarm system linked to Holmes Road police station. O'Neill and Davis responded to an alarm at 2.38 a.m. When they arrived the ram raid was still in progress. They called for backup and ran towards the shopfront. The Escort backed away fast, its back doors still open, and one of them hit Davis on the arm and side and knocked him down.

Meanwhile the other two offenders attempted to escape on foot and PC O'Neill pursued them. That's all we know. Davis saw PC O'Neill chase them down Crossland Walk. Five minutes later he found him lying unconscious in the alley at the junction of Crossland Walk and Anderson Way, directly behind the chemist's.'

She drew a breath.

'He has serious and extensive head injuries,' Fox said. 'He was clubbed with his own baton and was kicked and stamped on repeatedly, even after he fell unconscious.'

For a moment no one spoke.

'The store had video surveillance,' she went on. 'Unfortunately, the offenders were wearing balaclavas, so there's no chance of getting IDs. The camera picked up two offenders. The third was driving the vehicle. The video confirmed that the vehicle was a Ford Escort panel van.'

'Did we get a registration number?' Rankin asked.

Fox nodded.

'We got something right, then,' someone muttered at the back of the room.

'The car was found abandoned in Forest Road, Hackney, at 6 o'clock this morning,' Fox went on. 'It was reported stolen yesterday evening from Hainault Road in Leytonstone. Forensics are currently checking the vehicle for prints.'

'What about the stolen gear?'

Fox shook her head.

'How is PC O'Neill, ma'am?' someone asked.

'He's been transferred to the Royal London Hospital. He has extensive head injuries and is still on the critical list. That's all I know.'

'They did a real job on him,' James growled.

'So how do we play this, ma'am?' Rankin asked.

'I've pinned a duty roster to the board. Some of you will be going back to Kentish Town. Someone must have seen something. There were alarms going off, police sirens, you don't sleep through that, even in North London. PC O'Neill's assailants got away on foot. How? Where did they go? Did they get a cab, did they hitch? All the television and news stations are carrying a bulletin in their news reports, appealing for witnesses. Someone must have seen that blue Escort. There's a gap of over three hours between the time of the incident and when it was found, and the driver must have unloaded the gear somewhere. We are hoping for a positive response from the public. I also have a list here of every known fence in the borough. Some of you will be paying them a visit today. The scrotes who did this are running scared by now, and they'll probably try to unload the stuff fast. They're almostly certainly amateurs. Anyone likely to fence this gear for them, let them know the gloves are off. Make sure they know that this stuff is too hot to touch.'

'What are we talking about here, ma'am?'

Fox held up a typed A4 sheet. 'This is the complete list of the goods stolen: brands, sizes, serial numbers. About three thousand pounds' worth of televisions and videos.'

A few of them shook their heads. Was it worth getting your head kicked in for?

'How's Frank, ma'am?' Honeywell asked her.

'I haven't spoken to him yet.'

'He's going to take this hard,' James said.

'Let's just do our jobs,' she said. 'That's all we can do for him right at this moment.'

She pinned the list of stolen goods to the board beside the duty roster, and the meeting broke up. As the detectives gathered around the noticeboard she felt someone touch her lightly on the arm. It was James. 'We'll get the bastards, ma'am,' he whispered and gave her a reassuring smile.

She smiled back. All minor feuds were off. They were all together in this one.

✻   ✻   ✻

The alley where Tom O'Neill had been beaten was still cordoned off with blue and white tape. Fox and James fought their way through the spectators and the inevitable camera crews.

Fox looked around. The scene seemed much different in the daylight, neither as remote nor as lonely. She could hear the traffic on Kentish Town Road. Shops backed on to one side of the alley, a tangle of fire escapes and burglar alarms, the ramshackle wooden fences of Cambridge Street on the other, bollards and NO PARKING signs on the gates. She could see more than twenty windows from where she stood, a sign advertising the rear entrance to a chiropractor's office, an estate agent's hoarding. If this had happened in daylight she would have been confident of a score of witnesses.

But this had not happened in daylight. It had happened in the north of London, at night. Depressed, she looked down the alley. A red telephone box, one window smashed, the receiver hanging limp like a broken arm. Beside it a Borough of Camden rubbish bin, defaced with graffiti. A city in decay.

The weather had come in overnight. The sky was overcast, and a light drizzle had started to fall. The SOC officers were still at work, some of them on their hands and knees. There was a dark stain where O'Neill had lain. Fox turned away, sickened by her own imagination. The scene was eerily reminiscent of another alley and the sprawled rag-doll body of Kate Mercer.

'What the hell went wrong here?' she said.

James must have been thinking the same thing. He looked at her and shook his head in weary resignation.

It was late afternoon when she parked the car outside the Royal London on Whitechapel Road. The initial results on the house-to-house had not been encouraging. Of the twenty houses that backed on to the alley, residents at no fewer than eleven houses admitted to hearing shouts and the sound of a fight the previous night. Some of them saw scuffling in the alleyway, but they all insisted it was too dark to see what was going on. None of them had ventured outside for fear of getting hurt themselves.

A number of people had seen the two men running away from the scene, but at that time of the morning the best description they had was two black males, one tall, the other quite short. They had later been seen getting into a mini-cab on Brecknock Road. The search was on to find the cab driver.

Back at Crossland Walk the police tape was down, the SOCO team had finished, the spectators had drifted home, the TV crews were gone. Fox had the sense, as she always did, of things moving too fast for her. If you didn't get a result quickly, you often didn't get a result at all.

She found Marenko sitting on his own in a corridor outside the ICU, his head in his hands. She guessed the rest of the family were in the waiting room, further down the hall. She sat down next to him on a moulded plastic chair. He didn't even look up.

'How is he, guv?'

'The doctors don't think he's going to make it.'

'I'm sorry,' she said. What else was there to say?

'Massive subdural haematoma, they reckon. The doctor's way of saying they kicked his brain into porridge. He was in theatre for five hours.'

Fox stared at her hands.

'He was like a son to me.'

'We'll get them,' Fox promised him. 'We'll get whoever did this.'

Marenko took his hands away from his face. She was shocked by the expression on his face. 'Right now, I don't give a fuck what anyone does,' he said. 'But thanks for coming over.'

She nodded. He put his hands back to his face. She waited a moment but could think of nothing else to say, so she got up and left.

✳ ✳ ✳

When she got back to the car her mobile rang. It was WPC Stacey in the Incident Room at Hendon Road. A man had just walked in to Leyton police station, responding to the appeal on the 11 o'clock news bulletin on Radio 4. He had seen the blue Escort van in a neighbouring house at 4 o'clock that morning.

Fox put her Cavalier in gear and drove off fast, back to Hendon Road. She felt a thrill of anticipation. Kate Mercer was still unavenged and Flora Ellis's ghost followed her everywhere, but this one, at least, would not stay open. Their luck was due to change.

'They're always causing trouble. They play their music too loud, all hours of the night. I've told you people about it. You were never interested before.'

Arnold Simpson looked as if he had just got out of bed. He was in his seventies, and his grey, sparse hair had not been combed for some time, perhaps around the time he last had a shave. His breath made her gag. There was dried egg from his breakfast on his chin, and the hairs in his ears could have trapped a small moth. She found his voice so irritating she thought she would rather listen to someone drag their fingernails down a blackboard.

But at that moment Arnold Simpson was her single most favourite person in the world.

'Well, we are certainly interested now, Mr Simpson,' she heard herself saying.

'They're even worse than the last lot they put in there. I reckon they was on drugs.'

'What happened last night, Mr Simpson?'

'I was asleep. I heard this car pull in next door. I thought, 'ello, they're gonna have a party again. They always do that. Have parties in the middle of the night.'

'About what time was this, Mr Simpson?'

'I dunno. About four, I suppose.'

'Can you be a little more precise? Do you know what time it was or are you guessing?'

'No, I don't know what time it was,' Arnold Simpson snapped at her. 'Anyhow, I got up and looked out the window. There was this van parked next door. The front was all pushed in, and one of the lights wasn't working. I heard him open up the garage and then he backed it in and I heard him unloading things out the back.'

'You didn't see what he was unloading?'

'How could I?' he jeered. 'I told you. He backed it in. What am I, Superman?' Honeywell looked at Fox and sucked hard on his teeth to keep from laughing. 'Anyway I knew they was up to no good.'

'How did you know that, Mr Simpson?'

'They don't have a car, do they? Where would they get the money for a car? Had to be nicked.'

'Who did you see unloading the van, Mr Simpson?'

'Not the little one, the other one. The one with the big mouth with all the teeth. Bloody coons. If I had my way, I'd send 'em all back where they came from.'

'What happened after he unloaded the van?'

'Drove off, driving too bloody fast too. Don't know how he didn't wake up everyone in the bleedin' street.'

'And you're sure it was a blue Escort?'

'Of course I'm bloody sure. I might be getting on, but I'm not blind.' He fumbled in the dank recesses of his cardigan and pulled out a crumpled envelope. 'Here, I wrote down the registration number. Is that any good to you?'

Chapter Thirty-six

It was a run-down semidetached in Leytonstone. There was a rusted brown campervan in the street outside, a broken washing machine lying on its side in the front garden, and bedsheets across the windows in place of curtains. The front garden was overgrown with weeds. There was a rubbish bin lying on its side, a council sticker announcing: BOROUGH OF WALTHAM. TOGETHER WE CAN TIDY UP THE BOROUGH. There was also a padlocked garage built into the pebbledash frontage, peeling red-brown paint on the wooden doors.

The gear's in there, Fox decided.

She drove the lead car with James, Honeywell and Rankin in the car behind, two panda cars from Leyton following them with four uniforms. Fox jumped out and strode up the path to the front door. She turned to the police sergeant in charge of the uniforms.

'We'll take the front. You go around the side in case our boy's not in the mood for visitors.'

Fox saw curtains twitching up and down the street. She had grown accustomed to entertaining the locals.

There was no doorbell. She hammered on the door with her fist.

Almost at once she heard shouts from around the back. 'Stay here,' she said to Rankin and ran along the narrow path at the side of the house.

Vincent Barnes was lying on the ground, the sergeant and a uniformed constable sitting on him, cuffing his wrists behind his back. Predictably, he had tried to escape out of the back door. He was screaming obscenities while the sergeant attempted to read him his rights.

'You can't fuckin' do this! I ain't fuckin' done nuffin'!'

'Search the house,' Fox said to Honeywell.

'You got a fuckin' search warrant?'

Fox crouched down next to the struggling man and held a piece of paper in front of his face. 'There you are, Mr Barnes, we do have a warrant. You know what this is about, so let's stop pretending. Do you have the keys to the garage, please?'

'It's fuckin' padlocked, you daft cow. The landlord's got the keys. We never fuckin' use it!'

Fox dug her fingers into the trapezius muscles of the neck. She squeezed hard and Vincent Barnes cried and writhed like a child. 'Listen to me,' Fox said, leaning over his ear. 'A policeman was very seriously injured last night. We mean business, Vincent. So don't call me a daft cow. Now say you're sorry.' She squeezed harder.

'I'm sorry!' Vincent gasped.

'I'm sorry, *ma'am*.'

'Sorry ma'am!'

She relaxed her grip.

'That's police fuckin' brutality!'

'She never touched you,' the sergeant said.

She straightened. James was staring at her, but she could not decipher the look in his eyes. Was it respect or was it scorn?

Rankin was still waiting at the front. Honeywell had taken a crowbar to the padlock on the garage. It opened with a crack. As the doors sprung open, she peered inside. There were rows of cardboard boxes, stacked on top of each other, printed with manufacturers' labels: Baird, Sanyo and Ferguson She ripped open one of the boxes. The colour television inside was still in its protective wrapping.

'Little prick,' she heard James murmur from the doorway.
'Let's get him down the station,' Fox said.

Fox leaned her elbows on the table and stared at him. Twenty-one years old. Unemployed. Previous for shoplifting, burglary and driving without a licence. Definitely not a taxpayer.

Vincent Barnes kept his eyes on his Nike Air trainers.

'Look at me, Vincent,' she said. 'I said, *look at me.*'

Vincent peered up at her from hooded lids, a lizard peering out from under a rock.

'Tell me what happened, Vincent.'

'I ain't done nuffin'.'

'The televisions and the VCRs you stole in the ram raid on Brightwell's were stored in your garage. That wasn't very smart, was it, Vincent? You should have got rid of them. Don't you have a fence, Vincent?'

Vincent Barnes returned his gaze to his trainers. 'Some bloke came round and asked if he could store some stuff in our garage. I didn't fuckin' know what he was puttin' in there.'

Fox felt like laughing out loud. If it wasn't for what had happened to Tom O'Neill, such stupidity might be funny. Instead, it was sickening. 'What was his name, Vincent?'

'Who?'

'This man who wanted to store the stolen goods in your garage.'

'I dunno.'

'He uses your garage to store stolen property and you don't even know his name?'

Vincent looked up again, the quick, wide-eyed look of a cornered animal. 'I didn't know it was fuckin' stolen, did I?'

Fox glanced at James. OK, she would play along with his stupid games for a little while. 'His name.'

'Shankie.'

'Shankie. Shankie who?'

'It's his street name, ain't it? I dunno his real name.'

'When did he leave these boxes in your garage?'

'I don't remember.'

'Yesterday?'

'Yeah. Yesterday.'

'Where does he live?'

'I dunno. He's a friend of Tiny's.'

'You are referring to Paul Thompson, your flatmate, is that correct?' Again, the eyes scurried back to the floor. 'Is that correct, Vincent? For the tape.'

'Yeah.'

'Where is Paul Thompson?'

'I dunno.'

'He was with you last night when you ram-raided Bright-well's, wasn't he?'

'Ram raid? I don't know nuffin' about no ram raid.'

'OK. Let's see if I have this right. The televisions and VCRs that we found in your garage belong to someone called Shankie, whom you do not know. Shankie deposited these stolen items in your garage yesterday.'

Vincent looked blank for a moment. Then he said: 'Yeah, that's right.'

Fox stifled a yawn. 'Even though, when you were arrested, you stated that the garage was padlocked and you did not have the key.'

Vincent sniffed. His jaw hung open, caught in the lie.

'Shankie put these goods in your padlocked garage, to which you did not have access, twelve hours before they were stolen from Brightwell's electrical shop in Kentish Town Road. Is that what you're trying to tell me?'

He swallowed hard, his Adam's apple bobbing in his throat, a snake trying to swallow a small mammal.

Fox started again, slowly, trying to make Vincent understand the extent of his stupidity. 'Shankie brought round two dozen televisions and seventeen VCRs that were at that moment in the showroom of Brightwell's and put them in your garage with a key that you did not possess? That is what you wish me to believe, is that correct?'

Vincent put his head in his hands, trying to block out this nightmare. Fox guessed it must have seemed easy when it was put to him in the pub: *All you have to do is drive, man. We load the gear and you make yourself some easy dosh. OK?*

'Vincent?'

'I don't know nuffin' about it.'

'I'm afraid I can't accept that, Vincent.'

'I told ya. Shankie's a friend of Tiny's.'

'Let's stop playing games. One of your neighbours saw you unloading those boxes last night from a blue Ford Escort panel van that you stole in Leytonstone. We found the key to the padlock for the garage in your kitchen. We're going to find your prints all over it, aren't we?'

Vincent's eyes returned to the floor.

'Look at me. *Look at me!*' Fox got to her feet, her patience eroded entirely. She leaned across the desk. 'Did you know a police constable was badly beaten last night, Vincent? So badly beaten that he may never again be able to walk, talk or dress himself? So badly beaten that he cannot even recognise his own wife and family?'

'I didn't do nuff—'

'Shut up! We have you for the robbery. Your prints are all over the van and the padlock and the boxes. If you help us, a judge may take your cooperation into consideration at sentencing. So tell us, Vincent. Who was with you? There were two others, right? Was Paul Thompson one of them?'

Beads of sweat erupted all over him. No, she thought, he didn't touch Tom O'Neill. Vincent Barnes isn't hard at all.

'I'll give you five minutes to think about it, Vincent. The robbery charges are clear cut. That policeman might well die, Vincent. And that means if you can't think of the names of your two accomplices by the time I come back you'll also be making yourself an accomplice to murder. Am I making myself quite clear?'

'You know I didn't do the fuckin' copper!'

'Who did?'

Vincent's eyes returned to the floor.

'I'll give you five minutes. You'd better get used to sitting on your own in small cells, Vincent. If you don't crack smart pretty damned quick it's going to be a big part of your life from now on. Interview suspended 3.25 p.m.'

Fox walked out of the interrogation room, breathing hard. She looked at James.

He grinned at her. 'It's OK, ma'am,' he said. 'You're doing great.'

She walked back in and pressed the RECORD button on the tape. 'Interview recommences 3.31 p.m. Present, DI Fox, DS James.' She leaned her elbows on the table. 'OK, Vincent. Names.'

Vincent's face was sullen, immobile.

Fox tapped a pencil on the table. There was a long silence in the room, stretching almost to a minute. Finally she said, her voice as gentle as a mother's: 'Vincent, I'll tell you what I'm going to do.'

Vincent leaned forward slightly, looking for his out.

'I'm going to put you in for the robbery. When this comes to court the judge is going to take note of the fact that you tried to obstruct our investigation. If that policeman dies, it could make you an accomplice. You're looking at a whole shitload of bird here, to be frank. I think you need legal representation, Vincent. Would you like us to call a solicitor for you, or do you have your own brief?'

Vincent stared at her. 'What?'

Fox flicked the PAUSE button on the tape. 'You're in serious trouble, Vincent. You know how these things get when a cop gets hurt. How people get fitted up. You've heard the stories, right?' Fox stared at him, long and hard, calculating. Ah. A light turned on behind Vincent's eyes.

'We found the stolen goods in your possession. Also, while I was out of the room, I rang our forensic department. They found a trainer in your house with blood on the sole. The blood matches that of the constable who was beaten up.' It was a bluff. She hadn't heard from forensics yet. For all she knew they had found nothing.

But Vincent didn't know that. Vincent had heard the stories, what the cops did to black guys. His eyes were as big as soup plates. She was talking a language he could understand.

Fox leaned across the desk. 'Off the record, Vincent, I have pressure on me to put this case to bed. From the top. Are you with me? See, I don't care if I get the right person. As long as I can put someone inside for it. As far as I'm concerned, as far as anyone here is concerned, they found the trainer in your bedroom. Maybe it was Tiny who drove off in that van, picked you up later.'

Vincent's eyes flew wide. 'That's not my fuckin' shoe! I never went near that copper!'

She nodded. 'If I fit this to you, if I fit this to Paul, frankly, I don't care. Okay, Vincent?'

She sat back, slammed the tape back on and watched the wheels turning in his brain. She had nowhere near enough to take to the CPS for the assault on O'Neill. Vincent didn't know that.

'We can get you a court-appointed solicitor. I think one should be present before we discuss this any further. Don't you?' On an impulse, she reached forward and patted his hand.

Perhaps it was the implied threat. Or perhaps it was a policewoman patting his hand and telling him she was going to get him legal representation. Why would a cop offer you a lawyer unless they were really confident? And he had heard the stories, read the newspapers, knew how the cops like to fit up black guys for anything they could.

Whatever the reason, Vincent James Barnes, frightened, way out of his league, put his head in his hands and started to cry. And when he had finished crying he gave up Michael DeBruin and Paul 'Tiny' Thompson.

Chapter Thirty-seven

'It wasn't Tiny,' James said. 'I know him. Did him two years ago for breaking and entering when I was at Islington. He's a little scrote but he's not violent.'

'So that leaves Michael DeBruin,' Fox said.

Honeywell gave her the print-out. DeBruin had been in and out of juvenile court since he was thirteen. Now twenty-five, he had already served a two-year term for dealing in cocaine and had two other assault charges against him, for which he had served a total of six months.

Fox shook her head. The government spent a fortune every year persuading people not to drink and drive and they let people like this loose on the streets. What was the greater health risk? She handed the print-out to James.

'Any word on Tom O'Neill?' Honeywell asked.

'Nothing yet.'

He tossed the print-out on the desk. 'So that's it?'

'Thompson and DeBruin will finger each other,' James said. 'We need something from forensics to make it stick.'

'We have to catch these bastards first. Vincent gave us an address for DeBruin. There's a squad car round there now picking him up. But he still says he doesn't know where Tiny is. He reckons he never came back to the house that night.'

'He knew we'd be waiting.'

'So where would he go, skipper?' Honeywell said.

James shook his head. 'I don't know him. I just picked him up that once. Maybe there's something in his file. He must have some mates. I think his family came from Manchester.'

WPC Stacey put the phone down. 'Ma'am.'

Fox looked up.

'Just had a telephone call from a Mr Terry Richardson. He lives in Anderson Way. Says he thinks he has some information for us about the assault on PC O'Neill.'

Fox glanced at Honeywell and James. Nah. They couldn't be that lucky. She took the note from Stacey with Richardson's address and hurried out of the door, James following.

Terry Richardson had long hair, thinning at the crown to reveal an oval of pink scalp. He had on a leather jacket over a white T-shirt. Early forties, Fox guessed. His daughter Dianna was thirteen, a big awkward-looking girl with lank hair and acne. She sat on the sofa next to him, in a large shapeless jumper, her head down, sobbing.

They were in Richardson's living room. It was tiny, the walls covered with Tottenham Hotspur memorabilia – scarves and posters and photographs – the smell of frying sausages drifting from the kitchen.

'I slept right frew it last night,' Richardson said. 'Had a few jars at the pub and that's it for me. First I knew 'bout this rumble was when I looked out the window yesterdie mornin' and saw all the TV vans and everyfin'.'

'Right,' Fox said, wondering where this was going.

'I heard on the radio the copper wasn't lookin' too clever.'

'You have information you think might be able to help us?'

Richardson leaned forward. 'Look, let's get this straight from the off. I'm no grass, right. And I ain't no angel, either, I admit it. Got done a few years back for receiving, all right? But I don't hold with no violence.' He pushed his hair out of his eyes. 'They reckon this copper was married.'

'His wife's three months pregnant,' Fox said.

'You hear that?' Terry said and nudged the girl. 'His missus is gonna have a baby.'

The girl cried some more.

'It's me girl here. She saw it. She saw everyfin'.'

Fox turned her attention to Dianna. 'You saw what happened, Dianna? Why didn't you come forward before?'

The girl continued to drain her sinuses into a Kleenex.

Fox turned back to Terry Richardson. 'I believe DC Rankin spoke to your wife yesterday morning.'

'Yeah, that's right. I always tell her not to talk to the Old Bill. Old habits and all that.'

'She said no one had seen anything.'

'That's right. We didn't know, see?' He nudged the girl again. 'Tell him, girl.'

But Dianna just blew her nose and cried some more. Her eyes were pink and swollen. Fox felt sorry for her but also a little irritated as well. Get hold of yourself, she wanted to say.

'She reckons she's scared,' Terry went on. 'She only told me 'bout it when I got home from work yesterdie afternoon. I made her. Well, she didn't go to school, I finds out when I get home. Been in bed all day blubbering. Ker-ist, she had me dead worried. I fought she'd got herself knocked up. Then she lays this on me.'

Fox again concentrated her attention on the girl. She needed this in her words, not in Terry's. 'Dianna,' she said softly. 'Can you tell me what you saw, please?'

The story came out painfully slowly, and by the time Dianna had finished there were screwed-up tissues all over the carpet around her feet. She had woken up in the middle of the night, she said. She was having some problems at school and hadn't been sleeping well. Unable to get back to sleep, she had turned on the light and read a TV magazine while she listened to her radio, turned down low so her mum and dad couldn't hear. Then she heard shouts coming from the street.

The Richardsons' house was on the corner of Crossland Walk and Anderson Way and her bedroom window looked directly down the alley where the incident had taken place. There was a streetlamp at the corner, and from her window she saw two men run down Crossland Walk from the direction of Kentish Town Road and turn down the lane behind the shops. A few moments later she saw a uniformed policeman run into the alleyway after them. Then she heard shouts and the sounds of a fight.

One of the men reappeared. She now saw that he was wearing a balaclava over his face with slits cut for the eyes and the mouth. A short while later – how long? Fox had asked her; thirty seconds, maybe a minute, she said – the other man ran out and she saw his face clearly in the light of the streetlamp. He seemed to hesitate and the other man, the one with the balaclava, yelled something at him. The other man went back up the alley.

She heard a scream and then more noises. It sounded like someone throwing a cabbage against a wall, she said. Then the bare-headed man appeared again, holding something in his left hand. She couldn't see what it was.

'Would you recognise this man if you saw him again?' Fox asked her, hardly daring to breathe.

'His name's Tuffy,' she said.

'You know him?'

'I told you. It was Tuffy,' she repeated.

'Tuffy.'

'It's his street name,' Terry said. 'Everyone calls him that. His real name's Michael DeBruin. Thinks he's a regular little hard case.'

Michael DeBruin. She wanted to jump up and punch the air. Instead, she said: 'How do you know him, Dianna?'

'Me big bruvver knows him. They got in a fight once.'

'I see. When this . . . Tuffy . . . came out of the alley the second time . . . what happened then?'

'They ran off down the street. The bloke in the balaclava and Tuffy.'

'You're sure it was Tuffy who went back into the alley?'

'I told you. He was standing under the streetlight. It was him, all right.'

Fox imagined the events of that night. Whoever went back into the alley was the one who did the kicking. Had to be.

'Why didn't you tell us this morning?' James asked Dianna, trying to keep the frustration from his voice.

'I was scared.'

'You don't have to be scared of him,' Terry told her. 'Poxy coon. Comes near us, I'll fuckin' sort him out.' He looked at Fox. 'Not that he'll be goin' anywhere now, eh? How's this copper he gave the kickin' to?'

'He may die, Mr Richardson.'

'Ker-ist,' Terry said, and then he gave his daughter another shove. 'You hear that? Now stop snivelling. This family's not scared of nig-nogs, all right?'

Fox fought down a wave of disgust. Poxy coons. Nig-nogs. She wondered if Mr Richardson's altruism might be racially motivated. There was no doubt in her mind that the girl was telling the truth, for she had only confirmed what they already knew, or had guessed. But if her father was put on the stand in court, they would get ripped to bits.

'Thank you for coming forward, Mr Richardson,' Fox said. 'You and Dianna have been most helpful.'

'Just doin' my bit.'

'We may need to talk to you again, Dianna. And could you both please not speak to anyone about this in the meantime.'

'Not a word,' Richardson said, putting a finger to his lips.

Fox sighed. Even money it would be all over North London by the morning.

*　　*　　*

Fox was at Tolpuddle Street when they brought him in. He was a big, lithe man, perhaps six-two or six-three, muscular beneath the tracksuit and layers of fake gold chains, head shaved. His hands were cuffed behind his back, and he was screaming racial and sexual obscenities all the way.

Remarkable. He was just as she had imagined him.

Chapter Thirty-eight

A huddled knot of misery next to the nurses' station: Susan, Jules, Donna and Martin. Julia was at the hub of this mandala of pain, hunched over, a ragged tissue in her fist. The others looked up as he arrived. Jesus. Tom was gone.

It was a long walk from the lift, a long walk with his heart in his hand and his guts trailing along behind him on the floor.

'Jules?' he said, and his voice sounded a long way away.

Susan had her arm around their daughter. A look passed between her and Donna and then she got to her feet and came towards him.

'Is he gone?' he said. And he thought of all those times, in other people's houses, or in hospital wards like this one, where he had repeated the litany 'I am sorry for your loss' without ever understanding what loss was. And that was how it had to be if he was going to do his job, only now life had played this cruel joke and made him swallow his own jagged and bitter pills.

'They think he's going to make it.'

Marenko nodded, dully, not understanding.

'It may not be good news.'

He looked at Jules, his mind clunking through the gears, the scope of this tragedy dulling his brain.

'The doctors think he has sustained permanent damage, Frank. They don't know how bad the damage is just yet.'

Whoa. Stop. Let me take this on board. 'What?' He searched her face for answers. 'Can he talk?'

'The doctors have compared it to a massive stroke.'

Marenko sat down heavily on one of the plastic chairs. 'Jesus.' This was what he had feared most. This particular black shadow had been lurking in the back of his mind, but he had not wanted to confront it. *Vegetable.* Tom was going to be one of the slow ones who sat in chairs on the touchline at the football matches, the ones who were hard to look at, to accept into Frank Marenko's universe. He ran a hand across his face. Oh, Jesus holy suffering sweet Christ.

'But there's still a chance, right?'

He felt Susan's hand on his shoulder. A featherlight touch, a distant signal, a world away from absolution or even comfort. 'There's still hope,' she said, but her voice held out no shining beacon. 'The doctors have told us to pray for a miracle.'

'Right.' When doctors talked about miracles, you knew what they were saying.

He stood up, his knees weak, his balance unsteady, like one too many Guinnesses at the King's Head. Jules looked up at him and her eyes were swollen and pink and filled with a murderous loathing that shocked him to the core.

'You did this,' she said.

'Jules . . .'

'I didn't want him to be a copper. I married him because he had a nice safe job with regular hours. You wanted him to be a cop. He was your tousle-haired little boy, wasn't he? The son you never had!'

Donna held her tighter. 'Jules, let it be,' she whispered. Martin just looked embarrassed.

'He idolised you!' A deadly accusation. God forbid anyone should idolise me in my own family. *He idolised you, you made him like you and respect you and admire you and therefore you are guilty of this.* 'He wouldn't have joined the force if it wasn't for you!'

The sister at the nursing station looked over, concerned.

Thinking hysteria, no doubt, thinking sedatives. Susan knelt beside her daughter, put a consoling arm around her. 'Not now, Julia, not now.'

Not: you're wrong, Julia. Not: he's grieving too. Just: not *now*.

Marenko squatted down so that he was at a level with her face. He wanted to touch her, to hold her in his arms and tell her everything was going to be OK, as he did when she was a child, but he couldn't touch her without having her scream, and anyway nothing was going to be all right again, was it?

'We'll get the bastards who did this,' he said.

If he helped at all it was because he gave her a focus for her despair and her rage. She had stopped crying now, but her face was blotched and red. 'You don't get it, do you?'

'Jules . . .'

'It doesn't matter if you "get" anyone. It's not going to do any good, it's not going to change anything.'

He looked away.

'If anyone put him where he is now, it's you!'

Donna and Susan held her tighter, as if by squeezing her they could make the pain go away.

'Just go,' Susan whispered to him.

But Marenko did not want to go, because she was right. In some way he was responsible, and if he could not get absolution then at least he could take his punishment. Was that not, after all, what he believed in? You do the crime, you do the time.

'I always lost out to you,' Julia said.

A new accusation, another to add to the list of charges. This was a more familiar refrain, a charge sheet he knew by heart now.

'You were never home. The force was always more important than us, wasn't it, Dad? I always lost out to the cops. And now you've bloody done it again. Now you've taken Tom away and he's going to be gone for ever!'

And then a cry, directed towards the white-tiled ceiling and beyond, to the grey and indifferent sky that had set like a pall over the city. A howl of primal intensity, grief welling up like a malevolent gas and bubbling to the surface. Like a scream from a torture chamber, or the oubliette before the jailer slams the door for ever.

'Oh, Jules,' Marenko said.

Her eyes were screwed shut against the grief, there cradled in her family's arms, a family that no longer included the father. I thought I was on the side of the angels, Marenko thought. But the angels are not on the side of me.

He got up slowly, feeling the creaking in his knees, age and weariness setting like iron in his soul. He looked over at the nurses' station, at the sister, her face creased with a frown of professional concern. He had wanted to see Tom, had planned to go in and sit beside the broken body and talk out his pain and his guilt. But now he couldn't do it.

Martin was on his feet too. He looked both helpless and embarrassed. Inadequate to this process of grieving. He opened his mouth but no words came. This was a woman's business, after all, grief.

A man's business was revenge.

Chapter Thirty-nine

Marenko stared through the spyhole of the holding cell, his fists knotted in suppressed rage. The name DEBRUIN was chalked on the board next to the door. Twenty-five years old and already sent down twice, James had told him. A drug dealer and a hard man.

Scenes of Crime were right now swarming over the poxy terrace behind King's Cross where this piece of shit lived. What they had found so far was a small plastic bag with six amphetamine tablets, missing floorboards, a clogged lavatory and piles of trash, pizza boxes, plastic plates and takeaway chicken boxes feeding a generation of roaches.

That DeBruin couldn't care less. He lay on his back on his bunk, hands behind his head, staring at the ceiling, eyes half-lidded with sleep.

'What are you doing here, guv?' James said.

He ignored the question. 'Is that him, TJ?'

'We don't know yet. The driver grassed him up. We're still looking for the other bloke.' James hesitated. 'You shouldn't be here, guv.'

'Don't tell me what to do, TJ. All right?'

James got a call on his mobile. He took it out of his pocket and turned his back to answer it.

Marenko called over the custody sergeant. 'There's something wrong with this bloke, George.'

The sergeant walked over from his station and looked through the spyhole. 'Looks all right to me.'

'He was thrashing about. I think he had a fit or something. Better open up.'

The sergeant looked perplexed. He knew Marenko, but he didn't know the connection to this particular case or perhaps he would have had second thoughts. But this was a Detective Chief Inspector from Hendon Road and he wanted him to unlock the door. He reached for his keys.

As soon the door was open, Marenko rushed into the cell. DeBruin sat up, off guard, and yes, just for that moment, looking a little bit scared. But I've only just got started, Marenko thought.

He grabbed him by the throat and held him against the wall. His knee took him in the groin, and as he doubled over his fist crunched into his body just over his heart. DeBruin would have fallen, but Marenko held him upright with one beefy paw and smashed two more shots into his ribs.

The custody sergeant grabbed him and tried to pull him away. Then James ran in and together they hauled Marenko out of the cell.

'Guv, what the hell are you doing?' James shouted at him.

'I'll have to report this. It's assault,' the custody sergeant said.

'Don't be a prat all your life,' James told him. 'That scrote put his son-in-law in hospital!'

He could almost hear the gears clunking in the sergeant's head. 'I have to report it!'

'You do that,' James hissed, 'and you might as well find yourself another job.'

'He's going to tell his brief!'

'And you're going to fucking deny it!'

James stared him down. The custody sergeant looked at Marenko, who had his back against the wall, letting James hold him there. He was breathing hard.

'He's done twenty-seven years in the force. You're not going to fuck up his pension, are you?'

'He could have killed him!'

'But he didn't, did he?'

The custody sergeant thought about it, then went back into the cell. James heard him shouting at DeBruin, who was demanding a doctor. *You were asleep and you fell off your bunk. There's nothing wrong with you.*

He came out, locking the cell door. He stared hard at James. 'If he's hurt him—'

'He hardly touched him!'

'Get him out of here!'

James hauled Marenko down the corridor.

Marenko sat in his office staring at the London skyline. The overcast was breaking up and the sun was sinking down the sky, behind a dusty veil of orange and violet cirrus. Nothing like pollutants and toxins to put on a show. A pigeon strutted on the sill, peering at him with small and startled eyes.

The door opened and Fox walked in, breaking his reverie.

'Guv,' she said. 'What are you doing here?'

'Just thinking.'

She sat down. Marenko stared at her.

'Well?' he asked her.

'We have a witness,' she said.

'I'm listening.'

'A thirteen-year-old girl was looking out of her bedroom window. She saw Tom O'Neill pursue two men into the alley off Crossland Walk. She can positively identify one of those men as Michael DeBruin.'

'But she didn't see the assault?'

Fox shook her head.

'DeBruin's trainers came back positive for blood.'

Marenko shook his head wearily. 'How did this happen, Fox?'

'Only Tom can really tell us that.'

'Don't rely on him as a witness. It looks like he won't be able to tell you anything.'

It was what Fox had feared. For a moment neither of them spoke, and then she said: 'The way I see it, he caught DeBruin, tried to make the arrest. His cuffs were found lying a few feet from his body. Perhaps what happened was the other one, Thompson, realised it was a blind alley, started running back. DeBruin called out for help. Two against one, a scuffle, Tom goes down. Or maybe it was the other way round. DeBruin came back to help Thompson. Whatever. In the scuffle Tom pulled the balaclava off DeBruin's face.'

'How do you figure that?'

'The girl saw DeBruin in the streetlight. He went back into the alley, came back holding something. Must have been the balaclava. In the security video from the store, they both had their faces covered.'

'DeBruin went *back*?'

'She says he was there up to a minute and she heard . . . noises.'

Marenko's face went blank.

'He grabbed the balaclava, Tom was just lying there, he decided it was too tempting a target. And that's when the kicking started.'

Marenko turned back to the window. Fox wondered what he was thinking. James had already warned her that Tom was likely to be permanently brain-damaged. The doctors didn't think it was just one or two kicks. O'Neill had been stamped on, with force, and his head then crushed against the brick wall.

Marenko looked at her, his eyes grey and cold. 'Did James tell you what happened?'

Fox decided to lie. 'When?'

'This afternoon. At the Islington lockup.'

Lying was so easy. It was why interrogations were difficult. 'No, he didn't.'

Marenko stood up. 'I'd better be getting home. Or maybe I'll stop off at the King's Head. It's all yours till I get back. Don't fuck it up.' He stopped at the door. 'Where's this other scrote? What's his name?'

'Thompson. Paul Thompson.'

'Have you got him?'

'Not yet.'

'Better find him, Fox. I'll tell you now, nothing can give you grief like an invisible man.'

Chapter Forty

'I was fuckin' assaulted,' DeBruin yelled as soon as the tape was turned on and the interview under way. 'A big fuckin' copper with grey hair. He fuckin' assaulted me.' He held up his shirt so that Fox and James could see the bruises on his ribs. 'And he kneed me in the balls.'

'We don't want to see those, thanks,' James said.

'He was fuckin' there,' DeBruin shouted, pointing at James. 'He fuckin' saw it!'

James shook his head. 'I saw Custody Sergeant Thorpe and Detective Chief Inspector Marenko trying to restrain you. You were extremely aggressive. Custody Sergeant Thorpe told me you were throwing yourself around your cell.'

'That's a fuckin' lie! What do you fuckin' expect? All you fuckin' filth stick together!'

Fox waited until he had finished. 'If you wish to make a complaint, I will send someone down from internal investigation to take down your statement. Meanwhile I would like to continue with the interview. Do you realise the seriousness of the charges that may be laid against you?'

DeBruin leaned back in the chair, arms folded, legs splayed.

'Would you like to tell us what happened the night of the ram raid on Brightwell's?' James asked him.

DeBruin stared back through lidded eyes. 'Ain't got jack shit to say to you.'

'OK,' Fox said. 'We'll just go ahead and charge you then.'

'With what?'

'With the assault on PC O'Neill. Which may yet become a murder charge.'

'You can't fuckin' put that on me.'

'We have a witness, Michael. We have a witness who knows you, and who saw you being pursued by PC O'Neill shortly after the break in, and who is willing to testify in court. Do you know what happened to that police officer, Michael?'

'I don't give a shit about no fuckin' copper.'

Fox clenched her fists below the table. 'Whoever assaulted him kicked him in the head repeatedly, long after he was unconscious. They licked him so may times that he's now permanently brain damaged.'

'How can they tell?'

A long, cold moment. Fox heard the uniformed constable standing by the door suck in his breath. The muscles rippled in James' jaw.

'So I'm just going to go ahead and charge you, Michael.'

'It wasn't fuckin' me.' He looked at Fox, then at James. A flash of cunning appeared in his eyes, overlaid the contempt and belligerence. 'Your witness say they saw me do it?'

Fox said nothing. DeBruin's month split into a grin. There was a large gap between his front teeth. It should have been a disarming feature.

'You don't have jack shit.'

'Michael Joel DeBruin, I am charging you with resisting arrest and assaulting a police officer causing grievous bodily harm. I must warm you . . .'

'It was Paul Thompson.'

'You are stating that Paul Thompson is guilty of the assault on PC O'Neill?'

'Yeah, that's what I fuckin' said.'

'You are willing to testify to this in court?'

'Maybe.'

'Perhaps you'd better give us a statement,' James said.

'I want a solicitor first.'

'If Thompson assaulted PC O'Neill, why did you go back into the alley?'

'I said I want my fuckin' brief.'

Fox stood up. She leaned towards DeBruin, her fists on the table. Other threats, other acts filtered through her mind, phantoms of the revenge she would like to take on behalf of Frank Marenko, on behalf of the young man breathing through a respirator in the Royal London Hospital.

DeBruin met her stare.

'Interview suspended 6.43 p.m. Get him his brief,' she said to James and walked out of the room.

PART FOUR

Hendon Road.
A wet evening in late summer

Chapter Forty-one

Eight months and nothing. Nothing at all on Kate Mercer.

The case remained open, but there was nothing to be done and nowhere to go with it. The photographs that had filled the pinboards of the Incident Room the previous December with such terrible urgency had been filed away, along with the witness statements and pathology reports. The coroner had released the body in March and she had been buried in a private, family ceremony. Her twisted, tortured body had become a statistic, a memory now pushed aside by the detectives who had worked on the case.

On this wet and sticky summer evening, with the rain on the windows warping the lights of the city, turning the glass a kaleidoscope of refracted light, Fox sat alone at her desk, under the humming fluorescent lights, and stared at the rain-smudged pages of her notebook, the scrawled notes and crime-scene diagram she had committed to paper that cold, wet night.

It had always been a case on overload, she thought. She was convinced that somewhere in the morass of information they had obtained lay the one fact they had all overlooked, the one piece of evidence, the vital correlation, that would tie the case together.

The night cleaner came in, silently emptied the waste baskets and moved off.

Fox sipped coffee from a polystyrene cup, bitter and cold and foul. There was a dull pain behind her eyes. Without effort she was able to summon the images captured that night by the Home Office photographer in absolute detail; a dark lane, a child, lying on the ground like an abandoned doll, her eyes, half-lidded, staring in dull incomprehension at the camera flashlight. She tried to recapture the same feeling of rage that had almost overwhelmed her that night, groping in the darker places of herself for her emotions like a man at a foreign airport fumbling in his jacket for a lost passport, or a child ransacking a bedroom for a favourite toy. But it was gone, that outrage, and she felt that its passing had diminished her. Even Kate Mercer was something she had become inured to, and all that was left was a career professional faced with a personal failure and as yet unable to accept it.

Perhaps even that dull acceptance would come too, in time.

Marenko had laid it out for her. 'You're no bloody good to me going stamping about the place like you got PMT. Is that what you want? Is that what you think it's all about?'

'She was eleven years old, guv.'

'You didn't do it, Fox. You're not on our list of suspects. And you're not here to cry about it. If you're going to be a woman about this, you can walk right now.'

And he was right. The split in Kate Mercer's anus, that was evidence. The ligature marks on an eleven-year-old girl's wrists, that was evidence too. It was the job. You weren't priest or philosopher, and you weren't, God forbid, judge and jury. In the end it came down to what Marenko had said. *If you're going to be a woman about this, you can walk right now.*

She remembered when she was sixteen her father had given her a Rubik's cube for Christmas. She had spent all of Christmas Day and Boxing Day with the damned thing in her hands, fiddling with it, long after it had ceased to amuse her brothers and sisters. When she finally solved the puzzle, she immediately threw the toy in the bin. She felt that same cold determination now, brought to the mystery of Kate Mercer that same fierce and venomous concentration. She would crack this, find the one salient detail they had missed, open it up again, succeed where Marenko had failed. She wanted to do it for Kate Mercer. But also it was a matter of professional pride. Find the monster who did this and she would finally be accepted. She would no longer be a woman in a man's job, she would be Marenko's equal.

And so she had taken to worrying it, like a dog with a dead rabbit, muzzling it endlessly, turning it over, wanting it to spring back to life so she could chase after it again.

She had found James in the canteen one day.

'Hey, TJ,' she had said, 'the Katherine Mercer murder. You remember talking to the bloke who thought he saw a black saloon come out of the alley about 3 a.m.?'

He had stared at her with the wearied look of the veteran, the cynic, though in truth she had twelve months' longer service than him. His jaw fell open, revealing well-masticated sausage and chips. 'For fuck's sake, ma'am,' he had said, 'get a life.'

Get a life. What life? These days she went home only to sleep. There were no dates, no boyfriends, no lovers. Her membership of the health club had lapsed. Even her cat had left home. Perhaps it had been run over; more likely it had found a neighbour who kept more regular hours and was more forthcoming with food and milk.

She was losing weight. She was living on a diet of takeaway food, eaten hurriedly at her desk, pickles squeezing out of hamburgers and dropping on to witness statements, fried chicken stains on the corners of black and white crime-scene photographs, coffee rings on the corners of manila files. It was the Madeleine Fox Thirty-Day Plan, patent pending. You, too, can lose half a stone in weight and look like hell.

What had they missed in the Mercer case? What?

'We didn't miss fuck all,' Marenko had told her. 'We know who did it and we can't prove it. Welcome to the world of criminal investigation.'

They had spoken to the Candy Man's relatives, his two

former wives. *He has a problem with women,* one of them had said. *I don't know how to put it. But he was never gentle. Know what I mean?*

They spoke to another girl who had once worked for him in the sweet shop. She said he made her feel uneasy. He had never actually done anything, she said. But still, he was . . . creepy.

On its own, it was nothing, just another piece that slotted perfectly into the rest of the puzzle, another accusing finger pointing unerringly at the Candy Man. But not enough for the CPS.

What had they missed? What?

A spark, a spark of pure rage. He wondered how long that spark had been inside him, how long it had lain there dormant, waiting its moment. He had seen a lot in his twenty-seven years, wives lying battered on kitchen floors, young children with bodies covered in cigarette burns courtesy of their alcoholic mothers. But then one day he went to work and there was a young child lying strangled in an alleyway and the hot wind blew across the embers in his gut and he heard the distant crackle of flame. Then came Flora Ellis, murdered while her son slept in the next room, and then Tom, his head pulped while he lay unconscious; and the slow burn became a firestorm.

Marenko smashed his fist against the tiled wall of the lavatory.

He didn't hate the people who came through here. He treated most of them with indifference; the ugly, the arrogant, the stupid, the venal, it was all the same to him. He did his job and at night he went home and listened to his jazz records.

But for the first time he found he could not walk away from what he had seen and what he had heard. He had had twenty-seven years of police work, twenty-seven years of violence and briefs and stupid juries and lenient judges and career criminals and decrepit laws, and suddenly, almost overnight, it was too much.

So that night, instead of driving home, or walking over the road to the King's Head, he parked his brown Sierra outside the sweet shop on the corner of MacNaghten Row.

It was past 8 o'clock but it was still light. It was getting towards the end of summer, and the air in the city smelled of diesel and warm garbage. Marenko could smell his own sweat. Summer in the city left a haze over everything, air like a noxious gas with a taste and stink of its own.

An ice-cream van trailed past, wailing a painful rendition of 'Greensleeves'. There was a sign on the back of the van: MIND THAT CHILD. He looked across the junction at the newsagent's. The *Evening Standard* hoardings lined up in rows: a murder suicide in Kent; a divorced father of three had shot his wife and his kids before turning the gun on himself. Christ, Marenko thought. The world was top heavy with misery.

He turned away and stood with his hands in the pockets of his trousers and stared at the sweet shop. One of the windows was boarded up. To Marenko's knowledge there had been four separate incidents of vandalism on the shop since Kate Mercer's death. He didn't know how Henry Wexxler survived; none of the locals would allow their children to go into the shop any more. He had virtually no customers from one day to the next.

But he would not sell up, would not move out of the area. He faced the hostility of his neighbours with the same stoic passivity which he had brought to his interrogations at the station house in Islington.

What had they all missed? Where the hell was their crime scene?

Marenko stood there, looking around, trying to get the walls to speak to him. *What happened here?* He saw a curtain move at an upstairs window and saw the Candy Man staring down at him, watching. But he didn't come down, didn't say *What the fuck are you doing out there?* as any other civilian would do. He didn't shout, *Go fuck yourself, copper, I don't hurt little girls.* He just turned away from the window, and Marenko saw the ghostly blue flickering of a television set behind the curtains.

He waited another quarter of an hour for the Candy Man to come down, but he didn't, and so finally Marenko got back in his car and drove away.

He wondered who was toying with who.

He and Fox fed each other's obsession. It became a silent conspiracy between them: this case will not die. They never spoke about it to each other, for that would have broken the spell and they would have been forced to admit that the Candy Man had made them both a little crazy.

Finally it was Fox who came to him, who ended it. She had found their ace in the hole.

There was a pile of faxes and print-outs in Fox's in-tray, the pile growing higher every day. Marenko glanced at them from time to time but had not commented. But he had taken note of the direction of Fox's enquiry; case files from unsolved murders for the entire Liverpool area from 1983 to 1989, as well as every missing child report logged in that time. In the mornings, when he started his shift, at nights, when he left to go home, she was there, staring at the computer screen or reading through the files, empty polystyrene coffee cups piling up around her.

One day when he got in to the office, she brought him a cup of coffee and presented him with a Danish she had bought earlier that morning from the bakery across the road – something she did only when she was in a particularly good mood – and then sat down opposite him, her eyes shining. 'I've got something,' she said.

He tried the Danish. Not bad. And the coffee was hot. 'Shoot.'

'Henry Wexxler moved to London from Liverpool eight years ago. He lived in Everton for six years from 1983 to 1989.'

'OK.'

'I've been checking through the files on record, every missing person report of young girls in the Liverpool area in that period as well as unsolved child murders, rapes, molestations.'

'And?'

Fox produced a file with a flourish and laid a grainy faxed copy of a photograph on his desk. 'This is from the missing persons file on Caroline Lisa Stewart, aged ten and a half. Went missing in March of 1983. Has never been found. She lived two streets away from where Wexxler used to own . . . wait for it . . . a sweet shop.'

Marenko stared at the photograph, smudged with Fox's fingerprint. His face betrayed no emotion. 'Get the original sent down,' he said. 'I'll talk to Radford. Then we'll have one more crack at him.'

Chapter Forty-two

The tape recorder emitted a high-pitched beep and Marenko started talking. 'This is a recorded interview. I am Detective Chief Inspector Frank Marenko. Also present is Chief Superintendent James Radford, Detective Inspector Madeleine Fox and Mr George Layton, solicitor. We are situated in Room 4A at Kentish Town police station.'

Marenko turned to the Candy Man. 'Would you please state your full name, your address and your date of birth.'

'Henry Lincoln Wexxler, 48 MacNaghten Row, Islington. I was born on the fifth of December 1943.'

Marenko looked at Layton. 'Mr Layton, your client has not been arrested at this stage but is here of his own free will to answer questions and assist us in the investigation into the murder of Katherine Mercer on the fifteenth of December last year.'

And then they went in to it again. This time Marenko asked him where he had lived in Liverpool, how long he had lived there, about the sweet shop he had owned in Everton.

George Layton interrupted. 'Inspector, may I ask where this is leading?'

At that point Radford took over. 'Your client is helping us with our enquiries,' he said.

'Into the murder of Katherine Mercer?'

'That's correct.'

'You have uncovered new evidence?'

'Possibly.'

Layton glanced at his watch in irritation.

'When did you last see Katherine Mercer?' Radford asked him.

'When?' Henry Wexxler echoed.

'Yes, when?'

'I saw her lots of times.'

George Layton shook his head. 'Superintendent, I believe my client cooperated fully with you in the past. He answered that question to the best of his ability in your initial investigation.'

'I want him to tell me again.'

Layton turned to Henry Wexxler. 'You don't have to answer this. It's harassment.'

'I don't remember,' Henry Wexxler said.

'Try. Humour me, Henry.'

'On the Wednesday.'

'She was murdered on the Tuesday night.'

'I don't remember. Tuesday. She came in to buy sweets.'

A moment of stillness. The second time he had contradicted himself. The first time he had said she had not been in his shop that day, the second time he said he could not remember. Had he been lying then because he was frightened of putting himself too close to the dead girl and implicating himself? Or was he confused now and willing to say anything, give them any answer he thought they wanted?

'When we asked you about this in December,' Fox said, her voice deceptively gentle, 'you said you didn't remember her coming into your shop that afternoon.'

The Candy Man looked at her, then back at the other detectives. Then he looked up at the wall clock. He's going to say it, she thought, he's going to say what he always says when we corner him. But not this time. This time the Candy Man looked Fox right in the eye and said: 'I don't remember.'

Layton shook his head in exasperation. 'Is my client supposed to have a better memory of those events today than he did eight months ago, directly after this poor girl's murder?'

Radford reached into the folder on the table in front of him. This was their best shot. Fox and Marenko had convinced themselves it would tell them what they needed to know. They would look in his eyes and they would know if the Candy Man killed little Kate Mercer.

Radford removed the black and white photograph from the folder, his hand across it like a schoolboy in an exam, not wanting his neighbour to cheat. Then he suddenly flicked the photograph around, a gambler producing his ace. 'Remember her, Henry?'

A face like stone.

'Remember her? Caroline Lisa Stewart. She was ten years old.'

For a moment Fox watched the Candy Man disassemble in front of her. The mask slipped away, and she saw his lip tremble. He gripped the edge of the table as if he was afraid he was going to slip and fall. The moment lasted just a few seconds, long enough for Fox to be sure. But then, just as abruptly, Henry Wexxler remade himself, and his features returned to their former placid indifference.

'She's pretty,' he said.

Radford folded his hands. He appeared relaxed, but his knuckles were white. 'What did you do to her, Henry?'

The solicitor started to object. 'My client—'

Radford immediately changed tack. 'Do you remember her, Henry?'

The Candy Man sat there, his face set like cement.

'Come on, Henry. You owned a sweet shop in Everton two hundred yards from where she lived. You never ever saw her in eight years?'

He was gone, Fox thought, the man with the stained underwear and the bad breath, the dull-eyed monster they had found the day after Kate Mercer had died. The endless repetitions of 'What time is it?' had been a ruse, had thrown them as effectively as any lie. What she saw now was the eye of the devil, cunning and bright and intelligent. She thought for a moment he was going to smile.

'I don't remember,' he said.

Marenko leaned forward. Frustrated that Radford had decided to take over this final interrogation, he had been sitting there, stewing, ever since the interview began, and now he was red-faced and ready to explode. 'What did you do, Henry? Did you do the same things to her you did to Kate Mercer?'

'Inspector!' Layton almost shouted.

'They even look alike, don't they? Is that what gets you hot, Henry?'

'Inspector Marenko!' Layton was on his feet.

'Did you kill her like you killed Kate Mercer?'

There was a long and deathly silence.

The Candy Man looked up at George Layton, who was staring at Marenko, white-lipped with outrage. 'What time is it?' he said.

And Madeleine Fox knew. She had looked into those flecked brown eyes and she had seen the truth for herself. Henry Wexxler was a monster. And he was going to go free.

Chapter Forty-three

'Madeleine?'

This time she recognised the voice. 'Simon.'

'How are you?'

'Fine. How are things with you?'

'Fine.'

The small talk out of the way, Fox tapped on the edge of the desk with her pen and waited.

'Wonder if you could do me a favour. Well, it's more Sandy really.'

She hesitated. 'What kind of favour?' she heard herself say.

'She has this project for school. She has to interview someone, someone she admires. Apparently her father wasn't ever in the race. She wants to interview you.'

'Me?' Fox felt unreasonably flattered. 'Why me?'

'She thinks you're the coolest woman I've ever taken out – her words – and it seems I am on a par with the sloth and the green tree frog on the evolutionary scale for the way I treated you. I'm inclined to agree with her.'

'Is that an apology?'

'Yes.'

Another silence.

'So. Will you do it?'

Fox thought about it. On the debit side she didn't want to

continue any sort of relationship with Dr Simon Andrews, never mind the boyish good looks and the gorgeous body. On the plus side there was the tantalising promise of hero worship, something she had never experienced before.

'What time do you want me to come over?' she said.

This time they got their times right. Simon was waiting for her, wearing a faded blue denim shirt and tan slacks. He was shaved and groomed for her arrival. She detected the aroma of aftershave as he greeted her, and she wondered, not for the first time, if this so-called interview was not just an elaborate charade to arrange another date with her.

He led her inside and asked her if she wanted a drink. She specified black coffee. As he filled the kettle, Sandy appeared in the kitchen doorway, her school folder under one arm.

'Hello, Madeleine,' she grinned.

'Sandy.'

'Thanks for coming over. This is so cool.' She hopped on to a bar stool at the kitchen bench. 'It's for my English exams. It's twenty per cent of my end-of-year marks.'

'OK. Well, I'm flattered you asked me.'

Sandy flipped open her folder. 'Can I ask you anything I want?'

Simon shot her a warning glance.

'Almost anything,' Fox said.

'What made you join the police force?'

Fox looked at Simon, who smiled reassuringly at her over the rim of his coffee cup. 'I always had a highly developed sense of justice, I suppose. My father said that when I was a kid, my favourite expression was: "But that's not fair". I'm an idealist. I want to leave the world a better place than I found it. That sounds pompous, doesn't it?'

'No, that's cool,' Sandy said.

Fox looked at the cassette recorder. Sandy had left it on the breakfast bar between them, recording. She realised she enjoyed this much better when she was the one asking questions. 'Also, I could never imagine myself doing a desk job. Which is funny when you think how many hours I now spend doing paperwork. Plus, I thought I would be good at it. My father didn't like the idea much, but I went ahead anyway.'

The obvious question about fathers and their opinions hung in the air, unasked. Sandy seemed to think about it but then returned her attention to her notebook, where she had her questions neatly written out. 'Have you ever shot anyone?'

Fox smiled. 'No, police detectives in Britain don't carry guns as a rule. Not yet, anyway. If we have to arrest someone and we think they're going to be armed we call in a specially trained firearms squad.'

'Do you enjoy arresting people?'

'I don't enjoy it, as such. I mean, I don't enjoy being a bully or anything. But I mean I enjoy . . . I enjoy finding someone who did something wrong and being able to prove it. As I said, I'm an idealist. I'd like to think that people can't get away with hurting other people or stealing from them without being made to answer for it.'

Sandy barely waited for her to finish. 'What is the most interesting case you've ever worked on?'

'Oh, well, I'd have to think about that. There have been a lot.' She almost launched into a long explanation about a serial rapist they caught because he was an AB secreter and they finally trapped him with a DNA match on his sperm, but then decided that might be a little too explicit for a thirteen-year-old girl, even in the 1990s. So instead she told her about a murder investigation she had worked on as a detective constable in which forensics had cross-matched a print of a trainer found at the crime scene with a pair of Reeboks hidden in the wardrobe of a suspect they picked up for routine questioning. They then matched a flake of blood on the shoe with that of the victim and were able to lay charges.

She didn't tell her that when the case went to court the accused's barrister managed to convince the judge there had been irregularities in the chain of evidence and had their killer thrown back on the streets of London, where fifteen months later he bludgeoned to death a nineteen-year-old girlfriend with a base-ball bat.

Sandy returned to her carefully prepared list of questions. 'Why aren't you married?' she said.

Simon almost choked on his coffee. 'You don't have to answer that,' he said to her. He took his daughter's folder off her lap. 'What else have you got in there? Did no one ever teach you any manners?'

There were several more questions, of varying degrees of scrutiny; how many people she had locked up, how much she earned a year, what she would do if she wasn't a detective. Fox tried to explain patiently that she did not keep count of how many arrests she had made, that she earned more than a schoolteacher but much less than a doctor, and that if she wasn't a detective she would probably work in a hospital emergency ward, like Sandy's father, because the work was so much easier and the hours so much better, which brought a smile from Simon.

'Last question. How many people have you beaten up?'

'Sandy!' Simon said.

'I'm curious.'

'End of interview,' Fox said smiling, and snapped off the tape.

He walked her to the door. 'Thanks for coming round.'

'Happy to. I'm usually the one who gets to ask all the

questions. It was a novel experience being on the receiving end.'

'She thinks you're a pretty amazing person.' He hesitated and she waited a long moment for him to say what else was on his mind. 'So do I.'

She stared at him. Excuse me? She saw a silver-framed photograph on the hall table and she picked it up, giving herself time to think. It was Simon with Sandy and a woman she did not recognise, smiling, fresh-faced and beautiful.

'Is this your wife?'

'Her name was Anne,' he said.

'She was very beautiful.'

He gently took the photograph from her hand and set it back on the hall table. 'And she's gone,' he said.

'I'll see you around.' She turned for the door.

'Madeleine.'

She looked around, her face turned up towards him.

'Thanks,' he said.

And then he leaned forward and kissed her, briefly. It was nothing, a brush of the lips really. But she practically threw herself out of the door.

Carrie sat in reception like a schoolgirl outside the headmistress's office. She was wearing dark jeans and a shirt, and her best grey cotton jacket, the only one in her wardrobe without milk stains on the shoulder. The bright lit foyer was hung with industry awards, both to impress and to intimidate, Fox imagined, and busy men and women in power suits hurried to and from the chrome lift bank. Carrie started to bite a nail and then, realising what she was doing, hid her badly chewed nails behind her shoulder bag.

Fox leaned forward and smiled at her reassuringly. After all, that was what she was here for. Moral support. Carrie had been out of the business for a long time. Now Daisy went to nursery and Carrie was back at the bottom of the ladder, hopefully looking upwards.

Trying to take her mind off the upcoming interview, Fox said: 'I saw Simon again last night.'

'The doctor?'

She nodded.

'You sleep with him?'

'As if.'

'What happened?'

'His daughter was doing a project on weird and unnatural people, so naturally she decided to talk to a female CID detective. I went around to help her with her homework, basically.'

'And?'

'That was all.'

'That was all?'

'Yes. That was all.'

'So why did you tell me about it?'

'Just making small talk.'

'You like him, don't you?'

Fox stared at the three-foot-high photograph of one of the station announcers, mounted and framed. Ego City. 'It's impossible.'

'Nothing's impossible. Me getting this job, maybe. But you and a doctor. No, that's a green light.'

'You don't know him.'

'Introduce me. *I'll* sleep with him. How much does he make a year?'

'Be serious.'

'I'm a single mother, thirty-two years old with no career prospects and no fingernails. What makes you think I'm not serious?'

Fox forced a smile.

'What are you going to do? Are you going to see him again?'

Just then the receptionist put down the telephone and said: 'Miss Kennedy, Mr Regan will see you now.'

When Carrie came out half an hour later with a job as one of the station's news reporters the question had been forgotten. Which was just as well, for Fox still didn't know the answer.

Chapter Forty-four

The spectator gallery at court number one in the Old Bailey was full, the tourists and the regulars competing for the few seats with Tom's friends and family as well as half a dozen off-duty uniforms from Holmes Road. DeBruin's two brothers were there too, in their designer tracksuits and too much jewellery, eye-fucking Marenko.

Marenko watched the jury file in. Three West Indians, not a good sign. Of course, racial prejudice would not influence the decision of a jury in a serious court case. As it had not affected the verdict in the O.J. Simpson trial in America.

From where he sat Marenko could not see Fox, but he knew she was there, sitting behind the prosecuting counsel, along with James, as officer in the case. The defendant sat in the dock, facing the royal coat of arms and the High Court judge in his red sash. DeBruin had been kitted out with a well-tailored suit and a white shirt. Doesn't work, Marenko thought. He still looks like a gorilla in a penguin suit. He wondered who was going to be fooled by this pretence of the civilised man. The street gangster showed through in every little movement; the way he glared at the jury, even tried to stare down the judge.

One of the jury members, a young black girl, barely out of her teens, was watching DeBruin with a strange look on her face, excitement and fear and fascination, like he was a dangerous animal in a zoo. It seemed at least one member of the jury was mesmerised by the aura of menace emanating from the dock. No doubt she was wondering what Michael DeBruin looked like naked.

Julia O'Neill was wearing dark glasses when she walked into the courtroom, so Marenko could not see her eyes, could not tell if they were wet. He would have bet a year's salary they weren't. He knew his daughter. She would not have given anyone the satisfaction. She had her head held high, and she walked slowly, the broken thing in the wheelchair in front of her a source of defiant pride.

Oh, Tom, Marenko thought.

It was already hard to remember that this same Tom O'Neill was a young man who had once played rugby and basketball and squash, six foot two inches of bone and muscle with a ready smile and a handshake like a vice. Better off dead, were the words that kept echoing around Marenko's mind. The dead have dignity, they have headstones and obituaries and legends that are larger than life. Saliva doesn't leak from the side of their mouths, their wasted legs aren't covered with blankets, their eyes aren't glassy and don't roll in their heads.

Julia had dressed him in his best suit, blue serge with a muted grey silk tie. His black shoes were polished like glass. She had got a special dispensation to sit at the back of the court because of Tom's disability.

For a moment everyone in the courtroom and the spectator gallery turned their heads and stared. Even DeBruin turned around. Jules took off her sunglasses and looked him right in the eye, a look of pure venom.

He smiled back.

Because of her age Dianna Richardson's testimony was taken in camera and the videotape replayed in the courtroom. 'My name is Dianna Richardson. I live at 213 Anderson Way, Kentish Town.'

The prosecuting counsel, Dipak Patel, took her through it slowly, going through the usual establishing questions, where she went to school, how old she was, to get her used to speaking and answering. Then he went back to the events of that night in February that had reduced a uniformed constable to the wreck sitting in the wheelchair at the back of the court.

'What were you doing at the window, Dianna?'

'I couldn't sleep. I was awake, reading a TV magazine. I heard shouts in the street, and I got up to have a look what was happening.'

'What time was this?'

'Ten to three. I remember, I was listening to the radio. The DJ had just read out the time.'

'What did you see when you went to the window?'

Haltingly, Dianna repeated everything she had told Fox. The uniformed constable chasing the two men into the alleyway. The sound of a fight. The two men reappearing, one of them going back. Seeing his face in the light of the streetlamp.

'Would you know that man if you saw him again?' Patel asked her gently.

'Yes, I would,' she said.

'But it was dark,' Patel said, anticipating the defence. 'He was at least thirty yards away.'

'I'd know him anywhere. He hangs around our way a lot. They call him Tuffy, but his name's Michael. Michael DeBruin.'

The barrister appointed to defend Michael DeBruin was one Anthony James Ryder. Marenko remembered him from when he first arrived at chambers, dewy-eyed and pink-cheeked, the worst and best of the breed, an idealist. Susan had nicknamed him Crusader Rabbit. Under that wig there was a little grey in his hair, but Ryder was still a True Believer; he believed all policemen were stupid and corrupt.

Marenko hated him so much at the moment it made his bones ache.

Ryder's cross-examination was gentle. No judge would allow him to savage pre-pubescent girls. They left that for the men they were trying to defend, Marenko thought sourly. 'Miss Richardson, why did you not go to the police with this information straight away?'

'I did.'

'But according to my records your father did not contact the Incident Room at Hendon Road police station until early the next morning. In the interim, police had visited your house on two occasions asking for information. Is that not correct?'

Dianna looked panicked. 'I was scared.'

'Scared? Of what?'

'He's got a reputation around our street. You know.'

'Is it not true, though, Dianna,' Ryder went on, his voice soft, almost hypnotic, 'that you actually went to the police at the prompting of your father?'

'He told me I had to.'

Ryder nodded. 'He told you that you had to,' he repeated. 'Thank you, Miss Richardson. That will be all.'

The tape ended.

Chapter Forty-five

The prosecuting counsel laid out his case. Dr Charles Fenwick from the Metropolitan Police Forensic Science Laboratories testified that they had found blood on a pair of Reebok running shoes that had been recovered from Michael DeBruin's flat. That blood had since been cross-matched with that of PC O'Neill.

Vincent Barnes made a brief appearance to testify that he had driven the vehicle on the night of the ram raid, and that Michael DeBruin and Paul Thompson had been his accomplices. But he contradicted his earlier statements. Thompson had been the brains behind the job, he said. He and DeBruin just went along with it.

O'Neill's partner that night, PC Davis, also gave his testimony. He kept his eyes averted throughout. Marenko had heard he was thinking of leaving the force and had applied for a job with the London Fire Brigade.

Through the proceedings, Marenko kept his eye on the jury. There were seven men and five women and there was a strong racial mix. Three of them were black and two of them Asian. A young red-headed girl just kept staring at Tom with a wet tissue in her hand. There was a middle-aged white man with spectacles, who looked like an accountant and who was forever taking notes. Marenko doubted he would be very sympathetic to a man like

DeBruin. On the debit side the young black girl in the front row stared at the accused like he was Eddie Murphy.

He didn't have much time for the jury system. In the end you just measured one man's prejudice against another's.

Then it was the turn of the defence.

DeBruin lounged in the dock, a curious arrangement, like a pulpit with a plywood roof, as if the architect had expected it to rain in Old Bailey court number one. DeBruin was long and lithe, the suit hanging loose and alien on his frame, like the clothes had just fallen on him from the sky. He looked uncomfortable, as if even he was surprised at how they had got there.

Ryder took him through the events of that night. Yes, he had been involved in the ram raid, he said. He admitted that. But no one was supposed to get hurt. When the police had arrived, they had run. One of the constables had chased them into an alleyway.

'What happened then?' Ryder asked him in a tone of gentle concern, as if this was a predicament not of DeBruin's own making.

'I tripped, dint I? Next fing I knew this copper was pulling me hands behind me back and telling me he was arresting me. I thought, oh, well, that's it, then. It's all over.'

'You did not resist arrest?'

DeBruin looked sideways at the jury. 'Nah, I didn't fink there was any point.'

Ryder waited a moment, letting this declaration settle.

'What happened then, Michael?' Michael. As if this was a man you could talk to and reason with, a man you could like and respect.

'Then Paul came running back down the alley.'

'Paul Thompson,' Ryder said, and he glanced at the jury. He wanted them to remember that name.

Paul 'Tiny' Thompson.

Marenko knew what DeBruin was going to say. It had been

obvious from the start. What he had told Fox right at the beginning of the investigation had proved prophetic: *nothing can give you grief like an invisible man.*

In fact, they did not find Paul Thompson for three long months. They put photokits in national newspapers and on television, they launched a nationwide search, but Tiny had vanished. There were rumours that he was in Dublin; his friends said he had run back to Kingston.

He eventually turned up in Moss Side, Manchester, discovered propped against the wall of a warehouse by the nightwatchman, a needle hanging from his forearm and a tourniquet around his upper arm. The coroner's verdict was unequivocal. He had died from an overdose of seventy per cent pure heroin. There were no suspicious circumstances.

It was bad luck for Tiny but good luck for Michael DeBruin, because now Paul wasn't around to contradict his evidence. The dead man didn't care if he had the vicious assault of a police officer laid at his door. Nothing mattered to him any more.

'And what did Paul Thompson do when he came back down the alley and saw PC O'Neill arresting you?'

'He started in on the copper.'

Ryder looked perplexed, as if he was unfamiliar with the language of the street. 'Started in?'

'Kickin' him and that. He wouldn't stop. I yelled at him, tried to pull him away. But he wouldn't. He went crazy.'

'You pulled him away?'

'I thought he was gonna kill him. I mean, I don't love the Old Bill, and that, but I was scared.'

'What happened after you pulled him away from PC O'Neill?'

'We ran off.'

'You ran off. Out of the alleyway.'

'I pushed him in front of me and we ran, yeah.'

'But Dianna Richardson says she saw you go back into the alleyway.'

DeBruin glanced at the jury. 'I went back to see if the copper was all right. I was really panicked and everyfin'. But he was just lyin' there, making this gurglin' noise. I dint know what to do. Then I heard Paul shouting at me, so then I just ran. I was real scared, like.'

'Dianna Richardson said she heard other noises after you went back into the alley.'

'I reckon she made that bit up,' DeBruin said. 'Her old man's got it in for me.' He grinned at the black faces in the jury. They would know what he meant.

Marenko felt his fists tighten on the bench in front of him. You miserable little cunt, Marenko thought. A nice performance, you should get an Oscar. Tiny Thompson was half Tom's size. There was no way he could have done that to him. You're the one with the form for GBH. But the jury didn't know that, and under British law they would not be told.

After the incident in Crossland Walk they ran to DeBruin's flat where Thompson changed out of his clothes. Then he said he was going to try to get a cab on Brecknock Road. That was the last DeBruin saw of him.

DeBruin corroborated Barnes's characterisation of Thompson as the one who had planned the ram raid. That was why the stolen articles were found at the house he rented with Vincent Barnes.

Thompson had recruited him in the pub, he said. He hadn't even known which shop they were going to target until the night of the break-in.

Ryder sat down and the prosecuting counsel got to his feet and started the cross. But Marenko couldn't stand to sit there and listen to any more. He saw where this was going.

He stood up and walked out of the gallery.

Chapter Forty-six

Marenko stood on the corner of Anderson Way, staring at the vandalised telephone box, the graffiti on the walls, the empty alleyway. He kicked at an empty beer can. He imagined a cold February night, the blue strobes of the patrol cars, the ambulance sirens, the dark pooling of blood on the bitumen, the crackle of police radios. But today, in the daylight, it was just another drab London street smelling of dog shit. Impossible to think of it as the same malevolent place where Jules and Tom lost their future and their dreams.

A greasy sweat had erupted all over his body. He felt it soak into his shirt, stinging his eyes, making his head itch. The seamless summer afternoon followed him down the alleyway, fetid and breathless.

Why had he come here, what was he looking for?

He stared at the silent eyes of the windows in the attic roofs, listening to the barking of a dog in the next street, searching the dark tiles and the brown brick walls for what? Inspiration? Some unearthly glimpse into the past that would resurrect the events of that night and make them clearer? To see some sense in it all?

A warm wind blew down the alley, shuffling the loose rubbish, the empty crisp packets and ice-cream wrappers. This was where twenty-seven years of police work had led him, this dead end in Kentish Town, mute testimony to his own inadequacies, his own failure. But no, not just his own failures; the failures of the system, the system that had hogtied them all to the extent where a cold-blooded killer of little girls could walk the streets with impunity, and a man could order the murder of a widowed mother to save his own neck and thumb his nose at retribution.

As he walked out of the alley he tried once again to work out the odds for justice for Tom O'Neill. The outcome that Marenko didn't even want to think about was that DeBruin would walk. Paul Thompson's ghost hung over the case like a spectre, making an acquittal very possible.

Christ.

A young black man in a hooded sweatshirt and jeans was coming down the street towards him, his fists in the short pockets of his sweatshirt. Marenko stared at him, imagined Michael DeBruin in that same roll and swagger.

'What you looking at, granddad?' the boy growled at him.

'Just keep walking, shithead,' Marenko said.

The young man stopped. 'What you say to me?'

Marenko moved too quickly for the young man to react. He slammed his elbow in the kid's throat, turned him and pinned him to the wall. Oh, stop, a voice screamed in Marenko's head. This has nothing to do with this kid. This is not Michael DeBruin.

'I'm, not your granddad,' he growled. 'I'm a detective chief inspector, so have a bit of respect.'

The young man's eyes grew wide. 'OK, OK, man,' he said. 'Chill out.'

'Get out of here before I book you for disturbing the peace,' Marenko hissed and released him.

The young man staggered a few paces, clutching his throat. Then he straightened, shrugged his shoulders and put his street attitude back in place. 'Filth,' he spat and sauntered off.

A nice bit of community policing, Marenko thought. Christ, what's happening to me?

✳   ✳   ✳

Marenko was back in the Old Bailey the next afternoon, though he had promised himself he would stay away, was there to see Terry Richardson take the stand and change the course of trial. Terry Richardson, who had slept right through the whole thing, and who did not claim to have seen or heard anything. But it was his evidence that did them in.

'Mr Richardson,' Ryder said, and he stared at him for a moment, like a vulture surveying its next meal. He took in the leather jacket and the tie, the greasy hair trailing over the collar, the tattoo on the back of the right hand. They betrayed him somehow. 'Mr Richardson.'

The prosecuting counsel got slowly to his feet. 'M'lord, is my learned friend going to ask a question? We have established that this is indeed Mr Richardson. We do not contest it.'

A ripple of laughter among the jury. The judge told Ryder to get on with it. Ryder nodded in acknowledgement, taking the rebuke in good part and, apparently, in good humour.

'I shan't detain you for long . . . Mr Richardson.' More polite laughter around the courtroom, the first since the trial began. Ryder played up to it. 'You must be a busy man. Just a couple of questions.' Richardson smiled uneasily.

'Do you know the defendant?'

'Yeah, I know him.'

'How are you acquainted with Mr DeBruin?'

'From around the neighbourhood. You know?'

'Well, I'm not sure I do know. The two of you are . . . friends?'

'Not fu . . . not likely.'

'Not likely. Why is that not likely.?'

Richardson gritted his teeth. Marenko felt his insides turn to ice. Here it comes. 'We don't mix in the same circles,' Richardson said.

Ryder feigned puzzlement. Then he brightened, understanding vouchsafed. 'Ah, you mean — you are of different racial backgrounds.'

Richardson was looking increasingly uncomfortable. 'Yeah.'

'But you do know the defendant?'

Richardson wiped his hands on his trousers and leaned on the rail. 'He's got a reputation round the place. He thinks he's hard. Know what I mean?'

Ryder frowned, as if this didn't sound at all like the Michael DeBruin he knew. 'Is it true he had an . . . altercation . . . with your son . . . a few weeks before the incident in which Constable O'Neill was injured?'

'He had a what?'

'A fight.'

'He might have. So?'

Ryder raised an eyebrow, amused. 'I'll ask the questions, thank you. And what was the—'

Patel leaped to his feet. 'M'lord, I must object. Is any of this relevant?'

The judge looked at Ryder.

'M'lord, I believe the veracity of Dianna Richardson's evidence should be tested against the prior relationship that existed between the Richardson family and my client.'

The judge sighed. 'Carry on. But don't labour it.'

'Thank you, M'lord.' He turned back to Richardson. 'Is it true that your son got into a fight with the defendant, that your son sustained numerous cuts and bruises—'

'Cuts and bruises? He broke his fu . . . he broke his nose!'

'Quite. Is it not also true that afterwards you threatened to get even with him?'

Richardson hesitated.

'Is that not true, Mr Richardson?'

'I might have said that, yeah. In the heat of the moment.'

'And it was you that suggested your thirteen-year-old daughter go to the police the night after the brutal assault on this policeman?'

'That's right.'

'Did you try to influence her evidence in any way?'

'No!'

'I believe you, Mr Richardson.' He smiled and looked over his spectacles at the jury.

'I did not tell my daughter to purge herself!'

Ryder looked back at Richardson, delighted. 'Perjure, Mr Richardson. Purge is something that one does to one's bowels.'

The court reporters were laughing.

Richardson looked up at the judge, his face white with anger. He pointed at DeBruin. 'You're not going to let that black bastard get away with this?'

That black bastard. Marenko looked over at the jury. Christ Almighty. Suddenly, in the minds of the jury, the whole case had been painted as a private feud between a bigot and a black man. Ryder sat down, smiling and well satisfied.

Chapter Forty-seven

Prosecuting councel rose to give his final address to the jury.

This is more than just a crime, he began. This is an attack on the very fabric of our society. When a policeman is killed or maimed, then we are looking down the maw of anarchy.

Marenko stared at the faces of the jury. The white woman was still crying. The other eleven faces were impassive.

Patel summarised his case and once again begged the jury for a guilty verdict. He finished with an emotional personal address. 'Michael DeBruin is attempting to save himself by foisting the blame for this callous crime on the head of a dead man. A man with no record of violence, a man eight inches shorter and three stone lighter than the man he is alleged to have reduced to this state.'

He indicated Tom in his wheelchair at the back of the courtroom.

'A young police officer's life has been destroyed. Even if this man were not a police officer, it would be a tragedy. A senseless, brutal, evil act.

'Michael DeBruin is a liar. He lied to the police when he was first arrested, when he claimed he knew nothing of the crimes of which he is now charged. It was only when he was faced with a witness and forensic evidence that he decided to turn on his supposed friend and try to make him responsible for this horrific assault. Unfortunately, Paul Thompson is not here today to refute this lie.

'If PC O'Neill was able to talk, if his memory was still intact, if he could communicate in any way, I am sure he would tell us what happened that night. I am sure he would say that he captured Michael DeBruin and that DeBruin called out for assistance and Paul Thompson returned to help him. In the unequal struggle that followed, DeBruin succeeded in wrenching away PC O'Neill's baton and knocking him to the ground. But then, instead of choosing to escape, he used that same baton to batter the young policeman senseless.' He slapped his fist into his palm several times for effect. 'But that was not enough.' There was a long silence and an unearthly hush in the courtroom. 'Having left the alleyway, he then returned and stamped on the unconscious policeman's head several times. He then kicked his head against the wall with pitiless force. As if it was no more than a football.'

He looked each member of the jury in the eye.

'PC O'Neill pursued DeBruin and Thompson into that alleyway with reckless disregard for his own safety. He was doing his duty to you, the community. He did not let you down. Do not let *him* down. And tell me this. If you do not find the defendant guilty, as charged, can any of us go home tonight and sleep safe in our beds?'

Patel sat down, his magazine empty. Several of the jurors glanced at DeBruin, who was staring straight ahead, his face impassive. Marenko sensed it then, sensed they had won. It didn't matter about Paul Thompson. They had done enough.

Julia looked up from her position at the back of the courtroom and stared at Marenko. He tried to force a smile.

She stared back at him, her hatred undisguised.

Ryder got to his feet, fussing with his gown, and clasped his hands in front of him. 'Ladies and gentlemen of the jury,' he said, in a tone that suggested that each of them was fit for a position on the High Court, 'what has happened here is clearly a tragedy.

When any life is destroyed in such a way, there is no question but our hearts go out in sympathy, not only to the victim, but to the victim's family.'

Ryder paused to look around at the lolling head on the wheelchair and to take in Julia, eight months pregnant, her face set in stone, a tragic mural of despair. Marenko imagined that Ryder would indeed have lost a lot of sleep over Julia. The image of this tragic young madonna figure would perhaps turn the jury more eloquently than the ghost of Paul 'Tiny' Thompson.

'When something like this happens, our impulse is to look for revenge, to find a scapegoat for our fury. That is natural enough. But the danger is, ladies and gentlemen, that in looking for that scapegoat we become parties to another tragedy.'

You shit, Marenko thought, watching him. You don't know the meaning of tragedy. It's just your standard speech. You don't give one good damn about Tom, you don't know Jules's grief, you don't know . . .

'The tragedy is that we will take revenge on the wrong man. As sorry as we may feel for Tom and Julia O'Neill and their family, we cannot take away their pain by punishing the innocent.'

Marenko's hands balled into fists on the wooden bench in front of him.

Ryder outlined his case. Yes, Dianna Richardson had seen Michael DeBruin and Paul Thompson come out of the alleyway. What she said corresponded exactly to Michael's own testimony, but what she saw was open to interpretation. Terry Richardson had thought that the defendant had gone back to inflict further injuries on PC O'Neill. Could he not have gone back out of human compassion?

Marenko glanced sideways at James and Honeywell. They all sat stone-faced. Compassion. Hard to imagine such an emotion ever resided in Tuffy DeBruin.

Ryder did not dwell on the racial aspect of the case. Half the jury were white and he did not want to offeend them. But he did point out that DeBruin was a black man and it was hard for a black man to find justice in a white-dominated society. The police wanted a scapegoat for the injury to one of their own. Unfortunately, the real perpetrator, Paul Thompson, was dead, and so Michael DeBruin was to be that scapegoat.

'Ladies and gentlemen of the jury,' Ryder said, 'my client has pleaded guilty to the charges relating to the so-called ram raid on the electrical store. But as for the assault on PC O'Neill, you have to be satisfied *beyond* all reasonable doubt that he was guilty of this terrible attack on a policeman going about his lawful duty. The prosecution's case is clearly unproven, and I believe you have no choice but to find Michael DeBruin innocent.'

He sat down and smiled reassuringly over at DeBruin, to add weight to his performance, to try to persuade the jury that he liked this man, that he, too, was convinced of his innocence, that a great wrong had been done.

Trouble was, Marenko thought, it was all shit.

Chapter Forty-eight

Julia and Susan decided to wait it out in the public house across the road from the court. They found a table in a corner under an old framed Guinness ad, a toucan with a pint of stout balanced on its beak.

At least it tries to look like a pub, Marenko thought. There was an oak bar with a brass footrail, and gilt mirrors on the dark panelled walls. There were more framed advertisements around the walls: Kilkenny Beer, Murphy's Irish stout. There was a collection of old bottles in glass cupboards above the bar, as well as pewter tankards and old flagons.

Julia and Tom were joined, briefly, by some of Tom's former colleagues, from Holmes Road. Several of them attempted to shake Tom's hand, but he could not respond; his hand was limp and dropped back into his lap like cold meat. Julia clutched his other hand while his head lolled against the headrest of the wheelchair, his eyes staring vacantly towards one corner of the bar. Every once in a while she would take a paper tissue from her bag and dab dutifully at the saliva that pooled in the corner of his mouth. Susan sat on the other side, her arm around her daughter.

Tom's sisters, Leah and Rachel, sat a little apart, their eyes red from weeping, two young women looking as lost and bewildered as kids at a bus station. Donna sat with them.

Marenko ordered a double whisky at the bar.

One of the constables recognised him and came over. 'I'm sorry, guv,' he said, his voice a whisper. They might have been at an undertaker's.

'Part of the job,' Marenko said, like this was not his son-in-law they were talking about.

'They'll nail this black bastard. He's going away.'

'You think so?'

'It can't go any other way.'

Marenko nodded but said nothing. The young constable had the manner of a man who had to believe, who couldn't endure the thought that it could be otherwise. Marenko patted him lightly on the shoulder. 'When are you on duty again?'

He looked at his watch. 'I'm on late turn. I have to be getting back now.'

'Thanks for coming.'

He hesitated. Marenko knew he had something he wanted to get off his chest, but he wished he'd just leave it. 'He was . . . he was going to be a good cop.'

Marenko nodded. Yeah, right. Was.

He stared at Julia, hoping she would look up, offer him the vindication of even a glance. But nothing. Susan noticed his stare and came over. 'Why don't you leave, Frank?' she whispered. 'There's nothing you can do.'

'I can see this through,' Marenko said. Damned if he was going home.

He started over to where his family was sitting. Susan put a hand on his arm. 'Don't,' she said.

He pushed her hand away and walked over. Julia stared up at him with a mixture of surprise and hostility. 'You're still here.'

'Where else would I be?'

'Mum said you'd stay,' she repeated.

Marenko fought the tightness in his chest and his throat. 'It wasn't my fault, Jules,' he said.

'No.'

'You do believe that.'

Julia got up and tried to push past him. 'I need to go to the Ladies.'

'Please, Jules.'

She spun around. 'It's too late for that now! Don't come to me for absolution! I gave everything to the police force. When I was a child I gave it you. When I got married I gave it my husband. And now my son—' She put a hand to her belly. Her lower lip trembled and her voice sounded as if it would break. He took a step towards her. That was enough. It gave her the strength to recover. 'Don't. Don't come near me.'

Marenko held out his hands helplessly. He knew people were staring. That he should care about that. 'I'm sorry,' he mumbled.

'You can't take any of it back, Daddy,' she whispered. 'It's done. You can't make any of it better.'

Julia turned and hurried away.

Marenko left his whisky and stumbled outside into the street. He walked blindly, towards Ludgate Hill, found a newsagent's and went in and bought a packet of cigarettes. To hell with living a long and healthy life. Who needs it? He stood at the kerb, staring at the traffic, the black taxi cabs, the red buses. It crossed his mind to step out. No, he thought, not until I've put all this right.

He looked at his watch. The jury would be back soon. He gave them an hour at the outside. He started walking back, quickly, towards the great stone edifice of the Central Criminal Court. He looked up at the façade as he crossed Old Bailey. Funny, he had never noticed that before. He read: *Defend the children of the poor and punish the wrongdoer.*

If only.

Marenko watched the faces of the jury as they filed back into the courtroom. The white girl with the tissues crumpled in her fist was weeping openly.

It was late afternoon. The lights had been turned on in the

corridors. The jury had been out for almost five hours. What had taken them so long? The judge had warned them that if they did not reach a decision, he would have them sequestered overnight.

Five hours.

The clerk of the court got to his feet. 'Foreman of the jury, have you reached a unanimous verdict on the charge of attempted murder of a police officer in the course of his duty?'

'We have, sir.'

'And what say you to that charge?'

'We find the defendant not guilty.'

Marenko felt his gut turn to ice. DeBruin's brothers whooped and exchanged high fives. Marenko could not stand to watch, could not look at Tom or Jules or Susan, any of them. He stumbled outside into the corridor. He couldn't think, couldn't breathe.

Marenko was waiting for Patel as he hurried across the Great Hall, under the blue mosaics and lunettes of the dome.

'Patel?'

He was a tall man, balding under the legal wig. He wore spectacles and a perpetually harassed expression that gave him the look of an overworked post office clerk. His assistant trailed behind him, carrying his files. When he saw Marenko his face creased into a frown. 'Go home, Frank.'

'What happened? What happened in there?' He trailed after him like a beggar. 'How could they do that?'

Patel stopped and turned around. 'Frank, please, not now.'

'Just tell me what went wrong,' Marenko said softly.

He sighed. 'What it came down to in the end was DeBruin's word against a dead man's. I told your DI she had to find this Paul Thompson. Then we might have had a chance. Terry Richardson's testimony was a disaster.'

Marenko did not seem to be listening. 'How could they let him go?' he said.

Patel rubbed at his forehead with his fingers, the wig at a crazy angle on his head. 'While I was doing my cross of DeBruin the judge had to tell the bailiff to nudge one of the jurors awake. Some of them were bored by the whole thing, Frank.'

Marenko knew he shouldn't feel surprised. Twelve good men and true. Christ, where would you find that many in London these days?

Patel shrugged. He, too, looked weary to his soul. 'I'm sorry, Frank, I truly am. I did my best.'

Marenko watched him stride away.

And that was that.

Chapter Forty-nine

They held the wake at the King's Head. There was James, Honeywell, Rankin, every detective on Marenko's squad had the news within half an hour and had assembled over the road in the bar in a show of solidarity with their boss. Hell, none of them knew Tom, but he was a cop, and the verdict was a direct challenge to everything they stood for and believed in. They crowded round the bar and slapped their money on the polished oak counter and the drinks were lined up for Frank Marenko and together they damned everyone who had let them down, from the judge to the barristers to the bastards on the jury and every scrote in North London.

A few uniforms from Holmes Road were there too, even Davis, who was leaning on the bar, crying drunk, while the others slapped him on the back and told him it was none of his fault. Thirteen years a copper and this was what it came down to.

'He'll be out of the force within a year,' Honeywell said. 'If he doesn't jump, someone'll push him.'

'It wasn't his fault,' Marenko said.

'Why did it take him so long to find Tom?' James said, and this was really where the whole story began and ended. No one could explain it. Perhaps even Davis himself didn't know.

None of them saw Fox push her way through the crowd.

Suddenly she was beside them, throwing her money on the bar and lining up another round.

'Fox,' Marenko said.

'Life is shit,' she said.

The others watched Marenko, taking their cue from the big man. When she had first arrived at Hendon Road as their new DI they had resented taking orders from a woman. But she had proved herself capable in the last few months, and they wondered what Marenko would do now.

'Thanks for coming,' he said.

Fox ignored him. 'I'm sorry about what happened today.'

Marenko shrugged. 'Shit happens.'

'I still can't believe it.'

'The system sucks. Whether you're Joe Citizen or a cop, the system sucks. There's no such thing as justice in Britain any more. There's just fucking smart-mouth barristers and idiot juries who don't give a shit about us.' He snatched a packet of Benson and Hedges off the counter and put a cigarette in his mouth.

'You going to smoke that, guv?' Fox said.

'Yes, Foxy, I *am* going to smoke it. Today I don't give one brass shite about emphysema or lung cancer or myocardial fucking infarction. My son-in-law is a vegetable, and the guy who did it just winked at me in the courtroom. I am going to smoke this cigarette and suck every carcinogen in this damn thing into my lungs and I don't give a fuck any more.'

Fox snatched the packet out of his hand.

She shook one of the cigarettes into her palm and put it between her lips. 'Think I'll join you, then,' she said.

By the time Henry called last orders, those detectives who still remained had been in the bar for three or four hours. Through the evening the others had drifted away to their homes and families in the suburbs. The Tom O'Neill story would become just another tale in that long litany of injustice with which to regale their families and their friends when they drank too many pints at the pub.

The last ones to stagger out into the street were DCI Marenko, DC Honeywell, DS James and one DI Madeleine Fox. They went looking for more action in Soho, went to a club where Marenko's face was known and the doorman let them jump the queue and waved them through without paying. They stayed there drinking spirits until two o'clock in the morning, when they all squeezed into Fox's Vauxhall Cavalier, took out the two six-packs of Young's Bitter they had stashed in the boot and drove along High Holborn towards Smithfield Market. Fox turned off Holborn Circus and parked the car under a viaduct near one of the locked gates. The four detectives drank some more, sending the empty beer cans clattering on to the cobbles and cursing at the street people who stumbled past.

'You sure can hold your booze,' Marenko said to Fox.

'That's a compliment, coming from you.'

James laughed. 'You're a real unit, Foxy. Hey, guv, you should have seen her that afternoon we got Barnes. He called her a cow so she put some sort of martial arts hold on him and made him cry till he said he was sorry. You're a piece of work.'

'For a woman.'

'I never said that.'

'You thought it.'

He grinned. 'But I never said it.'

Fox shivered. It was cold out here; summer was nearly over. She saw huddled shapes in the arches of the viaducts, the homeless curled up for warmth under pieces of cardboard. England, my England. There was the pervading stench of urine. James tossed a can at a stray tabby, sent it scuttling away into the darkness.

'This country's going down the toilet,' Marenko said. 'Am I the only one who can see how fucked up this place is getting?' Fox waited but today there was no sardonic 'Excuse my French.'

For better or worse, she was one of the boys now. Language and all.

'No one gives a shit about anyone any more,' Honeywell said. 'Even the crims are changing. Once, if you had a shooter, you were really hard. Now every Yardie and dealer in North London packs an automatic. The new Britain! Too many people, too many housing estates, too many drugs.'

Marenko drained another can and crushed the aluminium in his fist. He threw it against one of the brick pillars. 'I wish that was DeBruin's head,' Marenko said.

'Or his bollocks,' James said.

'What will he get for his part of the ram raid? Three months? Six? He'll do his bird then he'll be strutting around the parish telling everyone how he done over a copper and got away with it.'

'Fucking bastard,' James said. 'He won't be walking around much longer.'

It was an idle threat, Fox thought. But then Marenko said: 'Maybe we should fix him up ourselves.' He peeled the tab off another can.

'Steady, guv,' Fox said.

'If the law won't give my little girl justice, then it's up to me.'

James and Honeywell were suddenly very quiet. He doesn't mean it, Fox thought. It's just the beer talking. 'You're not the law, guv.'

'No, but I ought to be.'

There was something in the way he said it that sent a chill up her spine. This wasn't the kind of conversation she wanted to be having at three in the morning, below a brick archway in the black heart of the city. 'It's time we went home,' she said.

'I knew it, Fox,' Marenko said.

'Knew what?'

'You don't have it. In here.' He hit his chest with his fist.

'You're foul and you're drunk.'

Honeywell sent another can rattling across the cobblestones. 'She's right, guv. Time to go.'

'Wouldn't it be something,' Marenko was saying, 'if I knocked him off, and I got to be the chief investigating officer on the case. The perfect crime.'

Fox looked at James, but she couldn't see his face in the darkness. Somewhere a siren wailed in the night, a dirge, for the city.

'Listen,' Marenko said, 'they're playing our song.'

Chapter Fifty

The sun rose in a dirty yellow haze over London. Marenko
negotiated the back streets in his battered brown Sierra, concentrating hard, wondering if it was worth his job and his
pension to drive this drunk and deciding he didn't really care. At
this time of the morning the city belonged to the street cleaners
and delivery trucks and the derelicts who selected their breakfast
menu from the rubbish bins.

He drove up Haverstock Hill towards Hampstead, turned on
to side roads just past the Royal Free. A few minutes later he
pulled on to the gravel drive of a terraced Victorian villa. As he
got out of the car he could smell the heath, wet grass and
decaying leaves. He breathed in the fresh air, cold and dew-
damp. His head started to spin. Jesus Christ. He had one hell of a
hangover coming.

Stone steps led up to a whitewashed portico. Marenko
stabbed at the buzzer, twice, three times. Finally he heard
footsteps in the hall and a voice on the other side of the door,
sounding frightened. 'Who is it?'

'One of Patrick Capper's victims. I've come back to haunt
you.'

'What? Who is this?'

'For Christ's sake. It's me, Frank.'

'Frank? It's half-past five in the morning.'

'Got a beer?'

The door swung open. 'You're drunk,' she said.

'Legless,' Marenko said and stumbled inside.

Susan had had the place remodelled after she'd bought it. It was an architect's wet dream: teak cupboards, slate floors, Italian ceramic, Florentine carpets. A black marble figure with a hole in its belly stood on a pedestal in the hallway. Art, apparently. There was a small garden at the foot of the stairs with a fountain at the centre. I've got water under the stairs in my place too, Marenko thought. It's called rising damp.

Susan was wearing a white silk dressing gown that shimmered as she walked. My angel of mercy, he thought. She led him to the kitchen and took two china cups from a smoked-glass cabinet.

Marenko looked around. The kitchen, he decided, was about as big as his living room. It was panelled in red cedar, and the bench tops were a display of almost every East Asian technological marvel: food processors, mixers, two microwaves. A one-woman energy crisis, Marenko thought sourly.

French windows looked out over the narrow but immaculately manicured garden.

'Got anything to drink?' Marenko said.

'Coffee,' Susan told him, spooning two heaped teaspoons in a cup and putting it in the microwave.

'Too poor to own a kettle?'

'Frank, it's half-past five. You didn't get me up to spar with you, I hope?'

Marenko shrugged and sagged against the refrigerator.

'Have you been drinking all night?'

'Not all night. I think I stopped about four. So technically—'

'Shut up,' Susan said.

Frank rubbed a hand across his face. 'How's Jules?'

'She's tough.'

'I know she's tough,' Marenko said, suddenly angry. 'But that's not what I'm asking.'

'I don't know, Frank. I don't know.'

'She blames me.'

'Yes, she does.'

'It's not fair, Susan.'

Susan shrugged. 'I know it.' The microwave chimed softly and Susan took out the coffee and handed it to him. 'You look like hell.'

'I'm nearly fifty years old. What does it matter?'

'Come and sit down.'

Marenko followed her through to the conservatory and slumped into one of the wicker armchairs. The sun was inching over the plane trees, throwing dappled yellow light through the windows. Susan crossed her legs and studied him with that look of pity and confusion that he knew so well.

'What's brown and looks good on a black man?'

'I don't know.'

'A German shepherd.'

'That's not funny.'

'Depends on your point of view.' He affected a lopsided grin. 'Let's review the day. We sure got DeBruin for the ram raid. He turned my son-in-law into a vegetable, but tomorrow that judge will teach him not to steal television sets.'

'Let it go, Frank. It's over.'

'It's not over, Susan. It's not.'

Susan was quiet for a long time. 'You're not going to do anything stupid, are you?'

'Like what? Like carry on as if nothing has happened?' Suddenly Marenko was angry again. His rage revived him, and he went with it. 'Why me, Susan? Why does she hate me? Why not you? It was one of your legal fraternity that got him off the hook! That stunt he pulled with Terry Richardson. It had nothing to do with anything!'

'He is entitled to challenge the credibility of any witness . . .'

Marenko ignored her. 'Do any of you people ever think about whether the bloke you're defending is innocent or guilty? Do any of you fucking *care* whether you're an accomplice to murder? Because that's what it is, Susan, every time you let one of these scrotes walk away from it, you're as guilty as they are.'

Susan stood up. 'What's this about, Frank? Is this about me, or Julia, or Tom, or DeBruin, or what? What is this about?'

'It's about everything. It's about why we can't get justice in this country any more! It's about everything coming apart!'

'Please, Frank, spare me the big speech. I've heard it a thousand times. Life's hard, then you die. Grow up.'

'Hey, that was your daughter in the courtroom today. Is that all you can say? *Life's hard?*'

'What do you want from me, Frank? You think I didn't want to put my hands around that bastard's neck myself? But once we start thinking like that, we go back to the jungle. The jury said he was innocent. No one can actually prove he did it. That's the law, *that's* what keeps this society from coming apart. There's nothing else we can do.'

'The law? The law's fucked! The law doesn't protect us any more! You think society works? You live in Hampstead! You're living in a fucking architect-designed bunker. You don't know what goes on in the real world.'

'I see the real world every day in court, Frank.'

'No, you don't. You see case loads and points of law and chain of evidence irregularities! You've got your head so far up your own arse you can't see daylight!'

'Is this why you came here, Frank? You want a fight, a shouting match? It's only just dawn. If that's what you want, you carry on alone. I'm going back to bed.'

She stood up and headed for the bedroom.

'No, wait,' Marenko said quickly. 'It's not you.'

Susan sensed the change in his mood and hesitated. After a moment she sat down. 'What is it, Frank?'

Marenko studied the carpet. 'What am I going to do about Jules?'

'There's nothing you can do. Maybe she'll come round.'

'You don't believe that.'

She shook her head. No, she didn't. 'Too much muddied water under the bridge now. What happened to Tom was . . . well, it was you who persuaded Tom to join.'

'Tom wanted to join.'

'He looked up to you. You were his hero. She blames you for that.'

Marenko spread his hands helplessly. What was he supposed to have done? Tom hated being a salesman. He had all the hallmarks of a cop. But Marenko had never canvassed him to apply for the police. Tom had his own mind. It was Tom who decided. How could she blame him for that?

'You lost her a long time ago, Frank. You can't bond with a child after twenty-four years of neglect.'

'I didn't neglect her, Susan.'

'She spent her childhood competing with the Metropolitan Police for your attention. And she lost. Yeah, Frank, it is a kind of neglect. Hey, Radford loves you. What more do you want?'

Marenko bit down on that one. They weren't talking about Jules any more, he realised. They were talking around some of Susan's hurt as well. Yeah, OK, he had been wrong. He thought his family understood that police work wasn't a nine to five thing. It had cost him his marriage. For him and Susan it was too late. He just couldn't accept that was true for him and Jules as well.

He closed his eyes, and the drink suddenly hit him and the anger drained out of him through his shoes. The trouble was, he didn't believe in any of it any more. Being a policeman had been the way he had defined himself for twenty-seven years. Now he felt as if he had been duped. He wasn't on the side of the angels after all. The devil had made him the court jester. He had been laughing behind his back all along.

'I'll make it up to her,' he mumbled.

A few moments later he was asleep.

Susan watched him. His jaw hung slack, his suit was crumpled, his thinning grey hair mussed. He was asleep, sitting upright, the coffee cup still clenched in his right fist. He looked like a statue, a war memorial.

The Old Cop. By Rodin.

She remembered all those years she had lain awake waiting for him to come home, fearing for him; during the Brixton and Broadwater Farm Estate riots in 1985, when that poor constable had been hacked to death; in 1987 at Wapping, when he had been one of the hundred and sixty-three policemen injured helping Margaret Thatcher and Rupert Murdoch get their way. They said he would have gone further if he'd been on the square. But he had never wanted to be a desk driver; he always wanted to be out there, where the action was, rather than get home at a decent hour and be with his family.

She got up and gently untwined the coffee cup from his fingers and left him. She went back to bed. When she got up a couple of hours later he had gone.

Chapter Fifty-one

He took her to Provençe, a French place in Richmond. Expensive. She had thought they were going Italian and just had on an M&S blouse and a cream skirt. She looked around at the heavy crimson velvet drapes on the windows, the plush banquettes, the yellow sconces on the walls, the scented candles. She felt underdressed and she wished he'd warned her.

'Like it?' he said, smiling.

'Great,' she said. I should have worn my black number. I feel like a lump in this.

He grinned at her. 'I made sure we got the non-smoking section. Just in case.'

Now he was smart-mouthing her. Oh, well. She deserved it. 'Watch what you say or I'll order the lobster,' she said.

The thing about her clothes put her in a sour mood. Their talk was desultory, and she could tell that he was bewildered and disappointed. It took a bottle of wine to straighten her out and mellow her. He told her a long story about something that had happened to him at the hospital, a prisoner who had been brought from Pentonville complaining of severe abdominal pain. While he was waiting to be examined he had eluded the guard who had escorted him and evaded the consequent search by hospital security by climbing into the crawl space in the roof. He was finally discovered half an hour later when the ceiling collapsed under his weight and he landed on a cardiac patient in the emergency room in a shower of dust and polystyrene tiles.

'You made that up.'

'It's true. Didn't you hear about it? Happened a couple of months ago. They managed to keep it out of the papers. The guy on the table died. Well, he probably would have died anyway, but it didn't help when that happened.'

'What about the prisoner?'

'Displaced patella.'

She gave him a quizzical look.

'Threw his knee,' he said.

The coffees arrived and he ordered two cognacs. She finally felt herself relax. Simon's eyes seemed to float in the candlelight. *I must have drunk more red wine than I thought.*

'Tell me something,' he asked her. 'Do you get lonely?'

'Living on my own?'

'Being a woman in a man's world.'

She blinked at him, surprised. 'Is it a man's world?'

'I was referring to the police force.'

'There are a number of women in the police force now.'

'Sure. How many are detective inspectors?'

She shrugged, taking his point. 'It's OK if you have tendencies to be a loner. Which I have.'

'I imagine the other detectives give you a hard time.'

'I give as good as I get. The worst thing is not being able to talk to other women outside the job. I always found it hard to make small talk anyway. But with this job . . . if I've spent all day on a murder-rape, I'm not much in the mood to talk about food or shopping or whatever. I certainly don't want to talk about men.'

'I suppose I know what you mean. About having normal conversations after hours.'

'Do you?'

'Sure. Ask me about my day.'

'How was your day?'

'I had a man come in with a dead cat attached to his person.'

Fox idly stirred sugar into her black coffee. 'How am I supposed to respond to that?'

'You see? I do understand what it's like.'

'A dead cat,' she said slowly.

'He had affixed himself to it in the search for sexual gratification. Its name was Cleo, by the way. Now Cleo, or any female cat for that matter, is not constructed to receive the sexual advances of an adult male *Homo sapiens* and died of internal injuries shortly after penetration. The cat's muscles then went into rigor and the man was unable to remove Cleo from his male appendage. So he put on an overcoat and visited us at the A&E and asked us to perform a . . . catectomy. Have I shocked you?'

'I'm not sure. Was it *his* cat?'

Simon laughed. 'You see. I couldn't imagine telling that story to anyone outside the medical profession, except a police detective. You people are shockproof.'

'No, you're wrong, I *am* shocked. I'm just not surprised. Nothing people do surprises me any more. When I was a DC in Kingston I was called to a shopping centre car park to investigate the death of a six-week-old baby. Hottest summer day for ten years. The mother had left it locked in a car, with all the windows up, for three hours while she went shopping. She couldn't understand what she'd done wrong.' She sipped her coffee. 'I was shocked by that. But I wasn't surprised. People are endlessly stupid and endlessly cruel.'

He gave her a crooked smile. 'You see what fun we'd have over the dinner table at night.'

'Yes, but I don't think it would be very good for your daughter to hear all this.' She leaned back in her chair. 'Is that an offer, by the way?'

'Do you want it to be?'

'I don't know. I don't think I've ever had anyone try to seduce me with stories of men violating cats. It's an unusual technique.'

The waiter arrived with the cognacs. I shouldn't be drinking this, she thought. I have to drive home tonight. I think.

'Can I ask you a personal question?'

'As long as it doesn't involve cats.'

'Why didn't you ever marry?'

'I don't know. I had one long-term relationship. It was like a marriage. I just never had the piece of paper to go with it. Or the hen party. I was with David for seven years. We always meant to get around to it.'

'The hen party?'

'The wedding.'

'So you did want to?'

She nodded. 'Not at first. I think he did. He would have liked kids, a greenhouse in the garden, nosy neighbours, the full monty. As it turned out I made the right choice. I'd still have the kids and he'd still be gone.'

'What stopped you?'

'I just wasn't ready.' She smiled. 'I have this thing about commitment.'

'That's novel.'

'You mean, for a woman?' She shrugged. 'I don't deny it's a dilemma. Sometimes I hear the biological clock ticking away and I get panic attacks. And then I think about getting married and having children and that brings me out in sweats as well. I'm what you would call a career woman. Half the prejudice in the force is because men suspect you're going to get broody. And when I think about walking into the DCI and asking for maternity leave I can hear them all sniggering behind my back saying: "I told you so." '

'Is that a good reason not to have children if you want them?'

'When I find a man who's willing to stay home and have the babies and let me go out to work, I'll marry him.'

'And you won't regret it? In ten years' time?'

'Whatever decision I make I'm going to regret. I know that. That's why it's called a dilemma.'

He smiled again. 'So what happened to him?'

'My old boyfriend?' She smiled. 'He married a model eleven years younger than I was. Traded up. She was in season, too, which must have pleased him no end. I hear she's pregnant.'

In season, she thought. Did I say that? Boy, that sounded bitter. She felt her cheeks burn with embarrassment and she looked away. The waiter broke the tension by removing the cheeseboard. They sat in silence for a while, Fox staring at the candle while Simon toyed with his coffee spoon. The *vin triste*, as the French called it.

'What about you?' she said finally. 'You must have been young when you had Sandy.'

'Sandy was a mistake. At the time I thought my life was over. I was at university studying medicine, Anne was doing nursing training. It wasn't as if we weren't careful. She was on the pill.'

'Where there's a womb, there's a way.'

He laughed at that. 'Where did you hear that?'

'I went to a girls' school. Our teacher said it in our sex-education class. She'd be delighted to know how it's burned itself into my memory. I think she wanted us all to be virgins until we got married. No, make that until we died. She was a frustrated spinster herself. That's the sort of talent Catholics look for to teach sex ed.'

'Anne was Catholic too. That's why we didn't . . . terminate.'

'So Sandy came along.'

'So Sandy came along. Anne dropped out of nursing and I studied medicine until three in the morning with an anatomy textbook cradled in one arm and Sandy cradled in the other. When she was a year old we persuaded Anne's parents to look after her during the day while Anne finished training. And we got through.'

'But you didn't have any more kids?'

'We decided to wait until Anne had qualified. As soon as she had the piece of paper she went off the pill and we waited for her to get pregnant again. And she never did. Life's funny.'

'Yes,' Fox said. 'A real riot.'

'Still, for a time we thought we were cruising. We had our lives all mapped out.'

She waited for him to finish the story but he didn't. He stared off into space, the thousand-yard stare she had seen before on the faces of the wives and husbands and mothers and fathers waiting outside hospital A&Es or in police interview rooms trying to make sense of senseless tragedy.

She thought of taking his hand, but it seemed like such an irrevocable step. So she waited and then said: 'What happened, Simon?'

His face was blank, a practised look devoid of all emotion. 'She was driving home from work late one night. By then she was a nursing sister. She was working at a hospital about five miles away, in Leicester. A car went through a stop sign at sixty miles an hour and ploughed into the driver's side door. The police say she died instantly. I hope so.'

There was a catch in his throat. He paused and drank the rest of his coffee.

'The boy driving the car was eighteen years old and he was drunk. He was also driving without a licence, which he'd lost on a previous drink-driving charge. He walked away from the smash with a few cuts and scratches. I think the judge sentenced him to two years. He was out after nine months.'

Fox waited, wondering if there was more.

'That's it, really,' he said after a while.

'You must be very angry.'

'What's the point of being angry? It doesn't change anything.'

'Did you ever speak to him? The driver?'

'I saw him in court. What can you say to someone like that? He looked—' He shrugged his shoulders. 'He just looked so ordinary. But I suppose what happened was ordinary. I see casualties from road trauma all the time. What happened to Anne and me was an everyday event.'

It sounded right, but when she looked in his eyes she could see the contradictions. There was a frenetic stillness to him and a tremor in his hands when he spoke. Rage was stalking around behind those ice-blue eyes, looking for somewhere to go.

Chapter Fifty-two

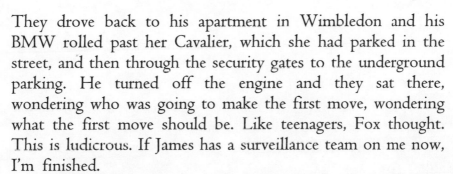

They drove back to his apartment in Wimbledon and his BMW rolled past her Cavalier, which she had parked in the street, and then through the security gates to the underground parking. He turned off the engine and they sat there, wondering who was going to make the first move, wondering what the first move should be. Like teenagers, Fox thought. This is ludicrous. If James has a surveillance team on me now, I'm finished.

'I have a confession to make,' Simon said.

'You're gay.'

'Almost.'

That took her off guard. She looked around and he gave her a shy smile and leaned away from her, resting his weight against the driver's side window.

'I mean, you are the first woman I have been out with since . . . well, for three years. I'm not quite sure what I should do right now. Do you kiss me on the doorstop and promise to call, or what?'

'You could invite me up for a cup of coffee.'

'Meaning?'

'Meaning black and two sugars.'

'OK.'

'Will your mother be waiting up?'

'Sandy? Probably.'

'Then you'd better be on your best behaviour.'

He was right. Sandy was waiting up. She was watching *Mad Max* on Sky and as soon as they walked through the door she jumped to her feet and rushed into the hall to greet them. 'So,' she said. 'How did it go?'

Fox heard Simon suck in his breath through his teeth. 'Shouldn't you be in bed?'

'I'm fourteen years old.'

'My point.'

'What was it like?'

'Have you eaten dinner in a restaurant before?' Simon asked her.

' 'Course.'

'Well, it was like that.' He looked at his watch. 'I thought I told you to be in bed by nine-thirty.'

'*Nine*-thirty. I thought you said *twelve*-thirty. They sound alike.'

Fox turned away, grinning. Poor Simon. Sandy had an answer for everything.

'Go to bed,' he said.

Sandy looked at Fox, her expression eager. 'I'm glad you had a good time.' She ran up the stairs, laughing. 'Good night!' she shouted from the top of the stairs.

They went into the kitchen. 'Sorry about that,' Simon said. He took out two coffee cups and fetched the milk from the refrigerator. He spilled some on the counter top. He was nervous.

'Don't get wound up. It's all right. I'm not going to sleep with you tonight.'

'Oh.'

'Is that relief or disappointment I hear?'

'A little of both.'

'I may be a police detective and I may be thirty-two years old, but I still don't sleep with a man on the first date.'

'Is it me or is it your Catholic sex-ed teacher?'

'Simon . . .'

'I know. You're scared of the commitment. You women. No wonder men turn gay.'

'You have a daughter. You've had a rough ride these last three years.'

'I haven't had *any* ride for three years.'

'Now you're being crude. I'm trying to be serious.'

He put the coffee percolator on the stove and the talk somehow drifted to former lives and the wrong directions they had taken. She told him about David, how he used to drive her crazy. 'It was the little things. He used to squeeze the toothpaste from the top of the tube and leave the wet bathmat on the floor after a shower. The day he said he was leaving I heard myself screaming all this stuff at him, things I could hardly believe I was saying, about what a slob he was. He just stood there, gaping at me.'

To her surprise Simon started talking to her about his wife. Anne had been the same, he said. She would always leave her underwear scattered on the floor of the wardrobe. 'When she died I left her things there. They were there for months. When she was alive, it drove me nuts. Afterwards, I missed it so much I couldn't bear to pick them up.'

'When *did* you finally pick them up?' she asked him. Listen to me, she thought. What else would a compulsive obsessive ask?

'I didn't,' he said. 'We moved house.' He even smiled when he said it. A good sign, she thought. The first time he had been able to talk about Anne without dropping into a black mood. 'Did you find it difficult . . . going out again, after David?'

'An old girlfriend of mine, she was divorced, she called me one Saturday night and we went to this dance club where we used to hang out. It was infested with schoolchildren, all under twenty-five. We stayed about half an hour. We felt like somebody's parents.'

'I know the feeling.'

'I started going to pubs. Occasionally I'd meet someone, he'd ask me what I did for a living. I heard myself saying I was a security consultant. I was afraid if I told them I was in the CID they'd run a mile. There was this one guy I went out with a couple of times, I don't know, we didn't really click. That was OK. But then, two months later I had to arrest him. He was involved in this credit-card fraud. Know what he said? "I guess it's just as well it never worked out between us." '

'I'm usually careful about telling people I'm a doctor. At parties they'll sidle up to me and start telling me about their haemorrhoids. Like I really want to know. I suppose you get the same thing.'

'No, people never tell me about their haemorrhoids.'

He smiled. 'You know what I mean. People probably ask you to help them get their parking fines cancelled, don't they?'

'All the time. Ian, my brother-in-law, does it all the time. Or I'll go to a party and everyone will be standing around laughing about the time they drove their car into a ditch or fiddled their VAT, and suddenly the talk will stop and everyone looks at me. Like I'm going to whip out a pair of handcuffs and arrest them, like I never speed on the motorway or park on yellow lines now and then.'

She laughed, and when she looked up he was leaning across the table staring at her. There was a look of frightening intensity in the steel-blue eyes. Suddenly it was hard to breathe.

He reached across the table and stroked her hand with his fingers. She stared at the fine golden hairs on the back of his arm.

'What are you looking for, Madeleine?'

'Probably another career cop like me, with no children, no ambitions to have a family and the ability to keep his mouth shut at work.'

'That's a bit general. Can't you be more specific?'

She smiled at that. He slid a coffee cup towards her across the bench.

'You realise I've been chasing you for almost a year.'

'You haven't chased very hard.'

'I'm not the kind of man who's used to chasing very hard. Perhaps that's why—'

'That's why, what?'

He shrugged and tried to make it sound casual. 'That's why I can't get you out of my head. God knows, I've tried. You insult me at dinner parties, start fights in my favourite restaurant—'

'I didn't *start* the fight—'

'—I've never met any woman quite like you.'

'That could be good or bad.'

'Or both.'

She hesitated. When they left the restaurant she had decided to stay the night if he asked her. But now they were here she felt suddenly reluctant. No, more panicked, really. 'Look, Simon, you're a very attractive man—'

'Now we're getting somewhere.'

'I worry about the baggage.'

'It's my freight, not yours.' He pushed his coffee away and walked around the bench. Here it comes, she thought. You either leave now or you make some sort of decision. Like always, you're just putting off making a choice. You don't like things as they are, but you hate changing anything. You don't like being alone, but as soon as there's the chance of a relationship you get scared and start making excuses.

He was standing over her. He put his hands on her shoulders. He was close enough for her to smell his cologne. 'Madeleine.'

Her chest felt tight and there was a physical ache in her heart and in her groin. The two empty places in my life, she thought.

She looked up. He kissed her, properly this time.

There was not enough air in the room. This was the moment. What was she so frightened of? He lifted her hair and kissed her neck and she heard herself moan with pleasure. His lips traced the contours of muscle and she felt his hot breath on her shoulder.

His arms were around her waist, pulling him against her. She felt his erection against her hip. Oh God, she heard herself murmur, over and over. She was wet, she could feel the dampness in her pants. Creaming my jeans. Wasn't that what they called it? A long time since that had happened. Even with David. She ached so much, she wanted him inside her *now*.

She turned her face up to his. He held her face in his hands and kissed her, his mouth wet and hot. She was hungry for him, and suddenly impatient. He slowly unbuttoned her blouse, taking too long about it. She didn't want him to be gentle. She pulled at his jeans and his shirt. Now is no time for the refinements, Simon, she thought. Just get them off.

She offered him her throat, felt his hot mouth on her neck. She felt his hand on her breast, and it was like an electric shock going through her. They slid to the tiled floor. He tugged at her skirt and she raised her hips so he could slide it off. She rolled on top of him and tried to take off his shirt, but her fingers fumbled with the buttons. He undid them for her as she dragged his jeans down around his hips. His penis was hard and smooth, a pearly drop of wetness glistening at the tip.

Oh, Christ.

She dug her nails into his chest, curling the fine hairs of his chest and his belly around her fingernails. Then she held him with her other hand and guided him towards her. She slid down on top of him at once, and the world seemed to explode. She couldn't believe how easily, how quickly, he fitted inside her.

She closed her eyes, waves of colour in her head, bright and angry. She rolled him on top of her, and he started to move very slowly, too slowly. She grabbed his hips and worked him faster and faster inside her. 'Maddy,' he groaned over and over. 'Maddy.' This is insane, a part of her was thinking. He's not wearing a condom. I'll get pregnant.

His hand was in her hair, pulling her head back. Yes, like that, like that, she thought. That's good. He gripped her arms above her head and plunged deep inside her, thrusting as hard as he could, and she could hear herself screaming yes, yes, in time with each stroke, and she heard him panting and knew what was going to happen.

I want his hot come inside me, Janie, her alter-ego, was screaming inside her head. Put on a condom, the other Madeleine was telling her, the one who would have to go back to the real world when this moment was over. You're like a teenager. How could you be so stupid?

She gasped aloud, arching her back, feigning her climax for him. He pulled out of her then and she moaned again, with disappointment and with relief.

Just in time. She felt the wetness on her belly and she held him in her hand, felt the powerful spasms between her fingers. Then he groaned and collapsed on top of her.

The world came back into focus through a haze of red gelatin. She held him tightly, her arms around his neck, so she would not have to look into his eyes. As always, she was overcome by a sense of mortal embarrassment, the feeling that she had not only exposed her body but a part of her soul. Guilt and frustration vied together for her attention, familiar baggage now.

It was always like this. Desire placed its nameless treasure within her grasp only to drag it away again at the last, leaving her desolate, as always.

PART FIVE

Clerkenwell.
A clear day in autumn

Chapter Fifty-three

Carrie was looking her old self again. There was colour in her cheeks, something flashed in her eyes. Good sex and plenty of attention, Fox thought. And she had a job. There was a mobile phone in her pocket and lip gloss on her mouth.

It was a bright, cool autumn day. From the snug in the Cat and Whistle they could hear jackhammers on Farringdon Road. A chalkboard menu offered Cumberland sausage and treacle sponge with custard. The health food of a nation. Occasionally a train rumbled into Farringdon station, shaking the bare wooden boards under their feet.

They sat at the bar with their gins and tonics. Fox noticed a man in a blue-striped shirt and a school tie draped over his beer gut watching her speculatively as he dribbled cigarette ash down his suit jacket. Men. They never stopped.

Carrie was buzzing. Her new job was working out, she was back doing what she did best, and there was a new man in her life. He was a marketing manager at the radio station, and last week he had asked her out for lunch. She had told him about her daughter and he didn't seem to mind.

'Are you going to see him again?' Fox asked her.

'I suppose so,' Carrie said. She looked suddenly embarrassed. 'I slept with him last night,' she said and waited for Fox's verdict.

'That was quick.'

'It felt right.'

Fox looked away so Carrie couldn't see her expression. Your funeral, she thought, but at the same time she told herself she was a prude. She couldn't be like Carrie, treat sex as casually as she did. What was she afraid of? Not just getting hurt, although that was part of it. She brought the same fatalistic attitude to Carrie's relationships as she did to her own; she knew they weren't ever going to last. But something in herself frightened her too. What she wanted from sex most men couldn't give her, and those who could were the kind of men she would never invite into her home, never mind her bedroom.

'I know what you're thinking,' Carrie said defensively.

'No, you don't.'

'He's different.'

'All men are different,' Fox said, 'until they start to do the same things.'

Carrie took out a packet of Pall Mall and lit one. She had got back a few bad habits along with her confidence. Like smoking and going out with men. Fox noticed her nails. They had grown back. She even wore polish on them.

'Are you still seeing Simon?' Carrie asked her.

She nodded.

'And?'

'I like him.'

'Is it serious?'

'I don't think so,' she said, and she wondered what it would be like to get into another serious relationship. Could she be a good cop, like Marenko, and still have time and energy to spare to be someone's lover, wife, whatever? Or was the job just an excuse these days, a way of postponing decisions about her personal life?

'Well, when you've finished with him, let me know,' Carrie said impishly over the rim of her glass. 'I'll have him.'

'He'd eat you alive.'

Carrie gave a disgusting laugh. 'I hope so,' she said.

Chapter Fifty-four

A row of drab terraced houses off Camden Road. Bonfire night, and bitterly cold.

When Fox arrived, the ambulance was still at the scene. In the swirl of the emergency beacons she saw uniformed constables putting up blue and white tape, while another interviewed a young Rasta and his girlfriend, writing down their names in his notebook.

A light rain had started to fall. As she got out of her car the chill hit her and she shivered inside her zippered jacket. Two paramedics were at work on a stricken form in the back of the ambulance. Their casualty was shaking, as if he was freezing to death. Rap dancing, Marenko called it. Not a good sign.

There was blood all over the stretcher; the floor of the ambulance was awash with it, dark and sticky. The two para-medics were trying to set up an intravenous line, another bad sign, a measure of true desperation. The man on the stretcher had massive head wounds. His blood pressure must be in a power dive. They were looking at murder here, no question.

She flashed her ID. 'Detective Inspector Madeleine Fox, Area Major Incident Team. How are you doing?'

One of the paramedics looked up and gave her an appraising glance. A woman, he was thinking, let's have a bit of fun. It was written all over his face. 'Not bad. Had a bit of a cold last week, but I'm feeling better now.'

A comedian. I've stumbled into another sitcom. *Paramedics Behaving Badly.* 'I mean the patient.'

'Oh, him. Stop the leak, pump up the tyres, you'll be able to ride him away.'

I don't believe this, Fox thought. This bloke needs counselling. The stress of the job has turned his head. Only young, too. Perhaps that's it. He thinks he's Jerry Seinfeld.

Just then the man on the stretcher shuddered and gasped. The paramedics rolled him quickly, but not quickly enough. Some of their patient's most recent meal hit the blacked-out window, the rest landing in Jerry's lap. He swore under his breath, while his partner grabbed for the suction and tried to clear the airway.

'Pizza delivery,' Fox said and backed off. This wasn't looking good at all.

Hallerton, the duty officer from Holmes Road, witnessed this exchange. He grinned at her.

'Good morning,' she said.

He nodded.

'Do you have the victim's name?'

'DeBruin, ma'am. Michael DeBruin.'

The world stopped. Fox ran a hand through her hair. Christ Almighty.

'We got a phone call. Whoever it was said they wanted to remain androgynous.' He waited, his face deadpan. 'So we don't know if it was a man or a woman.'

Any other time she might have laughed. But the name kept crashing around in her brain. DeBruin. Michael *DeBruin*. Please to remember the fifth of November. This one she would.

'Any witnesses?'

Hallerton shook his head slowly. The ambulance started to move off, sirens blaring.

'Anyone else here from Hendon Road?'

'Not yet, ma'am.'

'When DCI Marenko gets here, tell him I've gone to the hospital with the victim.'

He nodded. She jumped back in her Cavalier, started the engine and followed the flashing beacons along the dark, wet street. Michael DeBruin. Jesus.

He looked less like a corpse than an unfinished project. He was naked, the emergency team had cut his clothes off him. There was an endotracheal tube protruding from his mouth, heart monitor dots on his chest and his legs. More tubes hung from his arm and his groin. He looked up at the white acoustic tiles on the ceiling with an expression of dull surprise.

She imagined him as she had last seen him, standing in the dock at the Old Bailey, the olive-green suit hanging loosely on his muscular frame, looking around at her with that look of studied arrogance. He would indeed be surprised if he could see himself now, blood staining the sheet under his head, a small hole in his face under his left eye, another gaping wound on the side of the polished brown skull by the left temple, a considerable portion of his scalp missing.

She searched inside herself, rummaging through her emotions like an old trunk she had just found in the attic. To her surprise she discovered no feeling of triumph, no sense of elation at his death. Like Michael DeBruin, she found only dull surprise.

Leaning over him, she drew a dough man on a page of her notebook and marked the wound sites. There were powder marks on the gunshot wound below the left eye, indicating that it had been fired in close. The wound on the side of the head appeared to have been caused by a bullet that had furrowed the temporal skull without penetrating the brain. Was that the first or the second shot?

She stopped for a moment, perplexed. Who shoots someone under the eye? This was not a professional job. She formed a picture in her mind, saw the first bullet almost missing DeBruin, but the concussion enough to knock him down. She imagined the second shot being fired in close, but the hand that held the gun was shaking. Was that how it was?

'Police?'

Fox turned round. It was the emergency room sister. Fox nodded and took out her ID.

'Don't be long. When you're through we have to get him down to the morgue. He's taking up space.'

Fox almost smiled. It seemed a fitting obituary, somehow.

A woman was sitting in the waiting-room, stiff-backed, her dignity in savage contrast to her cheap clothes and scuffed shoes. Fox recognised her from the public gallery at the Old Bailey.

She went over.

The woman looked up. 'You're a detective,' she said.

DeBruin's mother. It was sometimes easy to forget, dealing every day with hard men and speed cases, that they had once been born, in the normal way and had not come into this word pre-fucked up.

'The doctors have seen you?'

Mrs DeBruin nodded slowly. 'I know he's gone. They told me.'

'I'm very sorry for your loss,' Fox began. They would need to speak to her, they would have to interview the whole family. But for Mrs DeBruin this was not the right time. 'Do you know who might have done this?' she said, as gently as she could.

The woman shook her head. She began to rock slowly backwards and forwards. 'I want you to catch the person who did this to my boy. He was a good boy.'

A good boy, Fox thought. That mean-mouthed, cold-eyed gangster. A good boy. 'We'll do our best,' she said.

And she would. That was the job.

Chapter Fifty-five

When she got back to DeBruin's house the street was still cordoned off but much of the crowd had dispersed. It was early in the morning and the rain was getting heavier and, besides, the body had gone. That's what police work had taught her. People like to see a body; it's what they hang around for. When the body's gone, people lose interest. Human nature.

Hallerton told her that DCI Marenko had arrived and wanted to see her. He was upstairs in the victim's bedroom, he said.

She slipped on a pair of white overshoes and went through to the kitchen. The back door had been jemmied open, by the look of the splinter marks around the door frame. A crude manner of entry, but effective. The SOCOs were busy dusting for prints.

She went upstairs and pulled on a pair of white overalls. When she walked in to DeBruin's bedroom Marenko was staring at the black sound system on a shelf. He put on a latex glove and gently touched the PLAY button on the machine to see if there was a disc in the player. Warren G. 'I Shot the Sheriff'.

James was in the room also, leering at the pretty Home Office photographer who was doing her best to ignore him.

'Fox,' Marenko said, looking up.

'Guv.'

'How's our poor victim?'

'He died in hospital.'

He gave her a wolfish grin. 'That's too bad. Did you hear that, TJ?'

'Yeah, too bad, guv,' James said.

Marenko noticed something on the carpet and he got down on his haunches for a better look. 'Now what do you think that is, TJ? I think it's his tonsils.'

'Nah,' James said.

'Could be. Maybe that's what it was. He got sick of waiting for the National Health and tried to remove his own tonsils.' Marenko bent over to take a closer inspection. He nudged the unidentified piece of pink matter with his gloved finger. 'Or his adenoids. Yeah, maybe his adenoids.'

'It's pizza, guv,' James said. 'See, there's an empty box on the table here.'

'Are you saying this is pepperoni?'

'Well, I suppose we'd better wait for forensics on that. But if you ask me, yeah, it's cold pepperoni.'

'How much?'

'A fiver.'

'Done.'

James looked up. 'Hey, Foxy, get over here. We got money riding on this. I say it's pizza, the guv'nor here says it's tonsil. What do you say?'

'I say we get on with our jobs.'

James shrugged, and he and Marenko grinned like naughty schoolboys.

Marenko stood up and looked around the room. A bed with off-grey sheets, an ancient wardrobe, a few ragged posters of rap artists and basketball players tacked to the walls, the carpet strewn with clothes and takeaway containers. That was it, aside from the ghetto blaster on the shelf.

'Must be tough to leave all this behind,' Marenko said.

Something on the bed caught Fox's eye. A magazine, hardcore porn. Fox glanced at it. How did guys get off on that sort of junk? she wondered. Maybe if you were a gynaecologist. A black woman with peroxide hair and a shaved pubis was squatting on what appeared to be a billiard table, naked. Her scarlet finger-nails had opened her labia. She was leaning back resting her weight on her other hand and was offering her vagina to the camera.

'Look at this,' she said.

'That's it,' James said. 'He recognised his mother and shot himself.'

Fox was disturbed by the atmosphere pervading here. 'Personal feelings aside, this is still premeditated murder,' she said.

Marenko shook his head. 'Don't ask me to lose sleep on this one. I may not even run up overtime.' He stood closer to one of the basketball posters, put on his spectacles for a better look. 'So how do you pronounce it, TJ? It is Shakwill or Sha-keel?'

'Sha-keel,' James said. 'Sha-keel. Rhymes with O'Neal.'

'Coincidence,' Marenko said, and he gave Fox a hard look. 'His hero's a guy named O'Neal.'

'He plays for the Chicago Bulls,' James said, and they took his word. He stayed up late at nights watching Sky channel and knew about these things.

Marenko returned his attention to the poster. 'Sha-keel. Strange name. Like DeBruin. DEE-bruin, or de-BRUIN. I guess it doesn't matter now. It's just DEE-ceased.'

'Right,' James laughed.

'DEE-bruin, DEE-ceased.'

'Guv,' Fox said. 'I don't think we should be talking like this.'

'Yeah,' James said. 'DEE-sist.' And they both laughed.

'You talk to the paramedics?' Marenko asked her.

She nodded. 'At the A&E.'

'What did they see?'

'When they got here he was lying slumped down between the bed and the wall. All he was wearing was a pair of underpants. They were around his knees.'

'He was facing which way?'

'Facing the door.'

Marenko nodded. 'So when the shots were fired he was standing beside the bed. Fell back, that way. Right?'

Fox took a closer look at the wallpaper. It was like someone had thrown a bucket of blood at the wall. But she could still make out a definite spray pattern on the wallpaper. The droplets were angled in such a way that the shot must have been fired from DeBruin's right. The bullet that left the wound in his temple must be embedded in the plaster. Sure enough, there was the hole. The SOCOs would extract that later.

She started to form a picture in her mind.

Murderer breaks in to the house through the kitchen. Michael does not hear him because he is lying on the bed with the music playing, masturbating. Murderer comes up the stairs, throws open the door. Michael is caught, literally, with his pants down. He jumps up, is too terrified to even pull his underpants up. He stands against the wall, the murderer comes towards him from around the bed. Perhaps there is a conversation. The conversation proves unsatisfactory and Michael is dispensed with. Or perhaps there was no conversation at all.

But for some reason it is not a perfect murder. Not as precise as it should have been. Emotion played a role in this, she thought, emotion and inexperience. The first shot almost misses his head. The second is enough to kill him, but not straight away, and is inexpertly done.

'Well, what do you think?' Marenko said to James.

James shrugged. 'I think the butler did it.'

'Yeah. Fucken' butlers. Got a lot to answer for. Excuse my French.' He put his hands in his pockets and rocked on his heels. 'Round up the usual suspects,' he said to Fox, and then, seeing the look on her face, he said: 'That was a joke.'

'Shall I put you and TJ on the list, guv?'

She had never seen that expression on his face before. He forced a smile, but his eyes were like chips of ice. 'If you like,' he said.

'What about Fox, guv?' James said.

'I don't think so. Women don't agree with violence. Do they, Foxy?'

She didn't answer him.

'Mind the tonsils,' James said to her as she followed Marenko out of the room.

She stood on the front step, shivering in the early-morning chill. Marenko was talking to Hallerton. He finished, glanced up at her, then walked back up the path.

'I didn't know DeBruin was out,' she said.

'Appealed his sentence and was given a special dispensation because his mother was sick. No one else at home to look after her, his brief said. The appeal judge bought it.'

'When did this happen?'

'Last week. I've been meaning to tell you.' He sucked on his teeth with his tongue. 'I know what you're thinking.'

'What am I thinking?'

'You're thinking a cop might have done this.'

She turned her collar up against the windblown rain.

'Say it.'

'Say what, guv?'

'What was I doing this evening between—' He looked at his watch '—11 o'clock and 12.30?'

'You're leading the investigation, guv. Not me.'

'I was in bed asleep,' he said, ignoring her. 'No, I did not have anyone with me who can verify that.'

She couldn't look at him. It was *precisely* what she had been thinking.

'What about you, Fox?'

'Guv?'

'Where were you this evening?'

'I was in bed, reading a book.'

'Did *you* have anyone with you who could verify that?' When she didn't answer, he said: 'There you are. We're even.'

She bit her lip.

'Don't worry about it, Fox. There's no way Radford would let us handle this one. It's a potential nightmare for all of us. He's black, we're white. He put a police officer, my son-in-law, into a wheelchair. It will have to go to another team.'

'You once said, in front of all of us, that you wanted him dead.'

'I've said the same about you, Foxy.'

He turned away. 'Jesus, I need a cigarette.' He walked back to his car. Fox shivered again in the rain and closed her eyes. My God. What a mess.

Chapter Fifty-six

Radford sat back in his chair and regarded them over the reading glasses he wore on a chain around his neck. He was a bear of a man almost fifty years old, with a full grey beard that reminded Fox of the admirals in the old black and white British films of the 1950s. The little half-moon glasses appeared an anachronism.

The file on Michael DeBruin lay open on his desk. As yet it contained only the initial reports from the pathologist and witness statements from the neighbours, hastily typed by WPC Stacey first thing that morning. Behind his head London had disappeared into the grey overcast of a November morning. Droplets of rain rippled and glittered on the window, catching the reflection of the strip lights.

'This Michael DeBruin. He stood trial for the attempted murder of Constable O'Neill?'

Marenko nodded. The silence turned to ice.

'He had a lot of enemies, sir,' Fox said. 'He thought he was hard. He has a number of previous convictions for assault.'

'Two months ago he was acquitted of the attempted murder of a policeman. A much-publicised case.'

Marenko shrugged again.

'Do you have any suspects at this stage?'

'It was bonfire night. Most people seemed to think it was fireworks going off. No one seems to have seen anything.

DeBruin's place backs on to King's Cross. We think the murderer went in and out over the back fence, down the embankment. We're waiting on the ballistics report. It may even have been a contract killing.'

Fox herself had interviewed the two constables who had responded to the call. What they said was substantiated by the two paramedics, Jerry Seinfeld and his pal. The man had made no dying declaration, they said, nor had they anticipated one. On examination they had slotted him into an unofficial medical classification known to them as a DBNY – Deceased But Not Yet. His brain had been mostly dead, they said, from the moment the bullet had entered his skull. If not before.

They had already traced the source of the anonymous telephone call. It had been made by DeBruin's girlfriend. She was not much more than a schoolgirl, and was at first unwilling to admit having been at DeBruin's house that night because her parents had thought she was in her bedroom asleep. It seemed that her late-night trysts with DeBruin were a regular feature of her secret life and that she had probably missed seeing the killer by only a few minutes.

Fox had questioned her for almost an hour at Kentish Town police station. She was fourteen years old and shaking, her attitude dissolved by the sight of her hard-case boyfriend with his blood and brains splattered on a poster of Shaquille O'Neal. Having her enraged father in the same room, watching over the interview, made her unusually cooperative. No doubt he only wished to get her back home to the bosom of her family where he could take the belt to her.

As far as the Inland Revenue were concerned, Michael DeBruin was unemployed; unofficially, it was common knowledge that he made significant profits from his own flourishing cottage industry, dealing in illegal substances. It was not a profession that always promised longevity. Perhaps he upset a supplier, Fox speculated, perhaps he got ideas above his humble station and tried to muscle in on someone else's territory and got mixed up with men who were smarter and harder than he could ever be. Another Elmore Crawford.

Or perhaps the notoriously violent DeBruin had fought with someone who had decided to even the score on a permanent basis. Terry Richardson and his son, for instance.

She hoped there would be a quick arrest on this one, before too many questions were asked about DeBruin's recent history. She told herself the murder had to be unrelated to the O'Neill case.

Radford turned his swivel chair around and stared at the London skyline, this dank, anonymous city where people could be shot in their own bedrooms without any of their neighbours becoming suspicious.

'I'm taking your team off the investigation,' he said to Marenko.

'Yes, guv.'

'You understand my reasons?'

'I sort of anticipated it, sir.'

Radford turned back to face him and his voice became softer. He and Marenko had known each other a long time. 'It is no reflection on you, Frank. It's just the way it looks.'

Marenko's face was blank. 'I suppose so.'

'And there's the race angle. That's why I want to bring in Venables.'

Fox almost smiled at the irony of it. Venables' mother was Jamaican, his father had been a diplomat. He had been born in Kensington, had received a university education and spoke English better than most of his Anglo-Saxon colleagues. In fact, Fox thought, he wasn't even very black. He was further removed from the Michael DeBruins of this world than men like Marenko and James, who at least understood the language of the street. But Venables was available, he had never been involved with the O'Neill case and he *was* black. Ish.

The interview was over. Fox stood up. Marenko stayed sitting. 'I'll see you downstairs,' he said to her.

She raised an eyebrow. What now?

'Something I need to talk about. In private.'

She felt an oily, sick sensation in the pit of her stomach. This is it, she thought. He wants me off the team. It's been coming for a long time now. She looked at Radford.

'Thank you, Inspector,' he said.

She went out, closing the door softly behind her.

Chapter Fifty-seven

'Why didn't you tell me?' she shouted over the thump of the bass from the CD jukebox in the corner. The King's Head was going downhill fast. You couldn't find a decent pub in London any more without one of the damned things. They wouldn't be satisfied until every old alehouse in the city had been turned into an amusement arcade.

'Tell you what, Fox?'

'That you'd applied for a transfer.'

'None of your business.'

'We've worked closely together for the last year. You were—' Was mentor too strong a word, she wondered, did it signify an intimacy and an involvement he did not feel? She let the thought go unfinished, unexpressed. 'Doesn't that count for anything with you?'

'I've worked lots of cases with lots of people. I'm not like you females. I don't have to sit down and pour my heart out over a cup of coffee every few minutes.'

There he sat, like a white moustached Buddha, his fleshy face immobile, spouting his misogynist philosophy from the angle of the bar as he always did, a Guinness and a double whisky at his right elbow. He produced a packet of cigarettes from the deep recesses of his jacket and lit one.

'I thought you'd given up.'

'Bollocks to that. I've given up four times in four years. A man has to know when he's beaten. At least if I die from these I'll know who did it. It won't be an unsolved mystery.'

She shook her head. He was deliberately baiting her and she knew it. And worse, she couldn't help but rise to the bait.

'What did Radford say?'

'He tried to talk me out of it.'

'And?'

'It's none of your business, Fox, but as you've asked, I've had enough. I want something with more regular hours. You know what it's like. First few murders you get, you bar up, well, blokes do. Feel the adrenalin start pumping. It's better than sex, right?'

She stared at him. No, he was wrong, it wasn't like that for her at all.

'Is this about the DeBruin case?'

He made a face. 'Fuck DeBruin, pardon my French. I just want a change of pace. I've been at Hendon Road a long time.' He drained his glass. 'I used to enjoy being a cop. But lately I've got tired of looking at mangled bodies and rape victims. I'm sick of locking up all the garbage we take off the street so some ponce with a fancy suit and a degree in law can put them back out there again. I've had enough of getting screwed by the system, having the Patrick Cappers of this world blow all over me, watching Michael DeBruins throw high fives in the Old Bailey. You were right, Fox. I shouldn't have got Flora Ellis killed for a scrote like Elmore Crawford. That's why I don't want to know about any of this any more.'

'Flora Ellis was a witness to murder. What else could you have done?'

'You know, the Yardies have got this rhyme,' Marenko said. '*The cops don't bang, the law don't hang, lock 'em up, not lang.* Know what it means? It's about why it's better being a crim over here than in the States. We've got no guns, no death penalty and the prison sentences are shorter. Great indictment of British justice, isn't it?'

'But the Drug Squad?'

Marenko made a face. 'Drugs don't get me hot under the collar. Dealers, users. They're all scrotes in my book. So who cares, right? Everyone knows prohibition's a joke. Policing drugs is like trying to cram an octopus into a string bag, but at least you start off *knowing* it's pointless. Not like this bloody place. I've had a gutful. I'm sick of trying to uphold the law. The law doesn't have anything to do with justice these days. They're laughing at us, Fox, blokes like Capper, and the Candy Man. DeBruin too, until someone wiped the smile off his face.'

'The law is there to protect the innocent as well as the guilty.'

'It's doing a fucking good job of protecting the guilty. But I don't know about the rest. If we bang up the wrong bloke, they call it a miscarriage of justice. But if some scrote gets off when he's guilty, they never call *that* a miscarriage of justice. And that's the way it happens far more often than us fitting up the wrong bloke.' Marenko finished his Guinness. 'Your round.'

Fox was feeling unsteady on her feet. It wasn't easy keeping up with Frank Marenko drink for drink. In spite of the grim conversation, the afternoon had taken on a rosier hue and the bar felt a warmer, more wonderful place. A dangerous sign when a public house in London seemed like a home away from home. But she nodded to Henry and another Guinness and a gin and tonic appeared on the polished bar.

'Take Capper, for instance,' Marenko went on, in his stride now. 'We know he topped Elmore Crawford, we know he topped Flora Ellis. We know it, he knows it, his brief knows it, the whole of fucking North London knows it. But we have to pretend like he didn't. That's the difference, isn't it? We read them their rights, give them the benefit of the doubt, a man's innocent until proven guilty, all that shite. And they laugh at us. They think the whole thing's a fucken' joke. Because they live in the hard, three-dimensional world, the real world. They don't play word games. You cross Patrick Capper, you don't get let off on a fucken' technicality. He doesn't ask you whether you got an alibi, or if you can be rehabilitated, or whether he might have confused you with someone else, or whether what he's been told about you is admissible or not admissible. You cross him and he shoots you down like a dog. In a way you have to admire the crims. At least they have a concept of justice. You fuck around with them, they fuck you. You won't find that in any law book, but at least it's a language everyone can understand. And justice is important, Fox. It can't bring anyone back, it doesn't ease the pain, but if people know they've got justice, at least they can get on with their lives.' Marenko finished his soliloquy and slammed the Guinness down on the counter. He was talking about Tom O'Neill now, she knew. 'Henry,' he said, 'give me another whisky. A double.'

'So is that what you're going to do about it, guv? Sit here and get drunk?'

'Can you think of something better to do?'

'Well, it's not going to make any of it go away.'

'Don't patronise me. I was doing this job while you were still wetting your knickers in kindergarten.'

He was getting beyond drunk. He was becoming volatile and vicious. She stood up to leave.

'Heard about Venables? Looks like he's got a prime suspect for the DeBruin murder.' He had a look on his face. Like he was taunting her.

'I'll see you, guv.'

'It's not a cop. Thought you'd be pleased about that.'

'I think we all are.'

'You thought it was me, you bitch.'

Fox felt the blood drain from her face. She leaned in close. 'I have taken a lot of shit from you, Detective Chief Inspector, but I will not just stand here while you call me a bitch.'

'Well, fuck off then.'

He didn't expect her to hit him. It wasn't hard. She didn't intend it to be. If he but knew it, she could have laid him flat on his back with his windpipe crushed and his testicles turned to hamburger mince. Instead she hit him with her right fist, bringing it up smartly from her hip and snapping his head back. He would have tottered backwards off his bar stool, but she was holding him by the lapel with her other hand. It was a smart, deft movement, executed without warning or fanfare, and attracted no attention at all from the other customers until Marenko's nose started to bleed.

'You can have my resignation in the morning,' she said.

He stared at her, then fumbled in his pocket for a hand-kerchief. He held it to his nose, astonished. Blood, for Christ's sake. 'That won't be necessary, Fox. I believe I tripped on a bit of loose carpet and fell. Besides, this time next week I won't be your boss any more.'

Everyone in the bar stared at her as she walked out.

Henry placed a whisky reverently on the end of the bar. 'You all right, Frank?'

He nodded, clutching the handkerchief tightly to his nose while he tilted back his head and drank some of the whisky. He nodded towards the door and Fox's departing shadow. 'PMT,' he said, and a few people laughed while Henry nodded his sympathy and understanding.

Marenko was right, it wasn't a cop.

His name was Andy Murray, aka Fat Boy. He was a friend of Michael DeBruin's and had been routinely interviewed early in the investigation. It was the forensics report on some asphalt fragments they found in DeBruin's bedroom that led Venables to his rundown semi off Balls Pond Road.

Murray had given his job as a handyman-fixer, and the detective constable who had interviewed him remembered that his front yard was littered with building materials, a cement mixer, piles of lumber, sand and, coincidentally, asphalt.

They went back and took a sample. Forensic at Lambeth told them it matched the material they had found at the murder scene. It was enough for Venables to effect a search warrant. When the team returned the next day they found, wrapped in plastic and hidden under another pile of lumber in the back yard, a pair of AirJordan sports shoes and a Glock 17L 9-millimetre semiautomatic pistol with a home-made silencer.

A mould of a print found in the garden of DeBruin's house exactly matched that of one of the shoes, and ballistics tests matched the bullet retrieved from DeBruin's brain with striations on the barrel of the Glock.

Four days after DeBruin's murder, Andy 'Fat Boy' Murray, still protesting his innocence, was charged with the murder of Michael DeBruin.

Chapter Fifty-eight

The lights were on in Regent Street, reindeer and angels frolicked in the windows of Selfridges. There was frost on the roofs and in the parks in the mornings, and the oaks and beeches in Green Park were bare. The air was brown and warm with the smell of roast chestnuts at the roadside stalls along Oxford Street.

Venables took over as their new DCI. Fox thought he looked like a skinny version of Clive Lloyd, with his thick spectacles and shoebrush moustache, his wiry hair flecked with grey. He had a good reputation as an investigator, but word was that he had neither Marenko's informal style nor his sick gallows humour.

It was Christmas, a time of goodwill to all men. Well, not in North London, and not this Christmas. Two men had been shot in a Kilburn pub over a drug debt, a woman was found bashed and murdered in a bedsit in Barnet. Within one twenty-four hour period there was a stabbing in King's Cross and two separate motor vehicle accidents in Camden Town and Belsize Park that resulted in five fatalities. The bodies started piling up in Gravedigger's Junkyard. Soon, James said, they'd be stacking them in the car park, leaning them up against the walls like pokers.

Prophetic words. Just three days later all hell broke loose.

Chapter Fifty-nine

They found Capper's body in an upstairs room of a small pub off Essex Road, the King George. He had gone into the establishment, alone, in order to do some business, leaving his minders in the car outside. When he had failed to reappear some two hours later, one of them went in to look for him. He found Capper lying on his back staring at the sagging plaster ceiling of an old storeroom. There were two bullet holes in his forehead and two more in his one-hundred-pound designer-label silk shirt.

By the time Fox arrived with James and Venables news crews were swarming around the police cordon getting footage, filming everyone who went in and out. Fox saw the mortuary van and Graveney's Jaguar among the police vehicles.

Venables flashed his ID at the uniforms and they went through.

Patrick Capper lay on his back in a dank and depressing room on the first floor, his brains, such as they ever were, decorating the wallpaper for a good three feet above his head. He lay half-twisted, his right arm and leg at an unnatural angle. The stench in the room was appalling. At the moment of death Capper had lost control of his bowel and bladder. Shooting victims always did. An ex-SAS mercenary had once confided to Fox that it was how he knew when a man was really dead. He didn't feel for a pulse, he just sniffed the air.

'Ma'am,' James said. 'Is that his brains on the wallpaper there?'

'I don't know, TJ.'

'Because, you know, I figured there wouldn't be that much.'

First Crawford, Fox was thinking, then Flora Ellis, DeBruin, now Capper. Their squad had caught four shootings in fifteen months. Not a lot for New York, but a lot for one AMIT in North London. There was a time when any shooting was automatically front-page news.

Capper was sprawled on the threadbare carpet, a pool of dark, congealed blood around his head. James and Venables contented themselves with viewing the scene from the doorway. Fox put on white overshoes and stepped carefully into the room.

'Alas, poor Patrick,' she heard James say. 'I knew him well. He was a scrote, Horatio.'

Fox studied the wall, marked the blood spatter on her notepad, the spray of brain and blood matter giving her an idea of the trajectory of the bullets. The pattern suggested he had been standing up when his attacker had fired his weapon. The droplets were not quite symmetrical; they were angled slightly up and away from the body. His murderer had been sitting down, in the chair by the window perhaps. The SOCOs would be able to give them a better idea.

She stared at his lifeless body. Without the customary swagger, he was almost unrecognisable. Parts of his ponytail were missing. She guessed forensics would find the remnants spread over the flock wallpaper.

One of the entry wounds at the front of his head was surrounded by sooty residue, which indicated the shot had been fired from close range. Judging by the mess on the carpets and the walls, the exit wounds at the back of the skull would be massive. There were two other wounds to the middle of the chest. Probably fired after Capper was already dead. A professional job. Like Flora Ellis.

Underworld legend had it that Capper had been born in a

room over a public house. The long and winding road had led him back here for the final act.

The SOCOs were dusting for prints, checking the carpet for trace evidence. Capper was virtually ignored, reduced almost to a bit player in the drama. Graveney had finished his examination of the body and was peeling off his gloves. He saw Venables and Fox and nodded a greeting.

'What's that on the floor?' Venables asked. After Marenko, Venables' plummy drawl made him sound like a BBC newsreader.

'It's his briefcase,' Graveney said.

'Has anyone opened it?'

'There's money in it,' one of the SOCOs told him.

'How much?'

'We haven't counted it. But it's bundles of tens and fives, tied with elastic bands. Quite a few thousand, I'd say.'

Venables rubbed his forehead, which creased into great, rubbery lines.

'Two bullet wounds to the head,' Graveney went on. 'Two more to the chest. No other obvious wounds or lesions. Contract killing, by the looks of it, but that's your call. We'll take him back to the lab and run the normal PM.'

'Time of death?'

'Three hours.'

Venables shook his head in bewilderment. 'Why does he walk in here with a briefcase full of money and leave his heavies outside? And why didn't the shooter take the money?'

'I have a theory,' Fox said.

Venables looked irritated that his rhetoric was being interrupted by his deputy, and a woman deputy at that.

'Perhaps he came here to pay for something and he didn't want anyone, even his own people, to know what he was doing. Capper was paranoid. For instance he might have come here to put out a contract. This could have been a regular rendezvous. He owns this pub.'

'Owns it?'

'Yes, sir. I know Mister Capper from a previous investigation.'

Venables frowned. 'I see.'

'By the position of the body I would speculate that he was shot as the walked through the door. So the shooter either already had the key to the room or it was never locked. You would have to assume that Capper expected to meet someone here, probably the murderer.'

Venables digested this angle. 'But then why didn't the assailant take the money? Why walk out and leave thousands of pounds in a briefcase?'

'There is something else you should look at,' Graveney said.

They eased their way around the contents of Capper's head. Someone had used the blood to write on the wall behind the door:

JUSTICE

The three detectives stared at it for a long time in utter bewilderment. A professional hit with an emotional aspect. It made no sense, no sense at all.

'Perhaps we should flake off the paper and send it for handwriting analysis,' Fox said.

Venables gave her a look that let her know her wit was not appreciated. Then he turned and walked out of the room. 'Oh, Christ,' he said. He looked down. He had found a piece of Pat Capper's ponytail. It had adhered to the bottom of his shoe.

'Christ, be careful,' one of the SOCOs said. 'That's evidence.'

Venables gave him a sour look and left.

Capper's two minders were still in the bar, slouching on two bentwood chairs, legs splayed. They were being watched in cold silence by two uniformed constables and a sergeant. The only other member of the good citizenry of London present at that moment was the publican. He was sitting on a stool behind the bar with his chin cupped in his hands, looking as if he was about to drop off to sleep. He must have an exciting life, Fox thought. The owner of his pub had just got topped upstairs and he still couldn't keep his eyes open. Been there, done that.

The bar smelled of stale hops and tobacco smoke. There was dark wood panelling, frosted-glass windows and old worn carpet. The inevitable poker machine by the door.

The two minders were flash, as always. They wore hand-tailored suits and freshly pressed white collarless shirts, and had gold Rolexes on their wrists. Almost certainly overpaid; Pat Capper would attest to that. Fox remembered them from her last visit to The Pieman, the day she and Marenko had bailed up Capper after the Flora Ellis shooting. In her mind she had labelled them Beauty and the Beast; the tall one, the younger of the two, with his spiky bleached hair, immaculately dressed, looked like an art dealer; his companion was balding with a blue jaw, built like a refrigerator with a head.

'Gentlemen,' Venables said.

They stared at him as if he was something they had found on the bottom of their Italian leather shoes.

'Hello, boys,' Fox greeted them.

The uniformed sergeant looked up at Venables. 'They were carrying, sir,' he said.

Venables nodded and turned back to the minders. 'Now why would two respectable-looking gentlemen like yourselves need firearms?'

'We're poachers,' the bald one said, and Fox compressed her lips to keep from smiling. Criminals these days. Such wags.

Venables perched himself on a bar stool. 'So. A bad day at the office, gentlemen.'

Cold stares.

'What happened?'

'You find out. You're the detective.'

'Don't you want to know who topped your boss?'

'We got nothing to say to you, copper,' the younger one said.

'A real hard man,' Fox said. The younger one had his feet planted on a chair. She pulled it out from under him, and his feet bounced on the floor. She brushed off the seat and sat down. 'You were Pat's minders, right?'

'What's it to you?'

'Didn't do a very good job.'

'He didn't want us—' the young one snapped back at her before he could stop himself. The bald one shot him a warning glance. Mr Young and Impetuous fell silent and leaned back in his chair, his lips compressed into a thin line, angry that he'd fallen for the bait.

'Didn't want you to what? He didn't want you to go in with him? Is that what you were going to say?' She leaned forward. 'Now why would he not take his minders with him? Because he knew who he was going to meet, right? He felt safe. Also, he was about to do some serious business and he always liked to do that alone, didn't he? He certainly didn't trust you bastards to keep your stupid mouths shut. Not after Flora Ellis, right? That got out, didn't it?'

They would have liked to have killed her. It was in their eyes, pure hate. Because they knew she was right. Pat was the man. They were just muscle and, no, he didn't trust them. Yes, Pat did think they were stupid. And they resented it.

'Who was he here to meet?' Venables asked them in his BBC voice.

'We got nothing to say to the filth,' the younger one announced.

'Because you don't know anything,' Fox said. 'You were just his bum boys, right?'

The younger one shot forward in his chair. Mr Ugly put a restraining hand on his arm. What a joke. As if he was holding him back. As if he had the bottle.

Fox hadn't moved. 'A quick temper. Fatal weakness, son.

Thin line between being a hard man like Pat and a total nutter. You should remember that.'

'That's enough, Fox,' Venables said.

Fox glared at him. *That's enough*. These guys were open books. Give her half an hour bear-baiting this one and she'd have chapter and verse. The ones who had so much to prove couldn't keep their mouths shut even when they wanted to.

'You'll both be charged with illegal possession of a firearm.' When they did not reply he nodded to James who was lounging by the bar with Rankin. 'Take them back to the station. Get their statements.'

'We want our brief,' the bald one said.

'You can have Perry Mason if you want,' Venables answered, revealing his vintage.

Fox watched them go, regretfully. Once they were at the station even the hard man would clam up. She had begun to miss Marenko, something she had once thought impossible.

Venables went over to the publican who gave them a broad grin and pretended to shake himself from a deep reverie. He was a big man with the build of a boxer gone to fat. A few teeth missing, Fox noticed, bad dentistry rather than bad boxing, judging by the state of the little enamel still remaining in his mouth. 'You're the publican?' Venables snapped.

'Norm Jarvis.' He held out a paw. Venables ignored it.

'I'm Detective Chief Inspector Venables, this is Detective Inspector Fox. I'm in charge of the murder investigation.'

'Can't believe it,' Norm said. 'Everyone loved ol' Pat. Why would someone want to do somefink like that?'

'You obviously didn't know him very well,' Fox said.

The smile fell away. 'I know he could be a bit of a lad, but he was a good boss. He did a few fings he shouldn't in his younger years, but he was strictly legit these days.'

'Please don't insult us, Mr Jarvis. Pat Capper was one of the biggest dope dealers and shakedown artists in North London.'

Venables shot her another glance. He obviously didn't

approve of her interrogation style. 'Did you hear anything this morning, Mr Jarvis?' he asked.

'Like a gunshot?'

'Yes,' Venables said testily. 'Like a gunshot.'

He shook his head. 'Not a fing.'

'What time did Mr Capper arrive here?'

'About ten. He walked in, shouted hello and went upstairs.'

'To do what?'

'I dunno. It's his pub.'

'But you must have wondered what he was going to do upstairs?'

Norm's eyes flickered, right to left, as some people's eyes do when they need time to think. Come on, Norm, Fox thought. Surely you've had enough time to figure out your story by now. I can't stand sloppy liars. 'Well, he sometimes does a bit of business here. Strictly legit, of course. But he likes to be private.'

Fox lost all patience with him. 'He uses one of those crappy little shithole rooms upstairs for a legitimate business meeting? Is that what you're telling us?'

Norm was outraged. 'Crappy little shithole?'

'Well, it's not five-star luxury, is it?'

'That's my office.'

'Look, we're not from Fodor or the RAC,' Venables snapped. 'Just give us the facts.'

'Did he use your office a lot for . . . these legit meetings?' Fox asked him.

Norm Jarvis nodded. 'Now and then.'

'Who did he meet?'

'I dunno. Like I said, it was private.'

'But to get to the room, he must have walked through the bar here.'

'Nar, there's a back way. He would have come in the back way.'

Fox shook her head. 'Are you telling us that people come in

and out through the back door of your pub at all hours of the day without you knowing about it?'

'Well, it's not my pub. It was Pat's, really. I just hold the licence. Christ knows what's going to happen now.'

'How often did this happen, Mr Jarvis?' Venables asked.

'I told you, I dunno. That was Pat's business.'

'So you have no idea at all who Mr Capper was meeting upstairs?'

Norm shook his head and grinned, apparently pleased that they were getting the idea.

'How did they get into your office?'

'I dunno. Maybe they had a key. It was—'

'I know,' Fox finished for him. 'It was Pat's pub.'

'Yeah.' He grinned again. Playing stupid, she thought. He was as stupid as Machiavelli. No way he was going to implicate himself as a witness in any of this, that was clear.

'How many people were in the bar at the time of the shooting, Mr Jarvis?' Fox asked him.

'Well, I can't be sure, because I don't know when the shooting happened, do I?'

Fox bit down her anger. 'This morning, then. How many customers were here?'

'About a dozen or so. They come and go.'

'Can you give us their names?'

Norm hesitated, then shook his head. 'They were all new.'

Even Venables looked up at that one. 'A wet Tuesday morning in December, you have a dozen customers, and not a single one of them is known to you? They couldn't all have been Japanese tourists.'

'Oh, they weren't Japanese,' Norm agreed. 'I would have known if they were Japanese. Their eyes are different.'

Fox wanted to reach across the bar and grab him by the throat. Norm was overplaying his role as simpleton. 'Surely you would only get regulars at that time of day.'

'Normally, yes. But this morning . . .' He shrugged. 'I didn't know one of 'em. Funny, innit?'

'Really odd,' Fox agreed.

'We'll need a statement,' Venables said. 'You'll have to come down the station with us.'

'Yeah, OK,' he said. 'I guess Pat won't mind if I shut up shop for a few hours. In the circumstances.'

'No,' Fox agreed. 'I guess he won't have a lot to say about it. In the circumstances.'

Chapter Sixty

Fox caught James as he was coming out of Room 4C at Islington station house.

'Have you got the statements?' she asked him.

'Such as they are.'

'What do they have to say?'

'They characterise themselves as the deceased's driver and personal assistant. They drove him to the King George at 10.45 this morning. He said he had business to attend to and asked them to wait outside. They have no idea what that business might have been, nor do they claim to know who he was going to meet. They waited for about two hours, then one of them, the bald one, went inside and found him in an upstairs room in an obviously redundant state. Being a public-minded citizen, he immediately summoned assistance through 999. Both their stories pretty much corroborate. They have been charged with illegal possession of a firearm.'

'That's it?'

'That's it. Well, we knew we weren't going to get much help on this one.'

'No doubt they'll want to sort this among themselves.'

'Maybe they really don't know who he was meeting there this morning. Capper was paranoid about getting grassed up.' He followed her down the hall to the coffee machine. 'Things are looking up.'

'How do you figure that?'

'DeBruin. Capper. Two major scrotes put in the freezer in the last six weeks. Cause for a celebration.'

She grabbed a polystyrene cup and put coffee in. Then she tried the sugar. Out. Didn't anyone ever service the damn machine?

'In fact a celebration sounds like a good idea. Want to come for a drink tonight?'

'Who's going?'

'Just me and you.'

'Don't give up, do you?'

'I'm tenacious. It's one of my endearing qualities.'

'It's your only one.'

James got a hot chocolate, two shots with powdered milk. Christ, must be like drinking mud. 'You still going out with Dr Death?' he asked her.

'His name's Simon.'

'That's the one. What's he got that I haven't?'

'Looks. Charm. Money. Sensitivity. Intelligence. A sense of humour. Do you want me to go on?'

'I have a sense of humour,' James said.

'Right.'

James sipped the chocolate and grimaced. 'It'll never work out.'

'For Christ's sake.'

'You know why?'

'You're going to tell me, so why ask my permission?'

'Because he's not a cop. He won't understand that your work comes first. He'll never understand that. He's a doctor. He think *his* work comes first. So you both come second. Get me?'

'You're wasted here. You should have been a philosopher.'

'You slept with him yet?' he asked, trying to sound casual, as if they were talking about the weather.

Fox felt her cheeks colour. Christ, men. They were obsessed

with sex. They bludgeoned you with it. It was a weapon. 'Is that any business of yours, TJ?'

'Yeah, I figured you had. Big mistake. Now you're going to get hurt.'

'What is your problem? You take a small condom size or were you picked on by other kids at school?'

'I'm just trying to highlight the problem for you. Everyone else can see it.'

'See what?'

'Why you have trouble getting blokes.'

Fox controlled her temper only with difficulty. 'I have trouble getting blokes because most of them are complete prats. Like you.'

James shrugged. 'I was only trying to help.'

'Don't,' she said and walked away.

Chapter Sixty-one

The Incident Room was crowded, the atmosphere thick with smoke, polystyrene coffee cups littered everywhere. Honeywell and Rankin had made up their own Christmas carol and had started singing it:

> Away at the Angel, they're piling up the dead,
> Poor old Pat Capper's been shot in the head.

As they walked in, Honeywell tossed the early edition of the paper at James. 'Have you seen this, skipper?' he said.

Capper had made the front page. There was a grainy photograph of his body being carried out of the King George and an inset in the bottom right-hand corner showed him attending the opening of a Soho nightclub with a certain showbusiness personality just a month before. The headline read: UNDERWORLD BOSS SLAIN IN LONDON PUB.

'Snappy headline,' Fox said.

'Brief and to the point,' James agreed.

He turned the page. There was more on the murder on page three, beside the obligatory nude. James read: 'The murder appears to be a part of an underworld feud, and it is rumoured to be a revenge killing linked to the shooting of Yardie gangster Elmore Crawford fifteen months ago, for which Capper was charged and later released. A Crown witness in the case was later found murdered. Police have failed to lay charges in either of these cases, and the senior inspector in charge of the investigations has since been transferred.'

'Where do they get this shite?' Honeywell hissed. 'The guv'nor asked for that transfer. They make it sound as if he was given the shove.'

'Do I get a mention anywhere?' Fox asked.

'Not unless that's you on page three,' James said.

'Do they mention that JUSTICE had been scrawled on the wall in Capper's own blood?'

James shook his head.

'We're in front, then.'

James tossed the paper in the bin. 'I was reading that,' Honeywell said.

There were photographs of Capper on the pin-board, for once not posing with London showbusiness celebrities in glossy magazines. In these particular three-by-five black and white glossies he was lying face up on the threadbare carpet of an Islington pub with two bullet wounds in his head and two more in his chest. The photographs had been taken from various angles around the room, and in all the shots the contents of Capper's skull featured prominently.

A wag had pinned a note to the board. *Dear Santa, Can I have a new head for Christmas. Love Pat. PS. I'd prefer one with a ponytail.*

There was also a floor plan of the pub and a street map of the area, enlarged several times.

Venables burst into the room looking pissed off. 'OK, settle down,' he shouted, and the room fell silent. 'You've all read the late editions, you know what they're saying about this. That it's the start of some underworld war. Journalistic nonsense. I'd like to wrap this one quickly and stick it right up them.'

Some of the men cheered Venables' uncharacteristic choice of language. Brave words, Fox thought. But if this is a professional hit we're going to need more than words, we're going to need a bit of luck as well.

He sat down. 'You've seen the map of the building on the board here. What we think happened is that Capper's assailant entered the building through this door here and made his way up the back stairs to the first floor. There is no sign of forced entry, so the room was either unlocked or he had a key. He may have even been given the key by the deceased himself, as there is every reason to believe Capper knew his assailant. We think he waited for Capper to arrive, and as soon as he walked through the door he produced a silenced pistol and shot him dead. We're still waiting on the forensic report, but I'm not holding my breath. This was a premeditated murder.'

Venables went around the room, checking on the progress of the investigation. Several of the team had been assigned to door-to-door enquiries. Nothing so far, they said.

'No one's going to talk to us anyway, sir,' James said. 'They've all read the papers. Who wants to be a witness in an underworld shooting and end up like Flora Ellis?'

'The skipper's right,' Honeywell agreed. 'This is the sort of thing that gets settled privately.'

Venables considered this, tapping the end of his Parker against his chin. 'This is what we do. I want a list of Capper's associates as well as his competition. We're going to hit them hard, their nightclubs, pubs, martial-arts clubs, the lot. Put the screws on. Hit them for inadequate fire safety, liquor licence irregularities, anything you can think of. Play it by the book, but make sure you make their lives a misery. We'll follow them around all day and fine them for littering until we get information on this one. Right?'

The men nodded. They were not enthusiastic, but they knew it had to be done.

'Now, what about this Elmore Crawford? I hate to say it, but the papers could be right. The two murders could be connected. We'll need to talk to his family, his close friends, business associates, find out what they were doing today between 10.30 and 11. Honeywell, Rankin, your job.'

The two detectives exchanged a look. Oh, joy.

'We also need to check on any personal enemies Capper may have had. Perhaps he's been sleeping with someone's wife. We have to cover all the angles here. I've worked out a duty list. I'll put it on the board. All weekend leave's cancelled. We stay with this one until it's sorted.'

The men climbed to their feet, stubbing out cigarettes and dragging on their coats.

Fox leaned in close. 'Sir, aren't we missing something?'

The expression on Venables' face was a picture. 'Yes, Fox?'

'The graffiti on the wall. JUSTICE.' That particular detail had been kept quiet from the press.

'What about it?'

'It doesn't make sense that this was a gangland murder. It seems personal.'

'That's why we're checking on the Elmore Crawford angle.'

Fox wondered why he was so aggressive. Perhaps, she thought, because he is as bewildered by this one jarring detail as the rest of us. 'Why would Capper meet privately with anyone connected to the Yardies? He'd take protection with him.'

'Thank you, Fox. Your point has been noted. Now let's get on. We have a lot to do.'

Radford stared at them over his gold-rimmed spectacles. 'Have you made any progress on this so far?'

'Not as yet, sir,' Venables said. 'We're keeping the pressure on the local firms, and we're getting all sorts of rumours. We still think it was a contract murder.'

'What do you have from forensics?'

'The ammunition was forty-five calibre hollowpoints. Home-made. Two of the four shells are not too badly mutilated, and ballistics say they can match the striations to a weapon, if we find it. A lot of other hairs and fibres were found in the room, probably too many. The room hadn't been cleaned in a while.'

'What about this graffiti that was written on the wall. JUSTICE. Is that the sort of thing a professional would do? Perhaps we should concentrate all our resources on some personal revenge motive.'

Venables fell silent. Fox stared at the ceiling.

'I'd like to cover every angle,' Venables said.

Radford shrugged. 'Well, you're in charge. Just get this sorted,' Radford said. 'I'll put whatever resources you need at your disposal. But just get this *sorted!*'

Chapter Sixty-two

Leicester Square was grey and bitterly cold. Michael was shivering inside his denim jacket. Fox sat beside him, as her alter ego Janie, in leathers and laddered stockings and cheap silver rings. A man had called to her from his car as she crossed Panton Street: 'How much?'

Thrilled, outraged, she tried to ignore him.

'Suck my dick for twenty?' he had said to her.

'You can kiss my arse for nothing,' she shot back.

He had beeped his horn and drew up again alongside her. 'OK,' he had said, beaming in almost boyish eagerness.

Now she sat there in the square, alongside all the crazies and the addicts and the toms. Tourists were queueing for tickets at the half-price booth near the underground. Pigeons strutted beside the benches pecking at crumbs.

Michael sat hunched up beside her, head down, a shadow of stubble on his cheeks and plum-coloured bruises under his eyes. He looked like hell.

'What do you know, Michael?'

His nose was running. He wiped it with the sleeve of his denim jacket. He was strung out, the worst she'd ever seen him. There was sweat on his upper lip and his breath was fetid. 'Old lady's got to have a hysterectomy.'

'I'm sorry to hear that, Michael.'

'She still blames me.' He leaned forward, put his head in his hands for a moment, then ran them through his long, greasy black hair.

Fox popped a wad of chewing gum in her mouth and sat there, her legs a little apart, both hands in the pockets of her studded leather jacket. Remember not to do this around the office, the thought. But there was a kind of freedom in it. Not every job let you flash your underwear in Leicester Square and still be a respectable taxpayer at night.

Michael sat up suddenly. 'You want to talk about Capper?'

'Who did it, Michael?'

'It was Mac.'

It was not the first time he had lied to her, she was sure, but it was the first time she had caught him out. Stuart Grayden may have murdered Flora Ellis, but he was not responsible for the death of Patrick Capper, of that she was certain. Grayden was in Marbella when Capper was shot, still was. He had recently bought a villa on the Costa del Crime and was spending the winters there. For his health, no doubt. In fact she knew who had killed Patrick Capper. It was a hard man from Birmingham, George Lennox, also known as Tank. Venables' campaign against Capper's underworld associates had indeed paid dividends, for he had been fingered by four different snouts. But they had no physical evidence, no witnesses, and not even Capper's associates knew who had paid Lennox to do the job. When Venables went to Birmingham to talk to him, he immediately lawyered up. The investigation had stalled right then and was going nowhere.

Fox decided to play along. 'How do you know it was Mac?' she asked him.

'I heard,' Michael mumbled.

'You heard.' Look at the state of him, she thought. Even if he did hear anything he was too wired to make any sense of it. He had just declared himself redundant. Pity. Snouts like Michael did not come along every day in a detective's life.

'Michael, when Capper died he had five thousand pounds with him in a briefcase. Why didn't the shooter take the money?'

'That would have been dishonest.'

Fox blinked, surprised. 'Dishonest?'

'He was paid to shoot him. He weren't paid to rip him off.'

'Paid by who?'

'The Yardies.'

'A name, Michael?'

'I dunno,' he said.

Fox shook her head. Another fabrication, she was sure. She took a last look at him, his nose running, his eyes sunken and bruised. She would miss him in a strange sort of way. 'Take care, Michael,' she said and stood up to go.

'Been hearing some strange shit,' he said.

She hesitated then sat down again. 'What kind of strange shit?'

'I was having a drink the other night. This bloke I know. Flash bastard. Lives out in Notting Hill.'

Fox said nothing, watched a bearded man, his T-shirt hanging out of his jeans, in a shouting match with a black girl, no more than fourteen years old. A tourist in a parka with a German flag sewn on to the hood was taking photographs. Like they were buskers.

'He said he's got this cop in his pocket,' Michael said.

Fox took a deep breath. Did she want to hear the rest of this? 'Who is this friend of yours, Michael?'

'Can't give you his name. But he's big. One of the biggest importers in the country, I reckon.'

Michael always did this, made it sound as if he was on first-name terms with every player in North London, when all he was doing was repeating a rumour. Still, some of the rumours were built around a kernel of truth, and she had made it a habit not to discount any of his stories completely.

Even now.

When she spoke again there was a hard edge to her voice.

'If you can't tell me his name, then what the hell good is it to me?'

Michael did not say anything for a while, his huge hands hanging between his knees, fingers knotting and unknotting around each other like worms in a bowl. 'His street name's Panther,' he said. 'His real name's Ahmed Khan. He's a Paki. Got connections at Heathrow, all right?'

She waited.

'Anyway, he was talking big, how he's got this cop in his pocket and he can deal as much shit as he wants and no one's ever going to touch him.'

'Who was he saying this to?'

Michael shrugged. 'He was just saying it.'

Fox could imagine the scene. This Panther with one of the local wide boys, Mickey the Flash or Charlie Williams at a billiards club or an illegal casino. Michael would be hanging around in the background, someone's gopher perhaps, or looking to move some stolen liquor. He would hear a few words, piece together a story with some other talk he'd heard, make up the rest to get her interested. Dangerous territory, this.

'What's this cop's name?'

'Friend of yours. That big bastard with the white hair. With the funny name. What was it? Marenko.'

Fox looked away, her mind whirling. The ravings of a junkie. Frank had made plenty of enemies. He was being set up. Had to be.

'See you around, Michael,' she said and walked away.

'It's true,' Michael said to her retreating back with what sounded to her like desperation.

Chapter Sixty-three

They met in the Anchor, by Southwark Bridge. It was a bitter winter's day. Fox watched a man down on Bankside struggle with the frame of his umbrella, blown inside out by a sudden gust of wind. The Thames was grey and forbidding, lighters and barges raising white caps at their bows.

It was superheated inside the pub. The trouble with an English winter, Fox thought. You were either too cold or too hot. Rain sparkled like diamond chips on Simon's Burberry overcoat. It was his day off, but she was in her working clothes, a black wool three-quarter-length overcoat and sensible shoes. Too cold for glamour. Her only concession to vanity was a Hermès scarf.

They sat in the Clink Bar downstairs under the Tudor beams, Simon nursing a pint to Caffrey's. The bar was filling with office workers. There was a Marvin Gaye song on the sound system, 'Sexual Healing'. Appropriate.

'I saw you on the news the other night,' he said, 'the gangland shooting. Are you hot on the trail or are you not allowed to talk about it?'

'We've rounded up the usual suspects,' she said.

He smiled. 'Sounds like New York or Chicago. It's still hard to think of you as a hard-bitten detective.'

She smiled. 'Then don't bite so hard.'

'*Is* it a gang war, like the papers say?'

She was hoping he would let it drop. Talking about her work still made her feel uncomfortable. She always sensed his disapproval. Or perhaps deep down she, too, felt there was perhaps something . . . well, strange . . . about a woman wanting to be a cop. 'I don't think so,' she said.

'You don't sound very enthusiastic about it.'

'I'm trying as hard as everyone else in the team to find out who killed Patrick Capper. But to be brutally frank I resent every hour I have to spend on it. Capper was evil, and he treated society with contempt.'

'In other words you don't have any leads,' Simon said, probably trying to make a joke, however lame.

But Fox took it seriously. 'We are in the familiar position of knowing who did it, but being unable to do anything about it. We don't know why this person did it, or who was behind it. It's not a whodunnit, it's a who-paid-for-it. But the hit man's hiding behind his brief so we'll never know. Sometimes I think it would be nice if we could bring back the rack.'

'Luckily I know you're joking.'

'Sure. Anyway, I meant for the lawyers, not the criminals.'

'It's not their fault,' he said. Like her, he didn't want to buy in to this but couldn't help himself.

'No, of course not. They just take the money and help contract murderers get back on the street, free to carry on with private enterprise. Just market forces, right?' Listen to her. She sounded like Marenko.

'Because you can't lock certain people up, you don't have to blame the whole legal profession.'

Oh, no. Here we go again. There's no value in this; keep your mouth shut. But the anger was burning in her belly, and she heard herself say: 'Of course. Stack the odds against the victims, then blame the police for being stupid. It's a great out, isn't it?'

Simon's face flushed. 'So what are you advocating? The thumbscrew as a means of routine interview?'

'I'm saying the law is weighted against the upholders of the law. Let me ask you this: if a brief knows his client is as guilty as hell and still gets him off, is he acting ethically? Is that in the interests of our society, of you and me?'

'Let's go back to solitary confinement and beatings.'

'Don't talk to me that way, Simon. Unlike you, I know what I'm talking about. I remember one kid I arrested back when I was in uniform. He had been in trouble with the law all his life — shoplifting, burglary, minor assaults — then one night he snapped and kicked the driver of a minicab to death over a six-pound cab fare. More likely he did it because the cabbie was Chinese. The jury called it GBH and the judge gave him two years. He was out on parole after nine months. This is justice? What about the cabbie's wife and family? They didn't lose a husband and a father for nine months; they lost him for ever. There's no clever barrister to hide behind when you're dead, no parole system when you're under the ground. You can't appeal when you've had your head kicked in by a little runt in Doc Martens. Three months after he got out he was arrested again for slashing someone's face with a razor in a pub brawl. Who's next? Me? You?'

'So let's bring back the Gestapo. That will solve everything.'

'It's not what I'm saying.'

'What *are* you saying? Because you sound like Himmler.'

Fox looked around. The people at the next table were staring, hearing raised voices. Time to stop, Fox thought.

But she had to have the last word. She lowered her voice. 'If I sound like Himmler, you sound like Michael Ball. Love changes everything, right?'

'You have to have laws.'

'Of course you do. Providing they work. Ours are patently spurious, and all they do is make a few unscrupulous cretins rich. By that I mean the lawyers and the criminals, and sometimes it's hard to tell one from the other these days.'

'You can't blame the ills of society on a few unprincipled men.'

'The ills of society derive from the rules that govern that society. Corruption has gravity, it filters down, not up. Would it be too much to ask that it was both legally as well as ethically incumbent on a lawyer to know and believe in his client's innocence before he represented him?'

'Everyone is entitled to legal representation. It's one of the foundations of our constitution.'

'Is it? So who is our constitution protecting? Hardened career criminals, child rapists, professional murderers?'

'Civil liberties is what makes our society civilised. It's what stands between us and the Hitlers and Stalins of this world.'

'Look around you. This is not civilisation; this is the veneer of it. It's like one of those Hollywood film sets: it looks great but it's all a façade, banged up with wood and a few nails. Our laws are being trampled on every day by people who don't give one hot fuck about civil liberties.'

'You're hysterical,' he said.

Until then it had been only her workday litany, a professional frustration at what she saw as the loading of the dice. What it was about this last comment that stung her she did not know. Perhaps the implied criticism against her sex. You are strident and female, therefore you are hysterical. But abruptly her frustration metamorphosed to rage, and when she was angry she became mean. 'What about your wife?' she hissed at him, and she saw the dismay on his face at hearing Anne's name brought up in this context. But she could not stop herself. 'What happened to the boy who killed her?'

'I hardly think that's the same thing.'

'The boy who did it was drunk. He was driving without a licence. Doesn't that make you angry?'

'There is nothing anyone can do about that now to change things. What would you do, hang him?'

'What did he get — twelve months? Does that seem just to you?'

'He has to live with what he's done.'

'You're making the huge assumption that his conscience still bothers him. Or is telling yourself that he's still sorry the only way you can get to sleep at night?'

Oh, she wished she could bite off her tongue. That was cruel.

'Vengeance wouldn't change anything,' he said.

'No, that's right. I don't believe in vengeance either. I do believe in protecting the innocent. There are monsters among us, Simon, and blowhards like you—'

'—blowhards?'

'—stick your head in the sand and seem to believe that everyone can be reformed. Well, they can't.' She leaned across the table. 'Do you want to know what that bastard did to Kate Mercer before he killed her?'

'No, and please keep your voice down. No one else on the South Bank wants to know the gory details either.' He drained his glass. 'Look at the time. Don't you have to get back to work?'

Remorse and embarrassment overtook her as quickly as her rage. She was suddenly acutely conscious of her surroundings. 'Yes, let's go,' she said and hurried off, Simon trailing after her, vainly calling for her to wait.

Chapter Sixty-four

James was standing by the bar with a pint of Young's. Rankin had moved away to the Gents. Fox took advantage of the moment and walked across with her gin and tonic and sat on a stool next to him.

James was so transparent. She could see what he was thinking. As if.

'How's things?' she said.

'Better for seeing you.'

'I'm not flirting with you, TJ.'

'Never crossed my mind, ma'am.'

'Where's Honeywell?'

'Went home early. His dog's sick. Got hit by a car.'

'Oh. I'm sorry.'

'It's all right. He doesn't like the bloody thing. It's just an excuse.' He watched her over the rim of his glass. 'So. You're looking great.'

'Thanks. I wanted to ask you about Frank.'

The smirk fell away.

'How's he going? Have you seen him lately?'

He shrugged. 'You know Frank. He won't ever change.'

'I would have thought narcotics is quite a change of pace.'

'Well. You know, he says it's like a drug.'

'Was that a joke? Sorry. I missed it.'

'He reckons it's the same people that are doing the homicides, but in the Drug Squad you get to see a different side of them. You know. Bend over while I put on these rubber gloves.'

Baiting her with their crudities again. Men. They never tired of it. 'It just surprises me, that's all.'

He gave her a quizzical look.

'I mean, I wonder why.'

'Something on your mind?' he said, and his eyes started to search the room for escape.

She chewed her lip. The question would not form in her mind. 'I've heard things.'

Since talking to Michael she had made discreet enquiries about the mysterious Ahmed Khan. It seemed that he was not a product of Michael's delirium but a real person with an import– export business and a warehouse in King's Cross, mainly carpets, silk and cotton. That was her first nasty surprise. The second unpleasant surprise was the discovery that Khan had indeed been under investigation by the Drug Squad but that charges had been dropped when videotaped evidence went missing. The chief investigating officer on the case was Detective Chief Inspector Frank Marenko.

'What sort of things have you heard?' James asked her.

'Nasty rumours. They involve a man by the name of Ahmed Khan.'

She watched the expression on James's face. Oh, shit. It was true. When he spoke, there was a hard edge to his voice, almost as if he thought she was trying to drag him into the conspiracy. 'Be careful what you say. He's a good cop. You don't want to believe everything you hear.'

'It's not whether I want to believe it. It's whether it's true.'

'There are always rumours when you work in the Drug Squad. Goes with the territory.'

Rankin came back, saying something about shaking hands with the unemployed. Fox ignored him, finished her drink and went home. She had always felt like an outsider, but never as much as she did right now.

Chapter Sixty-five

If he was taking bribes, he didn't have much to show for it. He wore the same grey suit she remembered, his tie spotted with a dark stain, perhaps gravy or ketchup from a police canteen. He looked bigger and heartier than she had seen him in years, more like a sales manager who'd let himself go than a senior police detective.

It was another cold and wet afternoon. The overheated bar near Victoria Station where they met was packed, mainly the after-work crowd. The place had the same jarring mix of dark oak panelling and garish poker machines as the King's Head.

He was standing with his foot on the brass rail nursing a whisky and dry.

'Foxy,' he said. He looked uncharacteristically cheerful.

'Good to see you again, guv.' Guv. It was a hard habit to break, even though he was no longer her boss.

'How's life treating you? How's the venerable Venables?'

'He's a complete misogynist and he tries to make my life a misery in every conceivable way. In fact, things are just the same as when you were there.'

He laughed easily, didn't even bite.

'Looking good, guv.'

'I have the same personal trainer as Terry Wogan. What are you drinking?'

'Usual.'

Marenko ordered a gin and tonic and another whisky and dry. He took a packet of thin cigars from his pocket and lit one.

'Cigars now?'

'If you're going to work in the Drug Squad you need to understand addiction. It's called going under cover.'

'Any big busts?'

'One of the plonks in the typing pool is pretty well stacked.'

Fox made a face.

'That was a joke.'

'Went over my head.'

'Look, I show up in the morning, I get through the day, I go home. I don't get too excited about it. You put away one dealer, there's another one waiting around the corner to take his place.'

'So what are you doing over there?'

'Treading water until pension day.'

The drinks arrived. Fox gulped at hers. 'How's Tom?' she asked him.

At the mention of his son-in-law's name Marenko's face underwent a transformation. The pain etched into the lines around his nose and mouth were plainly visible when the smile disappeared. 'He's fucked. I don't want to talk about it.'

'OK.'

'But thanks for asking. Some people have forgotten already. For a few weeks he's a battered hero. Then Jules takes him home and he's just another spastic in a wheelchair. Know what I mean? Nobody cares how he got to be that way. They just stare at the dribble.'

'It's a waste.'

'Yeah. Well. At least the piece of shit that did it to him isn't walking around mouthing off about it any more.' He took a deep breath to calm down.

Fox toyed with the lemon in her gin. There was a heavy silence. Marenko knew she wanted something, but he wasn't going to help her with it. How am I going to handle this? she wondered.

'I hear Venables has taken some heat over this Capper murder,' Marenko said. 'Bet that's really burning his arse.'

'There's a friendlier atmosphere at the Junkyard than Hendon Road right now.'

Marenko laughed easily, every inch the sales manager out with one of the staff. 'Someone else who got what was coming.'

'Shot in the head and chest four times.'

'How about that.'

Why did she feel as if he were taunting her? Oh, it had crossed her mind. She had made discreet enquiries. When Patrick Capper was murdered, Frank Marenko was involved in a drug bust on a warehouse at Heathrow. There were almost a dozen Drug Squad detectives with him at the time. Frank Marenko had not shot Patrick Capper. It had been a bizarre notion from the start.

'Forensics come up with anything?'

'Nothing we can run with.'

'Witnesses?'

'We found two people who thought they saw a man walking out of the fire-escape door at the back of the pub at around the time the murder was committed. One of them wears glasses and the other has a mental disorder.'

'Way to go.'

'Anyway, we think we know who did it.'

'Yeah?'

'Professional contract killer. Remember George Lennox?'

'He was a mercenary for a while. Angola. Two convictions for GBH.'

She nodded. Marenko's encyclopedic memory had always astonished her. 'We can't prove anything. He says he came to London to see *Phantom of the Opera*. Even has the ticket stub.'

'You talked to him?'

She nodded. 'He said he preferred *Les Mis*.'

Marenko finished his drink and ordered two more. 'Tough case.'

'At least with Capper dead we've closed the files on the Flora Ellis and Elmore Crawford shootings. That just leaves Kate Mercer.'

'The only one that really mattered anyway. That's the problem, Fox. The department pays for hundreds of man-hours looking for a bloke who topped someone we're all better off without. Why not write it off as a lucky break?'

'I guess,' she heard herself say. She thought about the fight she had had with Simon in the Anchor the other afternoon. Now it seemed it was her turn to play devil's advocate.

'You don't think so?'

'I had this same conversation recently. Someone put it to me that murder is murder, whichever way you look at it.'

'No, it's not. You put a gun in some guy's hand and send him off to Iraq and tell him to shoot people he doesn't know, you call it warfare and give him a medal. You do it in Camden Town, you send an SO19 squad round to arrest him. See? It's not black and white at all. Murder is a question of sanction and geography.'

'But it's not our job to decide whether a murder is worth investigating or not. You told me that.'

'Maybe I was wrong. What happened to Patrick Capper used to be called execution. Lennox was doing everyone a favour.'

'Only if he was sanctioned by law.'

'Well, maybe the law's wrong. If Lennox walked in here right now I'd buy him a drink.'

Fox looked into his eyes. Her old boss, her mentor and tormentor. The question was: Is he crazy? Worse, is he bent?

'Anyway, what was it you wanted to see me about?'

She felt her heart hammering in her chest. Here goes nothing. 'I'm hearing things, guv.'

'Your grass. Don't tell me. What's his name? Weasel?'

'Ferret.'

'I knew it was some kind of rodent.'

'He's been pretty good to us over the years.'

'You spend too much time with scrotes like him, you lose touch with reality. What's the point? You can't ever use them in court. I think you get a hard-on hanging around the underworld like that. That's how you get off.'

'I'm a woman, guv. I don't get hard-ons.'

'You don't know what you're missing.'

'No, but I can guess. Still, we're getting off-track here.'

'And what is the track? Which particular dead end are we exploring now?'

She took a deep breath. 'There's an Asian businessman in King's Cross sounding off that he has a member of the Drug Squad in his pocket.'

'Want another drink, Fox?'

'Guv?'

'What?'

'Why would he say something like that?'

'I don't know. Ask him.'

'I'm asking you.'

'You want me to dignify that sort of shit with a reply? Is that it?'

'I want you to tell me it's not true, Frank.'

His demeanour changed abruptly. She had seen him turn mean like this in interrogation rooms. It was no act. Deep inside Frank Marenko there was a fathomless reservoir of rage. He fixed her with a cold stare. 'If he's referring to me, no, it's not true. There you go. That's what you wanted to hear, right? Let me guess. Ahmed Khan.'

She met his stare.

'There's already been an internal investigation. I was cleared. And by the way I'm still a DCI and you're a detective inspector. You don't call me Frank.' He looked at his watch. 'Is that the time?'

'You know I've always admired you, guv.'

'Careful, Fox. That sounded like a threat. You hit me again, I'll make *your* nose bleed this time.'

'What *did* happen to the tape?'

'Not really your concern. I've got to be getting home. Cat needs feeding.'

They didn't say goodbye. She watched him walk out of the bar, turning up his collar against the rain. She finished her drink and left too, took the Circle Line to Notting Hill Gate. On the train she tried not to think about Frank Marenko taking payoffs from Asian drug dealers.

Christ. No wonder cops got burned out.

Carrie had got herself a new place, the top floor of a terrace in Fulham, all white gingerbread and a bell on the front door that actually worked. Fox sat in the living room overlooking the street and watched Daisy pulling all the books out of the bookcase while Carrie made tea.

Carrie had finally got her life straightened out. She had a job, she had a nursery for Daisy, she had a boyfriend who didn't drink too much, beat her up or have affairs with other women. Yet. Fox was happy for her but a little frightened too. It was selfish, but somehow it had been a consolation having a best friend who was a mess. It had somehow made her feel that her own life was together.

Now she was the one in freefall.

Carrie came back into the room with two cups, bone china, Fox noticed, not mugs. She put the cups down on the coffee table, then picked up Daisy and carried her over to the playpen in the corner. Daisy hung tenaciously to a copy of Salman's Rushdie's *Midnight's Children*. 'Might as well let her have it,' Carrie said after a half-hearted attempt to prise it from her small but determined grip. 'If she starts now, she might get to finish it by the time she draws her pension.'

Fox smiled and looked away out of the window. There was

snow on the brown tiles of Fulham and on the roofs of the cars in the street. She heard the steady drip-drip-drip from the eaves as the ice started to thaw. A grey mist hung over the street, the sky the colour of slush. The plane trees that lined the street were bare now, but Fox thought they must look wonderful in June, with the sun filtered through the leaves. Summer seemed so far away right now.

'You OK?' Carrie asked her.

She shrugged, not knowing where to start.

'How's things with Simon?'

'We had a fight last week. I haven't seen him since.'

'What was the fight about?'

'Things.'

'Yeah, right. That's always a hard one to get around.'

Fox smiled, acknowledging the inadequacy of her answer. 'Nothing important.'

'What's going on, Maddy?'

'I don't know. Things at work.'

'That job's killing you. When are you going to go out and get a life?'

'When we've caught all the bad people,' she said, but Carrie didn't smile. 'That was a joke.'

'I think you mean it.'

'I'll be OK.'

'You've got to get out and have some fun, Maddy. There's more to life than death. And you can quote me on that.'

'I love my job.'

'Your job doesn't love you.'

Fox wondered what to say to her. Sure, Kate Mercer and Flora Ellis were part of the problem. So was Marenko. But it wasn't just her job. 'I sort of go undercover now and then,' she said.

Carrie looked at her, puzzled by the relevance of this remark.

'I get scared. Sometimes I think I would like to be that person for a while.'

'And this is making you this unhappy?'

'It would be good to have no responsibilities. Just to run wild. Not worry about anyone but yourself.'

Carrie leaned forward eagerly. 'That's what I've been trying to tell you. You don't have to go undercover to get yourself a life, Maddy. Just kick back a while and do it.'

It all sounded so simple. But Carrie didn't understand.

'You need a holiday,' Carrie said.

Fox smiled. 'Sure,' she said. 'Maybe when all this is over.'

If it would ever be over. Really.

PART SIX

Camden Town.
An early morning in winter

Chapter Sixty-six

A familiar scene, blue and white police tape, blue strobes swirling in the rain, another body. This time their victim was slumped against a storeroom wall, in a sitting position, dried blood and brain matter sprayed across the wall above his head and over some empty confectionery boxes.

James stood in the doorway, hunched under the eaves, his black hair plastered over his skull by the rain, whistling tunelessly between his teeth as he watched the men in the white overalls do their work.

James saw her and nodded. Fox took shelter under the eaves beside him and stared at the peeling plaster. The word JUSTICE had been daubed on it in blood. It had leaked down the wall, carmine tears for the Candy Man.

She returned her attention to Henry Lincoln Wexxler, slumped in the corner of his storeroom, among the cardboard cartons of chocolates and cheese and onion crisps. Henry Lincoln Wexxler, a torch in his right hand, arms and legs sprawled in unnatural positions, like a string puppet that had been dropped onto the floor by a child. Henry Lincoln Wexxler, wearing that stupid half-lidded expression of the recently dead, already in rigor, the detectives who were to avenge him staring at him with the satisfaction of a lynch mob. Henry Lincoln Wexxler, sweet shop proprietor, wondering what time it is.

Time to die, Henry.

JUSTICE

A taunt, a statement? A droplet of rain squeezed between her umbrella and the collar of her coat and began its chill and tortuous journey down her spine. She shuddered. *Justice.* What did it mean? They were being taunted with a motive, but what did a professional gangster like Patrick Capper and a sweet shop owner with a record of minor sexual offences have in common?

'Stabbed ten times with a Weetabix,' James said. 'We think we're looking for a cereal killer.'

Fox ignored him. An old joke.

'The Chief is going to go apeshit,' she said.

'Why can't I get excited?' James said. 'Is it because I would have liked to have topped the dirty bastard myself?'

'Jesus, TJ. What the hell is going on?'

'You mean why is our victim not a woman or a little kid? You prefer it that way?'

'You know what I mean.'

'Whoever did it should have kneecapped him first.'

She let that pass. 'How was it done?'

'Popped him twice by the looks of it. They just levered a bullet out of the wall there. One as he came out of the house, probably the second when he was already dead, just to make sure. How about we go inside and do it standing up to celebrate?'

There were spectators in the alley, behind the police tape, in dressing gowns and wellington boots, holding umbrellas against the rain. Some of them were forgoing breakfast for this. The uniformed policeman guarding the cordon was hunched miserably in the downpour. Fox went back through the shop, saw a Sierra pull up outside, heard Venables' cultured voice barking orders at a policeman. Oh my. Seven o'clock and in a very bad mood.

DC Rankin went to meet him, holding an umbrella over Venables' grizzled head.

'Who is it?' Venables snapped at Fox.

'His name is Henry Wexxler, sir.'

'Is he known to us?'

'He was our chief suspect in the murder of Kate Mercer.'

'That's what I bloody thought.'

He followed Fox through the sweet shop, past the stairs that led to the upstairs flat and stared briefly at the body.

'The assailant came in the back way,' she said. 'Levered open a window with a crowbar. It looks like Mister Wexxler heard a noise and came downstairs to investigate. And he popped him.'

Venables peered through the yellow-lit doorway. He looked at the bloody message on the wall and his eyes narrowed into slits. 'Fox, we have to get this fucking lunatic before he ruins my career.'

'Yes, guv,' she said. She couldn't think of anything else to say.

'Are we finished up here?' Venables said to Graveney.

Gravedigger stripped off the latex gloves and dropped them on the floor. 'Your man was shot twice in the head. No other injuries that I can ascertain.'

'Was he raped?' James asked.

Graveney stared at him, mystified. 'No.'

'Pity,' James said.

Graveney shook his head. One sick puppy, she could see him thinking.

'Time of death?' Venables asked.

'We have first stage rigor, that puts it between two to twelve hours. Body temperature narrows it to around six to eight hours. It's cold in here. Say eight.'

'One in the morning,' Venables said. He turned to Fox.

'Who found him?'

'Delivery man. When he didn't get an answer at the front door he came round the back. Found the door half open and Mister Wexxler in his present redundant state.'

It looked like a professional hit. Yet the bloody letters left on the wall seemed to deny that. As did the identity of the victim himself. Who, in the name of God, would put a contract out on an impecunious shop proprietor?

They were loading the mortal remains of Henry Lincoln Wexxler into the mortuary van. Because rigor was by now well established and because he had been lying against the wall all night he now lay inside the body bag in a semi-reclining position. Ludicrous. It looked as if they were trying to put a covered armchair in the back of a removals van. She heard one of the attendants mutter something to his partner and they both started to laugh.

The obituary for the Candy Man. His death had been reduced to a furtive joke in the rain. She guessed he didn't deserve any better.

Venables was standing outside the shop waiting for her. 'I've called Honeywell.'

'Sir?'

'He was family liaison on the Katherine Mercer murder, wasn't he?'

She nodded.

'I want you to go with him and interview Katie Mercer's father.'

'Oh Christ, no.'

'I know what you're thinking. But we have to do it.'

'Yes, sir.'

'I don't like it any more than you do. But he has to be a suspect at this stage. Hopefully, we can eliminate him pretty quickly.'

'What about Capper? He wouldn't have shot Capper.'

Venables looked uncomfortable. He knew she was right. There was a common denominator to the two murders. It didn't make sense, threw all the normal procedures askew. It couldn't be a copycat murder because they had so far kept the details of the Capper murder out of the press. So what was going on?

'We still have to interview Katherine Mercer's father,' he said. 'Don't just stand there. Off you go.'

They pulled up outside Tolway Court. Fox turned off the engine and sat there chewing ~~his~~ lip. There were puddles on the pavement and a small lake had formed on the bitumen around the tree. Honeywell wiped the condensation off the windscreen. 'Jesus, I'm really looking forward to this.'

'He'll be happy to hear Wexxler's dead, at least.'

'Yeah,' Honeywell said. 'If I was him I'd want to ask us what the hell we're doing busting our guts looking for the bloke who did it. Where were you the night the pervert who raped and murdered your little girl was killed, Mr Mercer? Right. Who really gives a shit?'

'We can't have vigilantes running around taking the law into their own hands.'

'Christ, ma'am, who'd want to be a cop?'

'Me and you, apparently.'

'And I'm starting to get sick of it. That just leaves you, ma'am. Last one out turns off the lights at Hendon Road.' He took out his chewing gum and flicked it out of the window.

'Well no point just sitting here,' she said. 'Let's get this over with.'

Chapter Sixty-seven

The interview with Brian Mercer was even worse than she had anticipated. He had answered the door in his dressing gown. He had lost a lot of weight since she had last seen him; he had also lost his job, he said, although he did not explain how that had happened. Perhaps the medications piled on the kitchen bench had something to do with it. She had heard of people getting addicted to tranquillisers. Too many doctors in London who were prepared to pass them out like . . . like sweets, she caught herself thinking.

At first he seemed to think their purpose in informing him of Henry Wexxler's death was as some kind of solace for his pain. He started to thank them, quite profusely, as if they had pumped the bullets into the Candy Man themselves. When it became clear to him that he was a suspect in the case he jumped to his feet and started shouting and throwing things around the flat.

Fox understood how he felt.

Honeywell managed to calm him after a while. But when they asked him if he wanted legal representation he became violent again. She saw his wife and children watching through the doorway. As if they hadn't all suffered enough, she thought.

Finally they got a statement from him. He had been at home all night, he said. At 1 o'clock he was in bed, asleep. With his wife.

No, he didn't kill the bastard. He should have done. He'd thought about it.

So, what are you going to do? Arrest me now?

Fox tried to placate him, but he had worked himself into another rage. He hasn't take his tranquillisers this morning, she thought.

Get out of here, he screamed at them. Get out of here! Haven't I been through enough?

Mrs Mercer had ushered them out of the door. Just go, she had said. I'll be all right. I'll get him sorted. I've had plenty of practice.

As they left they heard something smash against the door.

They drove for a long time in silence.

'That went well,' Honeywell said.

'Brilliant.'

'Venables should have done it himself. It was his idea.'

'That's one of the perks of being the boss. You leave the minions to shovel the shit.'

'Poor bastard. I suppose he's got a point.'

Fox looked round at him.

'When he asked us why we were wasting time on this,' he said.

'Because that's what they pay us to do.' She stared through the windscreen at a grimy London morning, dirty rain on the glass, a city the colour of cold grease.

Honeywell flicked a piece of chewing gum in his mouth, offered one to Fox. She took it. 'It's a vigilante,' he said.

Fox tried to get it to gel in her mind. A vigilante. A vigilante with connections to Patrick Capper and Henry Lincoln Wexxler. A vigilante who wanted to make a point to society. Why else would he leave that one word, JUSTICE, written in his victim's blood?

Chapter Sixty-eight

Fox stared at the newspaper, as she had done a hundred times that day. As if she couldn't quite believe it, as if by just willing it she could make it go away. The headline jumped out at her in thick bold type: THE JUSTICE KILLER. Some living, breathing turd at one of the newspapers had written up the link between the Capper and the Wexxler slayings, revealing that JUSTICE had been scrawled on the wall in blood in both killings. Despite Scotland Yard's best efforts at keeping it quiet, despite their pleas to the proprietors of all the leading national newspapers to keep a lid on it, a small community newspaper had broken ranks first and then the *Sun* and *Mirror* had followed.

Now every crazy in the whole of the country with a grudge against society might be tempted to follow suit. The story had whipped up hysteria in the media, with the morning current-affairs and chat programmes speculating on the alleged links between the two killings. Some news commentators had furthered their own agendas by making the Justice Killer, as they had dubbed him, some kind of hero. They had him vindicated before they had even caught him.

None of this had done anything to aid the investigation. It had served only to make everyone at Hendon Road a focus of intense media scrutiny.

The telephone rang and she snatched it up.

'Hello, darling.'

'Who is this?' she snapped, thinking it might be James. Another joke.

'It's Simon.'

Oh. Simon. There was a long silence on the other end of the line. Probably not the sort of response he had hoped for. 'This is not a good time for me,' she said.

'Why, what's up?' What's up? Didn't they get newspaper deliveries in Wimbledon? James's words came back to her. *He's a doctor. He think his work comes first. So you both come second. Get me?*

'Have you see the newspaper headlines? We're under a bit of pressure here.'

Another long silence. She could almost hear him pouting into the telephone. 'I rang to see if you wanted to go out to dinner tonight.'

And fight again? 'I can't tonight,' she said, perhaps too quickly.

'Oh. OK. Well, I'll call you later in the week.'

'OK,' she said without enthusiasm.

'I hope you'll be feeling better then.'

He hung up before she could shoot back a response. *Feeling better.* Who said she wasn't feeling just fine?

James looked over and saw her expression. 'Doctor Death pull the pin?'

'Grow up, TJ,' she said and walked out of the room. As she closed the door she heard the catcalls from Rankin and Honeywell. She went into the Ladies locker room and splashed cold water on her face. She looked at herself in the mirror. She looked like hell. All night she had lain awake, thinking about the Capper and Wexxler slayings, and a terrible suspicion had insinuated itself into her mind.

She closed her eyes, saw Henry Lincoln Wexxler's wall. And it hit her. She realised what was wrong, what had jarred with her that morning. Without stopping to dry her hands and face she hurried back to the Incident Room and stared at the black and whites of the crime scene on the pin board. JUSTICE.

And she knew.

Venables looked around at the faces of his squad as they sprawled in chairs or leaned against walls. There was a curious tension to the room. She realised they weren't all going in the same direction; some of the men didn't really want to find the shooter on this one.

But there was nowhere to hide. It was one thing having two unsolved murders within a few weeks of each other, another having a serial killer on the loose and the tabloids running with the story. A lot of the more junior men would never have worked under this sort of pressure.

Venables briefed them on the latest development. It now appeared that the murders of Patrick Capper and Henry Wexxler had almost certainly been committed by the same person or persons. A vigilante, perhaps.

'What about Lennox?' James asked.

Venables shook his head. 'He can be discounted,' he said. 'We've checked him out. He was in a Birmingham hospital at the time of Wexxler's murder.'

'Someone take a shot at *him*?'

'Appendicitis.'

Fox massaged her temples. There was a dull pain behind her eyes.

'We cannot allow speculation at this stage to distract us from good, basic police work,' Venables said. 'We have to stop trying to guess why. Find out who did this, then we'll be able to put some rationale behind it.'

Nervous glances were exchanged around the room.

Venables looked over at Rankin, who had been in charge of the team going door to door around MacNaghten Row that morning. 'Anything?' he asked him.

He consulted his notebook. 'Nothing that really checks out. No one seems to have heard anything. He must have used a silencer. Like with Capper. A woman two doors down from the sweet shop thought she saw a man walking down the alley about midnight.'

'Did she get a look at him?'

He shook his head.

'Nothing else?'

'A man in the next street saw some kid hanging around and telephoned the police. That was about 10 o'clock. I wouldn't think it's the shooter. Just some punk looking for a video to steal.'

'That's all?'

'I interviewed another gentleman of the Irish persuasion who believed he saw a car pull out of the alleyway at about 1 a.m. and drive right past him.'

'Registration?' Venables asked hopefully.

Rankin shook his head. 'He can't even remember what make of car it was. In fact, when I questioned him a little more closely he wasn't even sure it was last night. I suspect he may have been drinking.'

Laughter, the first that morning.

Venables looked depressed. This was going to be a sticker. 'I just got a phone call from Dr Clark at forensics,' he said finally. He was nervous. He opened the file on his lap, and the crime-scene photographs slipped out on to the floor. Fox bent down, picked them up and handed them back to him. He didn't even acknowledge her.

He checked his notes. 'They found a number of footprints behind the shed at the bottom of the garden. They were made recently, and they don't match Mr Wexxler's shoe size. This would lead us to speculate that someone concealed themselves there on the night of his murder, may even have been there on previous nights, establishing his habits. So we may have to broaden the area of enquiry, find out if anyone in that area saw

anything unusual not only last night but over the course of this
week. We want a description of anyone seen acting suspiciously,
cars parked near the lane for a long period of time, that sort of
thing.'

'Problem is,' Rankin said, 'people aren't being very helpful.'
Rankin looked uncomfortable. 'I mean, a few of them actually
came right out and said it.'

'Said what?' Venables asked.

'You know, sir. That they didn't want us to find him.'

Venables pen beat a tattoo on the edge of the manila folder
in his lap. 'We have a job to do, ladies and gentlemen,' he said.

Dead silence in the room. Venables returned his attention to
his notes.

'The murder took place at approximately 1 o'clock in the
morning. Mr Wexxler was shot at very close range, the second
gunshot wound leaving powder marks on his forehead. His killer
broke in, waited for him to come down the stairs and then . . .'
He made a pantomime of a gun with his thumb and index finger
and pulled the trigger.

'What about Brian Mercer?' DC Jones asked, and was
rewarded with icy stares from around the room. James mouthed
the word 'Prat!' at him.

'DI Fox and DC Honeywell have already interviewed Mr
Mercer,' Venables said, as if it was their idea.

'He was in bed at home with his wife,' Fox said.

Venables started to fumble through the file on his lap. He
produced a print-out. 'Thirteen months ago police were called to
MacNaghten Row after the report of a disturbance. Brian
Mercer threw a housebrick through Mr Wexxler's shopfront
window. He was arrested by uniformed officers from Islington
police station for resisting arrest and being drunk and disorderly.'

James and Honeywell exchanged a glance. Fox knew they
were both thinking the same thing: I wonder how Frank
Marenko would have handled this?

'It seems to me,' Venables went on, 'that if he has been making visits to MacNaghten Row for thirteen months, he could well have been planning something like this.'

'That was an isolated incident, sir,' Honeywell said.

'Actually the inspector at Islington station has told me Mr Wexxler has made a number of complaints about Mr Mercer, that he has called the police on five different occasions to complain about him loitering at the front of the sweet shop or in the alleyway at the rear.'

Dead silence.

'I believe we have due cause to effect a search and seizure warrant on Mr Mercer to discover if there are any shoes in the flat that correspond to the prints found by the forensic team earlier this morning.'

This is a nightmare, Fox thought. How do I stop this?

Venables shuffled his papers again, consulting the notes he had made to himself from his telephone discussions with the forensics scientists at Lambeth a few minutes before. 'Dr Clark tells me that there were no shell casings found at the scene. As it is reasonable to believe at this stage that the murderer was using a silencer, then it follows that the assailant took the time to pick up the casings before he left the scene and took them with him, in order to make it more difficult for us to identify the ammunition used. It appears to be the work of a professional.'

'That gets Mercer off the hook, then?' Fox said.

'Perhaps Mercer employed someone to do the job for him,' Venables said.

'He doesn't have the connections. Or the money.'

'Maybe he cashed in an insurance policy. We should check that.'

'Yes, let's put him through hell all over again,' Fox murmured, saying what they were all thinking.

Venables looked up sharply. 'We have a job to do, Inspector. Even if we don't like it.'

'Sir,' she said through gritted teeth.

There was another long silence. Fox marshalled her thoughts. Her next outburst must not be an emotional one, not if she wanted to keep Venables' respect. 'What about Patrick Capper,' she said slowly. 'There is no possible connection to him. Yet we have this word scrawled at the crime scene in both cases. I believe we are looking for some . . . vigilante. We are wasting our time harassing Brian Mercer. We are only adding immeasurably to his grief at the loss of his daughter.'

Venables sighed. 'As I said at the beginning, we cannot allow ourselves to be distracted by the more sensational aspects of this case. Brian Mercer has to be eliminated from this particular investigation.'

Fox hesitated. 'Yes, sir,' she said.

But she didn't believe it. In fact, she thought she already knew who was responsible for the murders of Patrick Capper and Henry Lincoln Wexxler. But the idea was just so bizarre, so grotesque, there was no way she was going to put her name to it at that moment.

It was the first time Fox had stayed over at Simon's apartment. Usually, if she slept with him she slipped home again in the early hours of the morning. She liked waking up in her own bed, and that way she still felt in control of her life, not a part of someone else's.

But last night she had worked late because of the Candy Man investigation, and she had not got to Simon's until after eleven. They had talked for hours and by then she was too tired to drive home. So, for the first time, she stayed over.

She wondered what Sandy would think about it.

She knew that Sandy liked her, and it was obvious she approved of her father going out with her. But even so, that morning when Sandy walked into the kitchen Fox felt her cheeks burn. She and Simon were both standing at the breakfast bar, drinking coffee. Fox was wearing one of Simon's white shirts, which reached almost to her knees. It was a weekday, and Sandy was dressed in her school uniform. 'Hi,' she said casually, as if her father's girlfriends slept over all the time.

Their eyes met. I wonder what she's thinking, Fox thought. But Sandy smiled sweetly at her and said nothing.

'Having breakfast?' Sandy asked her, holding up a cereal bowl.

'I can't eat anything in the mornings. I just have a couple of black coffees.'

Sandy put two Weetabix in a bowl. 'That's not good for you.'

'I like living on the edge.'

Sandy opened a new carton of milk, but she poured too quickly and the milk spilled on to the breakfast bar. 'Shit,' she said.

'I beg your pardon,' Simon said.

'I only said "shit".'

'That's not language I want to hear from a young lady.'

Sandy gave Fox a conspiratorial wink. 'Of course. My mind is fresh and innocent and should not be corrupted.'

Fox and Simon exchanged a glance. That sounded like a shot across the bows. Never too early in the morning to start.

Sandy put the milk back in the fridge and turned the radio on. They caught the final bars of an Oasis song and then the announcer launched into a long and breathless announcement about Liam Gallagher appearing in person at the Virgin Store in Oxford Street on Thursday night.

'Can I go to that?' Sandy asked.

'You'll be at school,' Simon told her, taking a croissant from the microwave.

'I've got time to get home and get the train in.'

'Still no.'

'Why not?'

A fight coming, Fox thought. Suddenly they were both looking at her, seeking support. I want no part of this. 'I have to use the bathroom,' she said, but she wasn't out of the door fast enough.

Sandy fixed her with an imploring look. 'What do you think, Madeleine?'

'I think it's none of my business.'

Sandy toyed with her cereal, thinking of another angle. 'Didn't you go to concerts with your friends when you were my age?'

'Which is how old?'

'Fourteen.'

'When I was fourteen I was living in a little village of five hundred people and I still had a teddy bear.'

Sandy looked disappointed.

'In fact, I still have the bear.'

'Dad doesn't trust me.'

'It's not a matter of not trusting you,' Simon told her. 'I just don't like the idea of you going into London on your own. I told you, if you really want to go, I'll take you.'

'Go to see Liam Gallagher with my father?' Sandy shrieked, and put two fingers into her mouth and feigned throwing up to demonstrate her feelings about that idea.

'I think perhaps your father's right,' Fox said. 'There are lots of bad people out there. You're only fourteen.'

'What would you know?' Sandy said. 'You still sleep with a teddy bear.'

Take that. Fox wrestled with a smile. Simon just looked embarrassed.

'I think I'll take that shower now,' Fox said and escaped from the kitchen.

From the hallway she heard Sandy say: 'But it's Liam Gallagher.'

'I don't care if it's the Pope.'

'I wouldn't want to see the *Pope*.'

'The answer's no.'

'But why?'

'I've told you. You're not old enough. You're not going into the city on your own at night.'

'It's not night. It's afternoon.'

'By the time you get home it will be dark.'

'You don't trust me. Fourteen years old and you still treat me like a baby!'

Fox smiled. Exactly the words she had once used on her father. Keep it up, she thought. You'll wear him down in the end.

Chapter Sixty-nine

With the death of Henry Lincoln Wexxler, the Kate Mercer investigation was considered closed. Officially, it was still open because no charges had ever been laid or a conviction recorded, but in the minds of everyone who had worked on the Katherine Mercer AMIT, for detectives like James and Rankin and Honeywell, it was solved. As with Elmore Crawford, their prime suspect was dead.

Everyone was satisfied except one Detective Inspector Madeleine Fox.

Fox sat alone in her office, content in the perverse luxury of having the rest of the evening, and perhaps even the rest of that night, to work as hard as she wanted on whatever she wished without getting paid for it.

I must be crazy.

She had WPC Stacey collect all the files on the Mercer case and stack them on either side of her desk. Once again she read through the witness statements and the pathology reports, even though she was sure she now knew many of them off by heart. The fluorescent light buzzed irritatingly over her head, like a mosquito in a darkened room, like the one thing that was not right about this whole case.

If only she could work out what it was.

She got up and fetched another coffee from the machine and returned to her desk. She rubbed her eyes with her fingers. God, she was tired. She found the statement James had taken from the shift worker in number twenty-four MacNaghten Row, the man who thought he had seen a black saloon pull out of the alleyway the morning Kate's body had been found.

Irrelevant, she remembered Marenko saying after he was convinced that the Candy Man was their killer. But it was the one detail that did not mesh with everything else they had. James might be right, the man was drunk, he imagined it, he got the time wrong, even the wrong night, the whole thing could be irrelevant.

A black saloon.

Why keep going over it? There was no way of identifying the vehicle and tracing it, not now, not then.

She threw the file back into the cardboard box beside her desk and went back down the hall for yet another coffee. James was standing by the machine talking to Honeywell.

'You still here?' she said.

'Just leaving,' James said. 'What about you?'

'Catching up on my paperwork. Couple more things to finish off.'

Honeywell raised an eyebrow. 'The skipper's got a hot date with an underwear model tonight.' Being a married man, Honeywell seemed to have a vicarious fascination with the spills and thrills of James's love life, real and imagined.

'An underwear model,' Fox said. 'Male or female?'

James shook his head. 'Do I seem like anything but a red-blooded heterosexual to you, ma'am?'

'Depends on the light.'

James ignored the slight. Christ, she thought, it's impossible to insult him. He has a hide like an armadillo. 'What do you think, ma'am? This is my first date with her. Should I do French or Greek?'

'I assume you mean food.'

He grinned. 'Whatever.'

'Italian,' she said. 'Not too intimate, not too cheap, not too intimidating. Where does she live?'

'Hammersmith.'

'Plenty of good Italian places down Fulham Palace Road.'

'How do you know that?'

'I used to live there,' she said. *I used to live there.*

James and Honeywell were staring at her. 'Careful, ma'am,' Honeywell said.

'What?'

'Think you've got enough in there?'

She looked down. She was still holding down the bar for the hot water, and the coffee was spilling over the rim of the cup and pouring into the drip tray. She jerked her hand away.

'You OK?' James asked her.

'I used to live there,' she repeated, and she left the brimming polystyrene cup in the machine and hurried back down the corridor to her office.

'Hormones,' James said to Honeywell and shrugged his shoulders.

Why would anyone dump a body in an alleyway?

They had always assumed Henry Wexxler had left Kate Mercer in the lane behind his shop because he had no other choice, because it was convenient. As if hiding a body brought out the same instincts as going down to the corner shop to buy a carton of milk. Marenko had persisted with the theory that he had murdered her in the cellar below the shop, even though forensics had pronounced the place clean.

But it had never made sense to her that Wexxler would dump Katherine Mercer's corpse right outside his own back yard. Not if he was meticulous enough to murder her in his own shop and then remove every trace of evidence.

So why else would you dump a body in an alleyway?

What if it shifted suspicion *away* from you? What if the alley was miles away from where you lived, on the other side of London perhaps? Then it made sense to carry the body in the boot of your . . . black saloon . . . and dump it.

But how would Kate's murderer know about that alleyway behind MacNaghten Row? How would he know it was dark and rarely used? How would he know that Henry Wexxler was the sort of man who would be thought capable of the murder by his neighbours and the police?

Because he used to live there.

You're being stupid, Fox told herself as she jumped into her car. It's 8 o'clock at night, the case is dead in the water and you're not getting paid to do this. The man who killed Kate Mercer is six foot under the ground, and all you're going to get if you go back to MacNaghten Row tonight is abuse.

Perhaps Henry Lincoln Wexxler had been justly tried and convicted by his vigilante killer, but she had to be sure.

Chapter Seventy

Sandy heard the train rumble into the platform below, the announcer's voice drowned out by the squeal of the carriages. She and Kristen ran down the steps to the platform, hooting with nervous laughter. If they missed this train there might not be another for fifteen or twenty minutes. Then they might not get to see Liam Gallagher.

They launched themselves into the first carriage just as the doors were closing and slumped, out of breath, across the seats. The train was only half full. Most commuters were heading in the other direction at this time of the afternoon.

They had run to the station straight from school, and they still had their school uniforms on. There had been no time to go home and change into their street clothes.

'I thought your dad wouldn't let you go,' Kristen said.

'He doesn't know,' Sandy told her. 'He's working late at the hospital tonight. He won't get in till eight.'

'Won't he ring and check up on you?'

'I've left the answerphone on,' she said.

You have called Simon and Sandra Andrews' residence. Sandra cannot come to the telephone right now as she is doing her homework. Please leave a message after the long tone.

'If he gets home early you'll get grounded big time.'

'He never comes home early,' she said.

Serves him right, she thought. If he trusted her, she wouldn't be forced to lie to him. Anyway, she wasn't going to miss seeing Liam Gallagher. Not for anyone.

A few miles away, near Waterloo Bridge, a dark green Camry is cruising the streets. It is starting to get dark, the quick, early night of a London winter. There is a rim of orange across the Houses of Parliament, a grey twilight over the South Bank.

The driver's knuckles are white on the wheel. The tension has been building for months, and now he can stand it no more. The shackles that have held him this last year have been drawn to the stretching point, and tonight they are going to snap.

Chapter Seventy-one

They couldn't get within twenty yards of the Virgin store. There were yellow crowd-control barriers all along the pavement, and uniformed security guards at the doors to hold back the crowds of teenage girls who were milling around the entrance.

Sandy was disgusted. There wasn't a hope of getting inside. Over the heads of the crowd she saw a black stretch limousine pull up at the kerb, and for a moment she glimpsed a scruffy, unshaven young man, with a long scarf trailing, slip out of the back seat. Then he was gone.

Everyone around her was screaming with excitement. She tried to shove her way through, but it was hopeless. She couldn't even get near the windows to see inside. She looked around for Kristen but she had vanished.

'Shit!' This was pointless.

She turned around and fought her way back out of the crowd and started back towards the tube.

Fox stared at the computer screen, her pencil tapping a fast beat on the desktop. She had been working on this for three days now, all unpaid overtime, going door to door in MacNaghten Row and Hardinge Avenue, harassing every estate agent in the area, cross-checking the electoral rolls through the computer, compiling a complete list of everyone who had lived or rented one of the terraced houses in those two streets over the last five years. She eliminated anyone who had been checked in the initial investigation, but every new name was checked for a police record. She punched in the latest addition to her list.

She stared transfixed at the computer screen.

Martin Brian Lampard. Age thirty-nine. Ten previous convictions, ranging from molestation of a nine-year-old to carnal knowledge. Twice referred to psychiatric institutions, served three prison terms, ranging from three months for indecent exposure to one year for indecent dealings with a thirteen-year-old girl.

Lived at 39 MacNaghten Row until seven months before Kate Mercer was murdered.

Christ Almighty.

It was an overcast afternoon in January and already the buses and taxis crawling along Oxford Street had their headlights on. The Christmas lights seemed forlorn somehow. Commuters and shoppers hurried past her, dashing for the tube.

Sandy saw the sign for Tottenham Court Road station and went down the stairs, fumbling in her coat pocket for her purse and ticket. They weren't there. She stood rooted in the middle of the ticket hall as people pushed past her, scurrying through the barriers towards the escalators. She searched her other pockets, her blazer, her shirt, fighting down panic. Her purse was gone. She must have dropped it, or perhaps someone had picked her pocket in the crowd outside the music store.

How was she going to get home?

Kristen. She would go back and find Kristen.

The dark green Camry pulls off Blackfriars Road on to Webber Street. The driver sees a young girl in a maroon blazer at the side of the road and slows down. He winds down the electric window to speak to her, but she runs off down a side street. Disappointed, he drives away again, heading south. He is breathing fast, and his hands are shaking. He doesn't like to be disappointed.

Chapter Seventy-two

Crowds of teenage girls streamed past her, heading back towards Tottenham Court Road. It took her almost twenty minutes to battle her way through the crowds. When she got back to the Virgin store in Oxford Street, Liam Gallagher had left. She ran inside, looking for Kristen, but there was no sign of her, and she realised with frustration that she must have somehow passed her in the street.

Shit!

She fought down another wave of panic. How was she going to get home? She thought of approaching one of the security guards, ask him to have the store manager ring her father. No, she thought, don't be such a *girl*. Simon will kill me for defying him. And it will only prove to him that I'm still a kid, that I can't manage on my own.

She looked at her watch. Half-past five. He wouldn't be home until 8 o'clock. She could walk back over Hungerford Bridge, hitch a lift back from the South Bank somewhere. There was plenty of time. She could still get home by seven and Simon would never know.

Fox stared at her hands. They were shaking. Either too much coffee or perhaps the adrenalin. She remembered something

Marenko had said to her. 'I'm getting a hard-on,' she murmured. WPC Stacey looked up from her typewriter in the corner of the room.

'Ma'am?'

'Nothing,' Fox said. She sat forward, her face inches from the computer screen. Her heart was hammering against her ribs. She told herself not to get too excited. This is just speculation, she told herself; it's not evidence.

You could still be wrong about this.

A quarter-past six. It had taken her longer to get here than she had thought. It was a long walk from Oxford Circus; the rush-hour traffic around Trafalgar Square had been heavy, and it had taken her an age to get across. She was shaking. An old tramp had shouted at her on Mepham Street. He looked like a character out of Dickens, and the smell of him had made her gag. He had probably just wanted some money, but in the darkness she had lost her nerve and started to run.

As she headed down the road towards the Elephant and Castle and Newington Butts, it occurred to her that if she telephoned Kristen's father he might come and get her. But she had no money for the phone call.

She felt a little frightened now, away from the crowds and the lights of the city. There were few commuters in this part of London; instead there were people with orange hair, young black guys in track pants as well as a few drunks and rail-thin teenagers, not much older than herself, huddled in doorways. A light rain had started to fall, and the tyres of the passing traffic hissed on the wet road.

She kept her head down. Just stick your thumb out and start walking, she told herself. One ride, perhaps two, and you'll be home.

A car slowed. She saw the glow of the brake lights, the passenger side door swing open.

Chapter Seventy-three

None of the credit reference agencies had anything on a Martin Brian Lampard, but she tracked him down through his DSS records. He was currently receiving unemployment benefit.

She pulled up his traffic licensing records on the screen. SO18 at New Scotland Yard had replica copies from the DVLA with details of the registered owner of every licensed vehicle in the UK. Within minutes she had the registration number of Lampard's car – a current model Toyota Camry, dark green – and an address near the Elephant and Castle. Right on the other side of London.

A black saloon, she thought; that was what their witness had thought he'd seen. It was possible. At night, dark green could easily be mistaken for black. But it was a long shot. 'You're wasting your time, Madeleine,' Fox said to herself under her breath.

She looked at her watch. Half-past six. She should go home. She could talk to this Martin Lampard tomorrow.

No, she thought. I might as well call round this evening, get it done. Anyway, I won't be able to stop thinking about it all night if I don't do it. I can see Simon afterwards. It's on the way. Another situation that had to be resolved.

What would she say to Lampard? She had no official sanction for this.

She decided she would not even mention Kate Mercer. That would make him immediately wary. She would tell him she was investigating a robbery. That his car was seen near the scene, that a bystander gave them his registration number. That would throw him off balance. She would ask to come in, have a look around. Knowing he was innocent, he would be eager to clear it up, get rid of her.

And after she had spoken to him she would know if the file on Kate Mercer should be closed.

How will you know? she heard Frank Marenko sneering. Women's intuition?

'Maybe,' she said aloud. She picked up her bag and her car keys.

Chapter Seventy-four

She had always been scared of the dark.

She had been afraid of the shadows in her bedroom; with the flick of a light switch the dressing gown on the back of a door had become a monster, the boxes stacked on top of her wardrobe had metamorphosed, in her imagination, to red-eyed dogs crouched and ready to spring.

Which was why she had always slept with a night-light, even now.

But down here there was no light. Down here it was dark; swirling dark, dizzying dark, and cold, like death.

She heard a latch slide across a bolt, and for just a moment there was a glimmer of light, quickly extinguished as he put his eye to the shutter. She felt him watching her through the door, and she crouched further into the corner, her knees drawn up to her chest. She instinctively returned her thumb to her mouth. The teenager who owned the world returned to a dimly remembered childhood and cried aloud for her father.

She was back in her cot, unbidden memories crowding in from a long-forgotten nursery. She saw the pattern of leaves on the green and gold carpet, the brown wood of her cot, the shapes of animal stickers on the walls, Donald Duck, Goofy, Mickey Mouse.

She heard him laughing, and the sound of it jerked her away from those memories to a school playground. It was teasing laughter; she remembered his name, Billy Scanlon, Billy with the greased-down hair that reminded her of a wet rat's back, Billy of those big, crooked teeth. It was Billy Scanlon laughter, mocking and vindictive.

She sucked harder on her thumb.

A feeble halo of yellow appeared around the door. He had brought a light with him. A torch, perhaps. Some comfort in the light, even *his* light.

How long had she been here? She had screamed and screamed for what seemed like hours, her throat felt as if she had swallowed gravel. No one had answered her. Hadn't anyone heard?

Fragments dimly remembered, the car turning into a black side street, the smell of the chemical on the rag that had clamped over her mouth, the feeling of suffocation before the world turned black. It had all happened so quickly. She was stupid, so stupid.

Her clothes were wet, and the cold seeped through to her skin. There was a dull ache in her stomach, hunger and fear eating away at her, making her yearn for a smiling face, a warm place to lie. Mustn't cry.

She was shaking all over. Couldn't think; there was just this fear, blocking out reason. She shut her eyes. When I open them again it will be all over, she said to herself, I'll be back in my own bedroom where it's safe and light and dry.

She wanted her daddy, she wanted her daddy, she wanted her *daddy*.

She heard more Billy Scanlon laughter on the other side of the door. He was watching her.

Need to go to the toilet. But there was nowhere to go. Anyway, too late, too late now. She had wet her pants. She didn't care.

Don't be scared of the dark. She heard her father's voice from some long-ago time. *See, it's just the shadow on the wall. There's nothing to be scared of.*

But there *was* something to be scared of. There were monsters. There were monsters right here in the world. She had been right all the time.

She huddled further into the corner. Her hand touched a cobweb and she jerked away, screamed. She sat upright, rigid with fear, sobbing silently to the merciless dark.

I'm not here. This isn't happening. I'm not here, I'm not.

Fragments of lullabies came to her. *Go to sleep, little one.* She was breathing faster and faster, couldn't stop, there was tingling in her hands, her hands like claws, she couldn't move them, couldn't bend her fingers. I think I'm going to faint. Faint, leave this all behind, wake up when it's over.

Somebody help me. Daddy, please come. *Somebody, somebody help . . .*

Fox got out of the car.

Just another terraced house, drab, shit-coloured brick, a low wall, two steps to the front door. A few stunted rose bushes, coils of dog shit on the pavement right outside the little front gate. There were curtains tightly drawn at the window. No lights.

She rang the bell. As she waited she stared at the car parked in the street outside the door. A dark green Toyota Camry. She checked the registration number. That was it.

She rang the bell again. Still no answer. She went back into the street, peered through the windows of the Camry on the passenger side. A green air-freshener pine cone hung from the rear-view mirror; otherwise there were no personal touches at all, no spilled cassettes in the cosole, no food wrappings on the floor. Like a car on display in a showroom. He must have it cleaned regularly.

She went back and rang the bell a third time, pressed her face against the frosted glass. Dark. She tried to find a gap in the thick curtains, but they had been drawn meticulously and there were no gaps.

Feeling anyway that she was on a fool's errand, she gave up and left.

Chapter Seventy-five

———◆———

Instinct made her touch the car's bonnet. It was warm. She stopped, looked back at the house, at the second-floor windows. Did she see a curtain move? No, just her imagination.

But he had to be in there. Unless he had parked the car and gone straight out again. Was that likely?

Puzzled, she went back to her Cavalier, took a torch from the glove compartment. She went back up the path, knelt down and pushed open the letterbox, peered in, shining the torch into the hallway. She saw flock wallpaper, dark and stained with damp, linoleum peeling up off the floor. And what was that? She couldn't quite see. She pressed her face hard against the door.

An open suitcase, heavy-duty, with wheels. Beside it, a child's schoolbag.

Her heart was hammering in her chest now. She straightened, rang the bell again.

Then she heard it, or thought she heard it. A scream, a shout, something.

She reached into her shoulder bag, took out her mobile phone. She heard the phone ringing in the office. Five, six times.

'Come on,' she murmured under her breath. 'Come on!'

'Incident Room.'

'Bill!'

'Ma'am?'

'You're still at the office.'

'Paperwork.'

'Forget about it. I need you down here. Now. Before you leave, I want you to call the local plod and get me backup.'

She gave him the address and she told him what she was going to do. He told her not to. She hung up.

Was there time to wait? She had no weapon. Backup from a local panda car would take three, perhaps five minutes. And when they arrived the officers would want to do things by the book.

She stared at the window. How will this come out? she asked herself. Will they label it courage, instinct or recklessness leading to criminal damage? It depended on which way it went, she supposed. If you're wrong, she thought as she took off her shoe, if those screams are coming from a video player and Martin Lampard is sitting in there watching a Stephen King movie with a cup of cocoa in his hand, there goes your badge and your career.

She smashed the heel against the window as hard as she could.

The glass cracked but did not break. She tried again. Her shoe wasn't heavy enough.

She looked down. There was an old earthenware pot at her feet containing the sad remains of some plant, long since dead. She picked it up and hurled it through the window, then used her shoe to knock out the shards.

She ducked in, pushed aside the heavy drapes and rolled across the floor. She swung the torch in front of her, two-handed. The emptiness mocked her. Bare floorboards, an old fireplace, an empty grate, the smell of damp.

She threw open the door, expecting to see some badly shaven nightmare waiting there, holding a knife, a gun, an axe. But there was just the empty hallway. The child's schoolbag, carelessly discarded, lay at the foot of the stairs. She shone the torch up the staircase. No one.

There were no paintings on the walls, no furniture in the

hallway, nothing to indicate that anyone lived here. The torch beam groped back down the balustrade to the schoolbag, then along the dirty strip of carpet to the cupboard under the stairs. A door opened on to some steps leading down to a basement.

He was down there.

She kept her back pressed against the wall. Despite the cold, her hands were slick with sweat, and she almost dropped the torch. Christ, Madeleine, get a grip.

'Help me, help me, *help me!*'

The shouts were coming from the basement and it wasn't a video. Fox felt her knees give way under her. She should have waited for backup. Too late now.

She reached for the latch on the front door and let it swing open. An escape route for her, a way for the backup to get in. Her mouth was as dry as bone. She took a deep breath to steady herself, then she took her first tentative steps towards the door under the stairs.

She imagined him down there, waiting, the light from her torch making her an easy target. Yes, please, he was thinking, come to me, come to me, come to me.

A car drove past in the street outside. A board creaked under her foot. She waited.

There was a sudden noise to her right and she jerked around, thought she was trapped, but it was only the refrigerator humming to life in the kitchen.

Why doesn't he come up the stairs, she thought? Of course. He must think I have a weapon. Why would anyone break into a house unarmed? Only a fool. He doesn't know I am alone. He is thinking, he is waiting, but soon he will understand why it has taken me so long to come after him and he will start up those stairs.

How long since she had called in for backup?

Her arms and legs were shaking almost uncontrollably, her heart banging wildly in her chest, the blood pounding so loudly in her ears she couldn't hear anything else.

Calm down. You must be able to hear him, hear what he does.

Was that a police siren she could hear in the distance? It would panic him, make him move, shake him from his caution.

Another scream from below.

And then she saw it, the switch for the cellar light, there by the stairs, caught in the beam of her torch. She knew what she had to do.

She flicked on the light as she ran past and threw herself blind down the steps. She was running down cement steps into an ancient coal cellar, saw a padlocked wooden door against the far wall. And there he was, directly below her, legs braced, blinking in the unexpected light, an ordinary-looking man in workman's overalls, eyes wide like a dog running from a fire. He stared at her down the barrel of a revolver, half turning to shoot out the bulb, then changing his mind and turning back towards her, fractions of a second, all that she needed as she closed on him.

The sound of the revolver in the tiny basement was deafening, she thought it was just one explosion, and she felt nothing, a brush of wind against her face, that was all. Adrenalin drove her the rest of the way down the stairs, and as she closed on him she pushed the gun away with her left hand and hit him twice, as her martial arts instructors had taught her, ignoring the gun, going in behind it and over it, hands flat, fingers bent at the second knuckle, aiming for the throat with her right hand, then the heel of her left hand driving up under the base of the nose. She kicked out as he went down, the knee, the groin. Over in seconds.

He lay at her feet, trying to suck in air through his shattered windpipe, his nose destroyed, spitting blood through his mouth. He rolled over and over on the floor, writhing and grasping at his genitals with both hands.

Fox kicked the gun away across the floor and sagged against the wall.

There was something sticky on her shirt. She looked down, saw the blossoming of blood on her chest and arm. Her knees started to give way. When you're shot you're supposed to fall over, a voice told her.

The room was spinning. Someone was still screaming, on the other side of the door, but now it seemed to come from a long way away.

Shock, she thought. I'm going into shock. She tried to pick up the gun, lost her balance, fell on to her knees. She fumbled for the handkerchief in her pocket so that she would not get her fingerprints over it. She picked it up by the barrel. Must be careful, she thought, don't want to shoot myself, and she started to laugh as she crawled up the stairs.

She was aware of the sound of keening from behind the locked door, and the man grunting and choking on the floor, making another sound from his chest, shrill, like a scalded pig.

Fox was halfway up the stairs when she passed out.

Simon pulled out of the gates of the hospital car park and drove up to the lights on Rosslyn Hill. He punched a number on his phone's speed dial with his spare hand.

You have called Simon and Sandra Andrews' residence. Sandra cannot come to the telephone right now as she is doing her homework. Please leave a message after the long tone –

He felt a stirring of unease. She wasn't there, the little scamp. She might have sneaked out to Kristen's. He braked at the lights and punched in another number.

'Hi, Glynn, it's Simon. Is Sandy there? . . . I thought she might be with Kristen . . . well, I can't get any answer at home . . . can you go and ask her . . .' An ambulance, beacons flashing, rolled through the red light heading towards the hospital. 'No, it's OK. Thanks, Glynn.'

He folded the mobile back in his jacket pocket. She might have sneaked out to use her friend Danielle's Internet chat line –

which he strictly forbade – or gone round to Michelle's house on the pretence of doing homework together. He was sure it was nothing to worry about.

The two officers who had been sent to the scene from Vauxhall found the house in darkness, the front door yawning open. Several neighbours were gathered in the front garden, but none of them had summoned up the courage to enter. The two PCs heard a girl screaming in the basement. They shone their torches into the hallway, looking for the light switches.

All they knew was that a murder-squad detective from Hendon Road had asked for backup on an arrest. A DI Fox. They called the name and went down to the basement.

They found her halfway up the stairs, her blouse and jacket saturated in blood. A man lay writhing and kicking on the cement floor a few feet away, his face turning blue. Someone was screaming on the other side of a padlocked metal door.

'Fuck me,' one of the constables said. He knew enough first aid to drag the semiconscious detective up the stairs to the hallway and lie her flat.

Meanwhile his partner called in for an ambulance and asked for extra backup.

His partner crouched over the wounded detective, his hands and his uniform tunic covered in bright blood. 'I don't think she's going to make it,' he said.

Chapter Seventy-six

Simon latched the door behind him and took off his jacket.

'Sandy!'

He waited, his heart hammering painfully against his ribs, his mouth sour with fear.

'Hi, Dad.' She stood there, in the kitchen doorway, an uncertain half-smile on her face. He knew the look: guilty as hell.

'I tried to call you half a dozen times. The answerphone was on.'

'I was doing my homework,' she said. 'I must have forgotten to turn it off.'

Her jacket was on a hook by the door. He touched the sleeve. It was damp. It had only started raining in the last half an hour. He turned to look at her, but she had already gone back into the kitchen. He was about to say something but a wash of relief overcame him, and he was too tired to compose another lecture. He decided for once to let it go.

'Sorry I'm late,' he said.

'It's OK. I've started tea.'

He felt a sudden rush of gratitude, was thankful for the dinner smells from the kitchen, the reassuring chatter of the television, the glow of yellow lamps in the living room and the knowledge of the warm breath of a loved one.

Chapter Seventy-seven

Fox studied her reflection in the driver's mirror. She looked a little pale. But not bad for three months down the track. As James had said, it could have gone the other way. 'If you'd spent the last three months decomposing you'd look worse. Well, marginally.'

Still another three months before she could go back to work. Longer if the doctors had their way. But it was hard being at home day after day. At least in the hospital there had been regular visitors and the odd enema to look forward to.

Carrie had put her head in almost every day. She had a great job, great sex and a new wardrobe. Hard not to hate her, lying in bed with a tube in your arm, another up your nose and your hair not washed for three weeks.

Simon had been another regular visitor. They were awkward with each other. They both knew it was over between them, had been finished with before she had been wounded. Now his decency and her helplessness enforced an uneasy truce on them, a delay before moving on. It would make it harder on Sandy.

Sandy. She visited every weekend. She never once asked her about what had happened. Instead, they made small talk about the hospital food, about Sandy's teachers, why Fox had a plastic identity tag around her wrist.

'That's because I've nowhere to put my ID. This way I can

just hold out my wrist. Police! Stand quite still and tell me what you've got in that bedpan!'

She laughed, but not very much. There was something behind her eyes. Somehow, a little piece of her innocence had gone.

Lampard had picked up his victim on Blackfriars Road around 5 o'clock while Fox was still hunched over the computer, chasing down his records. Her name was Belinda Bryant. In her statement to the police, Belinda admitted she had skipped school that day and spent the afternoon in the city with two friends. She had been trying to hitch a lift back to Kingston. She had done it several times before without incident.

Lampard had seemed nice at first, she said. It was getting dark when he suddenly pulled off the main road on to a side street, behind a textile factory. He told her he worked there and he had to pick up some papers from the office. Belinda could see clerks and typists moving around behind the bright lit second-floor windows of the factory office. It reassured her, and she resisted the urge to run.

Lampard was fiddling with something in the boot. Suddenly he returned to the car, and as he got in the driver's side she saw he was holding a rag in his hand. He clamped it over her mouth. She remembered a strong smell of chemical and the feeling she was suffocating. She tried to scratch at his eyes and then she blacked out.

The next thing she remembered was waking up in the basement.

She had come in once, with her mother, to thank her. They were both barely able to talk through their tears. Fox found the episode embarrassing and awkward. All she wanted to say to the girl was: *How could you have been so stupid?*

*   *   *

It was on her last day in the hospital that Sandy broke the news to her.

'Dad has a new girlfriend,' she said.

'I know.'

'She's a doctor. She works in this place somewhere.' Sandy sounded bewildered more than hurt.

'It wasn't working out between us,' Fox told her. 'We decided . . . well, we decided before this happened.'

'He should have waited. I mean, until you were better.'

Fox smiled. 'Why? It's what we both wanted.' She took Sandy's hand. 'I'll always be your friend. You get into trouble, you can always say: *I know someone in the police, so watch yourself.*'

Sandy brushed away a tear with the heel of her hand. She needs a mother, Fox had reminded herself. And I'm not it.

She grimaced now at the memory. She guessed she would miss Sandy more than she would miss Simon. She brushed the thought aside, applied a touch of lip gloss and got out of the car. Strange to be back at Hendon Road again after all this time. Spring again. Vapour trails in a cold blue sky, the first buds shooting on the plane trees.

She met Marenko in the King's Head. It was not yet eleven and there was only a handful of people drinking at this hour, the diehards and the alcoholics. Which just about covers me and Frank, Fox thought, as she walked across to the bar.

She had on a long-sleeved blouse, which hid the scar on her forearm, still a pink and livid thing on her skin. The bullet had removed a piece of muscle the size of a 50p coin. She would always have a scar there, as souvenir. The puckered scar over her right breast, where the bullet entered, was only a little smaller; the larger incision from the operation that repaired her lung had been made under her breast. The plastic surgeon had told her that it would heal well and that the scar would fade quickly and become barely noticeable.

'Only close friends will know,' he had said to her.

'If I can make any of those kinds of friends looking like this,' she said. 'I feel like the Elephant Man. Should I prepare these close friends in advance? So they don't faint?'

'It won't always look as it does now. The cicatrix will fade. It will always be there, but it won't be disfiguring. And we can do a few things later on that will help.'

'Like turn out all the lights?'

The scar on her neck was not as pronounced. It had creased the skin without damaging major blood vessels and nerves. Which was fortunate, the doctors had told her, because if it had you'd be dead. But still, for her meeting with Marenko she wore a Hermès scarf to hide the damage. In fact, she had spoiled herself and bought several. When you've nearly died, running up debts on your credit card did not seem the terrible disaster it once had.

Marenko stood at the bar, a goofy, lopsided grin on his face. Almost as if he owned a part of her now, as if they shared some kind of secret. Which perhaps they did.

'Guv.'

'Looking good, Fox. They put Humpty Dumpty together again?'

'As far as I know there's no bits missing.'

'That's good. Drink?'

'Usual.'

He nodded to Henry. Fox sat down on the bar stool beside him.

'Well,' he said.

'Well.'

'Last time I saw you, you had tubes sticking out everywhere. I was about to start tracing you out with chalk.'

'Sorry I didn't say hello.'

'Yeah, you weren't much company. Had to eat the grapes

myself. You slept through the whole hour. I didn't take it personally.' The drinks arrived. 'Want peanuts or anything? I mean, are you back on solids?'

'I don't know. Are you?'

He grinned. 'Lost none of the old edge.'

'No, can't lose that.'

He watched her over the rim of his glass. He was still smiling. 'I have to know. How did you do it?'

'Just good, solid police work. It was tedious and I didn't get paid for it.'

'You finally understand what being a murder detective is all about.'

'I guess so.'

Yes, she thought, good, solid police work. Everyone thought so. Even James and Honeywell conceded that she hadn't done a bad job. They did a lot of the follow-up work on the case while she was lying on her back in St Thomas's.

Neighbours they interviewed said Martin Lampard was quiet and kept mostly to himself. He didn't play loud music or gun the motor on his car at 7 o'clock on a Sunday morning and so was considered an ideal neighbour. He dressed in a suit and tie and drove a late model car and everyone assumed he was a sales rep. In fact, the car had been bought with the money his father had left him when he died three years before. Martin Lampard was unemployed.

He brought his heavily drugged victims into the house in a large suitcase. Neighbours had seen him once or twice and thought he kept his samples in it. Which in a way he did.

Beneath the house was a small cellar, and he had spent the rest of his inheritance soundproofing it. His private Idaho, as James had said. He must have spent a lot of time down there. Apart from a television, a video player, a large selection of illegal pornographic videos and magazines, and a mattress in the front parlour, the house was largely bare of furnishings.

Lampard had now been tentatively connected to the murders

of children in Manchester, Leeds and Sheffield. The full extent of his evil might never be known because Lampard had suffered a severe hypoxia due to the trauma on his throat and was now destined to spend the rest of his days in a maximum-care facility dribbling food down his front and staring without comprehension at the ceiling.

'You said you wanted to see me,' Marenko said.

'The Candy Man,' she told him.

'What about him?'

'He was innocent.'

'He was a pervert.'

'But he didn't kill Kate Mercer. He didn't kill anyone. Kate was in that cellar, Frank. They've cross-matched hairs and fibres they found in that place. It was Lampard who killed her.'

Marenko shrugged. 'So. I was wrong. You were wrong. We were all wrong about him. Doesn't matter now. He's dead.'

'That's my point.'

'Sorry. What is your point again?'

'Did you ever get a case where you know someone did something but you couldn't prove it?'

'I've had dozens of them. We all do.'

'That's why I wanted to talk to you. I wanted your advice.'

'Shoot. If you'll pardon the expression.'

'Patrick Capper.'

'Are you still wasting your time on that?'

'Why would someone shoot Patrick Capper and then write "Justice" on the wall? They were making a point, right?'

'They were making the point that even though he put himself above the law, someone out there was keeping score.'

'Exactly. So who did it? Could be anyone. Right?'

'Don't let this Lampard thing go to your head, Fox. You're not Sherlock Holmes. My guess is the Capper and Wexxler files won't ever get closed.'

She ignored him. 'That's why they bother me. I mean, Capper looked like a professional hit. And then the Candy Man gets topped. Someone writes "Justice" on the wall in his blood. Just like they did with Patrick Capper. Doesn't make sense.'

'Copycat killing, maybe.'

'A copycat hit-man. I don't think so. Anyway, no one knew about the graffiti before the Candy Man was murdered. No, I think it was the same man, making the point that you can't get beyond justice, even if you go beyond the law.'

'So you think it was Lennox?'

'Lennox was in Birmingham when the Candy Man was murdered. Anyway, he doesn't believe in anything except money. You think he's going to waste his time on rock spiders?'

'So. Your point?'

'There was one other thing. I kept looking at the photographs of the two murders. The writing's different.'

'You what?' he said, looking at her as if she was crazy.

'The Capper murder scene, there's a stroke on top of the "J". In the second one, there isn't.'

Marenko ordered two more drinks. He reached into his pocket and lit a cigarette.

'Back on the cancer sticks?'

'Cigars were getting too expensive.'

'You almost quit once.'

'I almost quit a lot of times. You got to die of something. You were saying. About the different "J"s.'

'Why would a contract killer write "Justice" on the wall anyway? Supposing it *was* a hit man.'

'I don't know. Why?'

'Because he was paid to.'

Marenko didn't say anything.

'That would explain the different writing. Two different hit men.'

'So you're into writing analysis now?'

'It's the only thing that makes sense.'

'We're talking about letters scrawled on a wall in blood.'

'Blood. Ink. It's something you write with.'

Marenko shook his head. 'Don't let normal people hear you talk like this.'

'The question is, who would put out two different contracts, one for Patrick Capper and one for Henry Wexxler?'

The drinks arrived. Marenko took a long swallow of his whisky. 'You got me. Who?'

'Someone who believes in justice. Their version of it, anyway.'

'Come up with any names?'

Fox finished her first gin and tonic and picked up the second. She toyed with draining that one too. She couldn't meet his eyes. A deep breath. 'I was right, wasn't I? You are taking money from Ahmed Khan?'

She wondered what he would do. Would he get angry? Would he rage, would he lower his voice and threaten, would he throw his drink at her and walk out? But the smile stayed in place. 'You still on that, Fox? You should be careful.'

'It's true, isn't it?'

'You wired, Fox? Did Internal Affairs ask you to nail me?'

'You can search me, if you like.'

'Please, Fox. I'm a divorced man, celibate for three years. You shouldn't say things you don't mean.' It was meant to be playful, but it didn't sound that way. There was a hard edge to Marenko's voice now.

'Michael DeBruin,' she said.

Marenko drained his whisky and slammed the glass on the bar. 'The case is closed. Andy Murray just got fifteen years. Anyway, what has one thing got to do with the other?'

'Let me run this past you. A senior police detective is having a very bad run. One of his witnesses is killed, and he thinks it's his fault. His son-in-law is badly beaten while on duty, and he finds himself investigating the brutal murder of a little girl and cannot find the evidence to put away his prime suspect. He's been doing this job for twenty-seven years and he's tired and frustrated. Some people may say he's a stress case. His family life is to hell, and he feels his whole life's been wasted. Then the man who put his son-in-law in a wheelchair is acquitted and virtually laughs in his face. So he decides enough is enough. Who better to commit a murder than a murder detective? He knows how hard it is to solve a premeditated murder, and he knows what to do to make reasonably sure he'll get away with it. If he's lucky he might even end up investigating the murder himself. Even if he leaves any trace evidence behind at the scene, which he knows not to do, he's still covered. Perfect.

'But it's not as easy to kill another human being as he thinks. All his life wading around in blood and decomposing flesh and when it comes down to it his hands are shaking so hard he nearly botches the job. But he's right about one thing. It *is* hard to close a premeditated murder. So hard that the investigating detectives are happy to seize on the crumbs he leaves lying around. He already knows the victim's associates from the previous investigation, knows where they live. So he knows how and where to leave a trail.

'But in his mind he's crossed the line. Deep down he feels a sense of guilt. Not about the murder, but about betraying the job. So he transfers out of the department. Now he finds there's people wanting to put money in his pocket if he'll turn a blind eye to crimes he doesn't really give a damn about anyway. So he does it, he takes the money. But not for himself. He's an honest cop, one of the good guys, he's on the side of the angels. So he uses the money where it can do most good.'

Marenko ran a tongue around his teeth. 'You know how this sounds?'

'I know how it sounds. But it also fits the facts. Got any better ideas?'

'Keep going.'

'He knows several hard men from his years trying to arrest them for underworld murders. But this time he's the one putting out the contracts. He uses the dirty money to nail Patrick Capper and the Candy Man. The scales of justice have been loaded against him all these years, but now they start to swing up again. Everything's just beautiful. He's balanced the ledger. Except for one thing. The Candy Man was innocent.'

'You've spent too long on those cases, Fox. Suck something long enough and it loses its flavour.'

She finished her drink. 'I don't think so.' She stood up to leave.

'What are you going to do?'

'About what?'

'About this bedtime story you just told me.'

'Nothing I can do. I have no evidence, no material witnesses. It's all that matters, right? You taught me that. This isn't Agatha Christie. There *is* such a thing as the perfect murder. You knew that all along.'

Marenko shook his head and looked away. It was as close to a confession as she knew she would get.

'You have to stop, guv.'

'Stop what?'

'I told you. The Candy Man was innocent.'

'He was a child molester. He's no loss to the world.'

'You cannot set yourself up as judge and executioner.'

'I think I'm pretty well qualified, actually. In my book, justice is when someone gets what's coming to them, even if it's for something they didn't do. You don't want another drink?'

'It's not even lunchtime. You have to know when to stop, Frank.'

'Yeah,' Marenko said after a while. 'I guess you do.'

Fox got in behind the wheel of her Cavalier. What a tip. Time she got herself another car. She put the key in the ignition, but instead of starting the engine she laid her head back on the headrest and closed her eyes.

Justice.

The hunt for those responsible for the murders of Patrick

Capper and Henry Lincoln Wexxler would continue for another few weeks, all routine lines of enquiry would be exhausted and then the AMIT would be wound down. There would be another murder or another serial rapist to track down and new black and white glossies to fill the noticeboard in the Incident Room. The newspapers would find other stories to fill their front pages.

The Justice Killer would become just another story told over drinks at the King's Head.

Justice. Was there justice for Tom O'Neill? Nothing was going to give him back his life, nothing would give Julie back her husband or her baby son its father. But if it had been left to the jury and the legal professionals, the man responsible for it would still be walking the streets, signifying with his loping walk and cocky grin that society put little value on the life of anyone, least of all a policeman.

Did he then deserve to die? Did Patrick Capper deserve to die? Her former lover, Simon Andrews, would say that no one deserved to die that way, that society had no right to murder anyone.

But that same caring and egalitarian society had been powerless to do anything about him and men like him. Was society better off without men like Pat Capper? In her opinion the answer was yes.

And then there was the Candy Man. Not, as James would have said, a taxpayer. Certainly no credit to the society that had spawned him. But had he deserved to die too?

There are monsters among us, as Marenko had once told her, and it was why she, like him, wished to be on the side of the angels. But for now she was just grateful that it was over. She had peered into the heart of darkness and she was yet glad to be alive on this crisp London morning, on this day in the life of the world.